James Burks

Bird & Squirrel

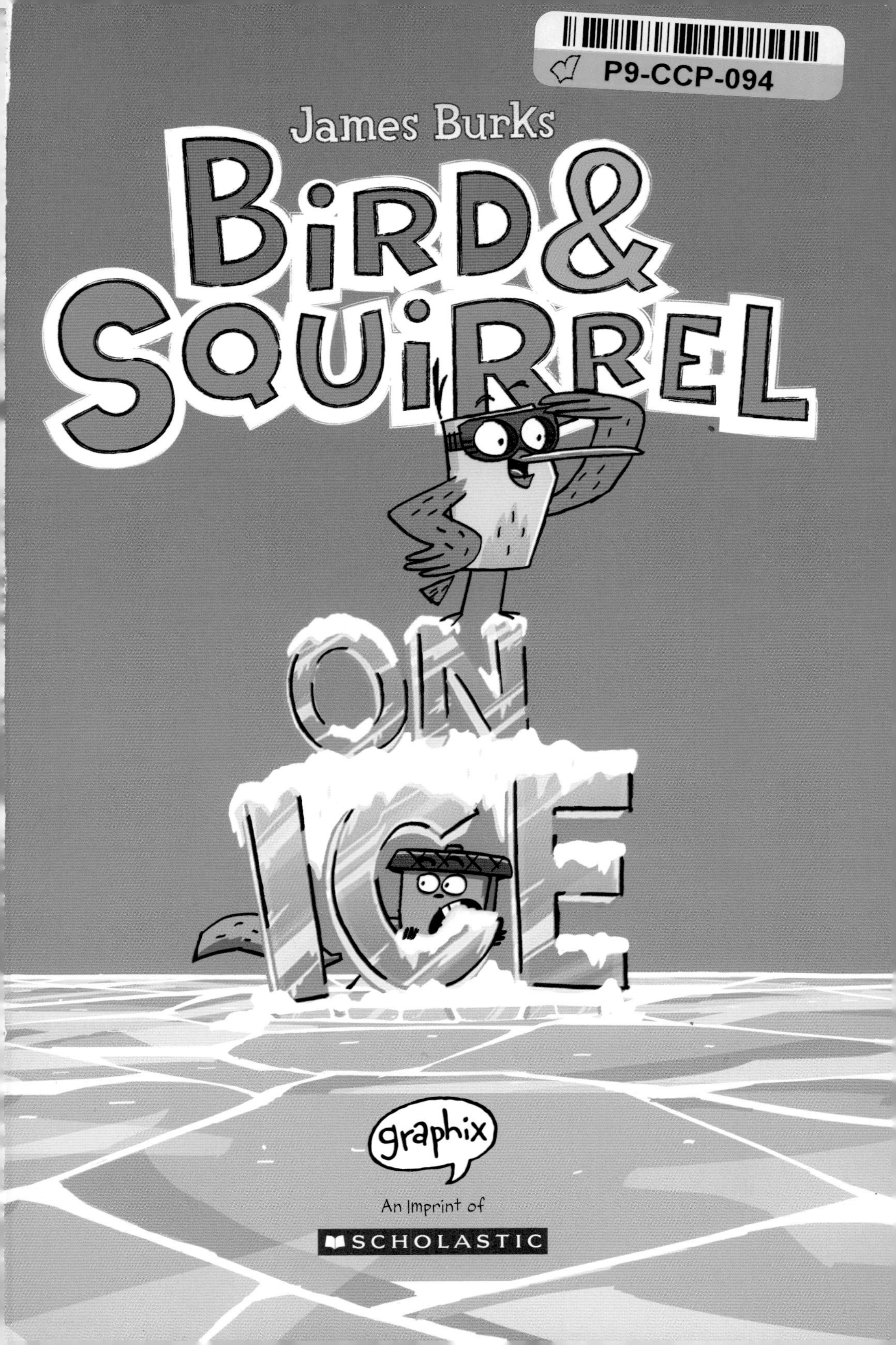

On Ice

graphix

An Imprint of

SCHOLASTIC

For Kelly: You're the best. Onward and upward!

All rights reserved. Published by Graphix, an imprint of Scholastic Inc., Publishers since 1920. SCHOLASTIC, GRAPHIX, and associated logos are trademarks and/or registered trademarks of Scholastic Inc.

Library of Congress control number: 2014931610

ISBN 978-0-545-56318-5

10 9 8 7 6 5 4 3   19 20 21 22
Printed in China   62

First edition, October 2014

Edited by Adam Rau
Creative Director: David Saylor
Book design by Phil Falco

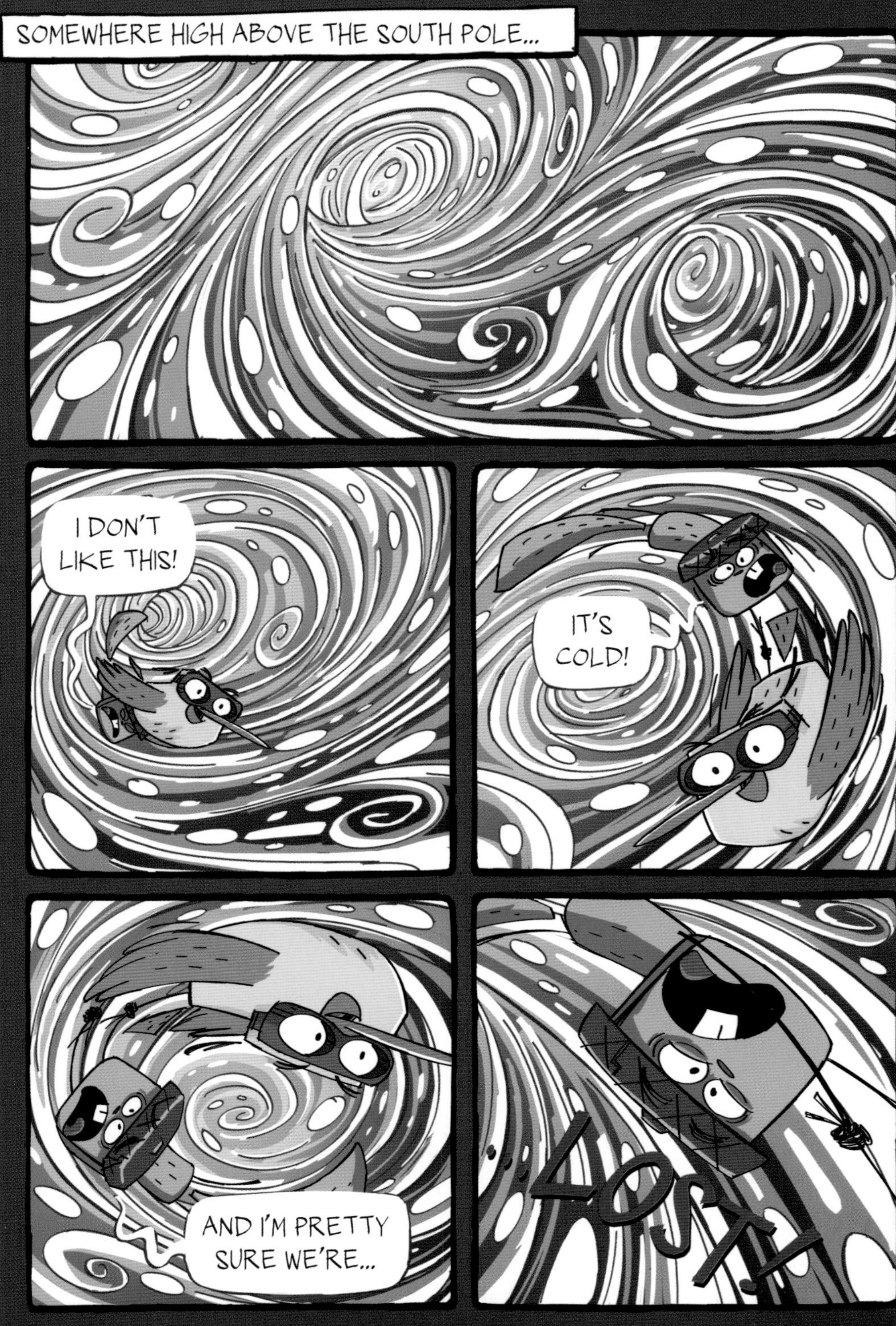
SOMEWHERE HIGH ABOVE THE SOUTH POLE...
I DON'T LIKE THIS!
IT'S COLD!
AND I'M PRETTY SURE WE'RE...
LOST!!

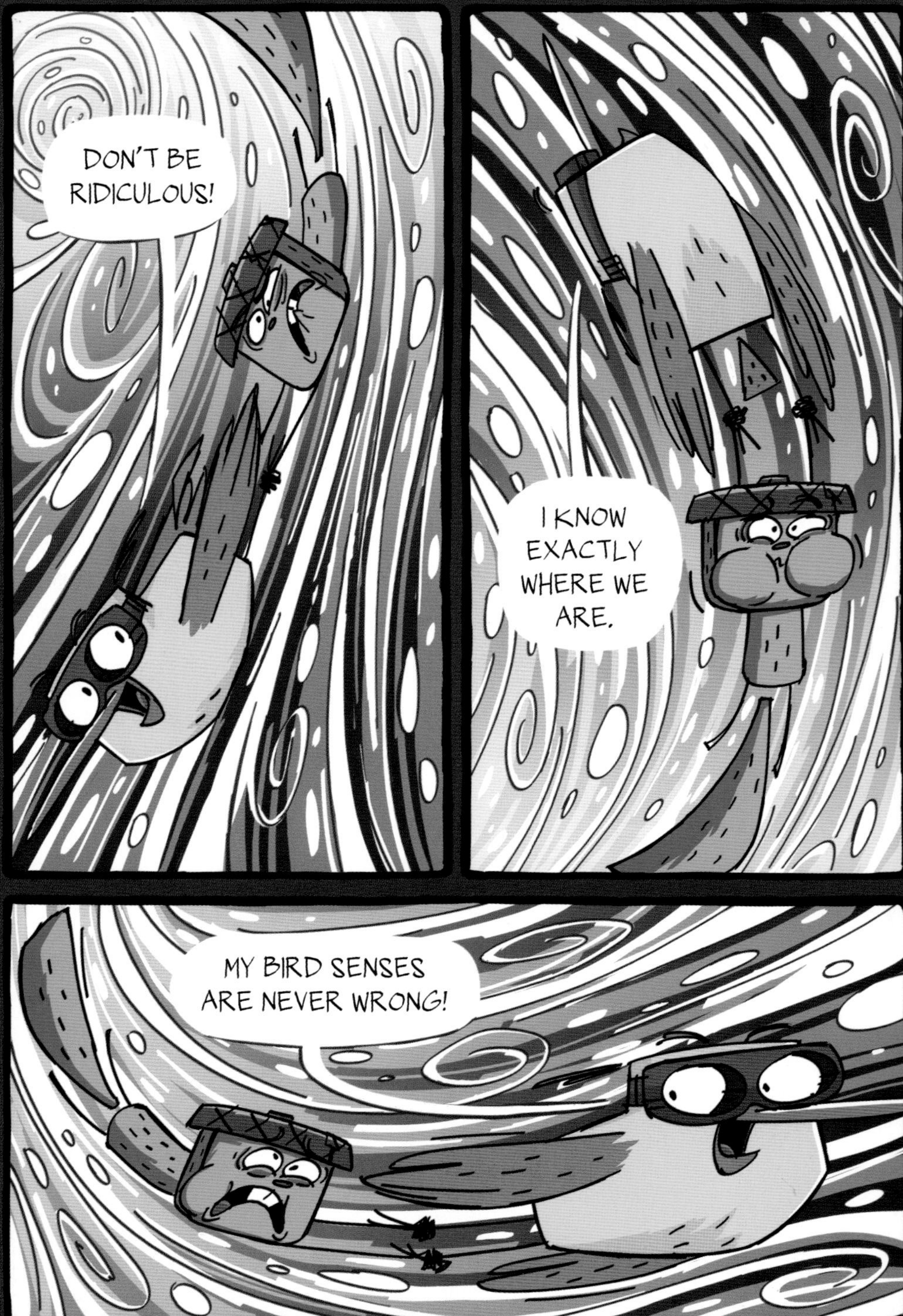
DON'T BE RIDICULOUS!
I KNOW EXACTLY WHERE WE ARE.
MY BIRD SENSES ARE NEVER WRONG!

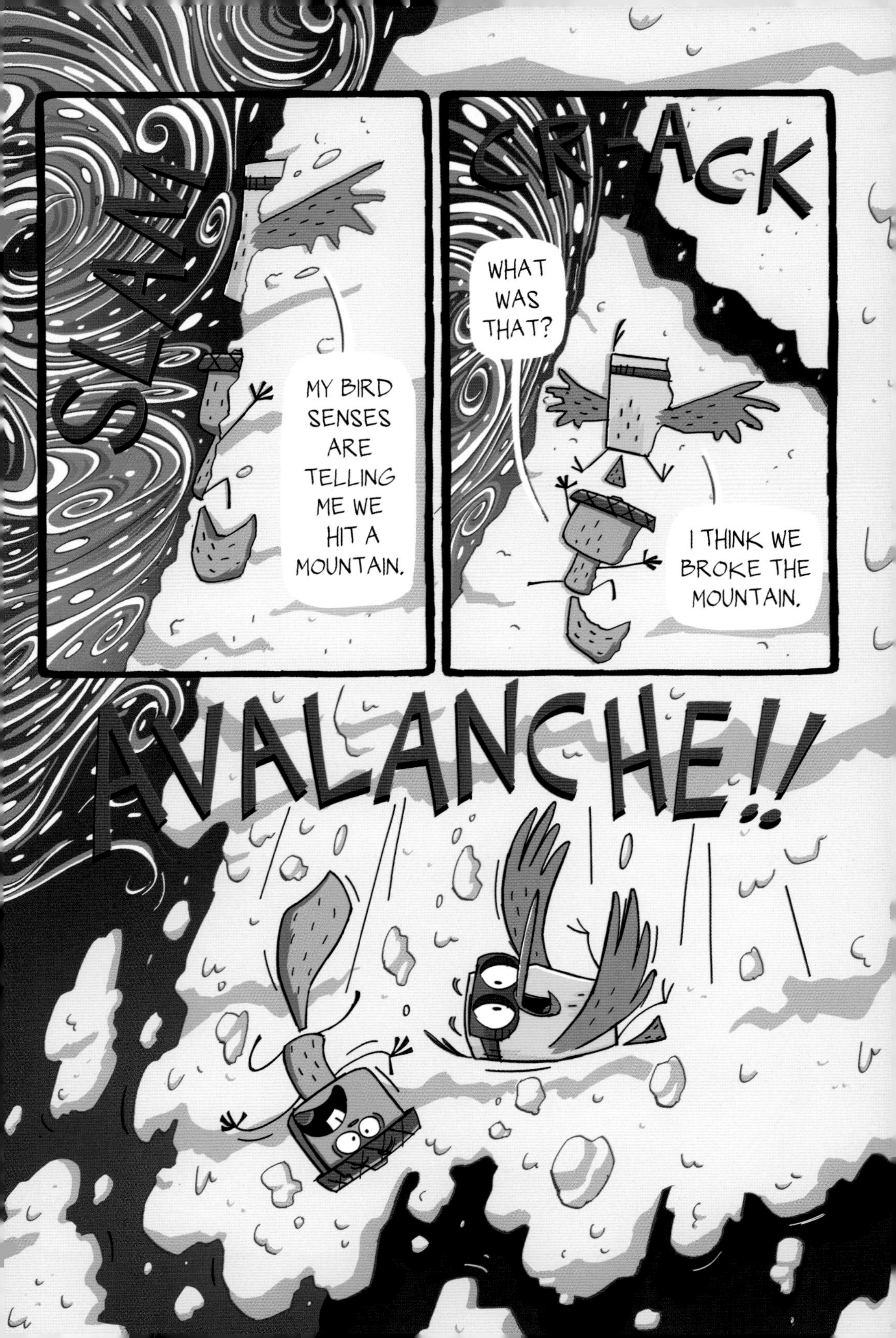
SLAM
MY BIRD SENSES ARE TELLING ME WE HIT A MOUNTAIN.
CR-ACK
WHAT WAS THAT?
I THINK WE BROKE THE MOUNTAIN.
AVALANCHE!!

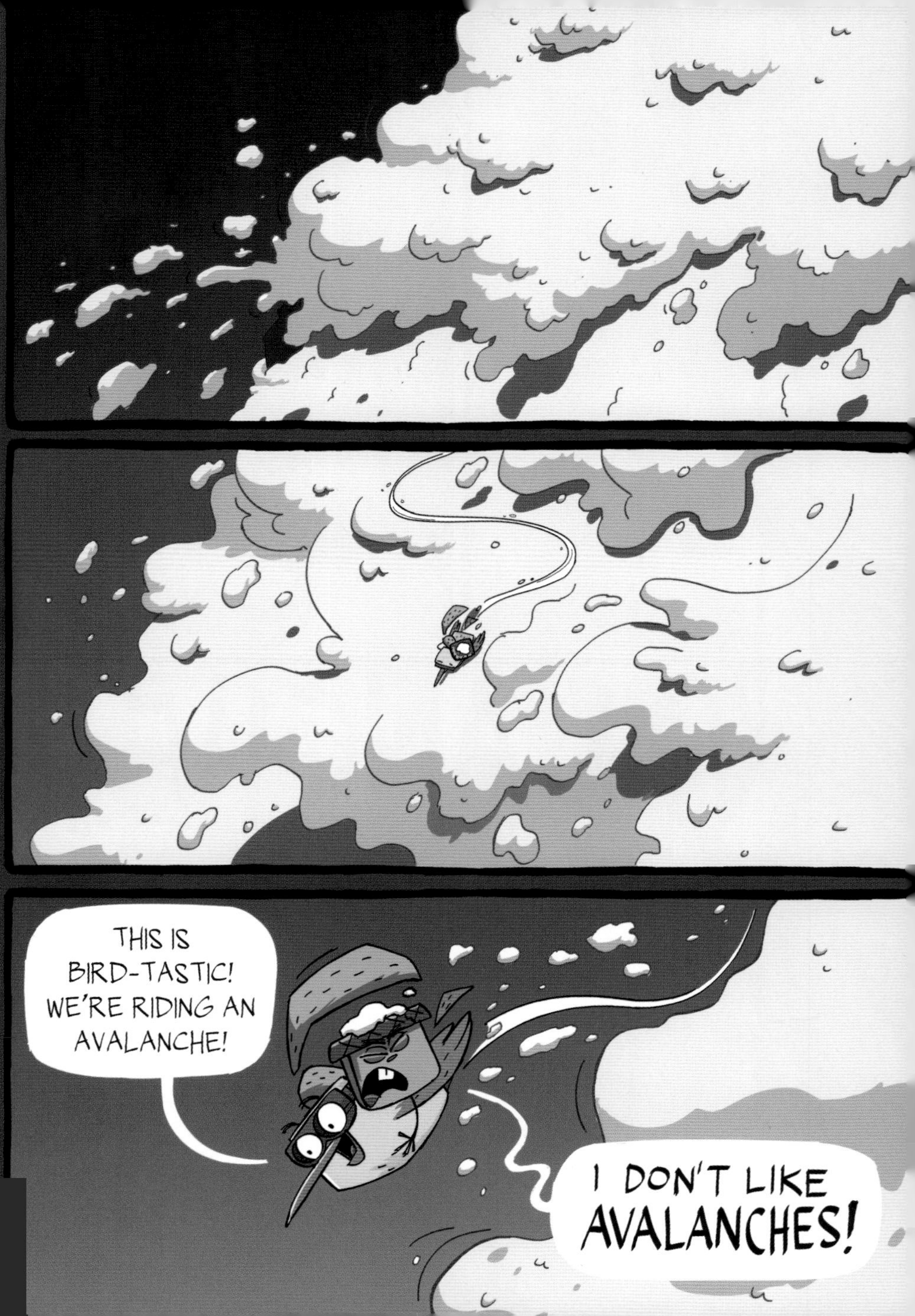
THIS IS BIRD-TASTIC! WE'RE RIDING AN AVALANCHE!
I DON'T LIKE AVALANCHES!

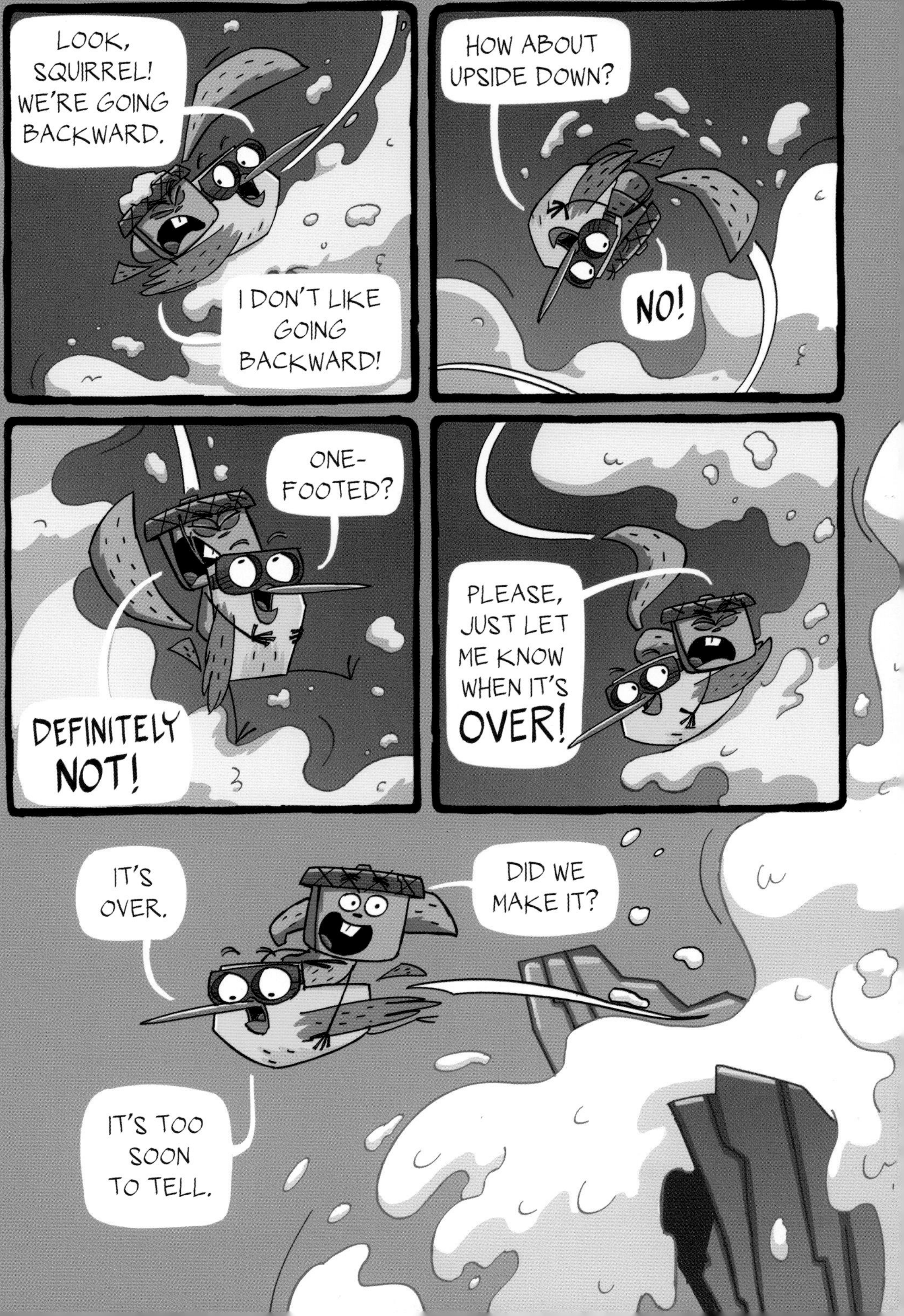
LOOK, SQUIRREL! WE'RE GOING BACKWARD.
I DON'T LIKE GOING BACKWARD!
HOW ABOUT UPSIDE DOWN?
NO!
ONE-FOOTED?
DEFINITELY NOT!
PLEASE, JUST LET ME KNOW WHEN IT'S OVER!
IT'S OVER.
DID WE MAKE IT?
IT'S TOO SOON TO TELL.

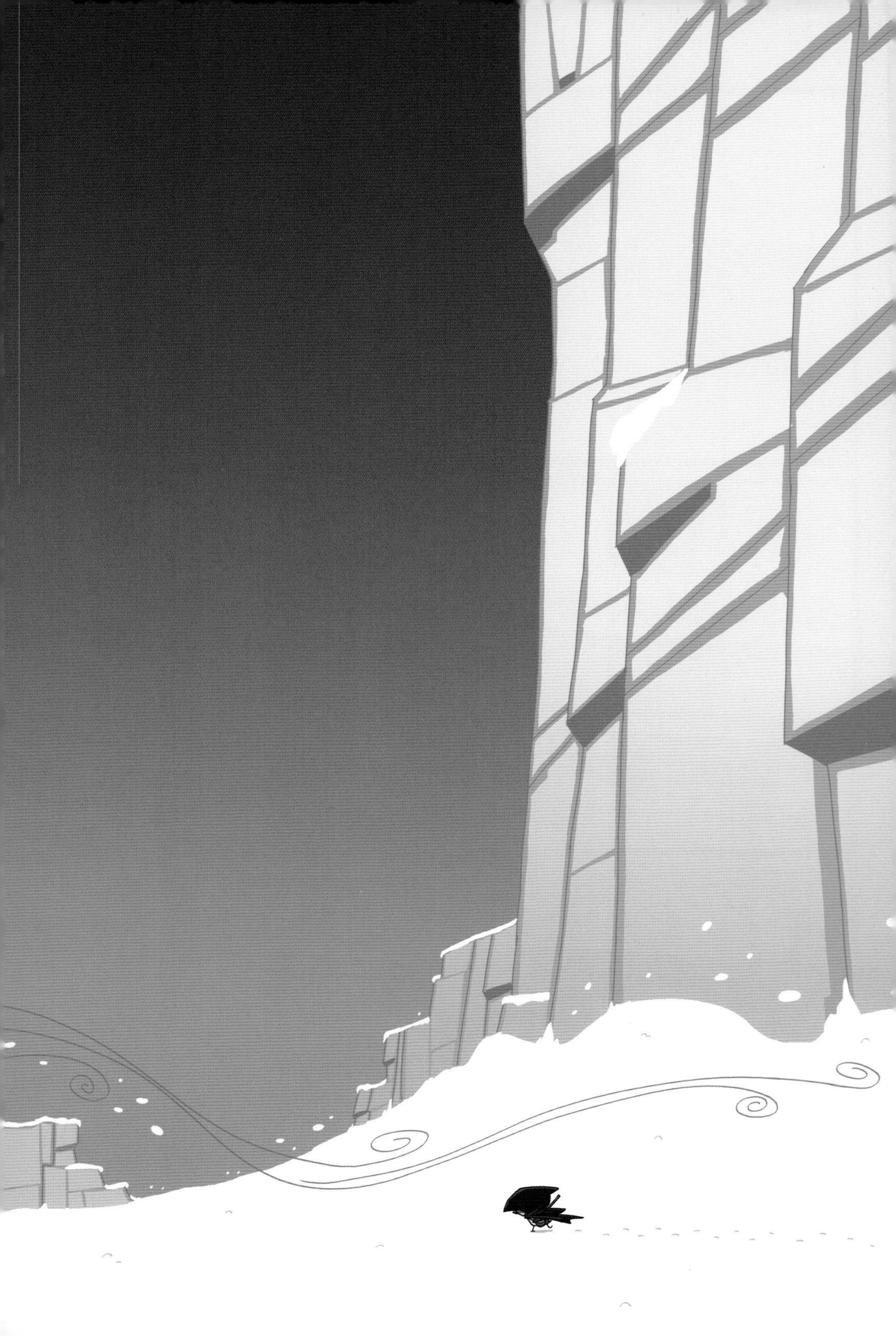

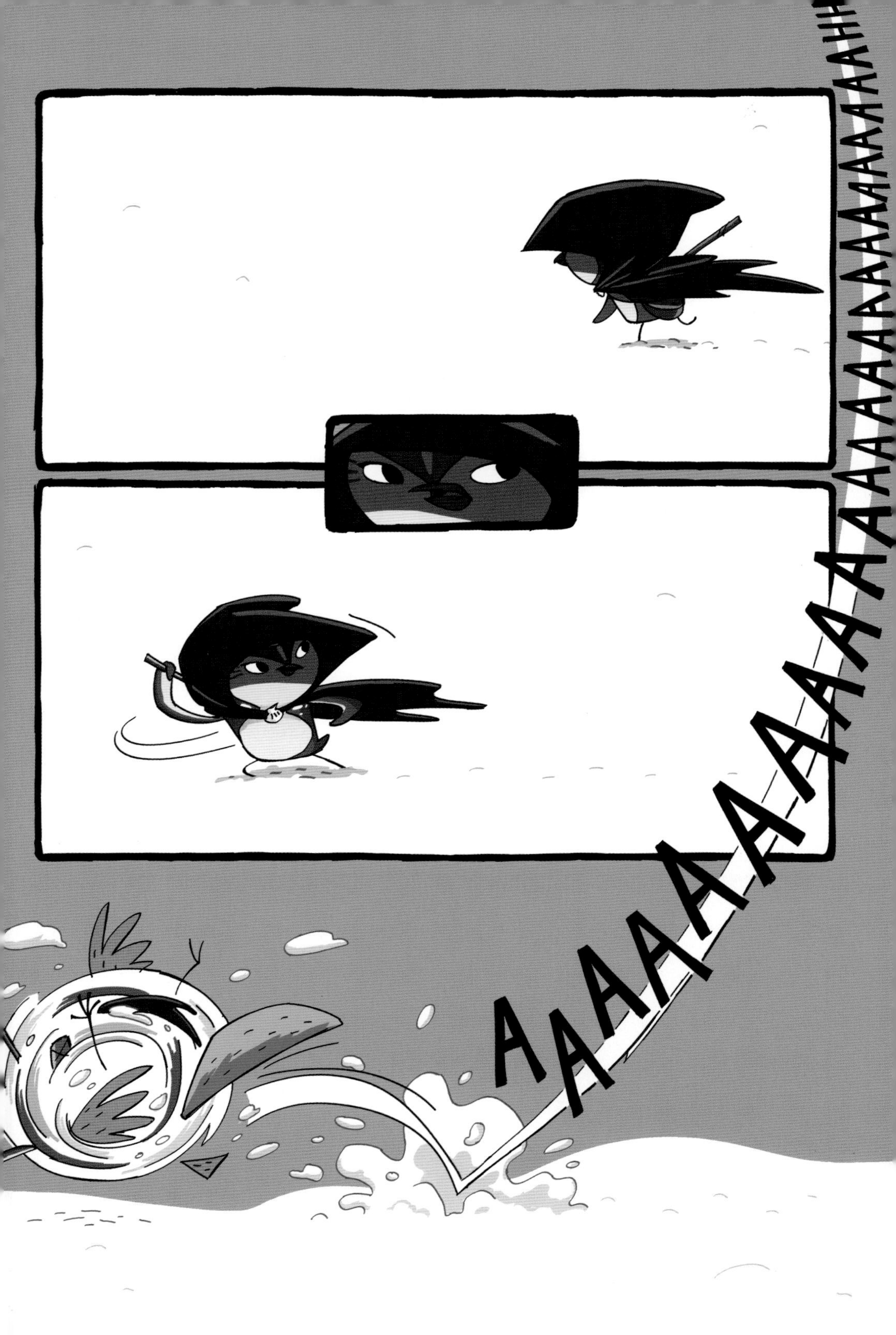
AAAAAAAAAAAAAAAAAAAAAAAAAAAHH

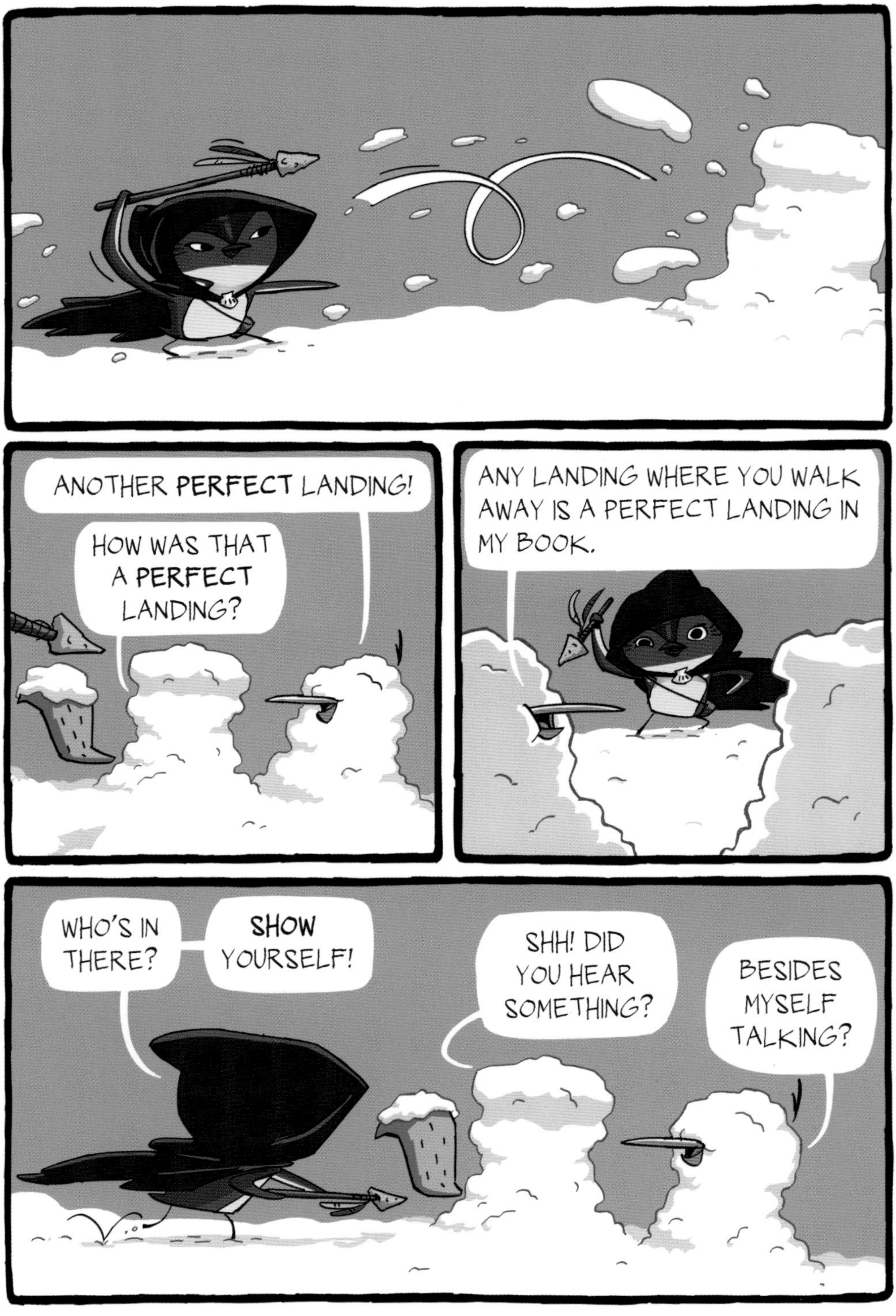
ANOTHER **PERFECT** LANDING!
HOW WAS THAT A **PERFECT** LANDING?
ANY LANDING WHERE YOU WALK AWAY IS A PERFECT LANDING IN MY BOOK.
WHO'S IN THERE?
SHOW YOURSELF!
SHH! DID YOU HEAR SOMETHING?
BESIDES MYSELF TALKING?

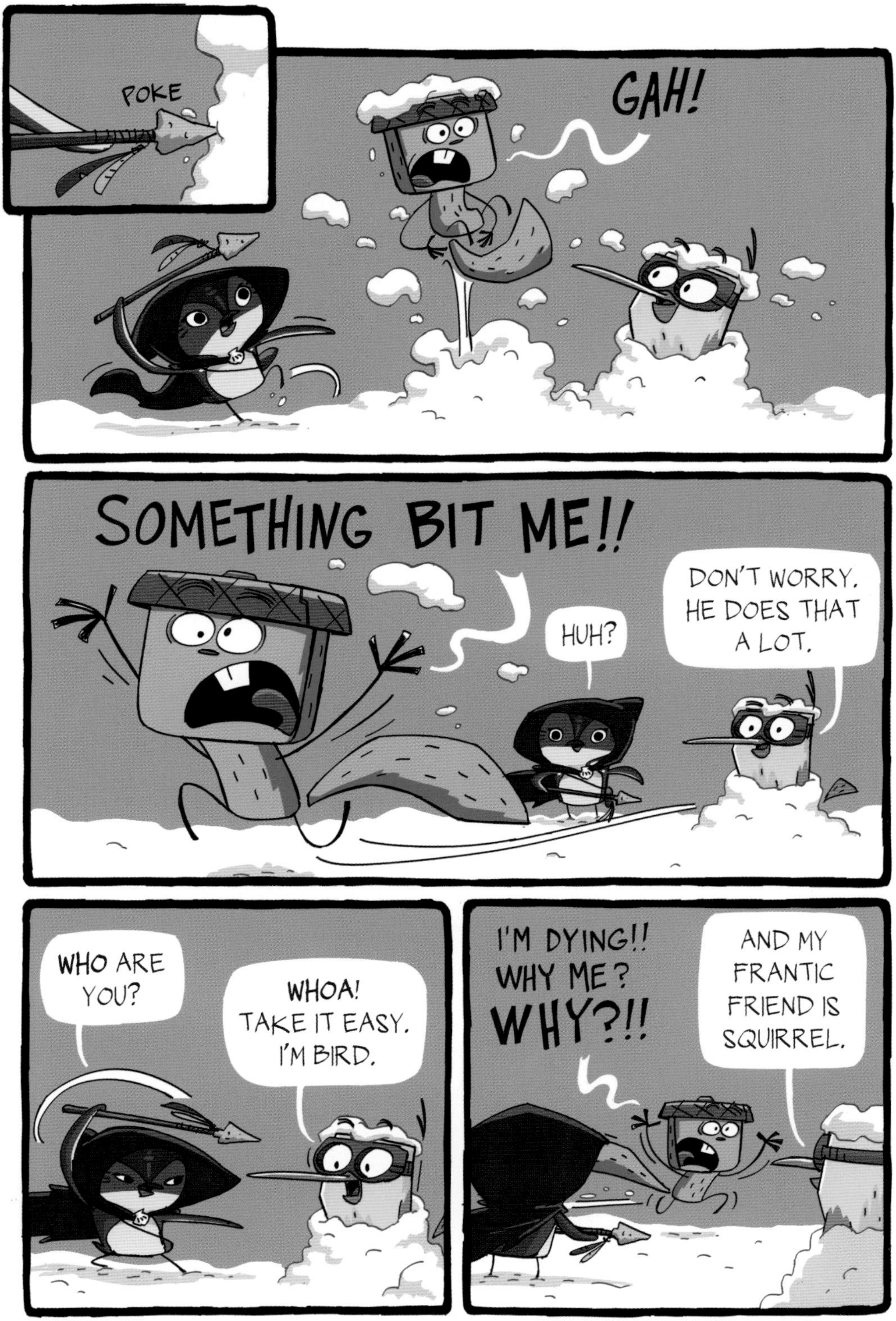
POKE
GAH!
SOMETHING BIT ME!!
HUH?
DON'T WORRY. HE DOES THAT A LOT.
WHO ARE YOU?
WHOA! TAKE IT EASY. I'M BIRD.
I'M DYING!! WHY ME? WHY?!!
AND MY FRANTIC FRIEND IS SQUIRREL.

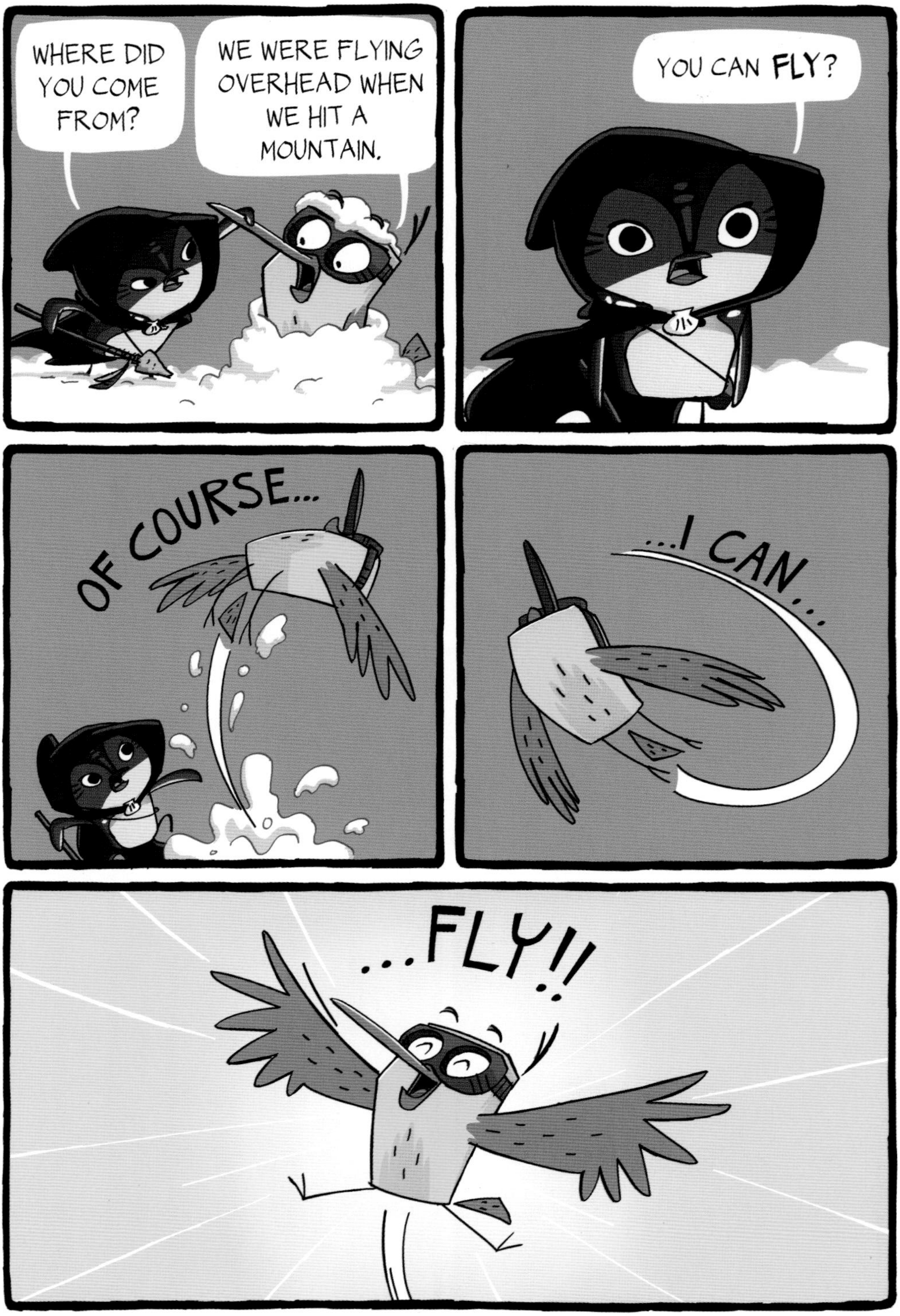
WHERE DID YOU COME FROM?
WE WERE FLYING OVERHEAD WHEN WE HIT A MOUNTAIN.
YOU CAN FLY?
OF COURSE...
...I CAN...
...FLY!!

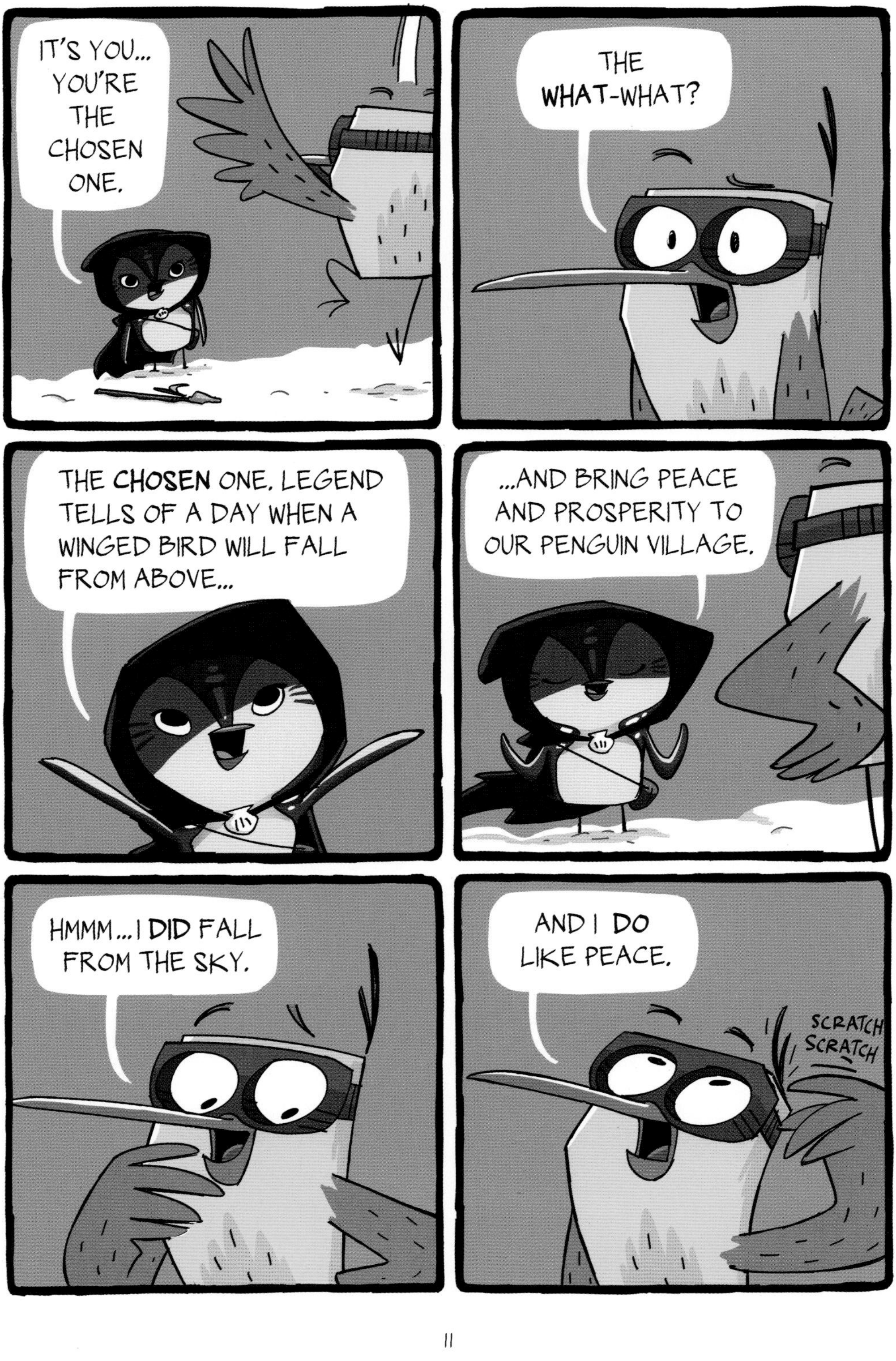
IT'S YOU... YOU'RE THE CHOSEN ONE.
THE WHAT-WHAT?
THE CHOSEN ONE. LEGEND TELLS OF A DAY WHEN A WINGED BIRD WILL FALL FROM ABOVE...
...AND BRING PEACE AND PROSPERITY TO OUR PENGUIN VILLAGE.
HMMM...I DID FALL FROM THE SKY.
AND I DO LIKE PEACE.
SCRATCH SCRATCH

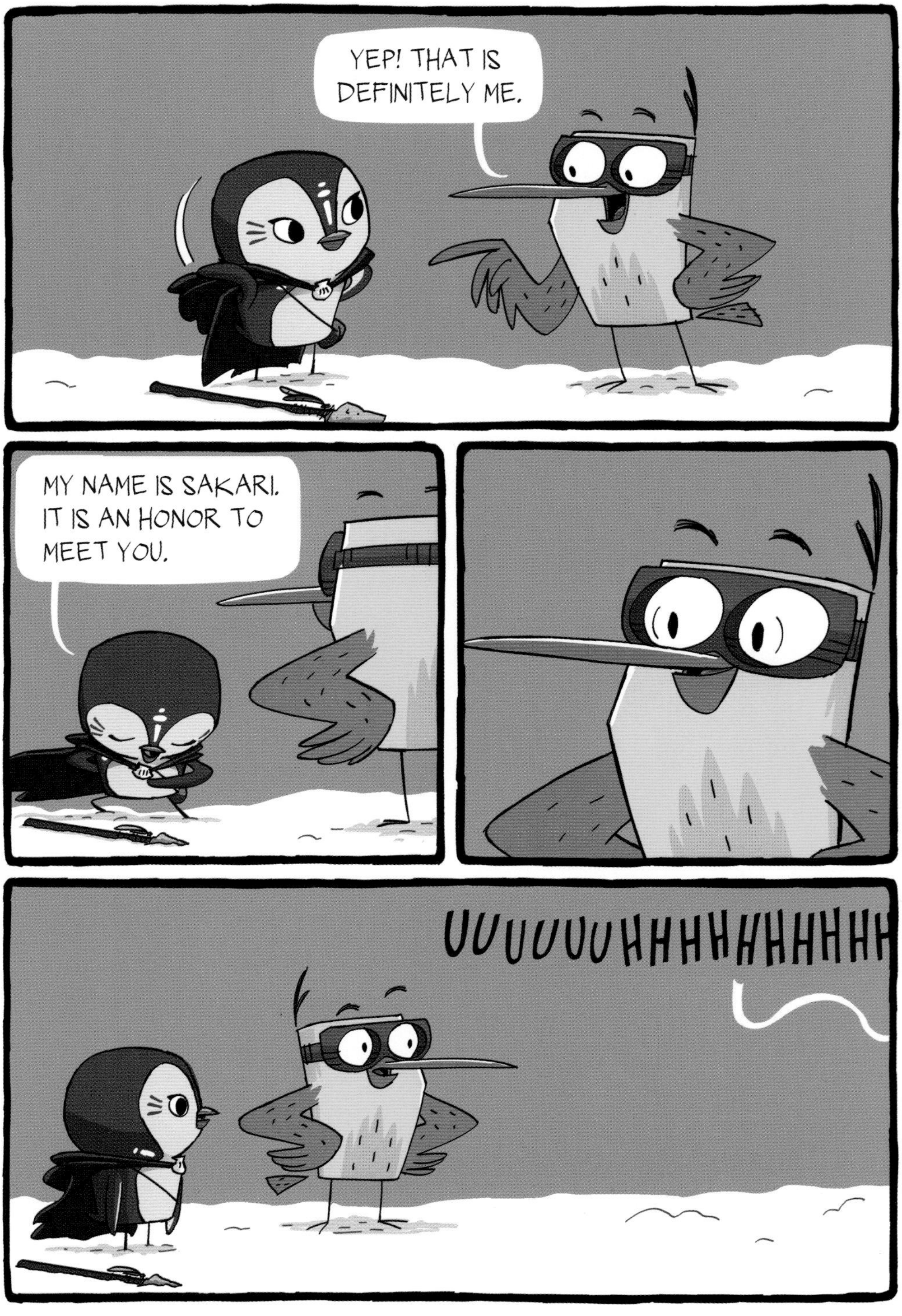
YEP! THAT IS DEFINITELY ME.
MY NAME IS SAKARI. IT IS AN HONOR TO MEET YOU.
UUUUUUHHHHHHHHHH

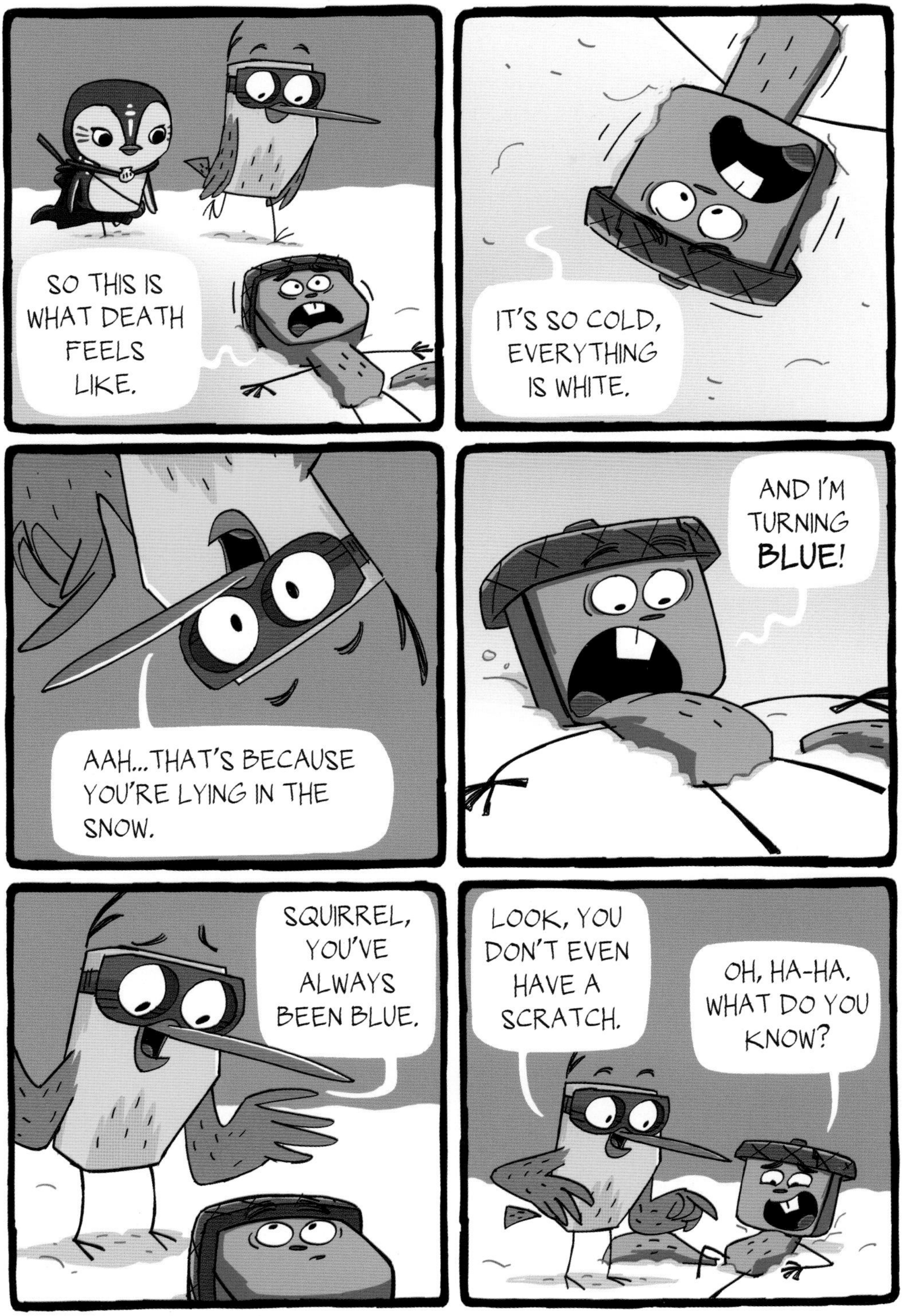
SO THIS IS WHAT DEATH FEELS LIKE.
IT'S SO COLD, EVERYTHING IS WHITE.
AAH...THAT'S BECAUSE YOU'RE LYING IN THE SNOW.
AND I'M TURNING **BLUE**!
SQUIRREL, YOU'VE ALWAYS BEEN BLUE.
LOOK, YOU DON'T EVEN HAVE A SCRATCH.
OH, HA-HA. WHAT DO YOU KNOW?

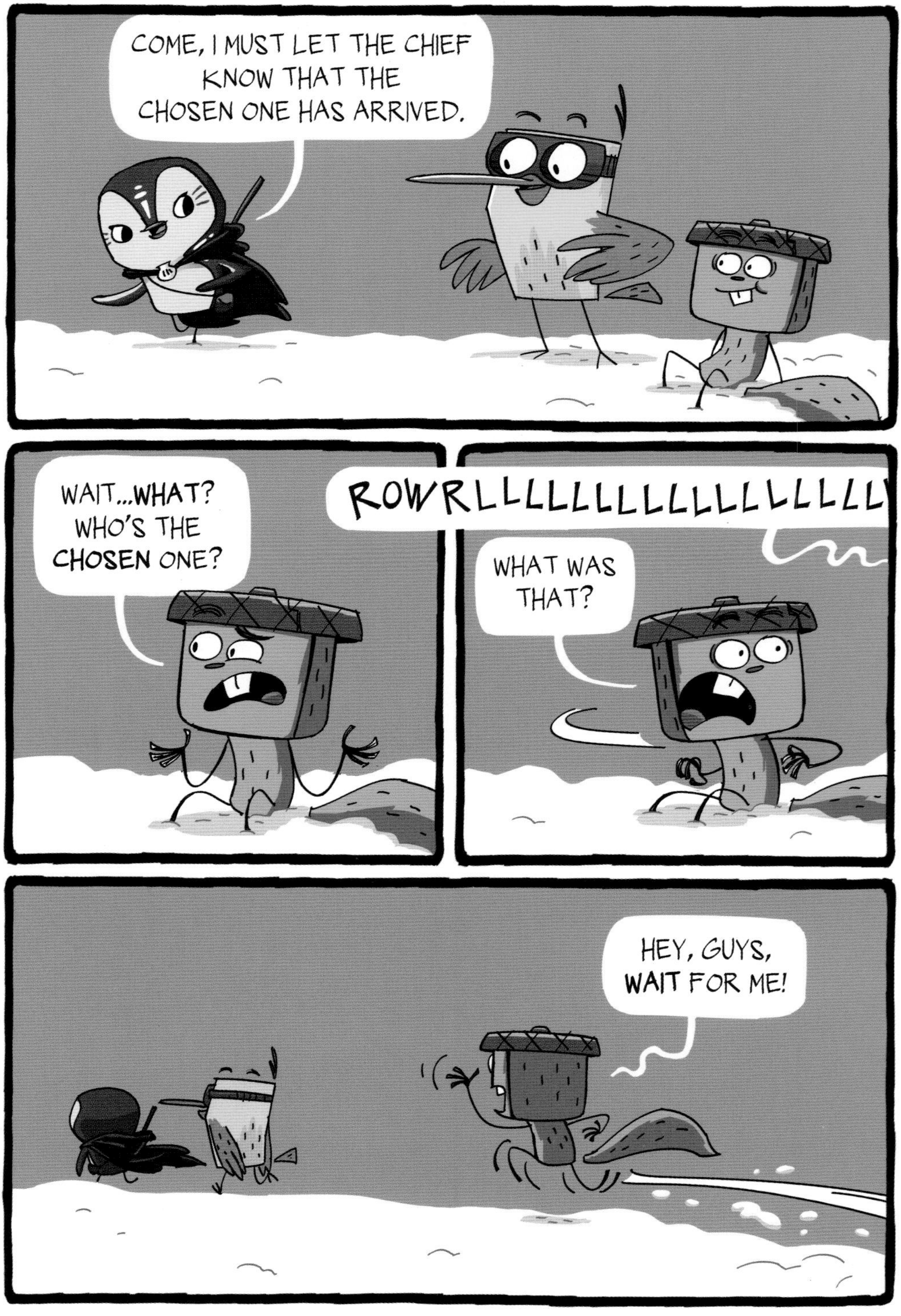
COME, I MUST LET THE CHIEF KNOW THAT THE CHOSEN ONE HAS ARRIVED.
WAIT...**WHAT?** WHO'S THE **CHOSEN** ONE?
ROWRLLLLLLLLLLLLLLLLL
WHAT WAS THAT?
HEY, GUYS, **WAIT** FOR ME!

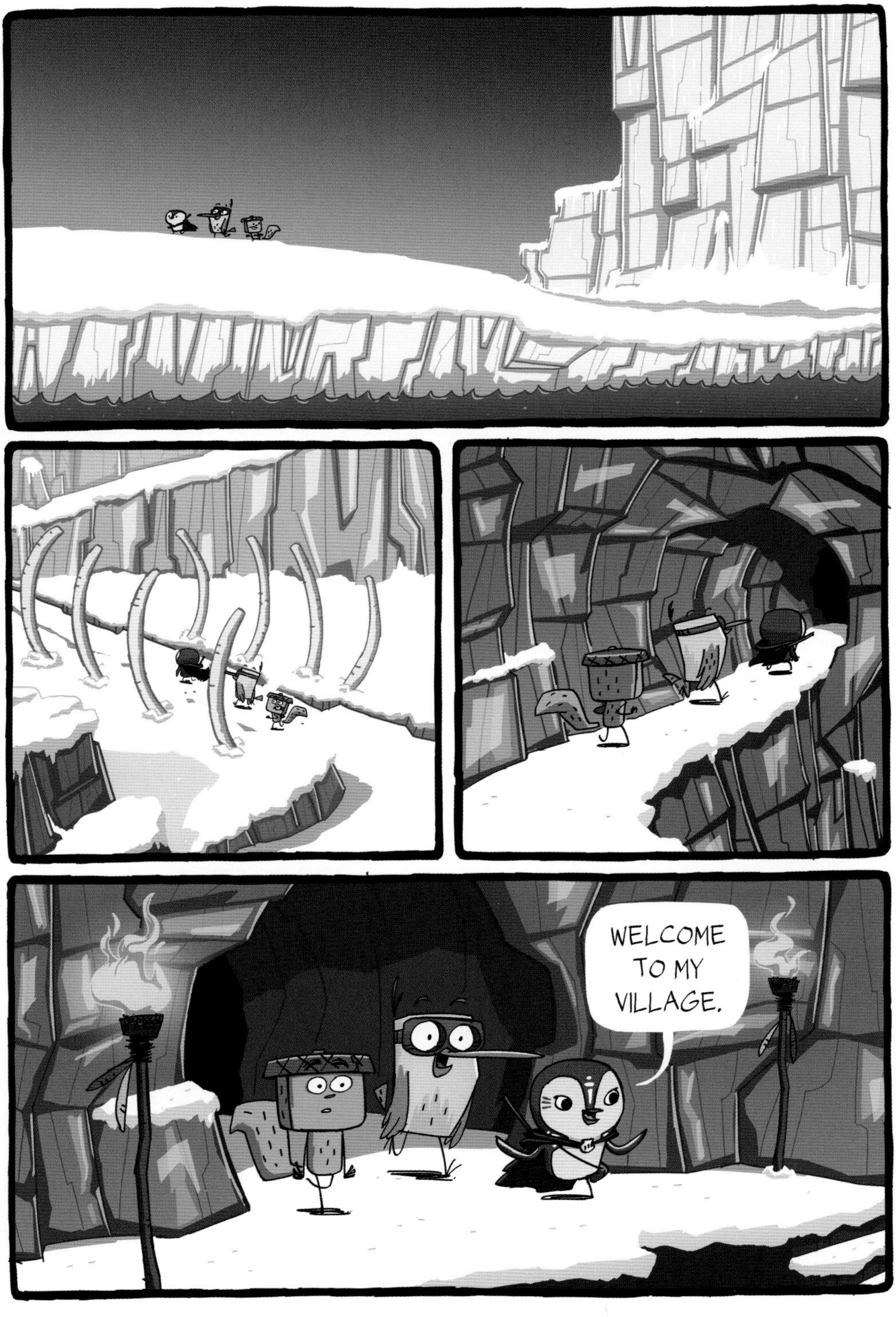
WELCOME TO MY VILLAGE.

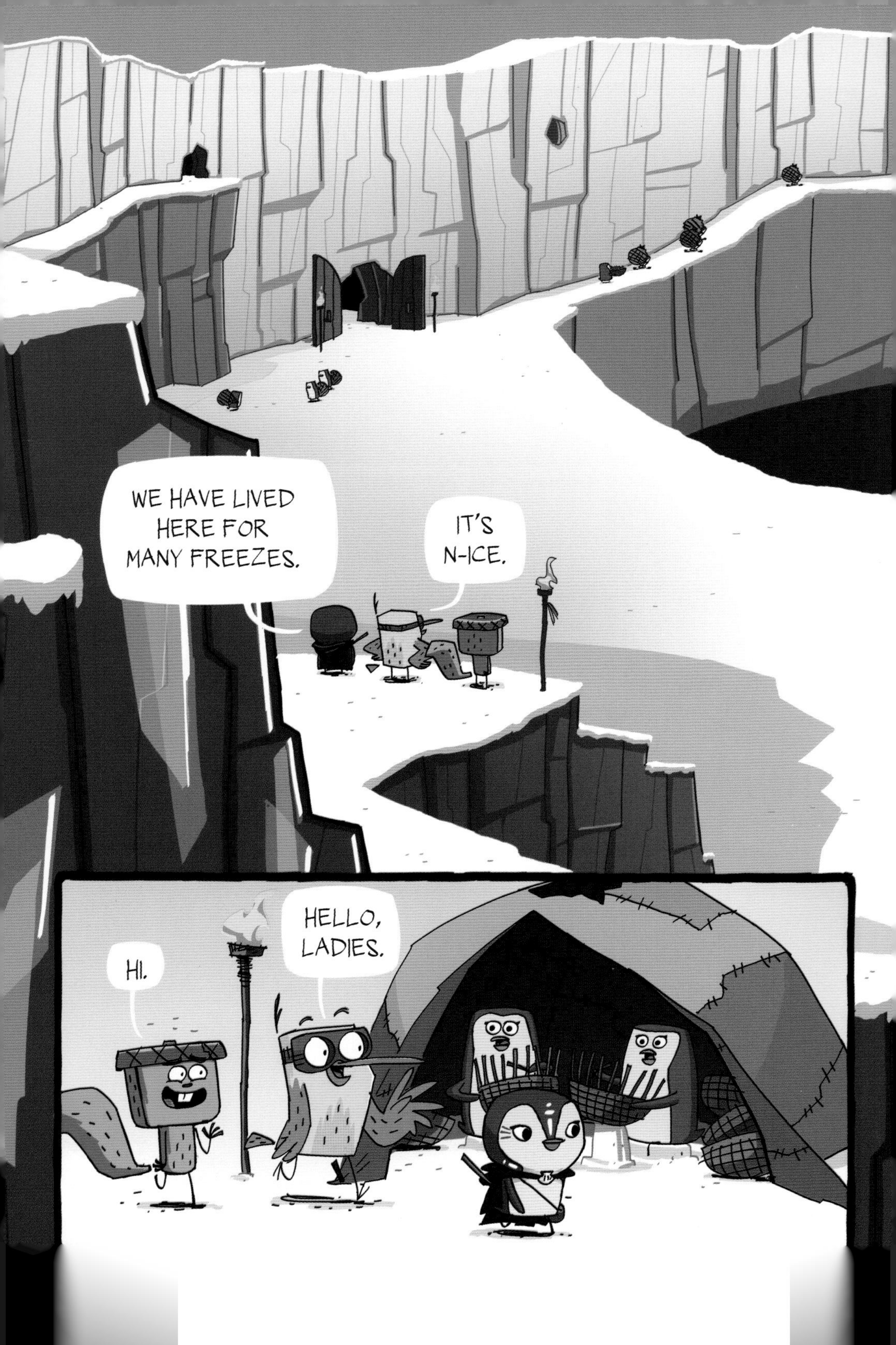
WE HAVE LIVED HERE FOR MANY FREEZES.
IT'S N-ICE.
HI.
HELLO, LADIES.

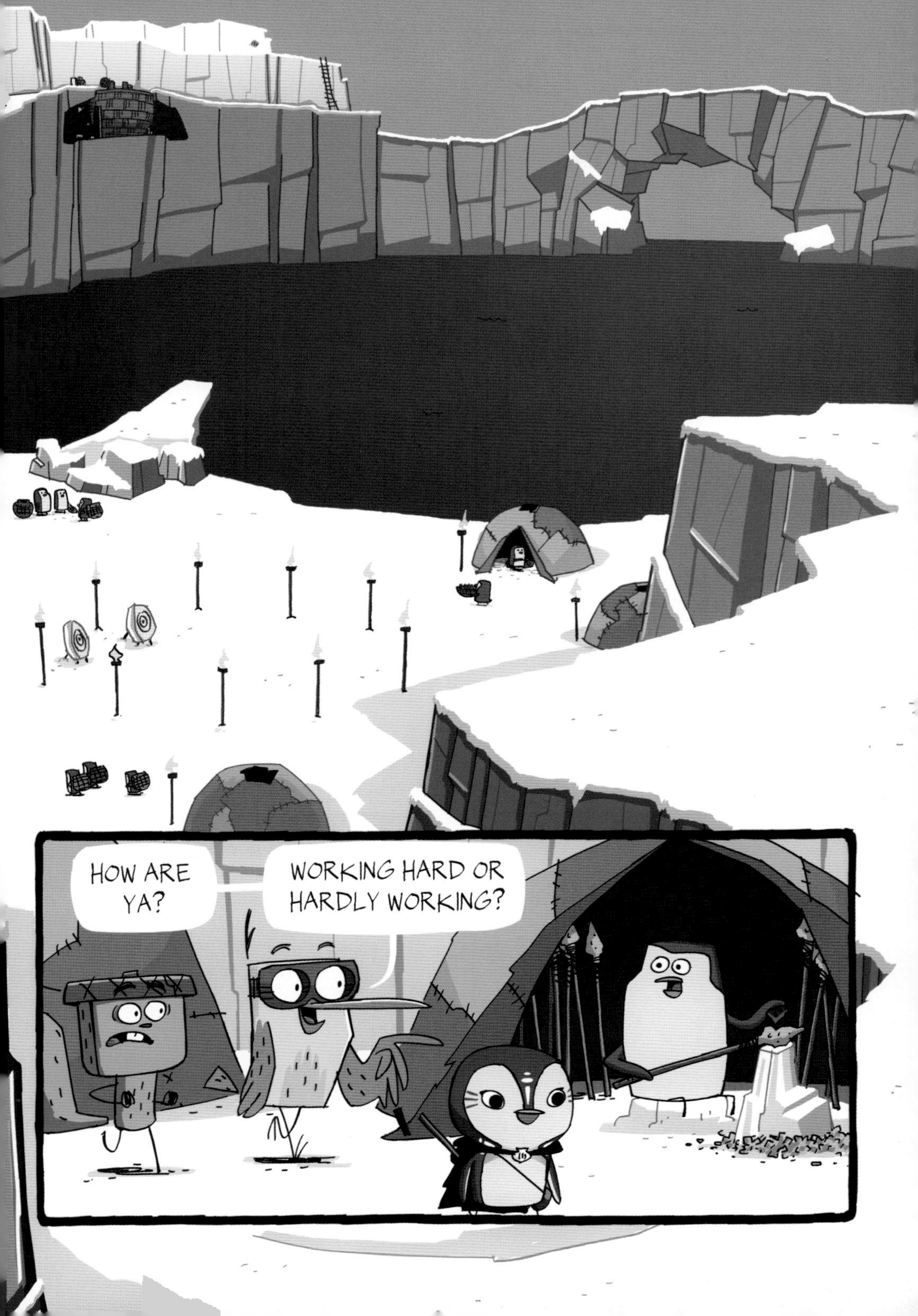
HOW ARE YA?
WORKING HARD OR HARDLY WORKING?

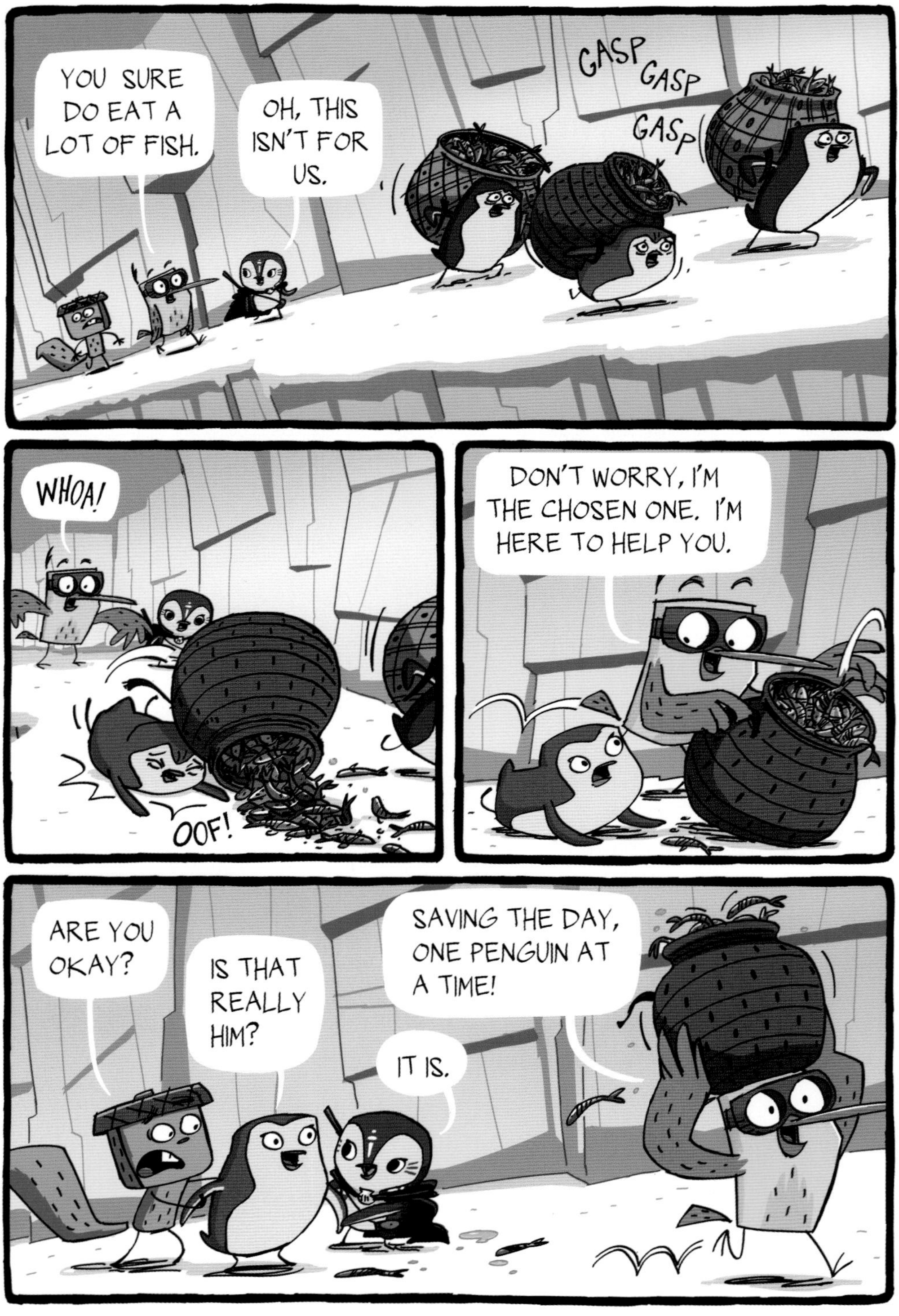
YOU SURE DO EAT A LOT OF FISH.
OH, THIS ISN'T FOR US.
GASP GASP GASP
WHOA!
OOF!
DON'T WORRY, I'M THE CHOSEN ONE. I'M HERE TO HELP YOU.
ARE YOU OKAY?
IS THAT REALLY HIM?
SAVING THE DAY, ONE PENGUIN AT A TIME!
IT IS.

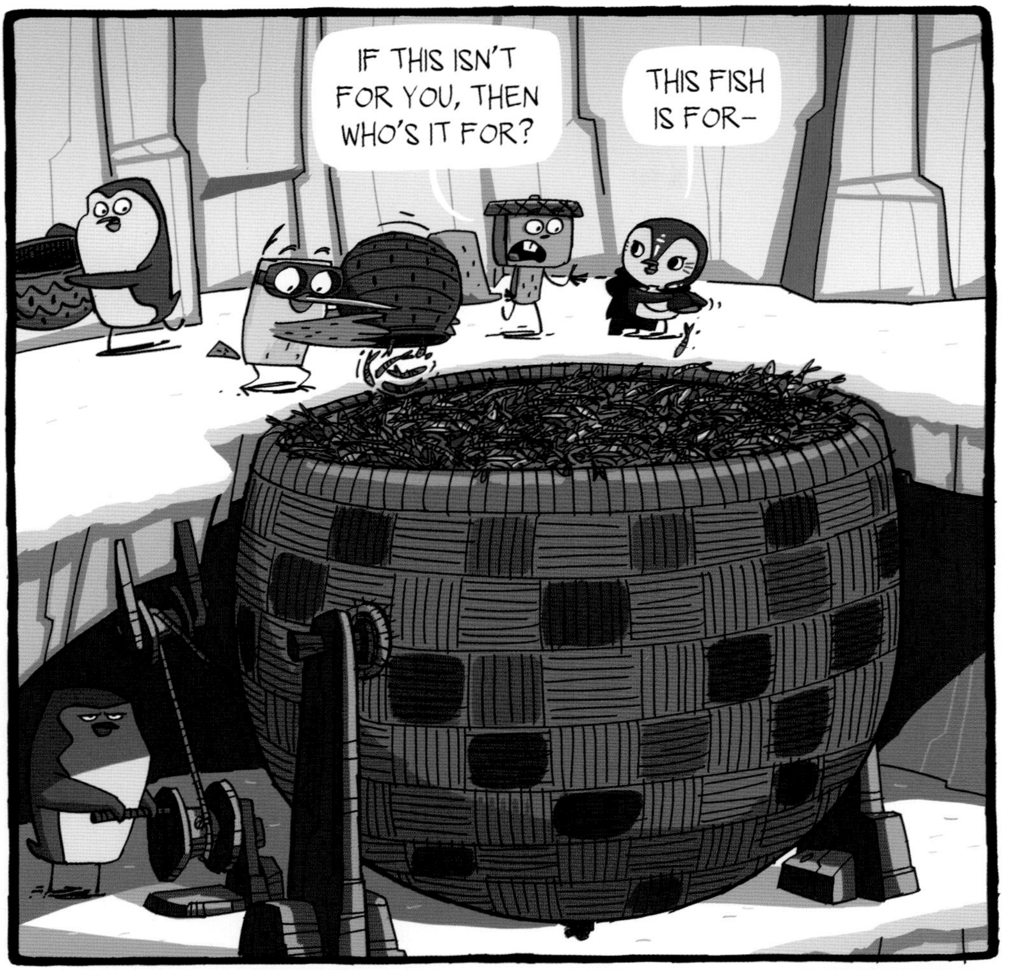
IF THIS ISN'T FOR YOU, THEN WHO'S IT FOR?
THIS FISH IS FOR–

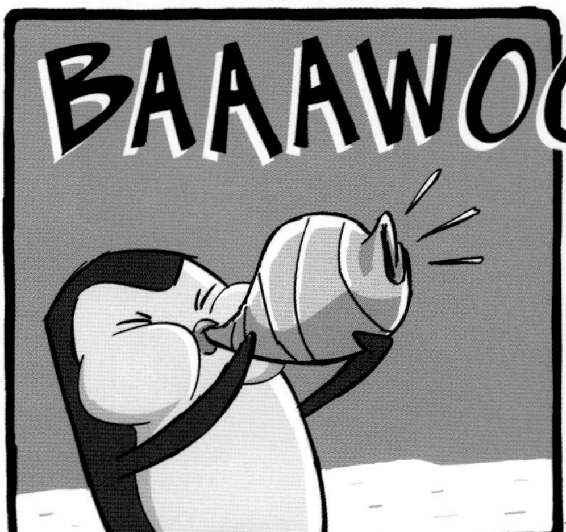
BAAAWOOOOOOOOOO

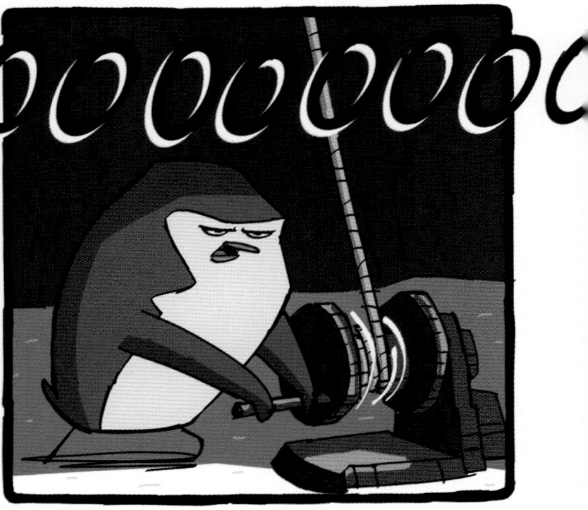

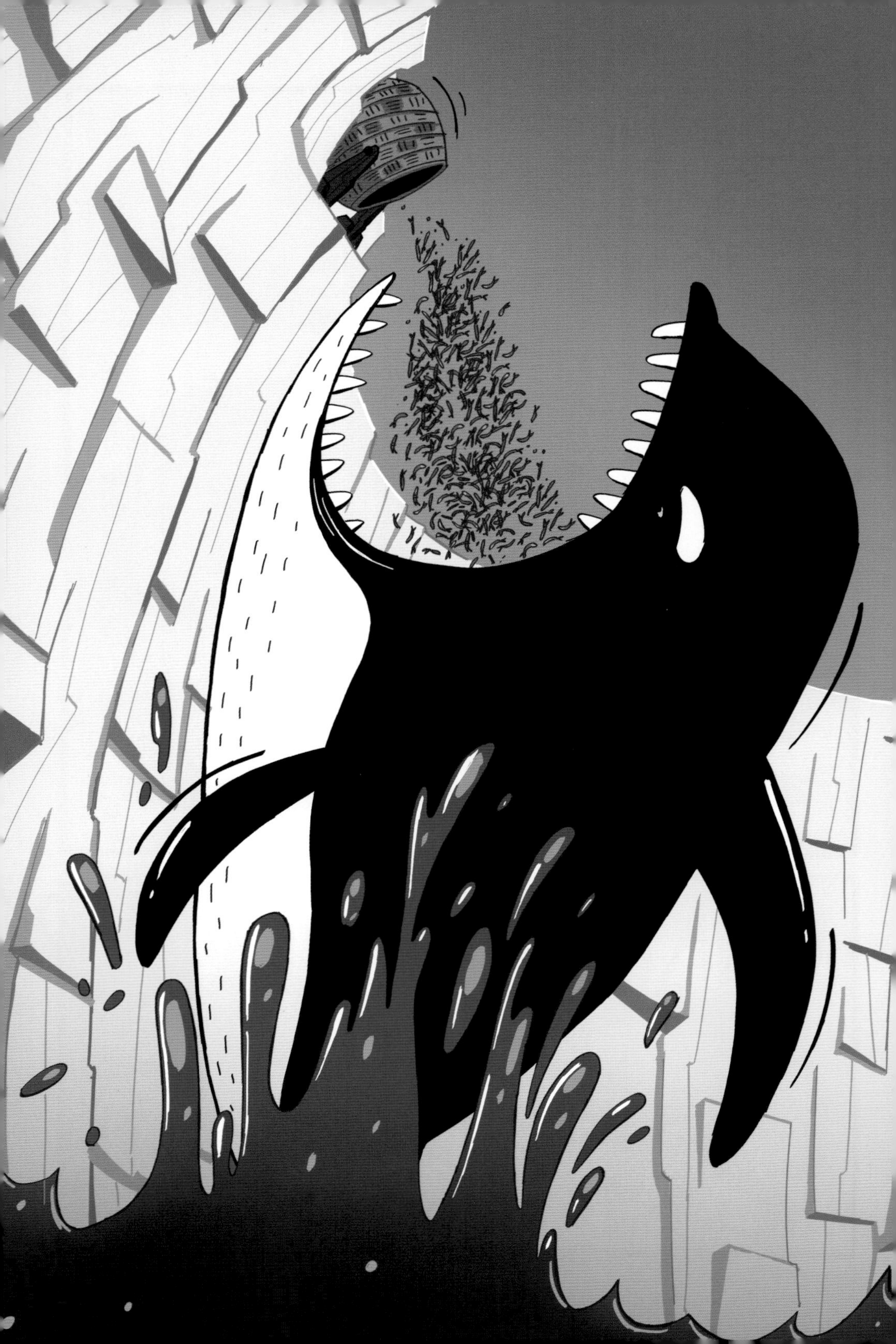

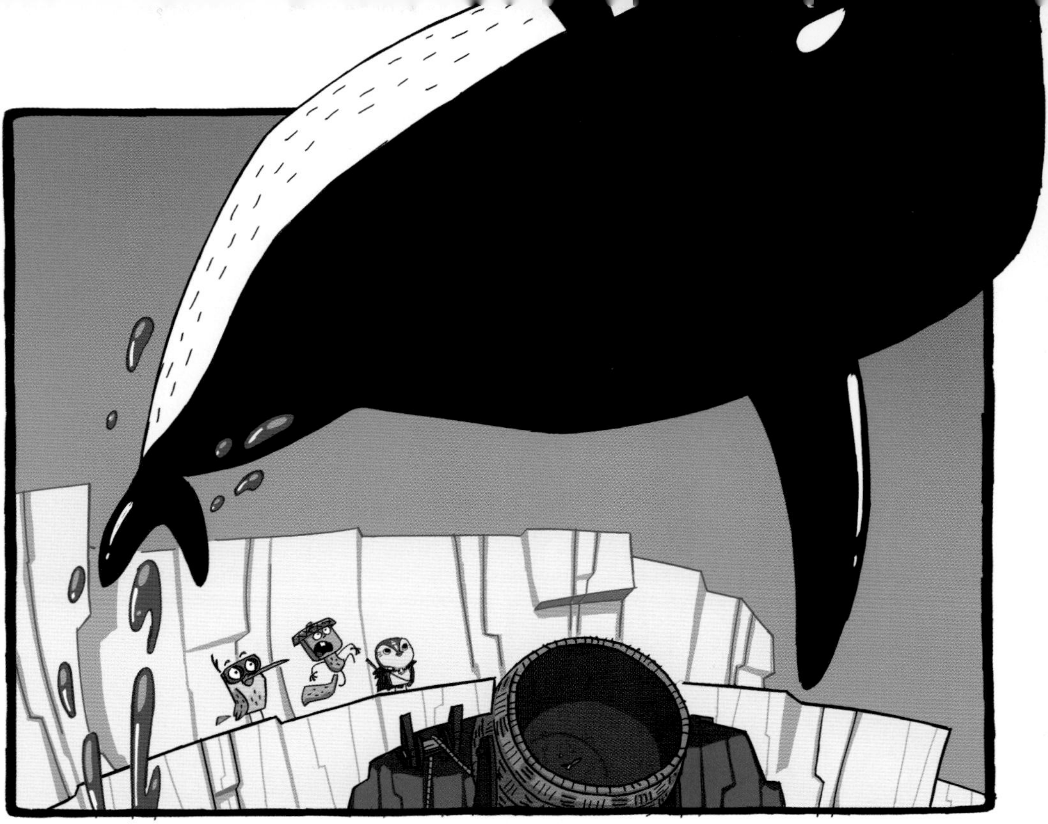

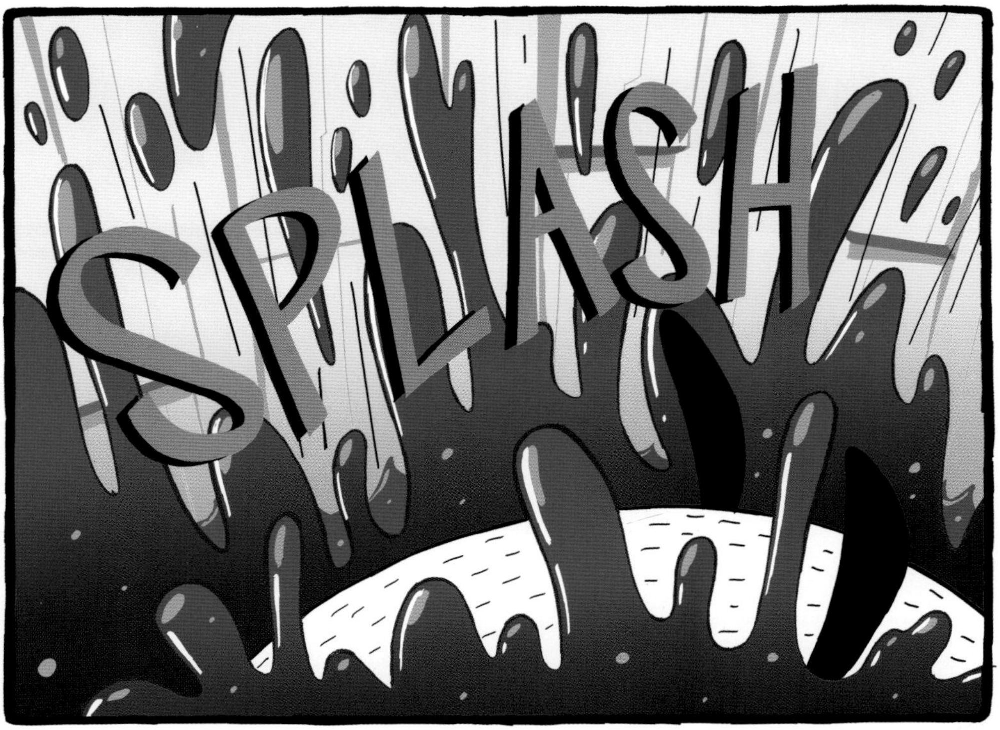
SPLASH

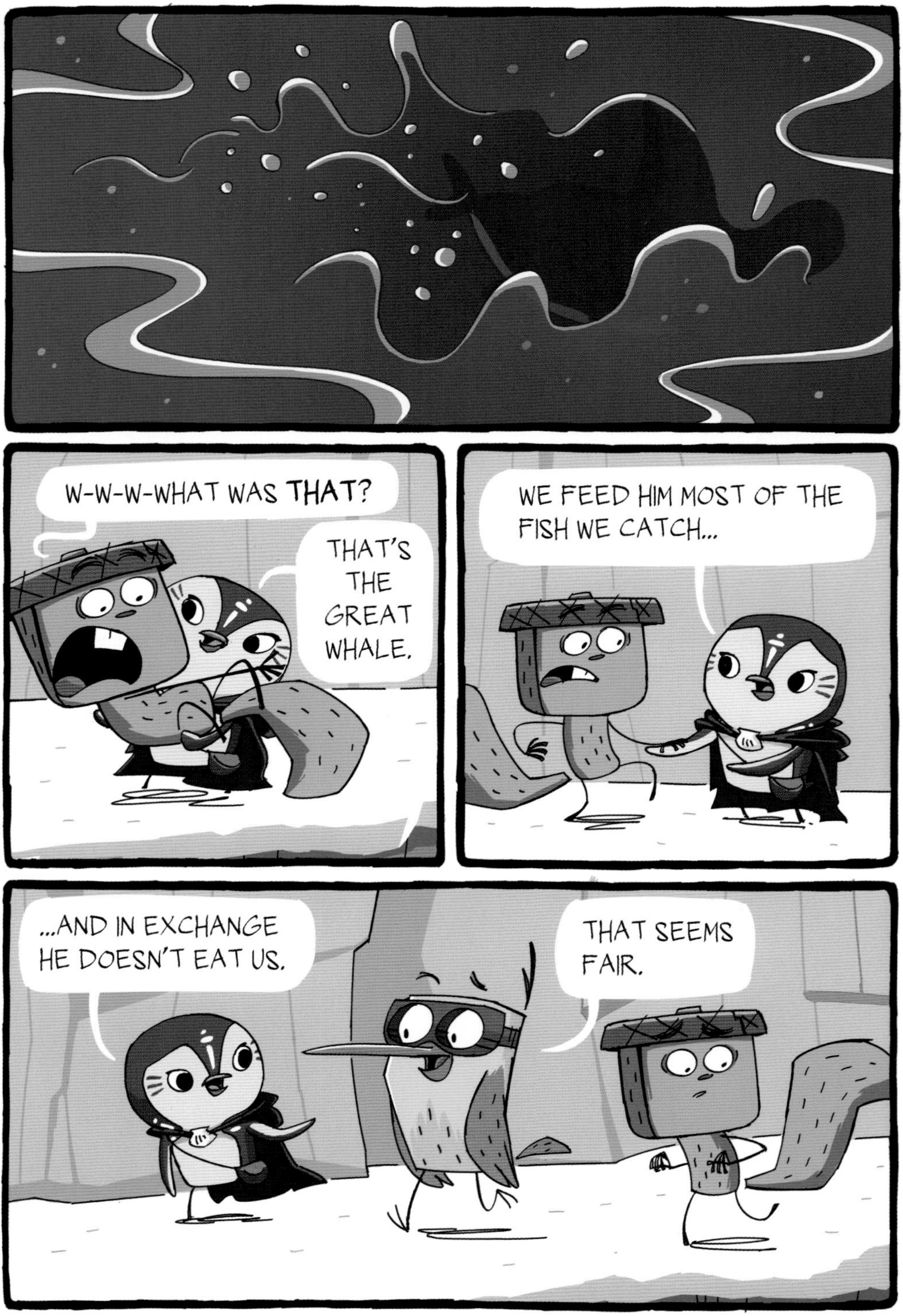
W-W-W-WHAT WAS THAT?
THAT'S THE GREAT WHALE.
WE FEED HIM MOST OF THE FISH WE CATCH...
...AND IN EXCHANGE HE DOESN'T EAT US.
THAT SEEMS FAIR.

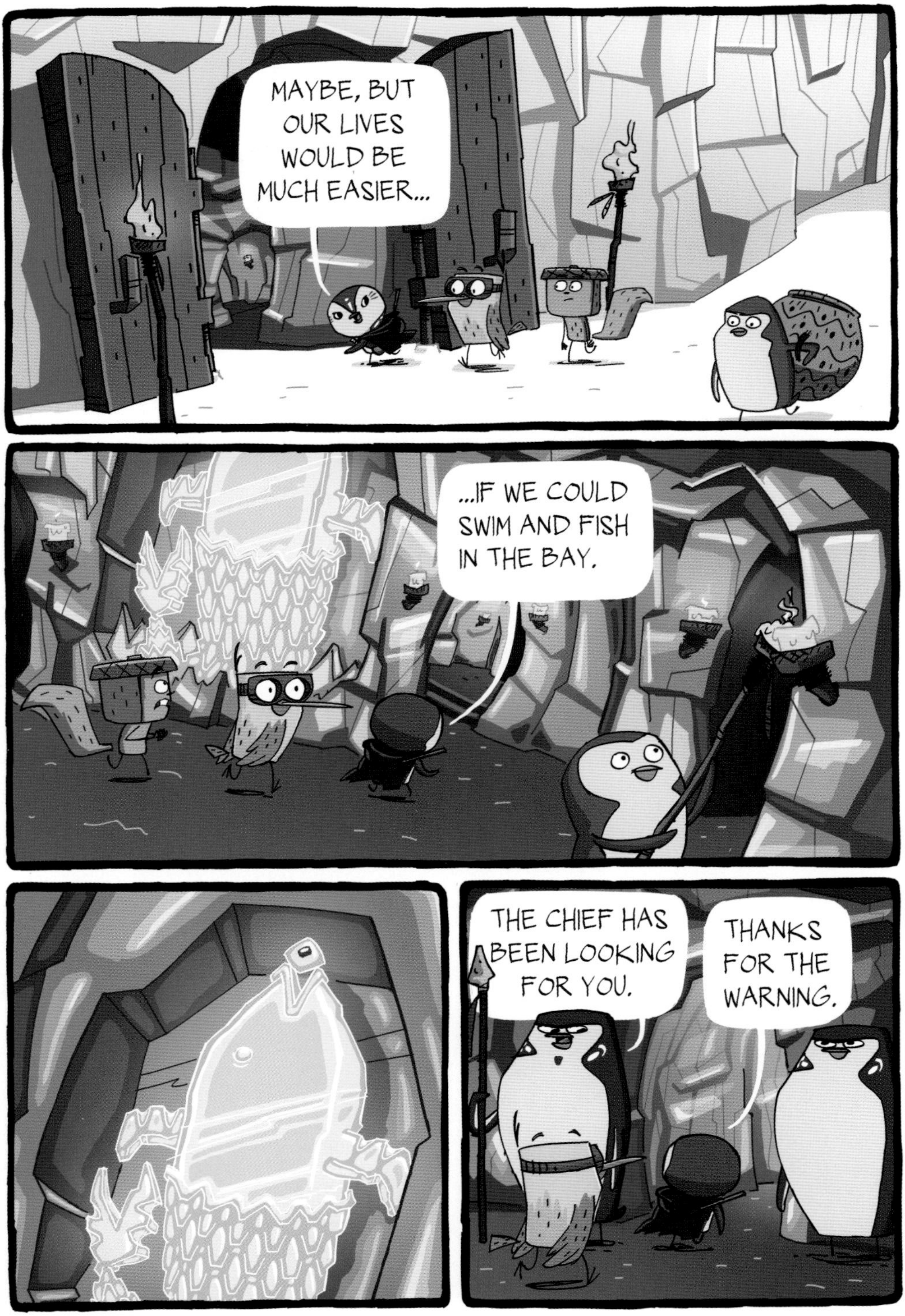
MAYBE, BUT OUR LIVES WOULD BE MUCH EASIER...
...IF WE COULD SWIM AND FISH IN THE BAY.
THE CHIEF HAS BEEN LOOKING FOR YOU.
THANKS FOR THE WARNING.

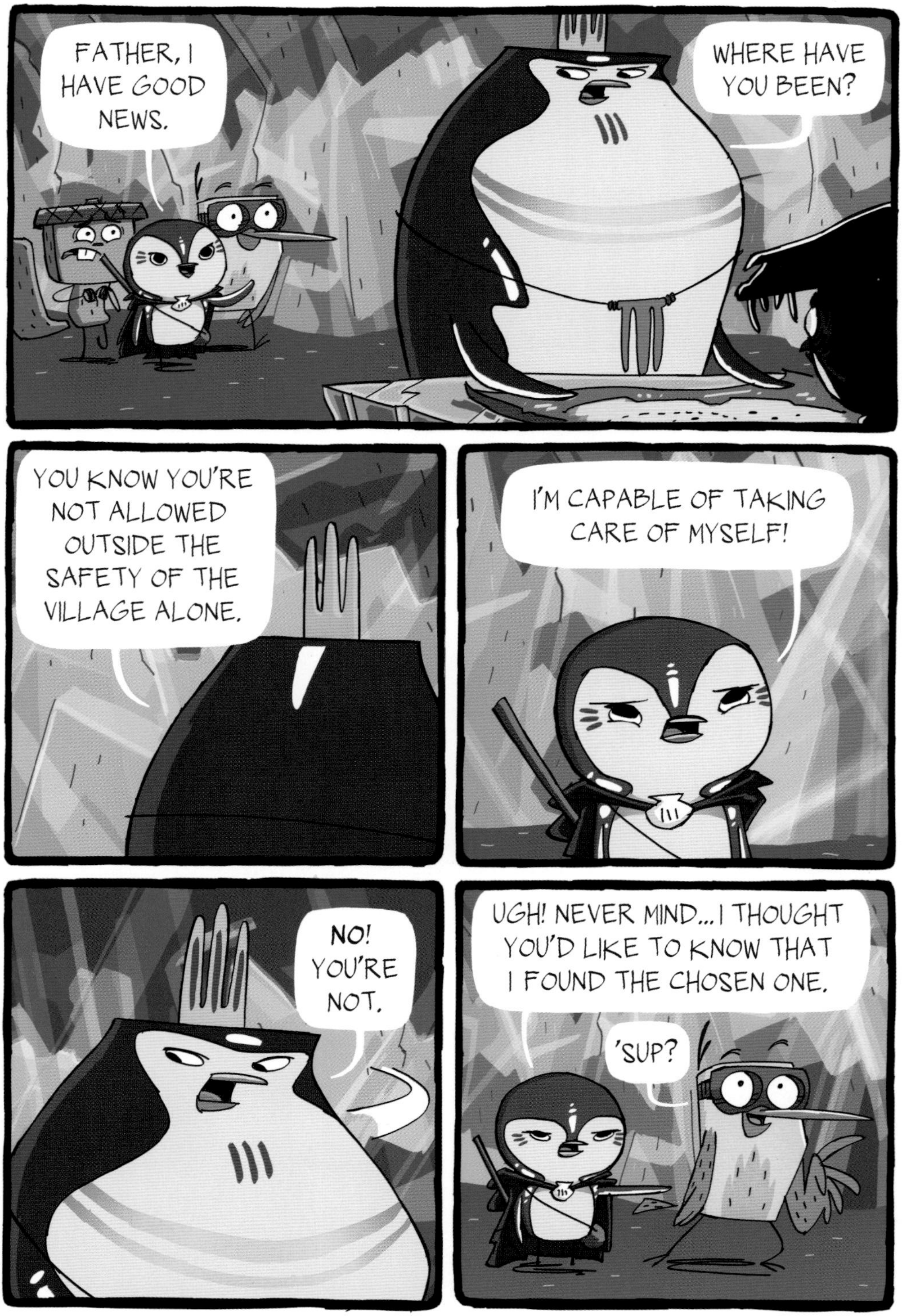
FATHER, I HAVE GOOD NEWS.
WHERE HAVE YOU BEEN?
YOU KNOW YOU'RE NOT ALLOWED OUTSIDE THE SAFETY OF THE VILLAGE ALONE.
I'M CAPABLE OF TAKING CARE OF MYSELF!
NO! YOU'RE NOT.
UGH! NEVER MIND... I THOUGHT YOU'D LIKE TO KNOW THAT I FOUND THE CHOSEN ONE.
'SUP?

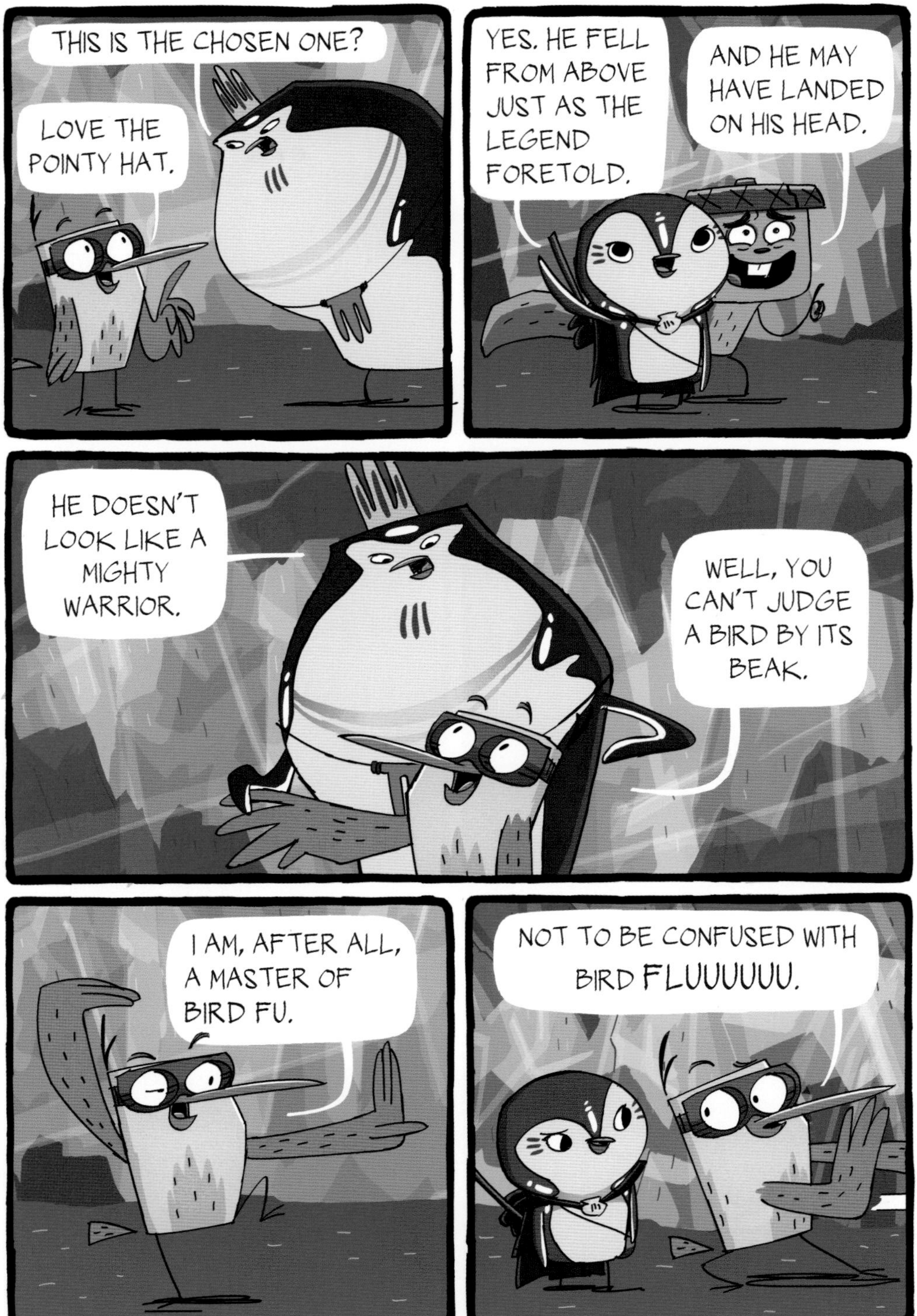

THIS IS THE CHOSEN ONE?
LOVE THE POINTY HAT.
YES. HE FELL FROM ABOVE JUST AS THE LEGEND FORETOLD.
AND HE MAY HAVE LANDED ON HIS HEAD.
HE DOESN'T LOOK LIKE A MIGHTY WARRIOR.
WELL, YOU CAN'T JUDGE A BIRD BY ITS BEAK.
I AM, AFTER ALL, A MASTER OF BIRD FU.
NOT TO BE CONFUSED WITH BIRD FLUUUUUU.

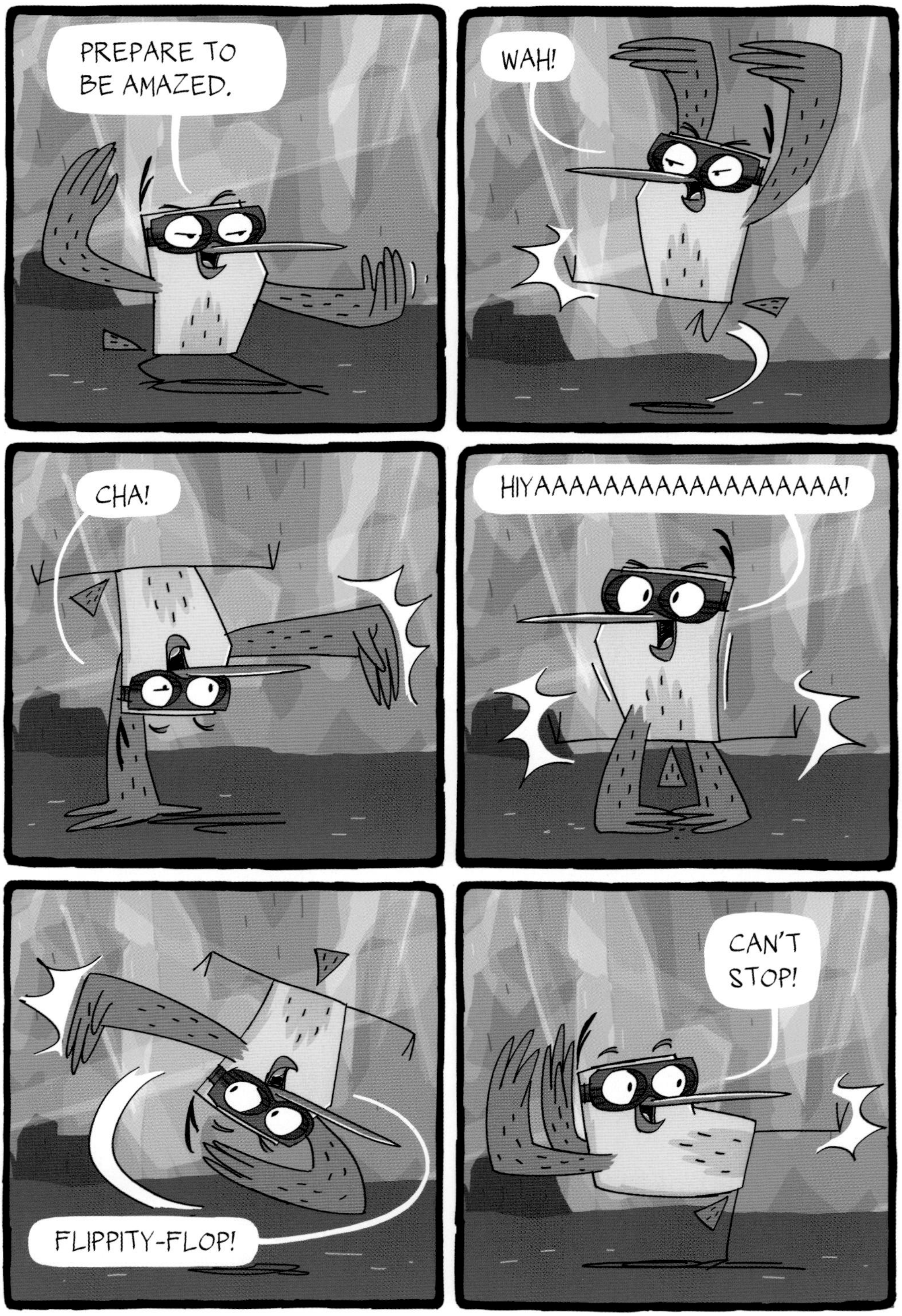
PREPARE TO BE AMAZED.
WAH!
CHA!
HIYAAAAAAAAAAAAAAAAAA!
FLIPPITY-FLOP!
CAN'T STOP!

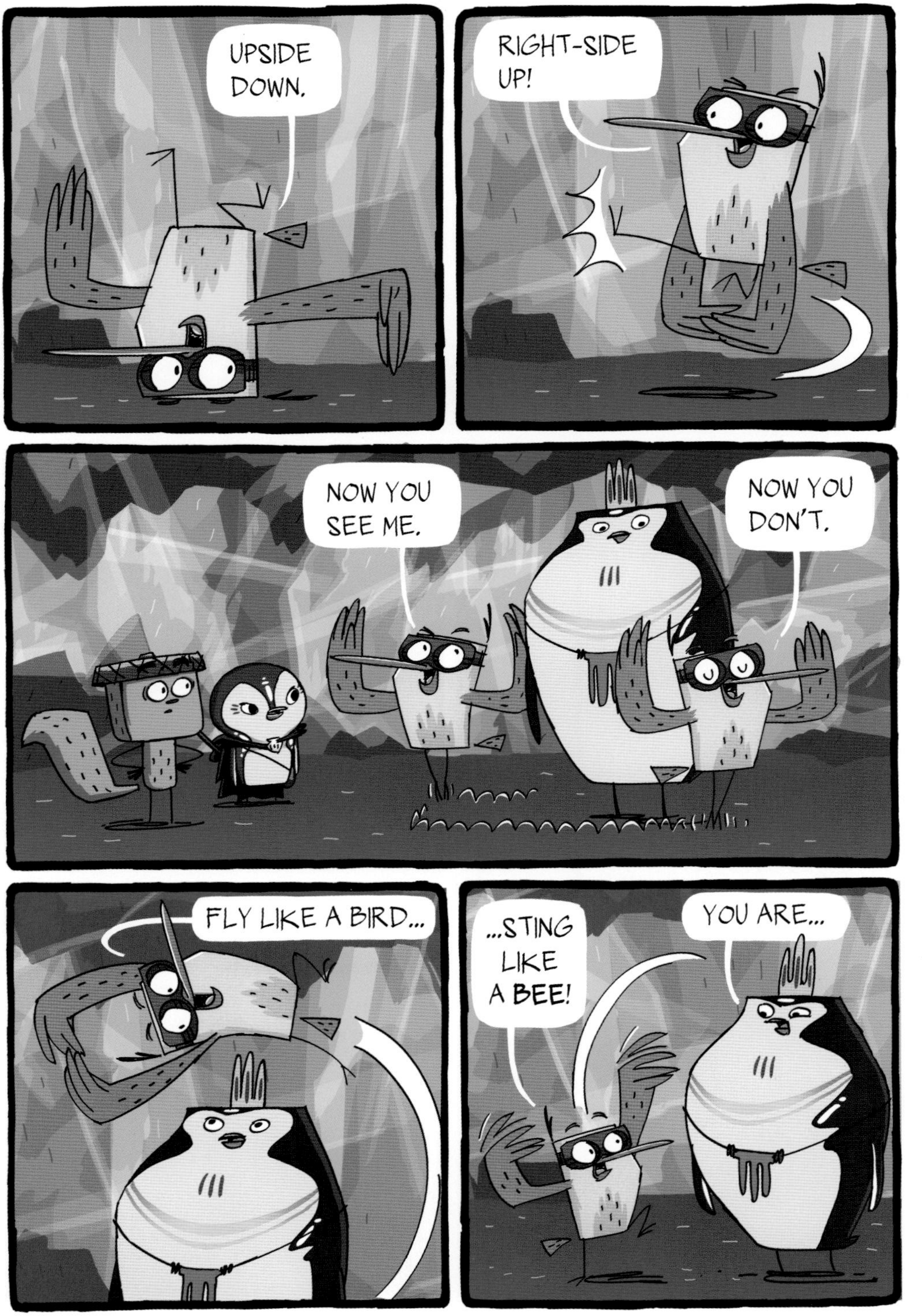
UPSIDE DOWN.
RIGHT-SIDE UP!
NOW YOU SEE ME.
NOW YOU DON'T.
FLY LIKE A BIRD...
...STING LIKE A BEE!
YOU ARE...

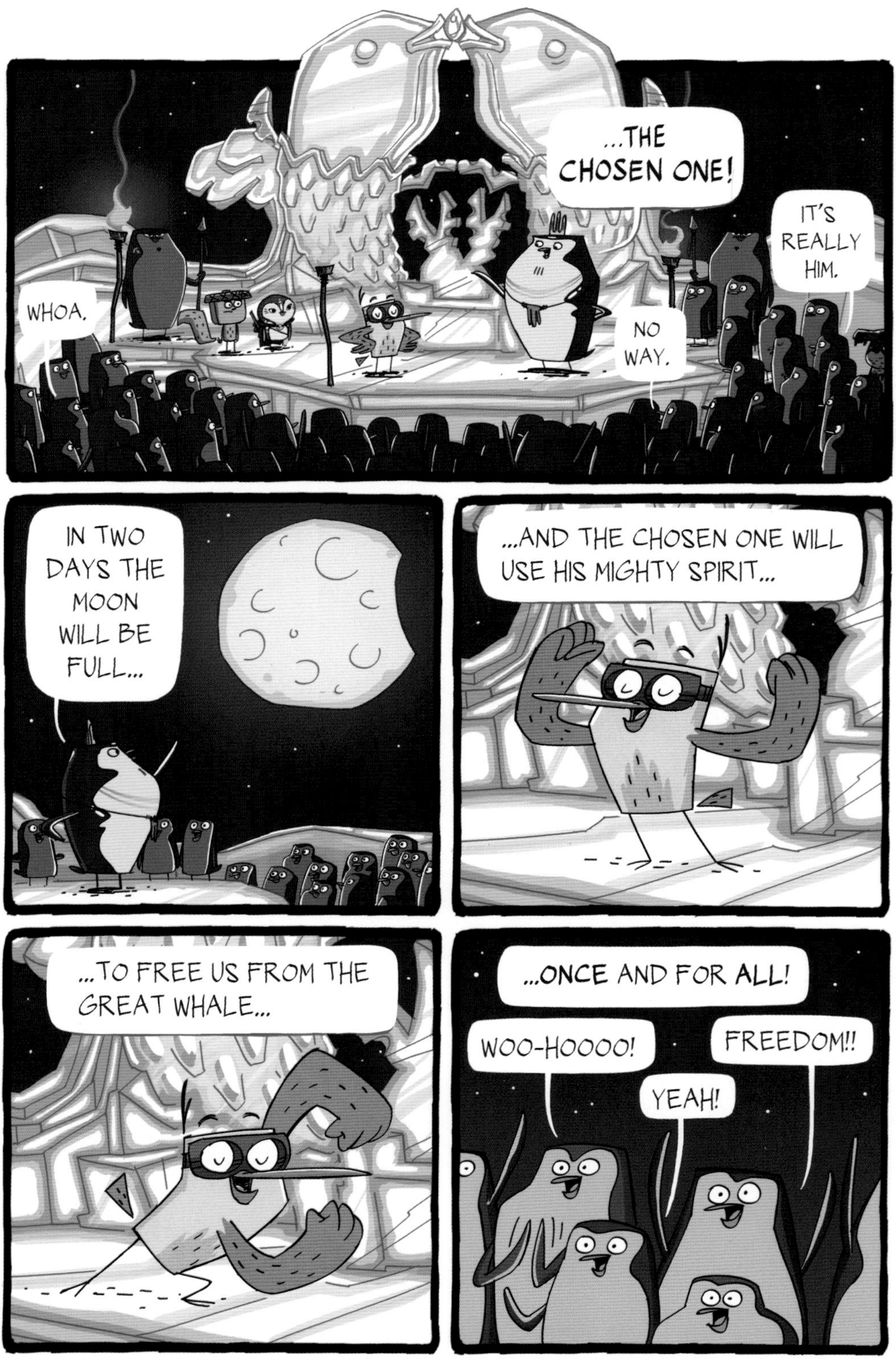
...THE CHOSEN ONE!
IT'S REALLY HIM.
WHOA.
NO WAY.
IN TWO DAYS THE MOON WILL BE FULL...
...AND THE CHOSEN ONE WILL USE HIS MIGHTY SPIRIT...
...TO FREE US FROM THE GREAT WHALE...
...ONCE AND FOR ALL!
WOO-HOOOO!
FREEDOM!!
YEAH!

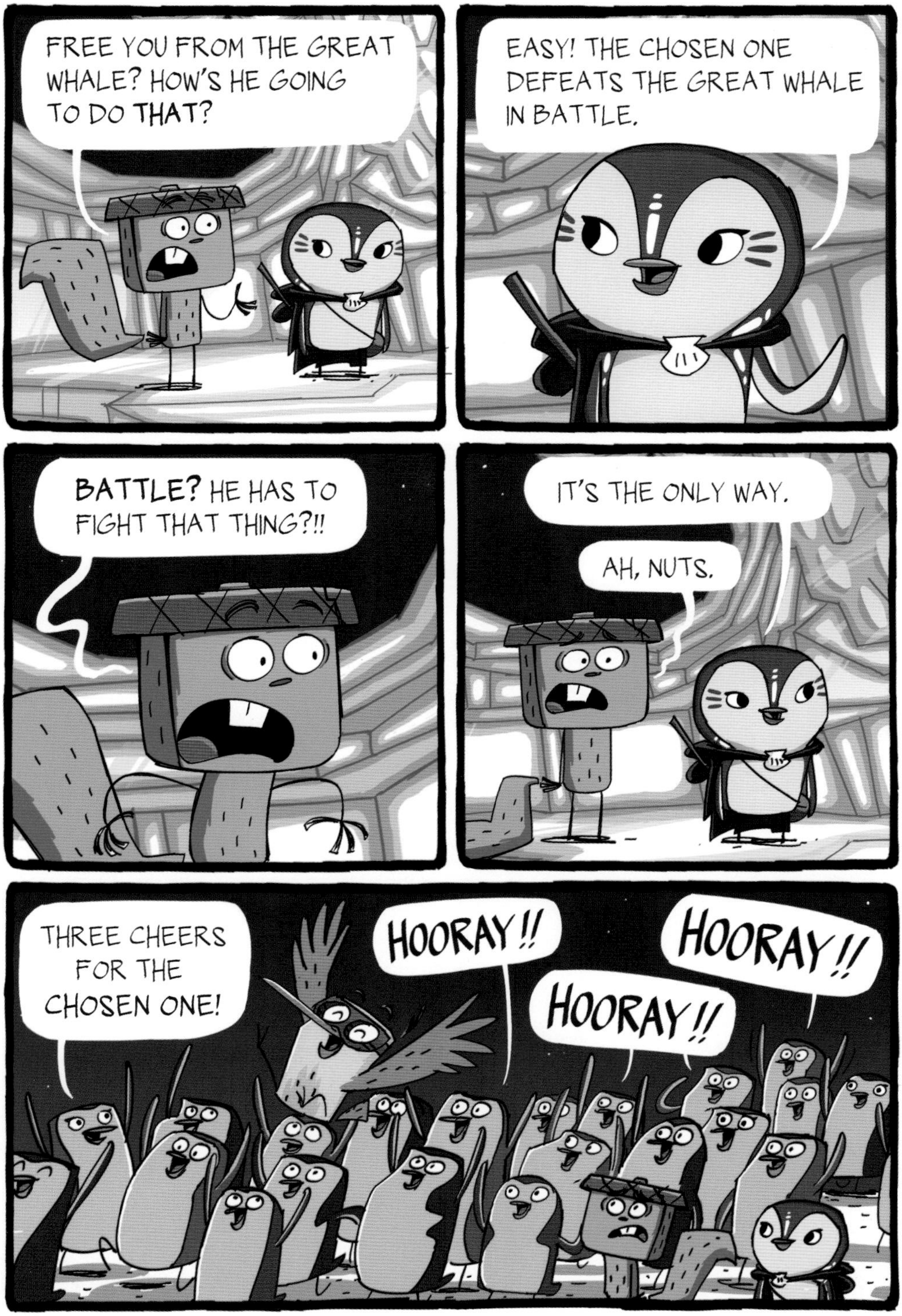
FREE YOU FROM THE GREAT WHALE? HOW'S HE GOING TO DO THAT?
EASY! THE CHOSEN ONE DEFEATS THE GREAT WHALE IN BATTLE.
BATTLE? HE HAS TO FIGHT THAT THING?!!
IT'S THE ONLY WAY.
AH, NUTS.
THREE CHEERS FOR THE CHOSEN ONE!
HOORAY!!
HOORAY!!
HOORAY!!

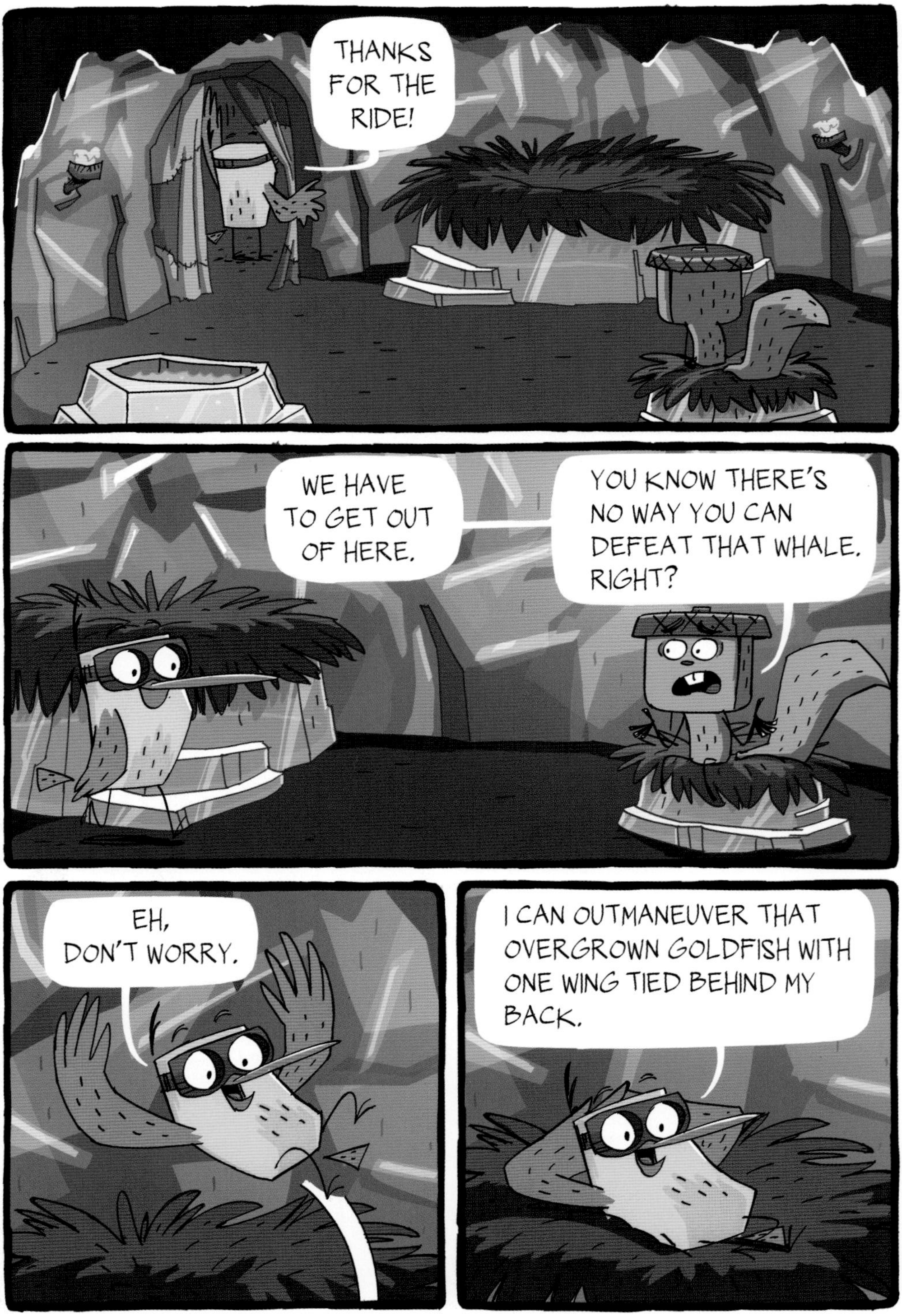
THANKS FOR THE RIDE!
WE HAVE TO GET OUT OF HERE.
YOU KNOW THERE'S NO WAY YOU CAN DEFEAT THAT WHALE. RIGHT?
EH, DON'T WORRY.
I CAN OUTMANEUVER THAT OVERGROWN GOLDFISH WITH ONE WING TIED BEHIND MY BACK.

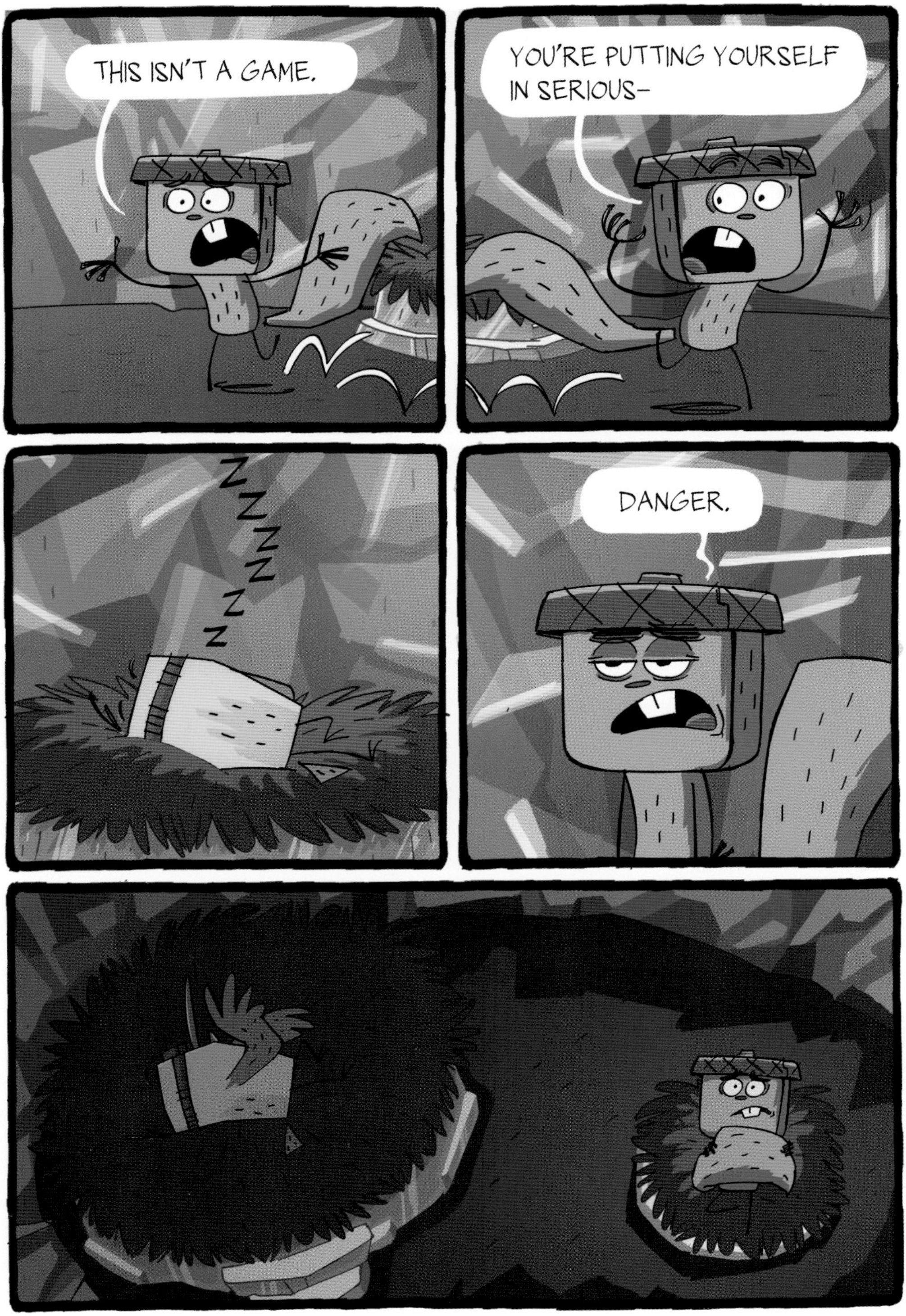
THIS ISN'T A GAME.
YOU'RE PUTTING YOURSELF IN SERIOUS–
ZZZZZZZ
DANGER.

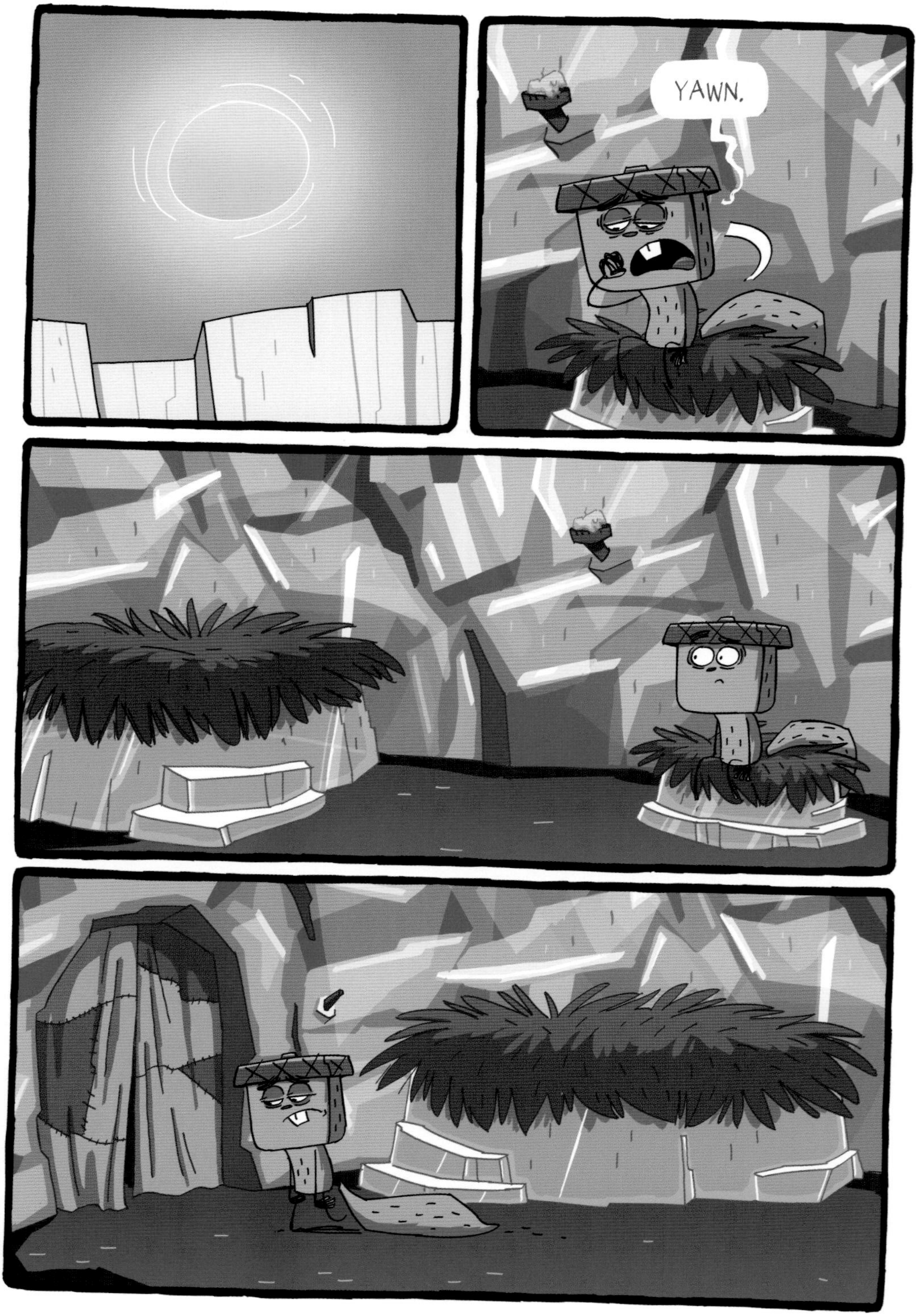
YAWN.

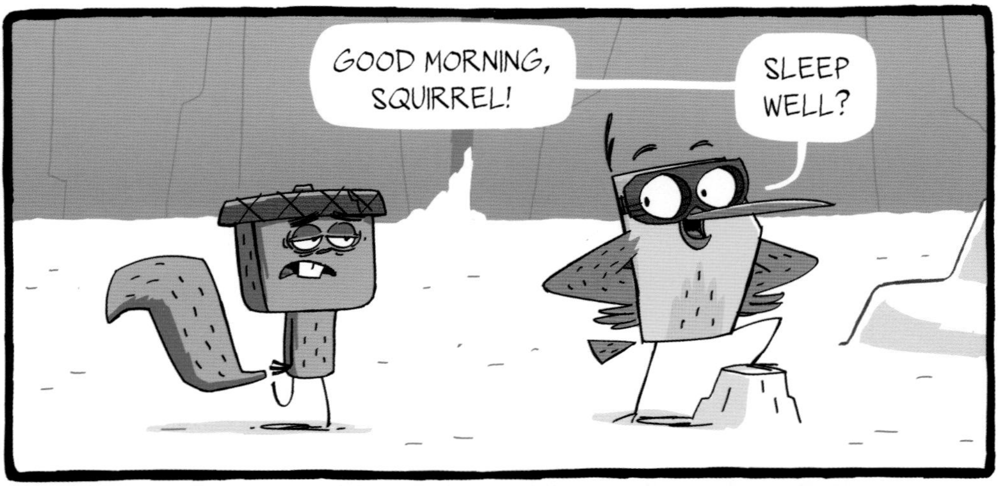
GOOD MORNING, SQUIRREL!
SLEEP WELL?

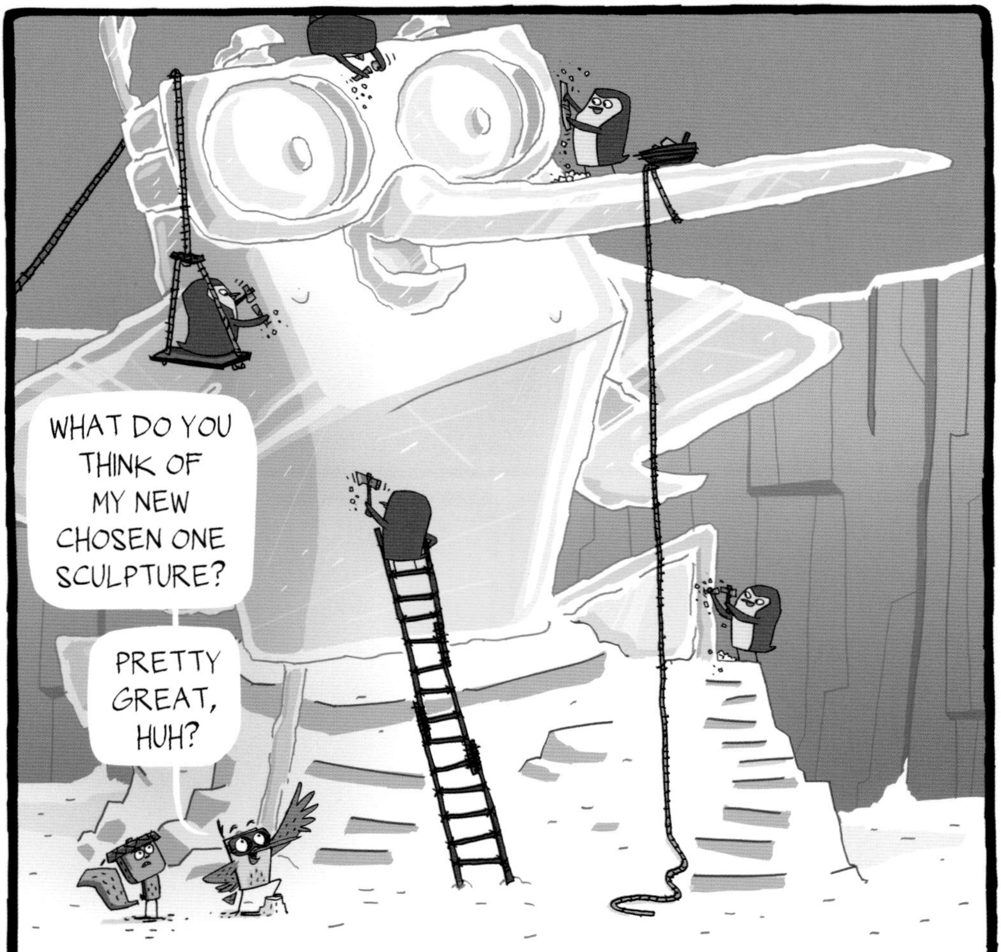
WHAT DO YOU THINK OF MY NEW CHOSEN ONE SCULPTURE?
PRETTY GREAT, HUH?

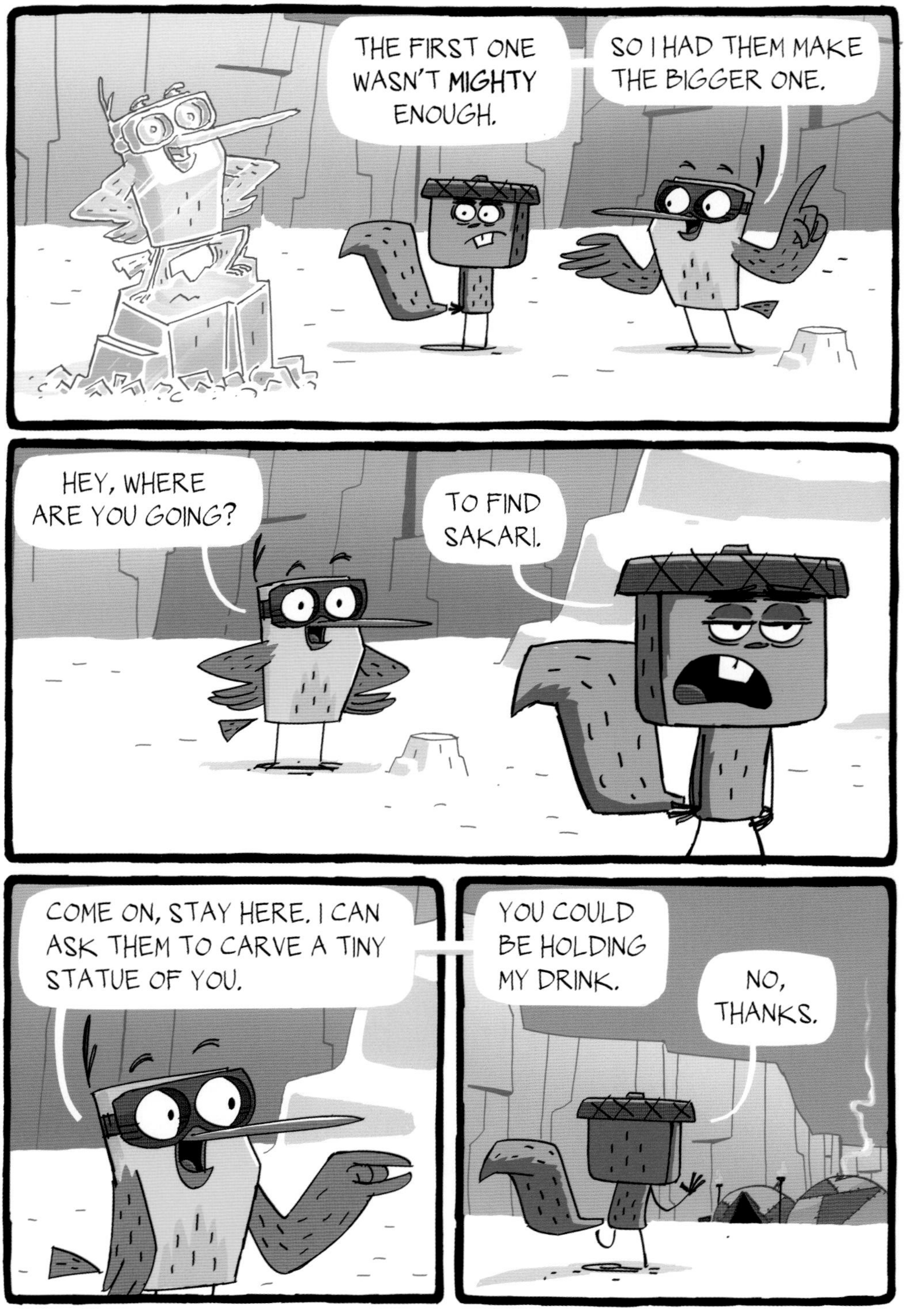
THE FIRST ONE WASN'T **MIGHTY** ENOUGH.
SO I HAD THEM MAKE THE BIGGER ONE.
HEY, WHERE ARE YOU GOING?
TO FIND SAKARI.
COME ON, STAY HERE. I CAN ASK THEM TO CARVE A TINY STATUE OF YOU.
YOU COULD BE HOLDING MY DRINK.
NO, THANKS.

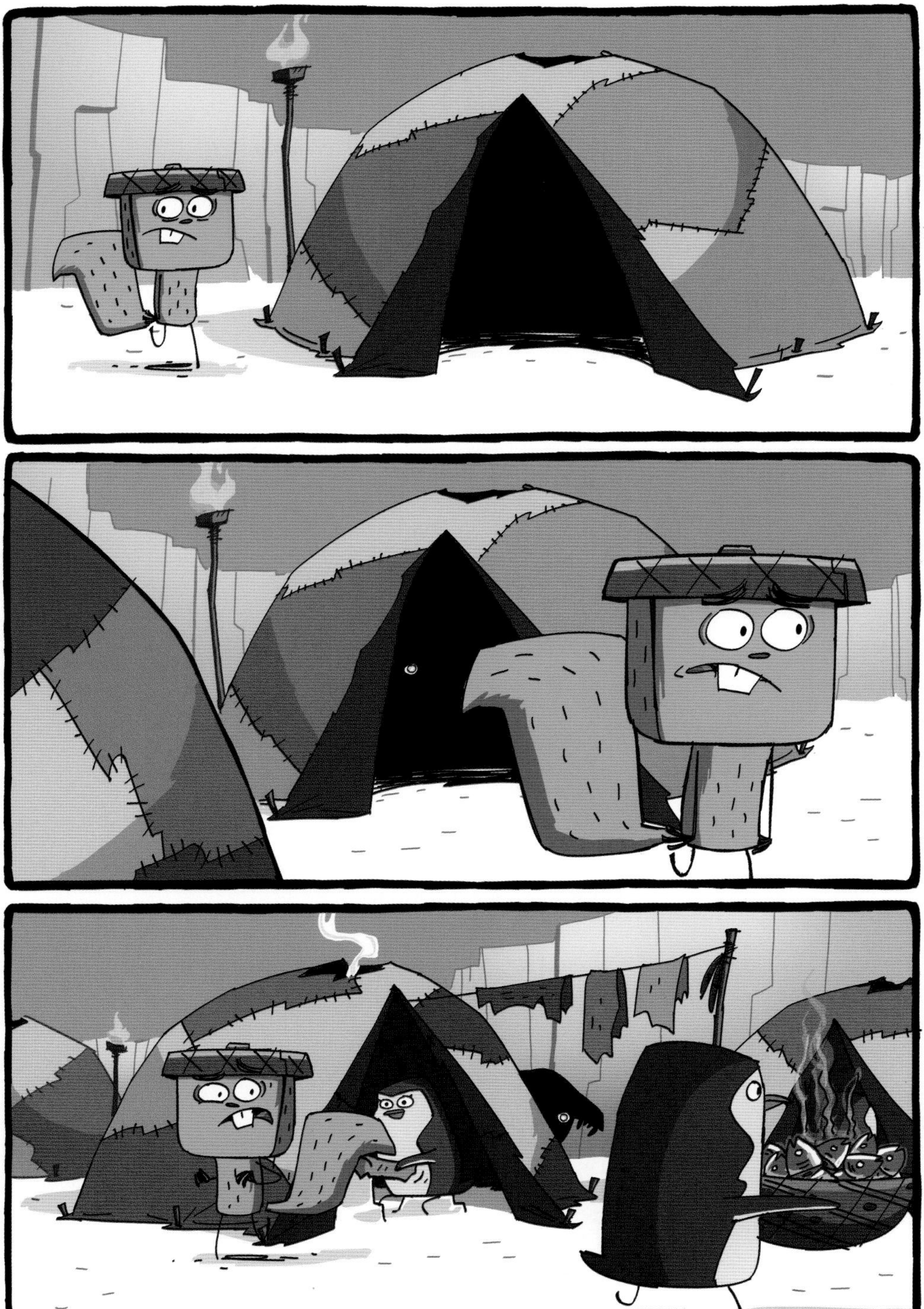

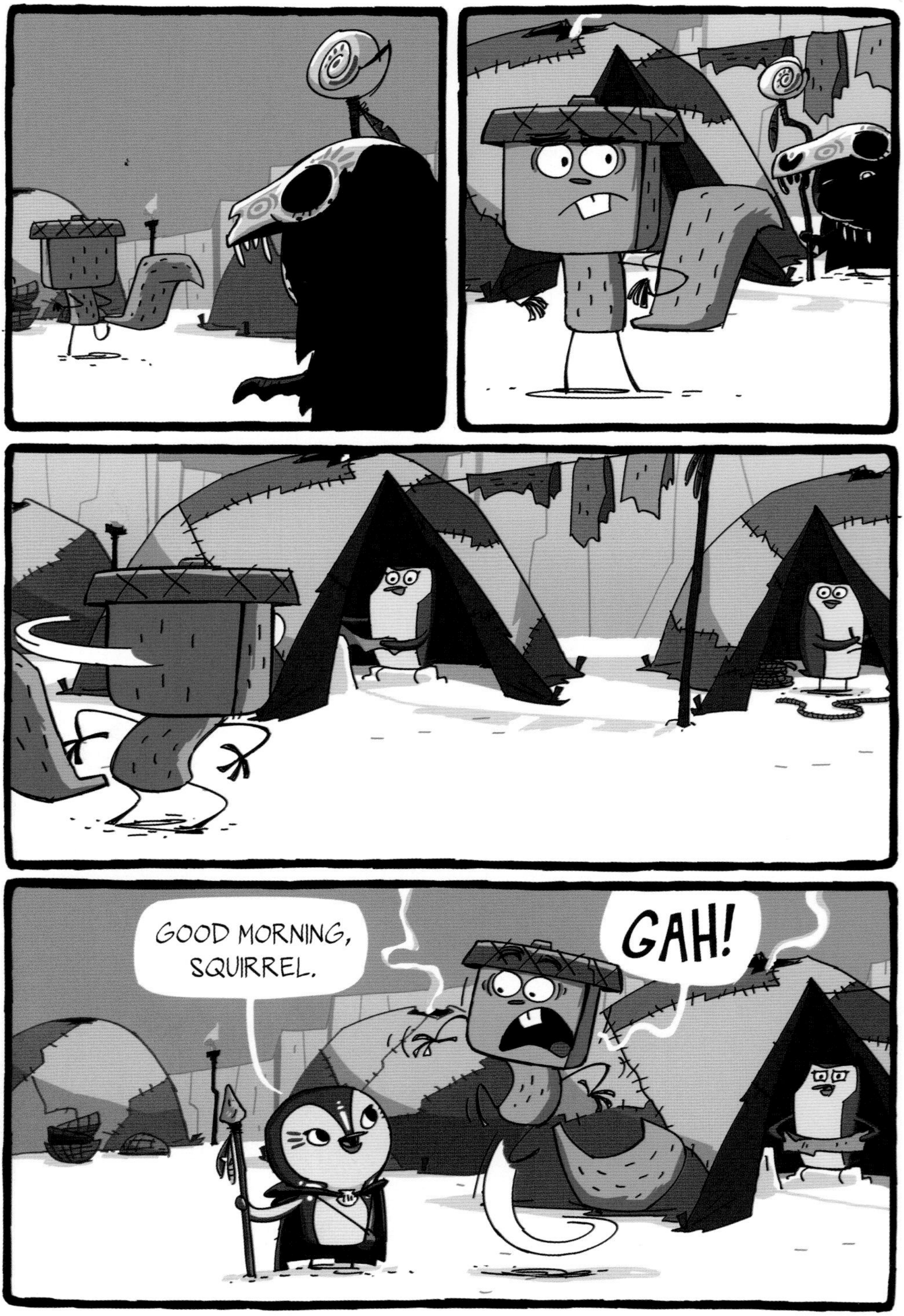
GOOD MORNING, SQUIRREL.
GAH!

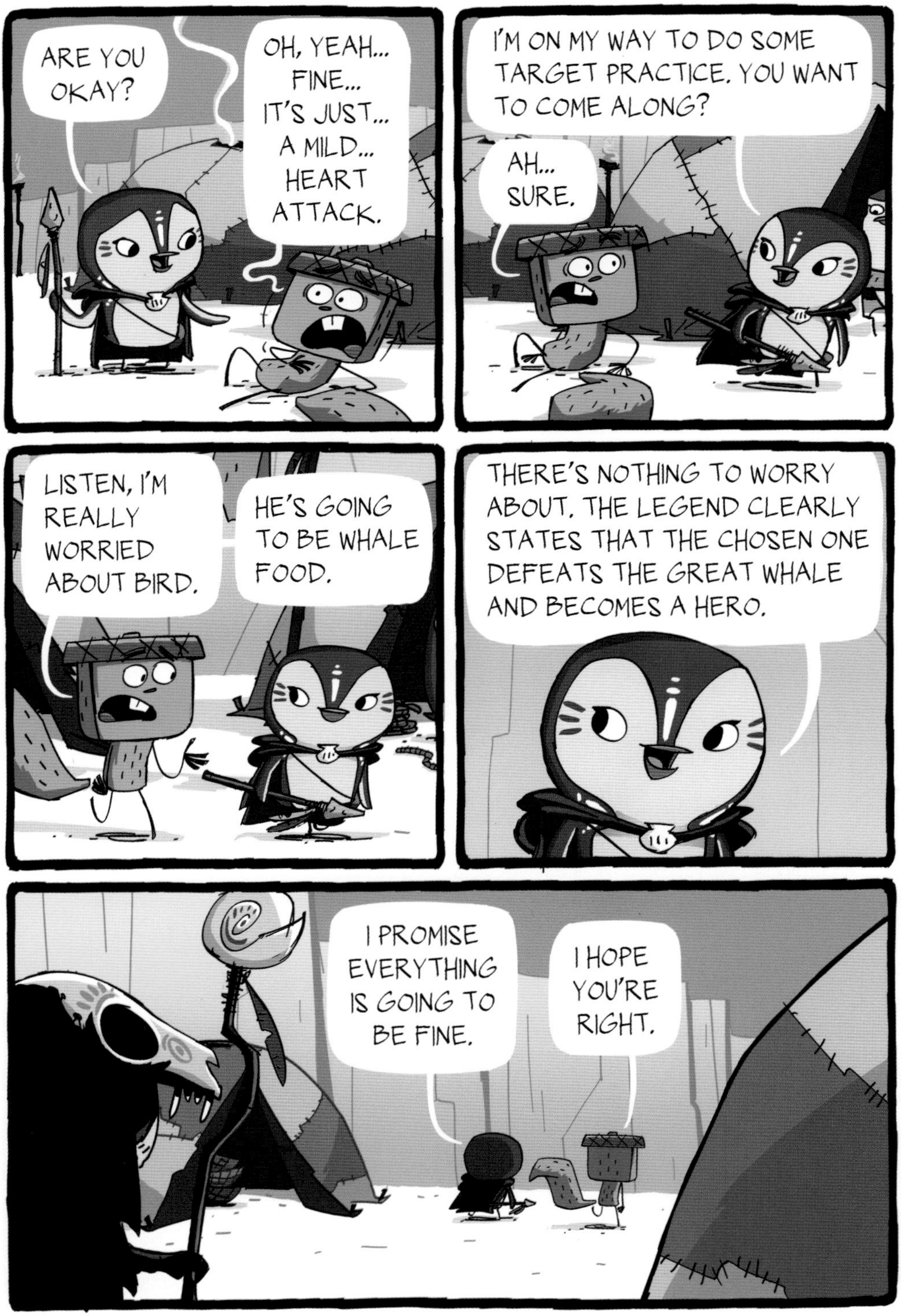
ARE YOU OKAY?
OH, YEAH... FINE... IT'S JUST... A MILD... HEART ATTACK.
I'M ON MY WAY TO DO SOME TARGET PRACTICE. YOU WANT TO COME ALONG?
AH... SURE.
LISTEN, I'M REALLY WORRIED ABOUT BIRD.
HE'S GOING TO BE WHALE FOOD.
THERE'S NOTHING TO WORRY ABOUT. THE LEGEND CLEARLY STATES THAT THE CHOSEN ONE DEFEATS THE GREAT WHALE AND BECOMES A HERO.
I PROMISE EVERYTHING IS GOING TO BE FINE.
I HOPE YOU'RE RIGHT.

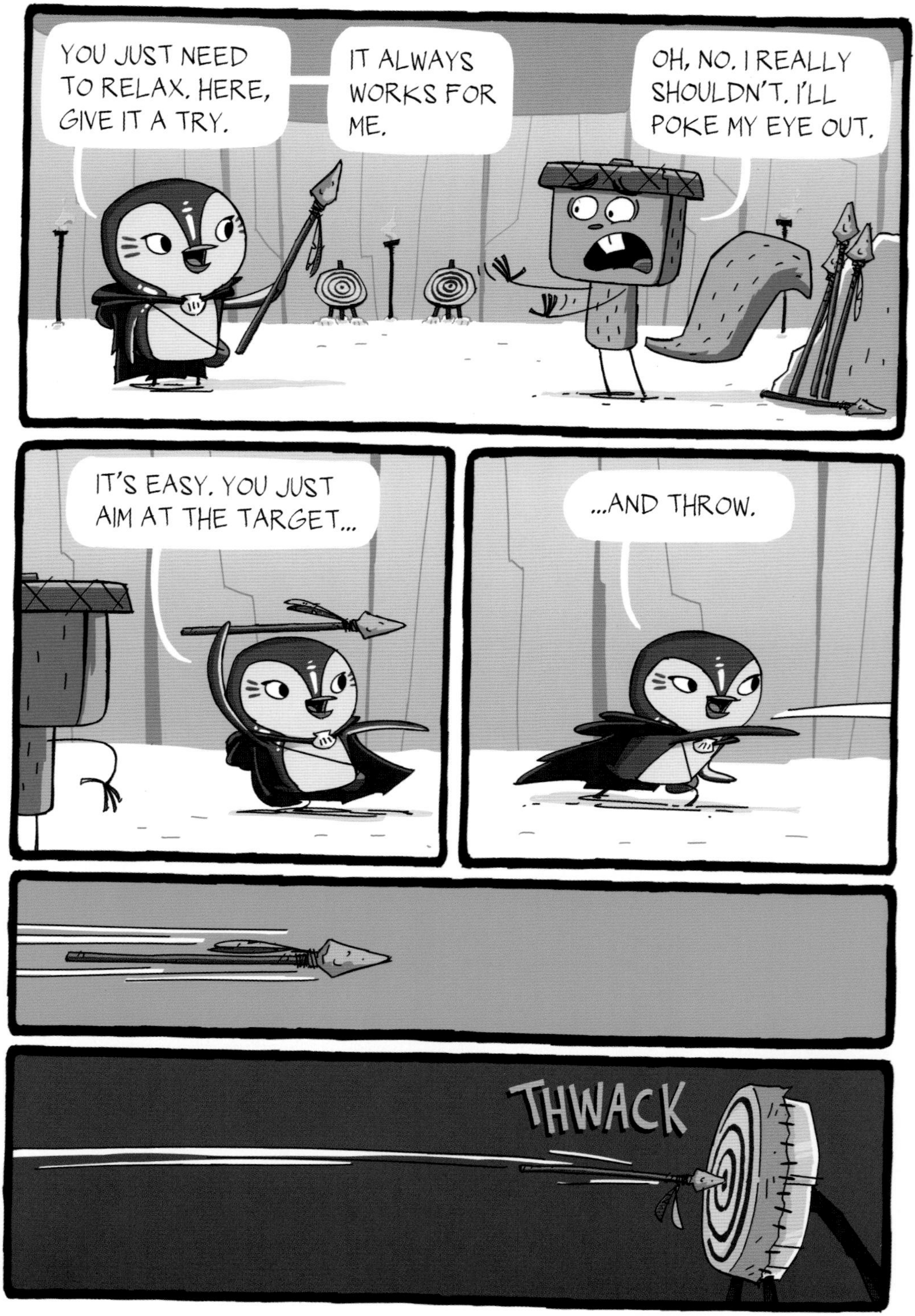
YOU JUST NEED TO RELAX. HERE, GIVE IT A TRY.
IT ALWAYS WORKS FOR ME.
OH, NO. I REALLY SHOULDN'T. I'LL POKE MY EYE OUT.
IT'S EASY. YOU JUST AIM AT THE TARGET...
...AND THROW.
THWACK

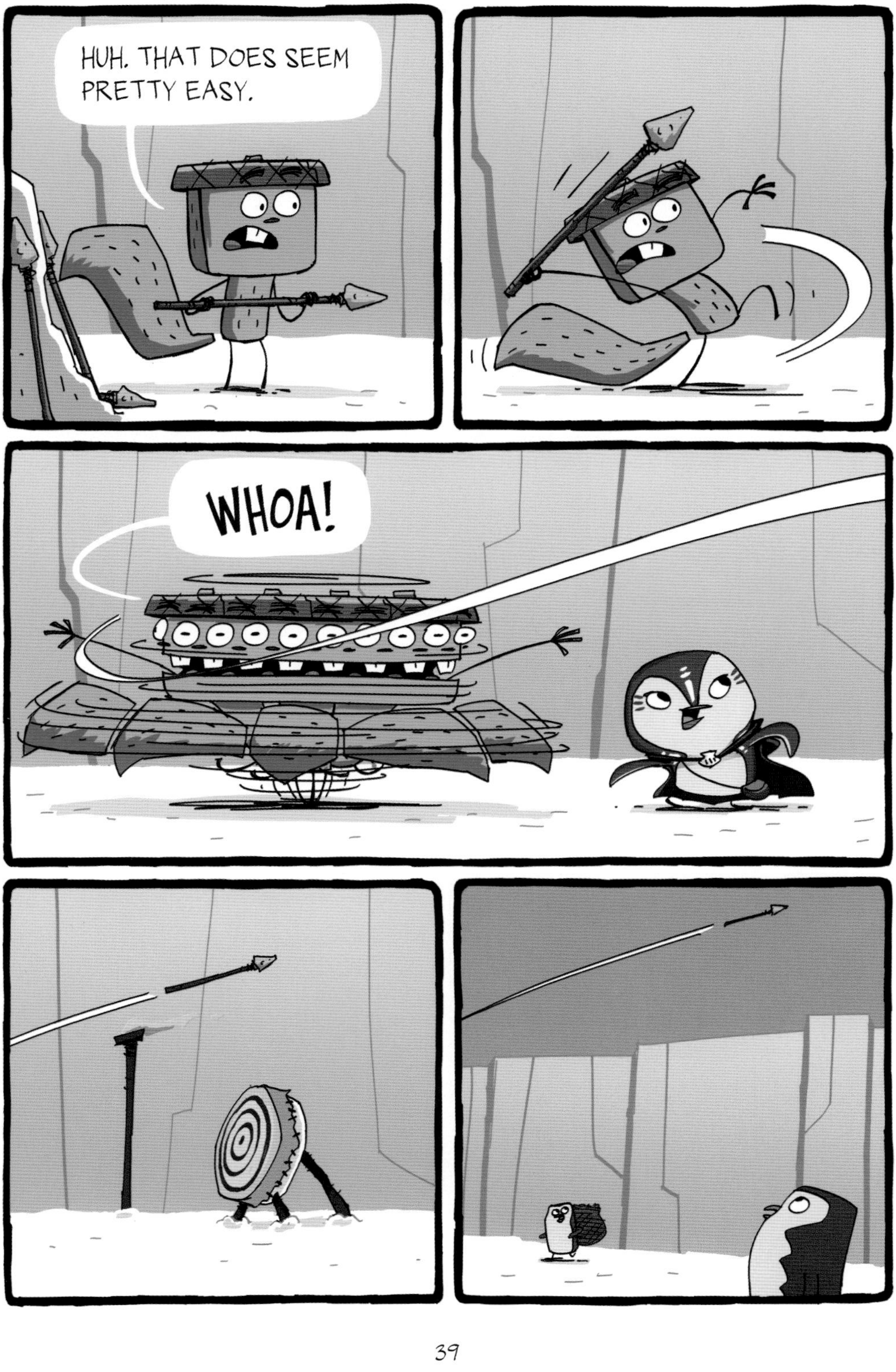
HUH. THAT DOES SEEM PRETTY EASY.
WHOA!

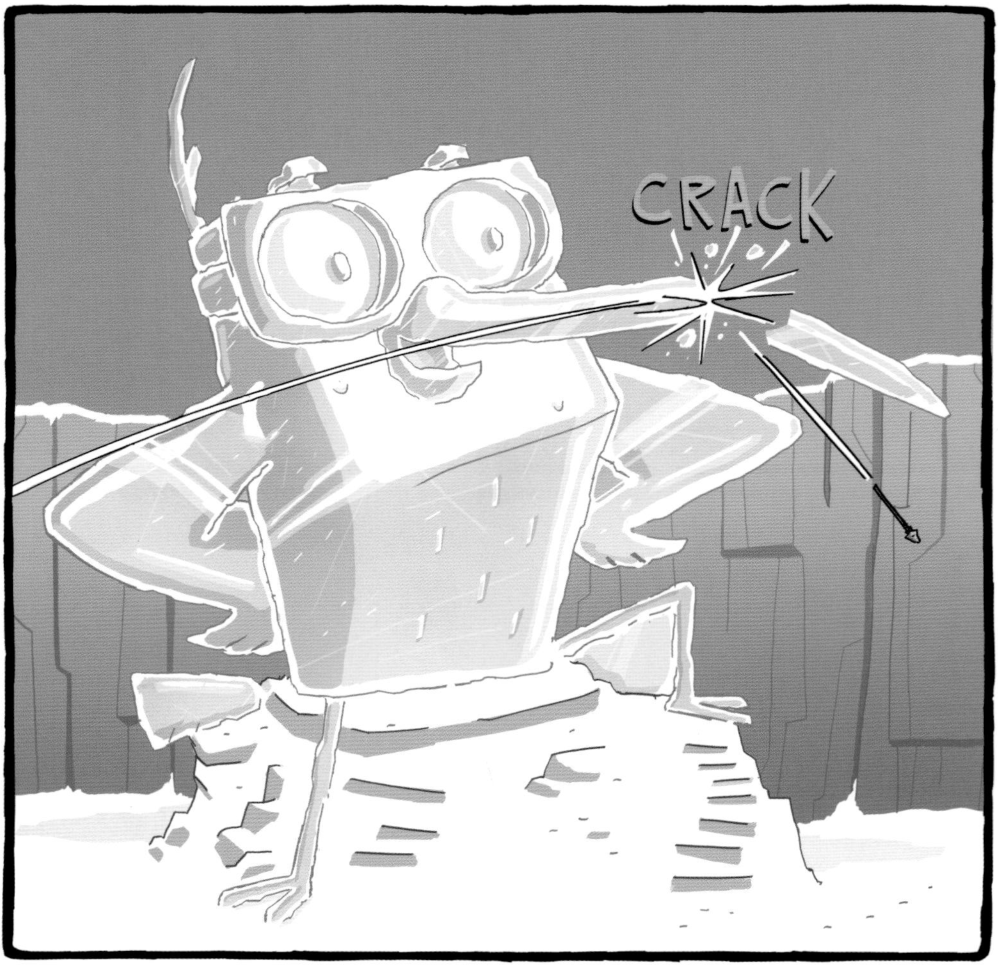
CRACK

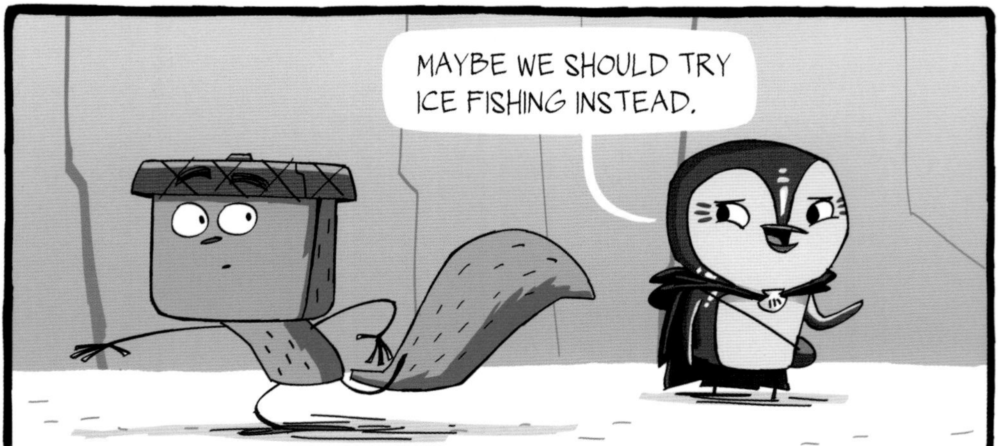
MAYBE WE SHOULD TRY ICE FISHING INSTEAD.

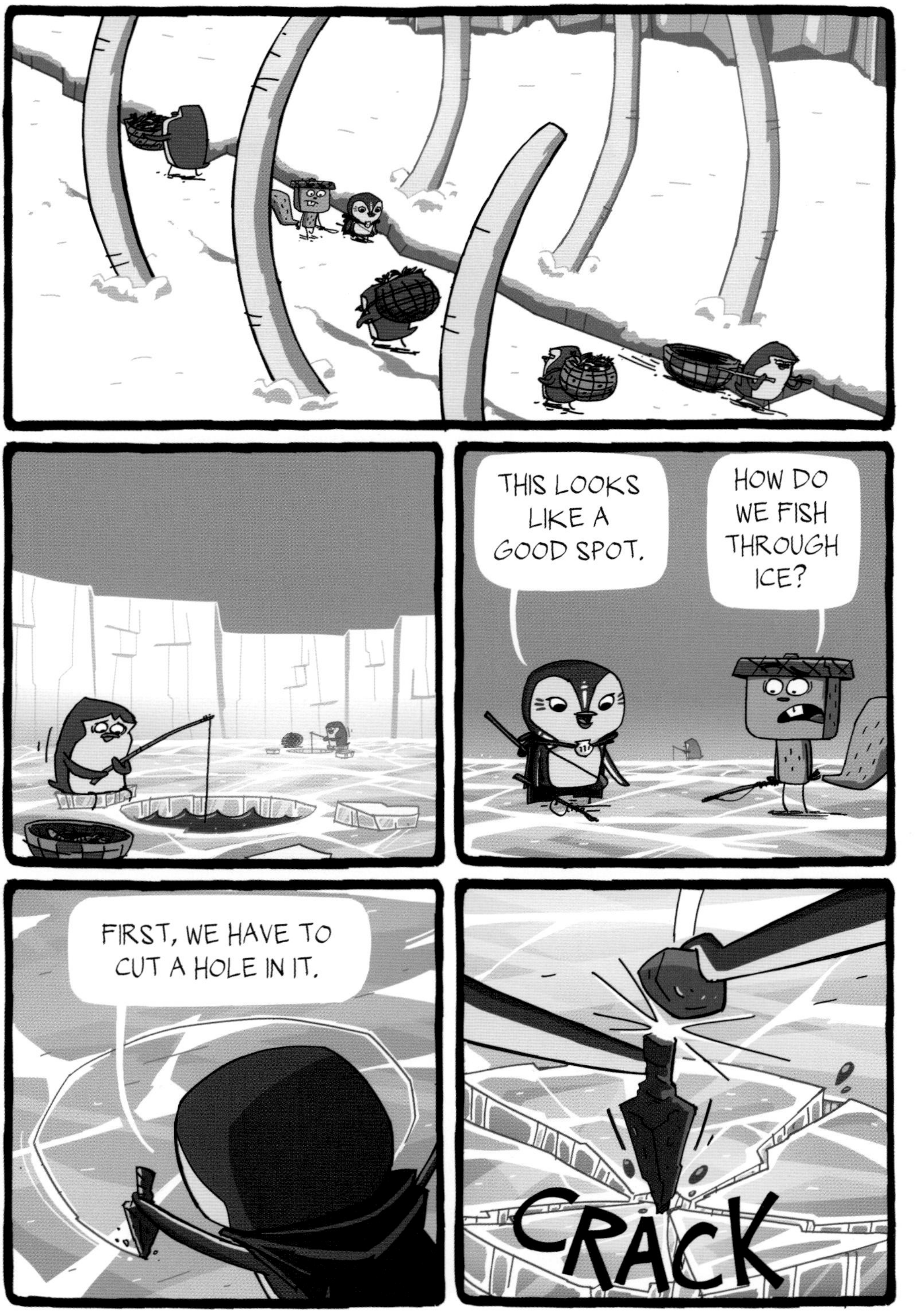
THIS LOOKS LIKE A GOOD SPOT.
HOW DO WE FISH THROUGH ICE?
FIRST, WE HAVE TO CUT A HOLE IN IT.
CRACK

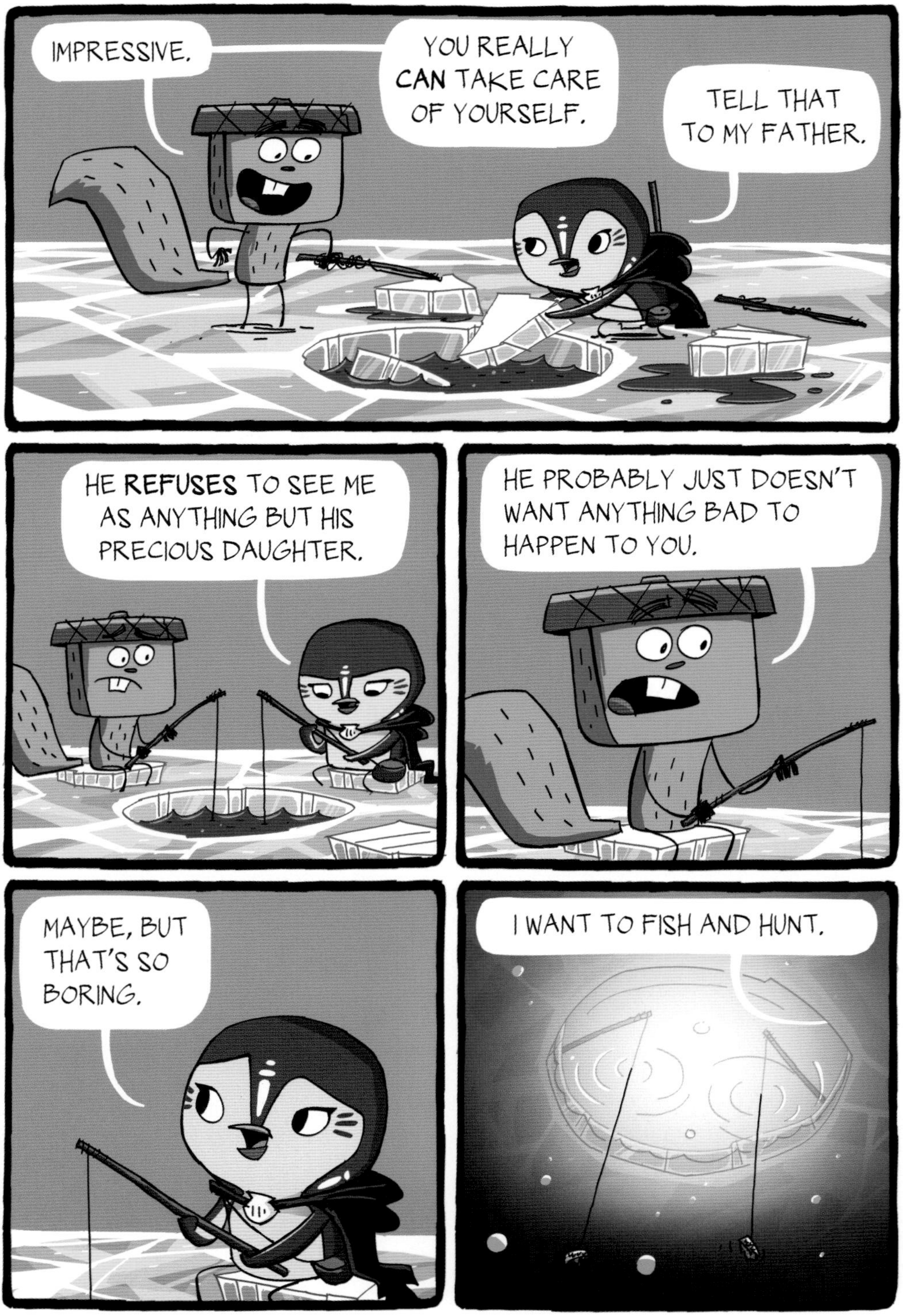
IMPRESSIVE.
YOU REALLY **CAN** TAKE CARE OF YOURSELF.
TELL THAT TO MY FATHER.
HE **REFUSES** TO SEE ME AS ANYTHING BUT HIS PRECIOUS DAUGHTER.
HE PROBABLY JUST DOESN'T WANT ANYTHING BAD TO HAPPEN TO YOU.
MAYBE, BUT THAT'S SO BORING.
I WANT TO FISH AND HUNT.

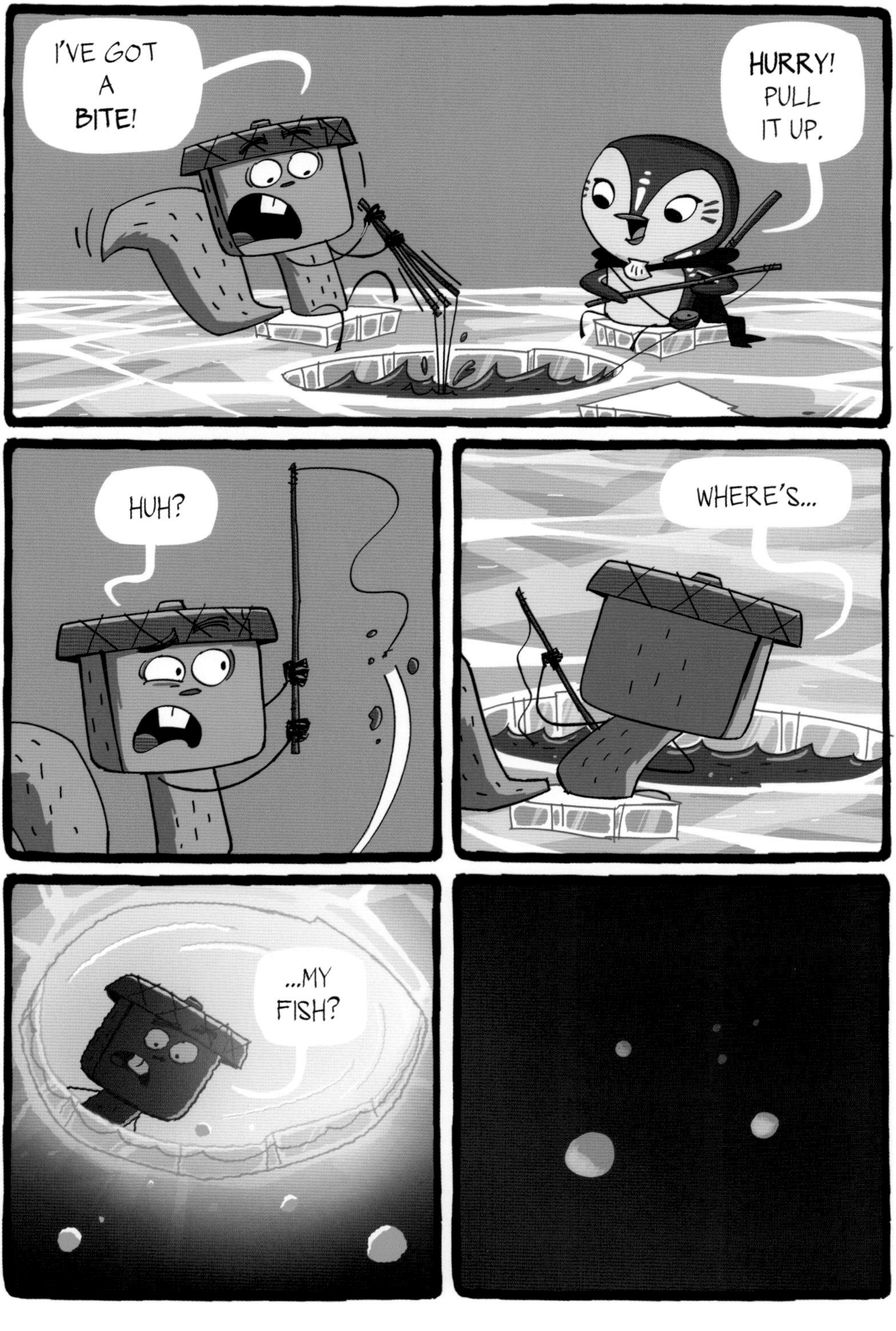
I'VE GOT A BITE!
HURRY! PULL IT UP.
HUH?
WHERE'S...
...MY FISH?

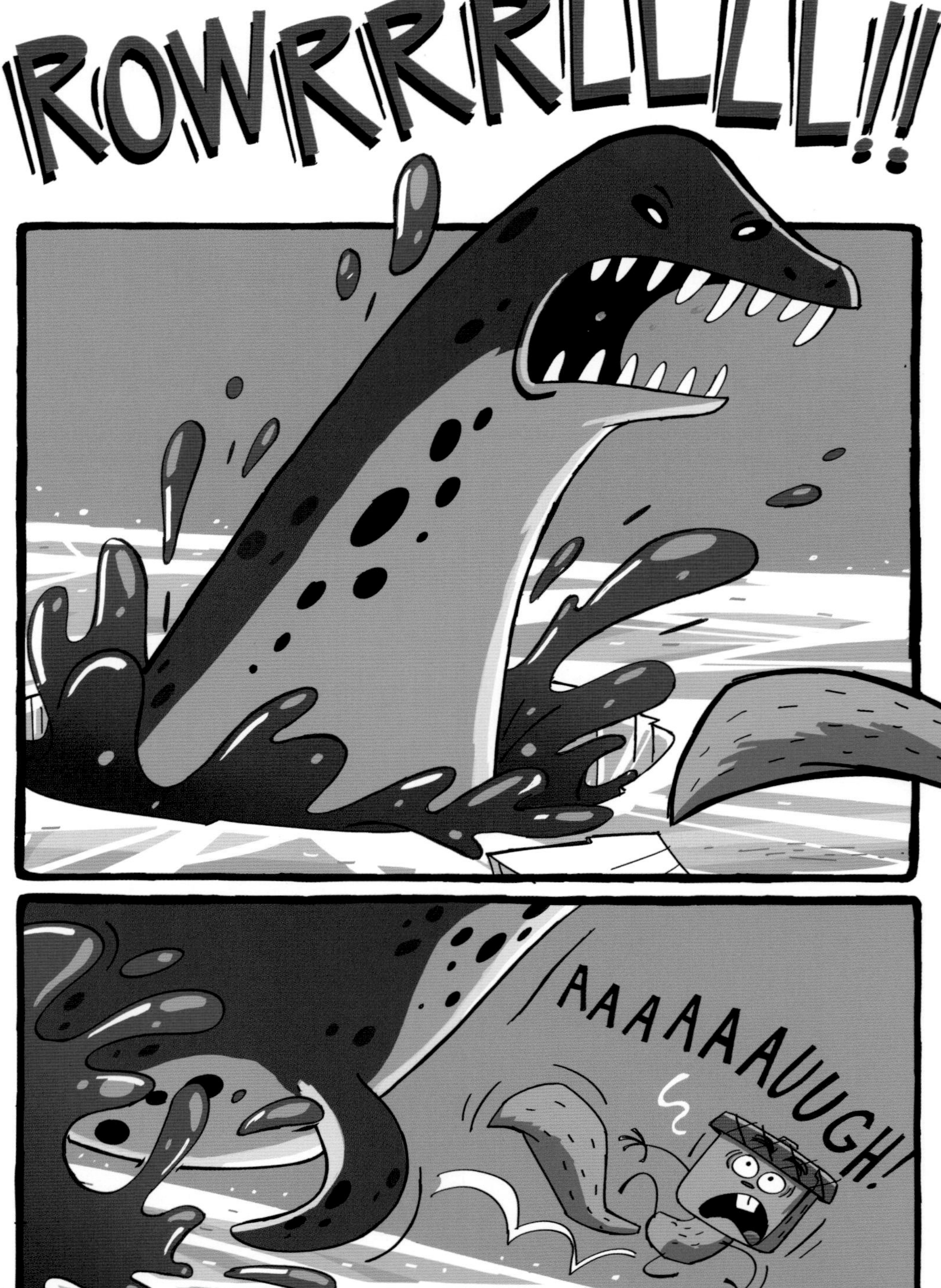
ROWRRRRLLLLL!!
AAAAAAUUGH!

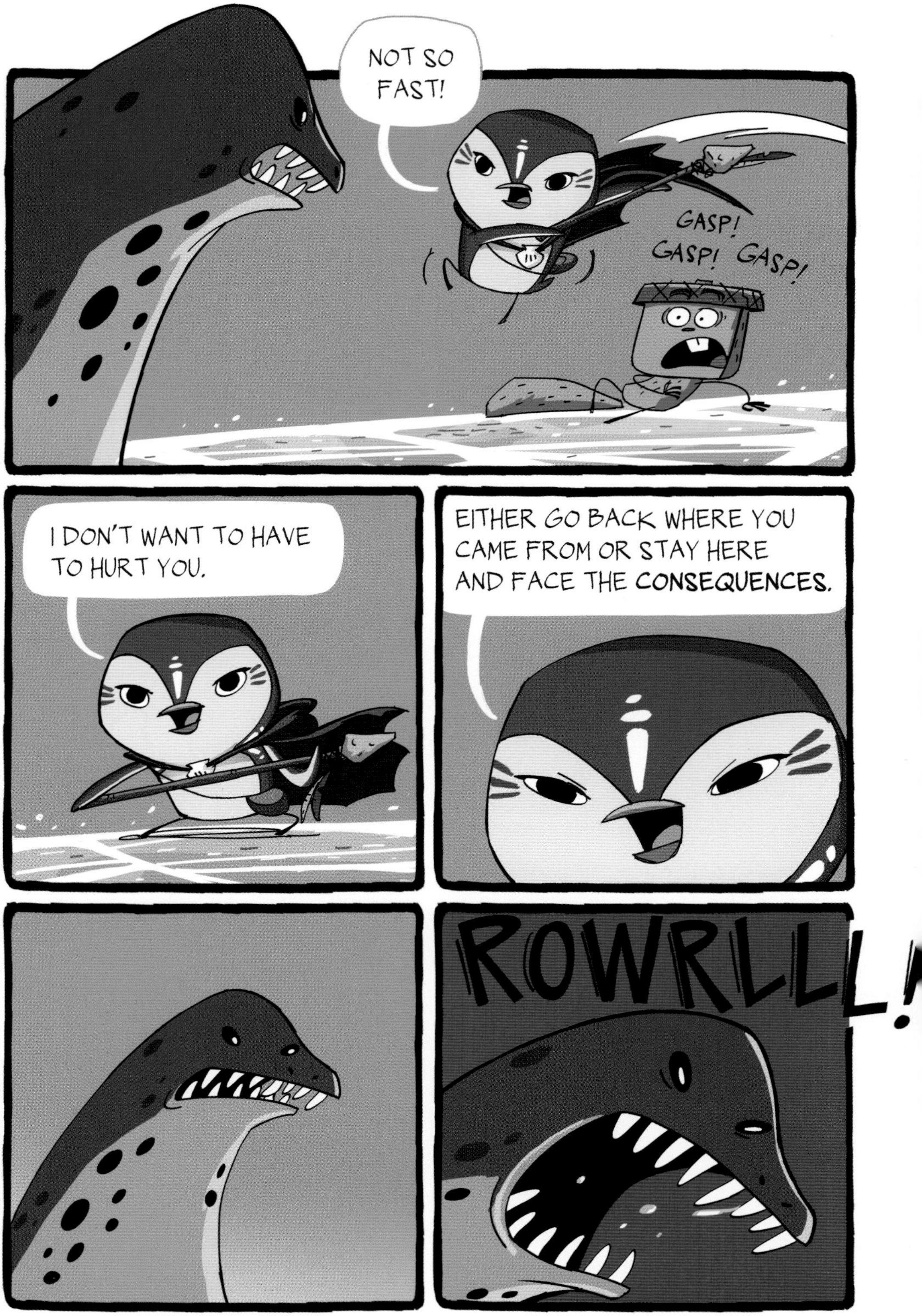
NOT SO FAST!
GASP! GASP! GASP!
I DON'T WANT TO HAVE TO HURT YOU.
EITHER GO BACK WHERE YOU CAME FROM OR STAY HERE AND FACE THE **CONSEQUENCES.**
ROWRLLL!

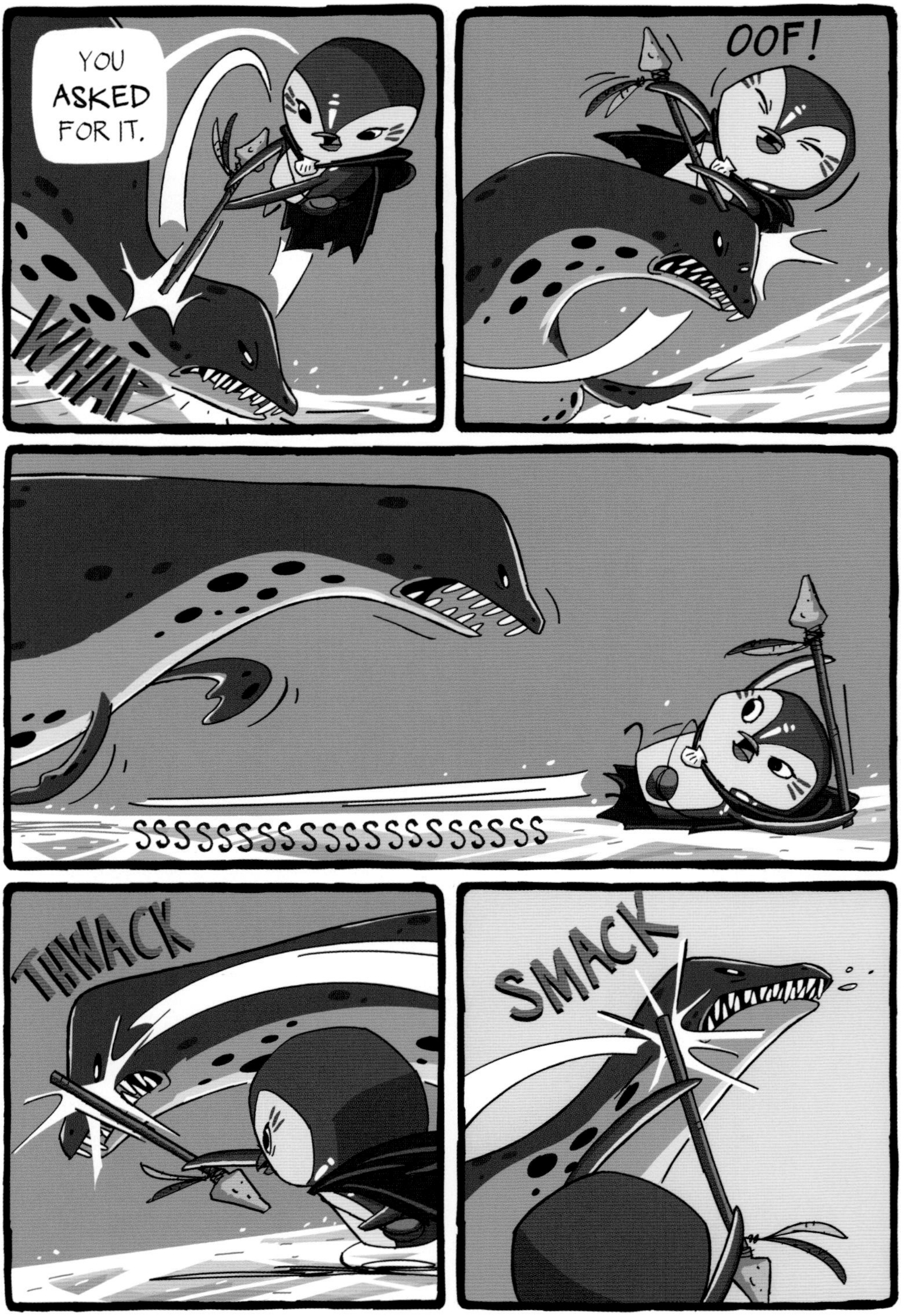
YOU ASKED FOR IT.
WHAP
OOF!
SSSSSSSSSSSSSSSSSSSSS
THWACK
SMACK

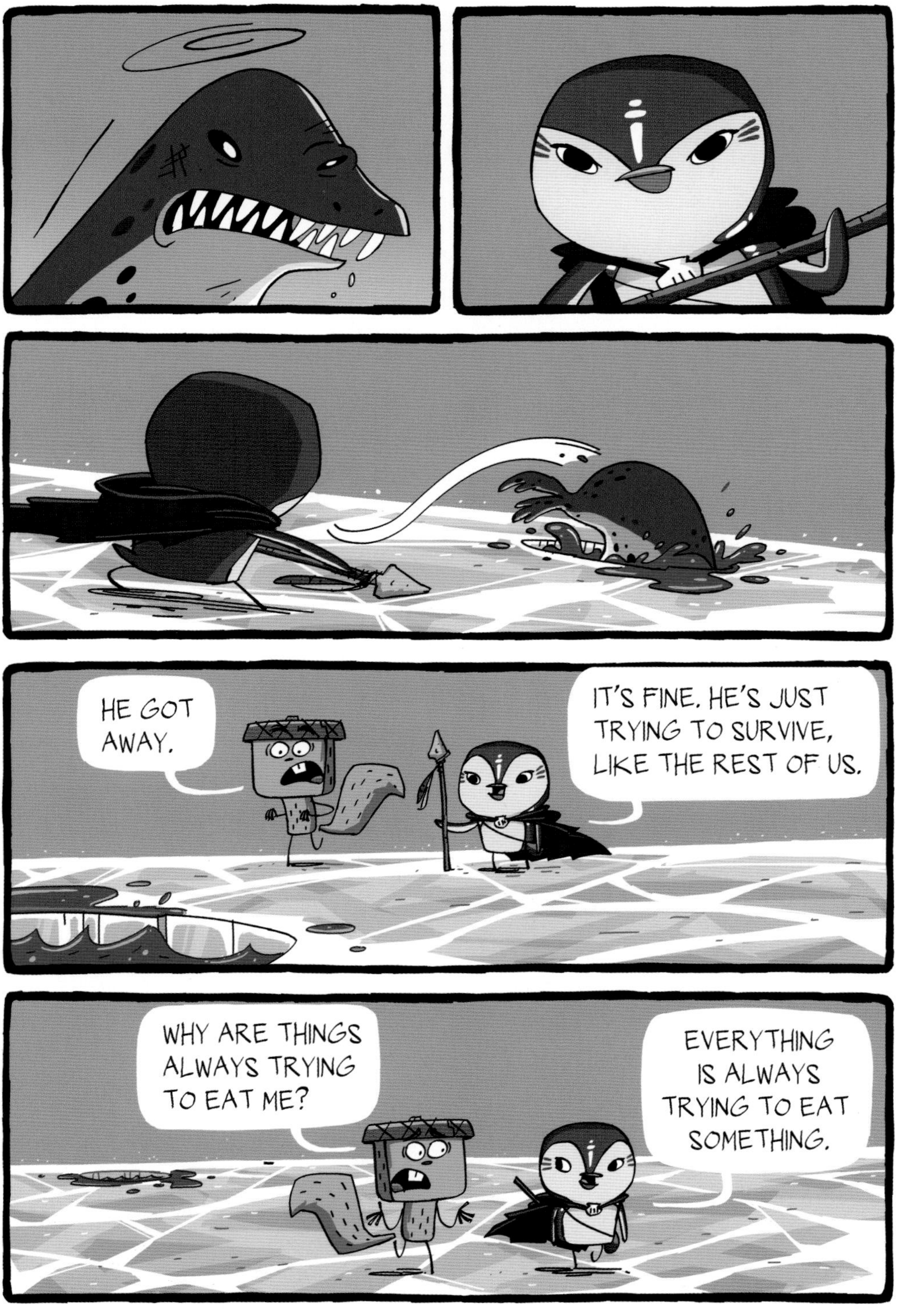
HE GOT AWAY.
IT'S FINE. HE'S JUST TRYING TO SURVIVE, LIKE THE REST OF US.
WHY ARE THINGS ALWAYS TRYING TO EAT ME?
EVERYTHING IS ALWAYS TRYING TO EAT SOMETHING.

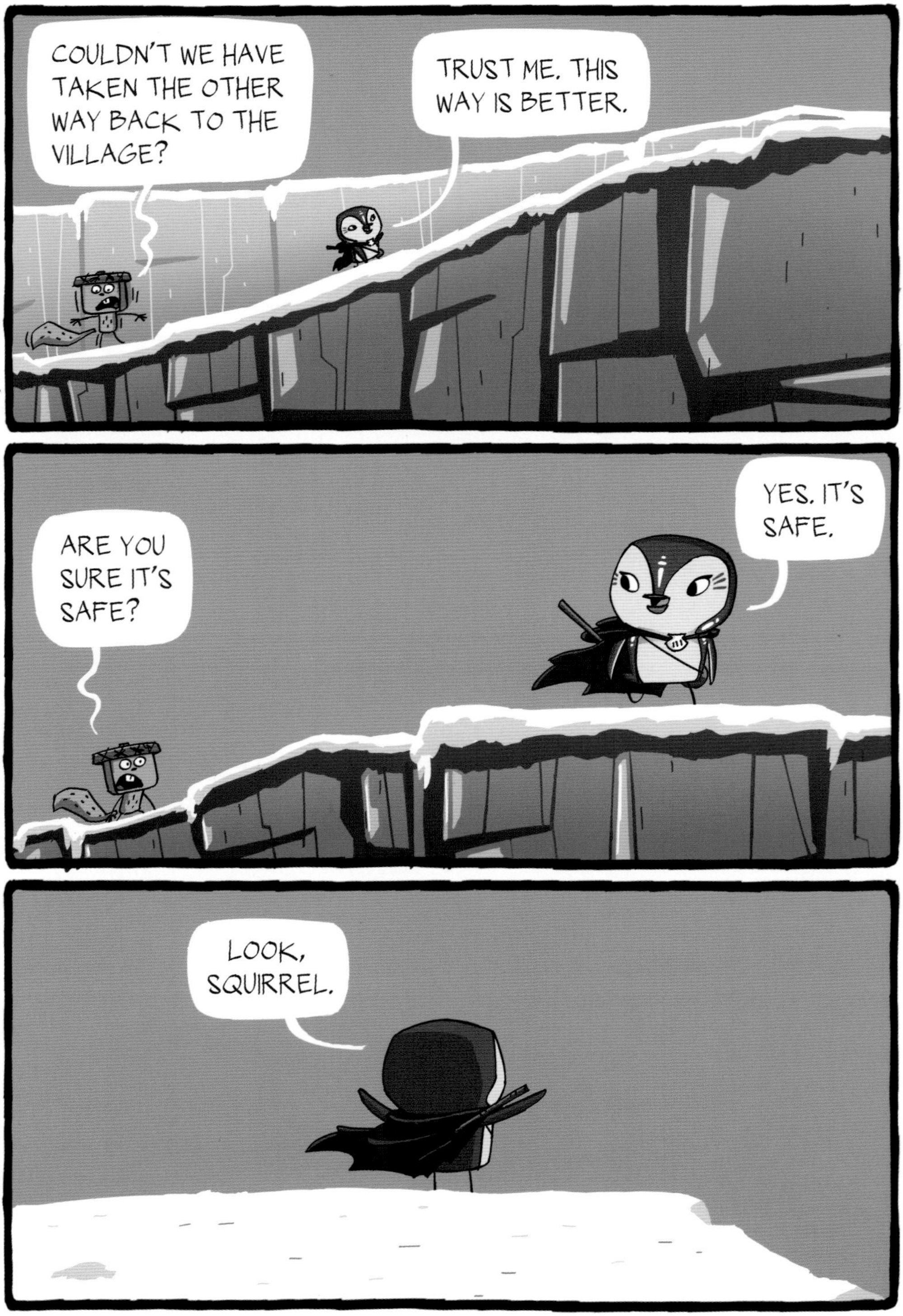
COULDN'T WE HAVE TAKEN THE OTHER WAY BACK TO THE VILLAGE?
TRUST ME. THIS WAY IS BETTER.
ARE YOU SURE IT'S SAFE?
YES. IT'S SAFE.
LOOK, SQUIRREL.

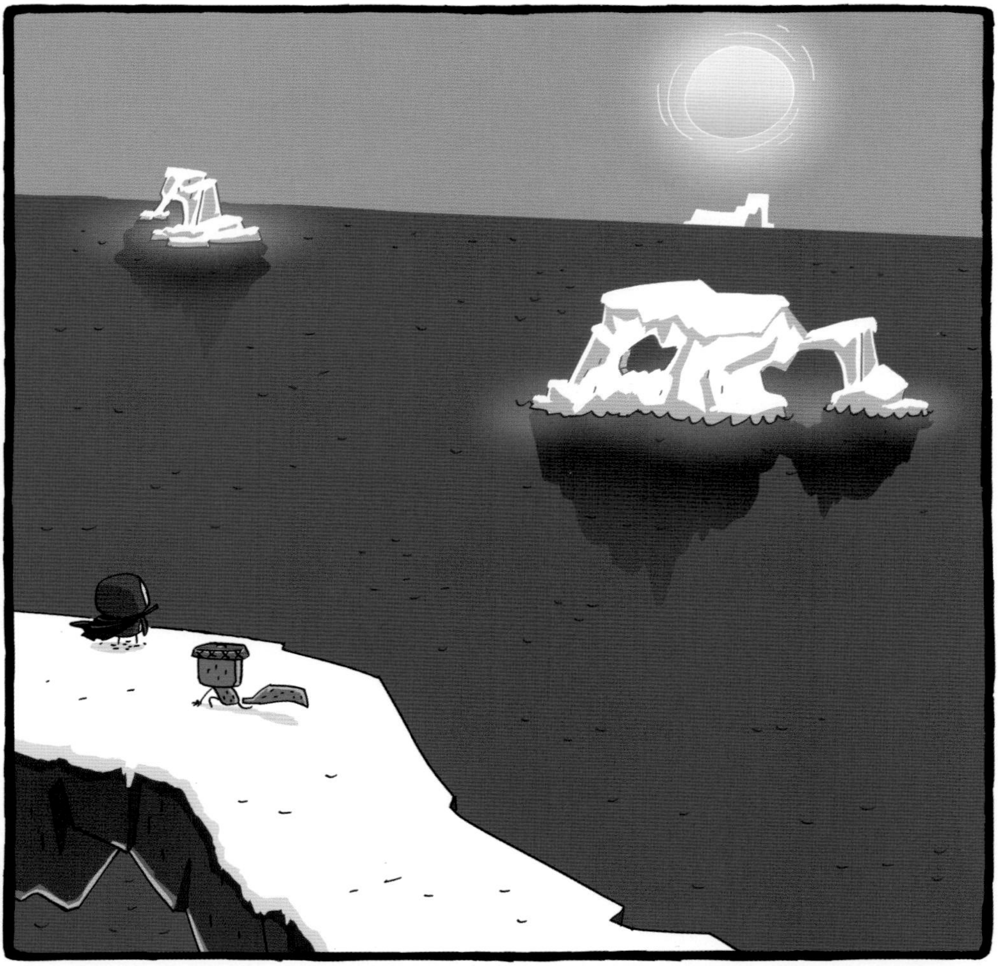

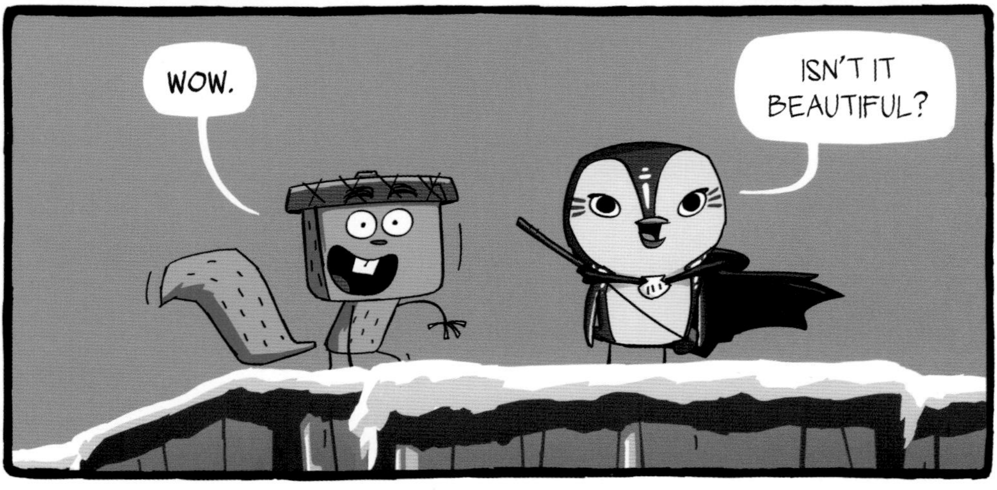
WOW.
ISN'T IT BEAUTIFUL?

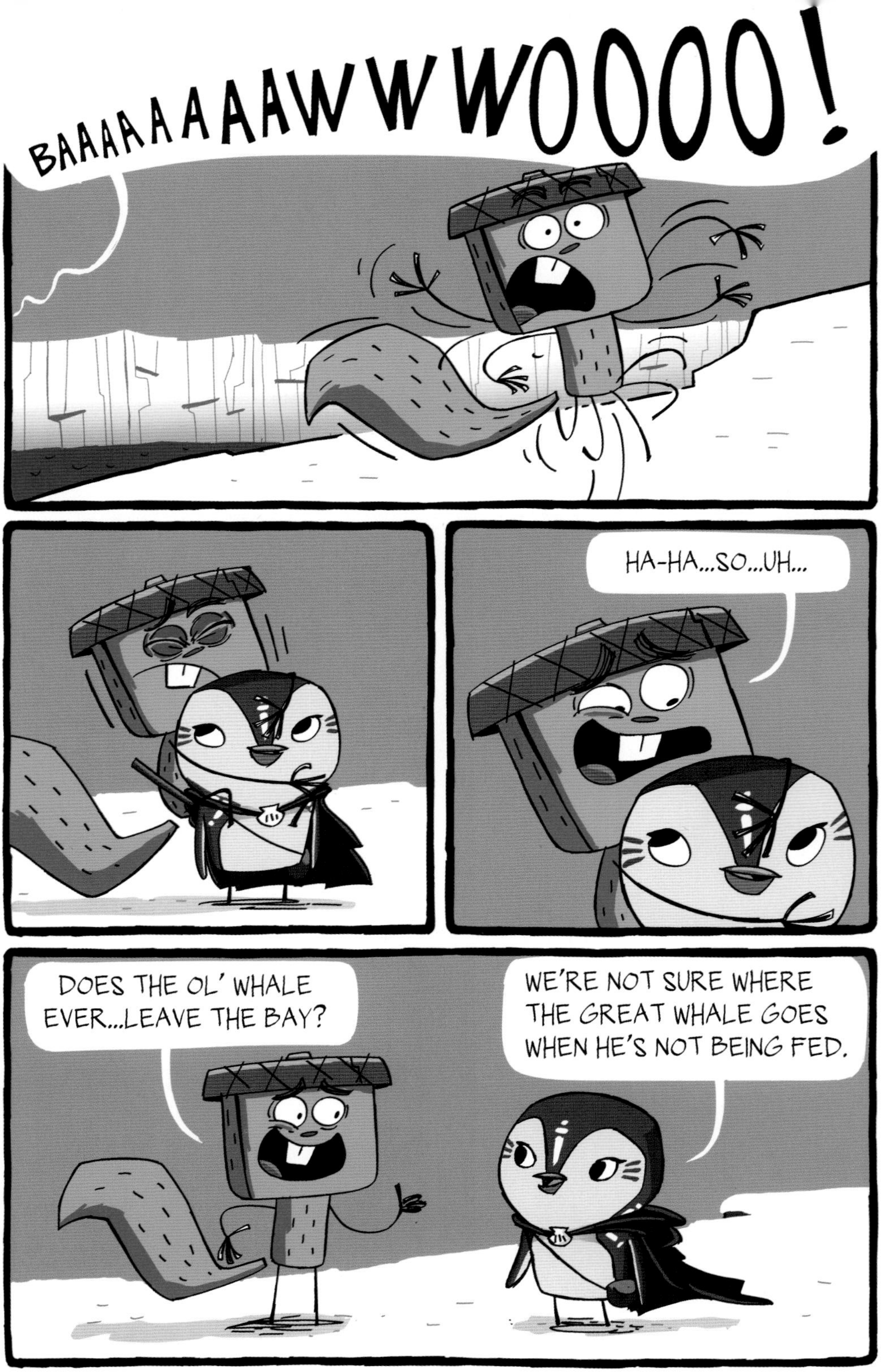
BAAAAAAAAWWWOOOO!
HA-HA...SO...UH...
DOES THE OL' WHALE EVER...LEAVE THE BAY?
WE'RE NOT SURE WHERE THE GREAT WHALE GOES WHEN HE'S NOT BEING FED.

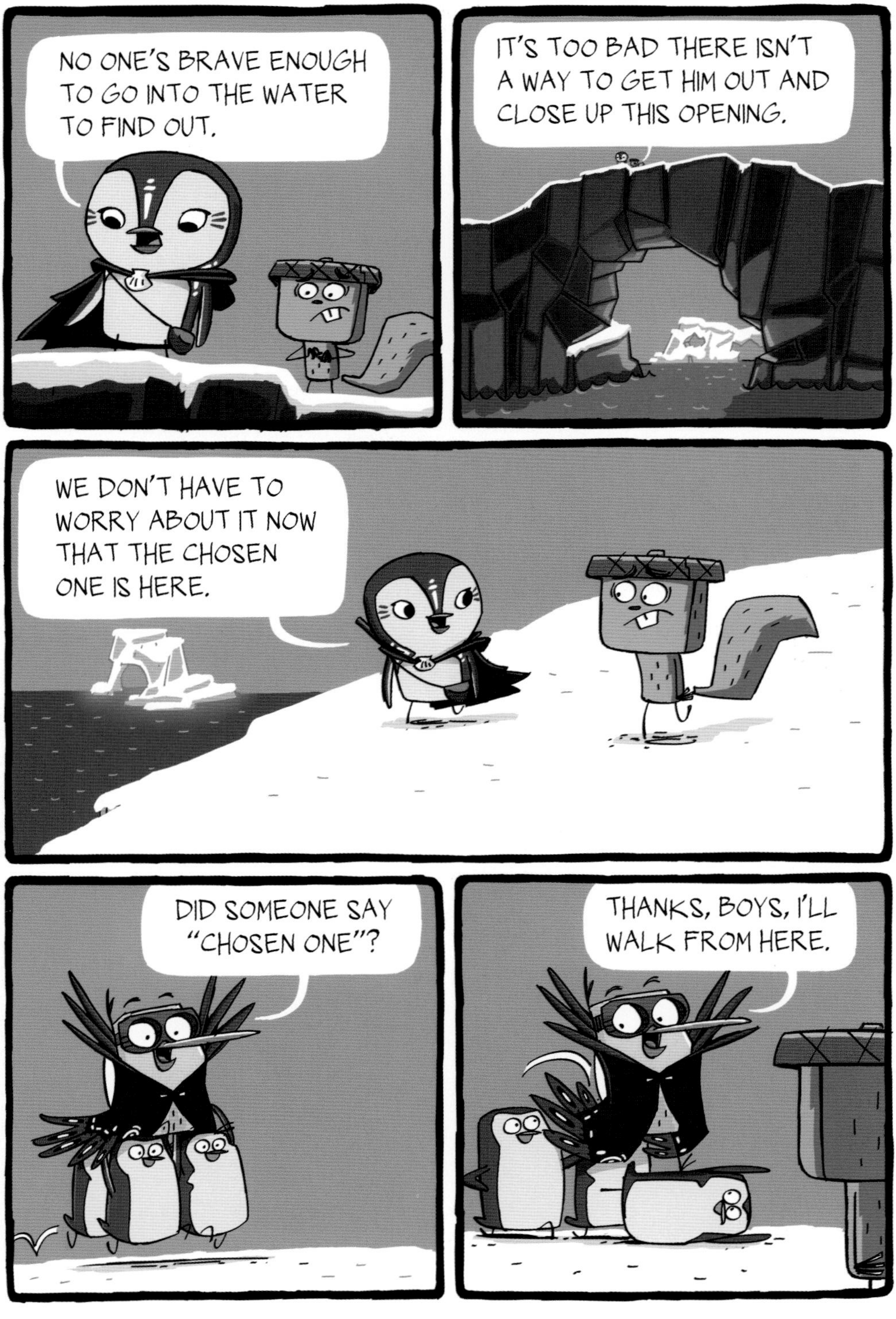
NO ONE'S BRAVE ENOUGH TO GO INTO THE WATER TO FIND OUT.
IT'S TOO BAD THERE ISN'T A WAY TO GET HIM OUT AND CLOSE UP THIS OPENING.
WE DON'T HAVE TO WORRY ABOUT IT NOW THAT THE CHOSEN ONE IS HERE.
DID SOMEONE SAY "CHOSEN ONE"?
THANKS, BOYS, I'LL WALK FROM HERE.

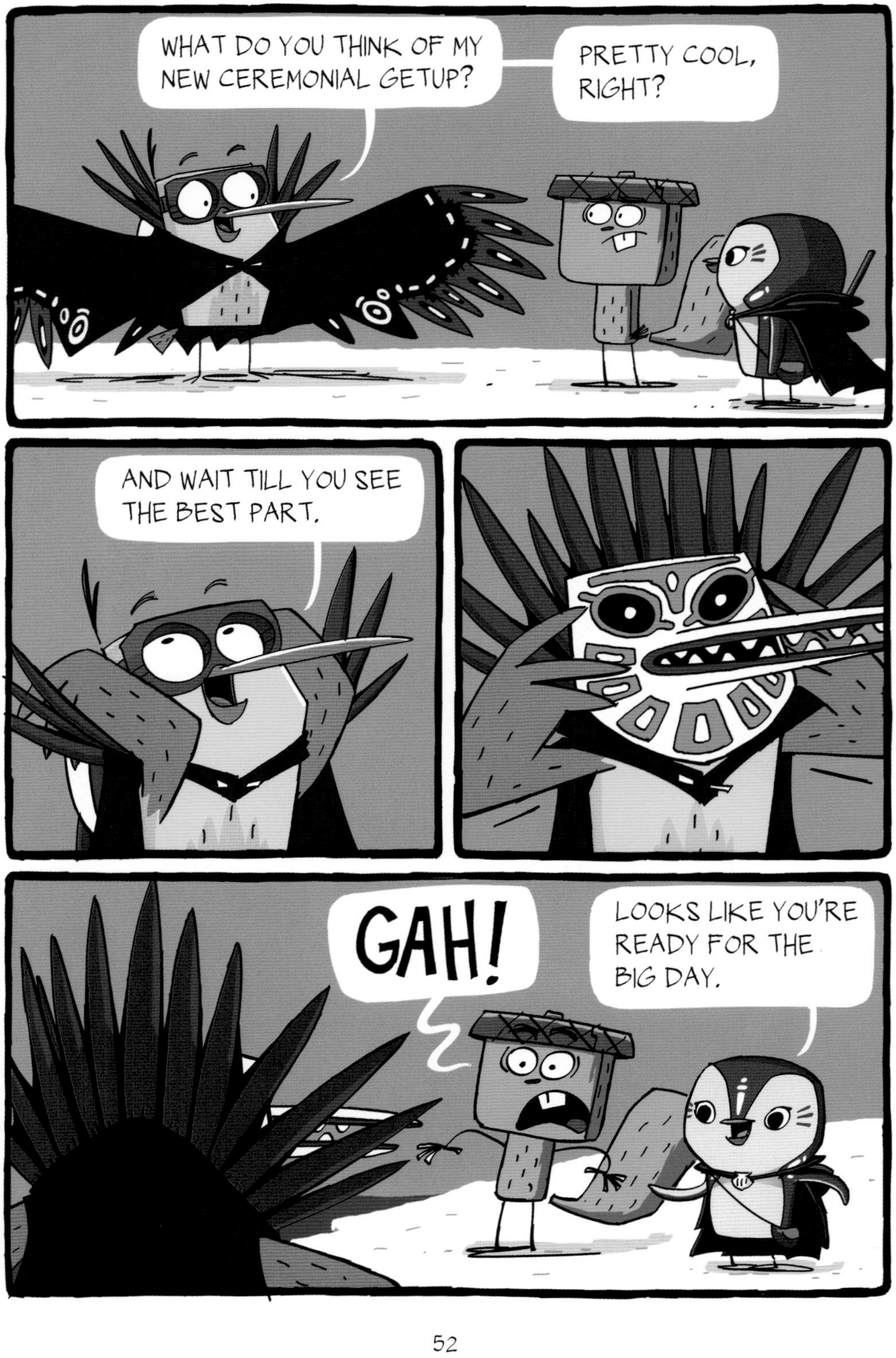
WHAT DO YOU THINK OF MY NEW CEREMONIAL GETUP?
PRETTY COOL, RIGHT?
AND WAIT TILL YOU SEE THE BEST PART.
GAH!
LOOKS LIKE YOU'RE READY FOR THE BIG DAY.

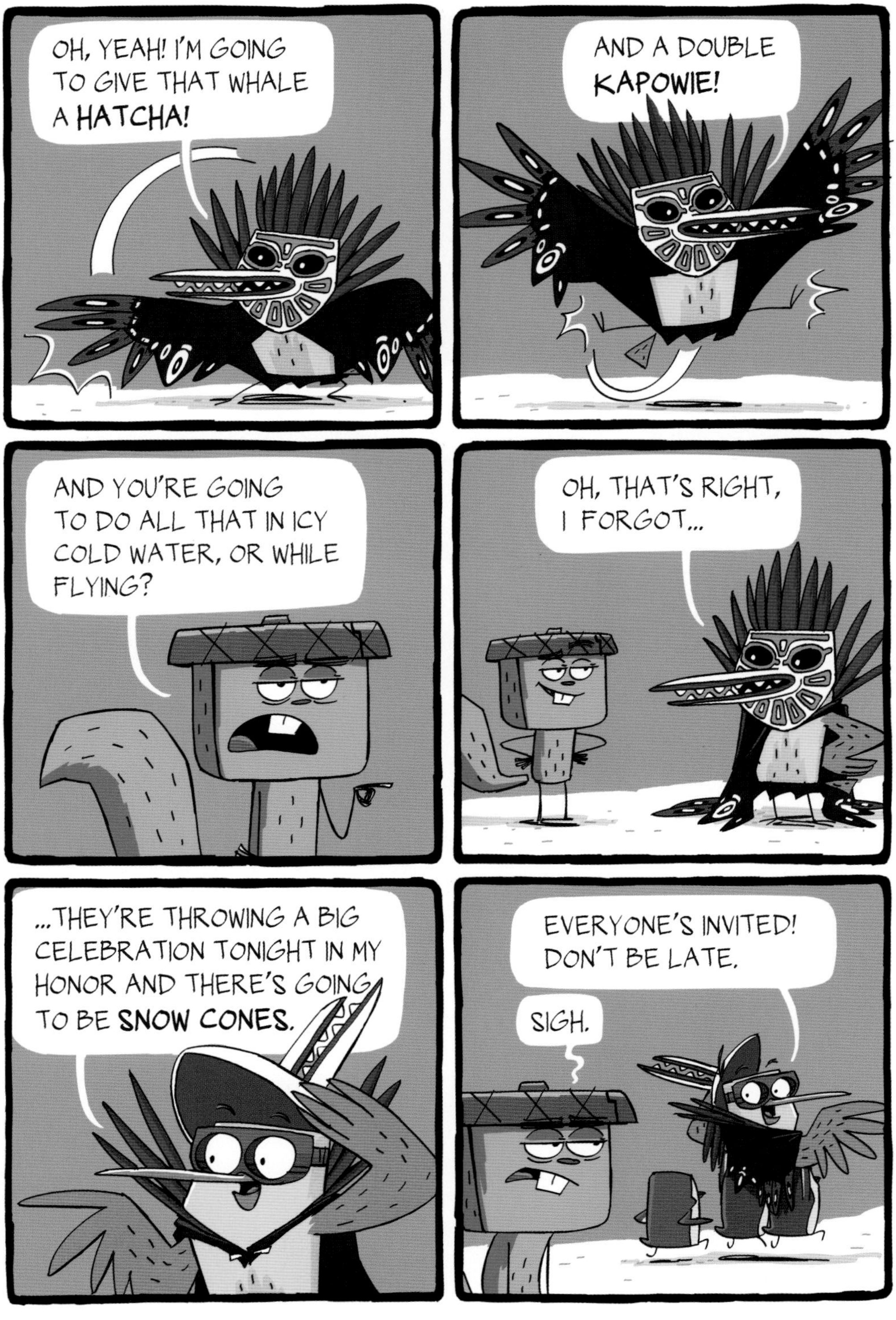
OH, YEAH! I'M GOING TO GIVE THAT WHALE A **HATCHA!**
AND A DOUBLE **KAPOWIE!**
AND YOU'RE GOING TO DO ALL THAT IN ICY COLD WATER, OR WHILE FLYING?
OH, THAT'S RIGHT, I FORGOT...
...THEY'RE THROWING A BIG CELEBRATION TONIGHT IN MY HONOR AND THERE'S GOING TO BE **SNOW CONES.**
EVERYONE'S INVITED! DON'T BE LATE.
SIGH.

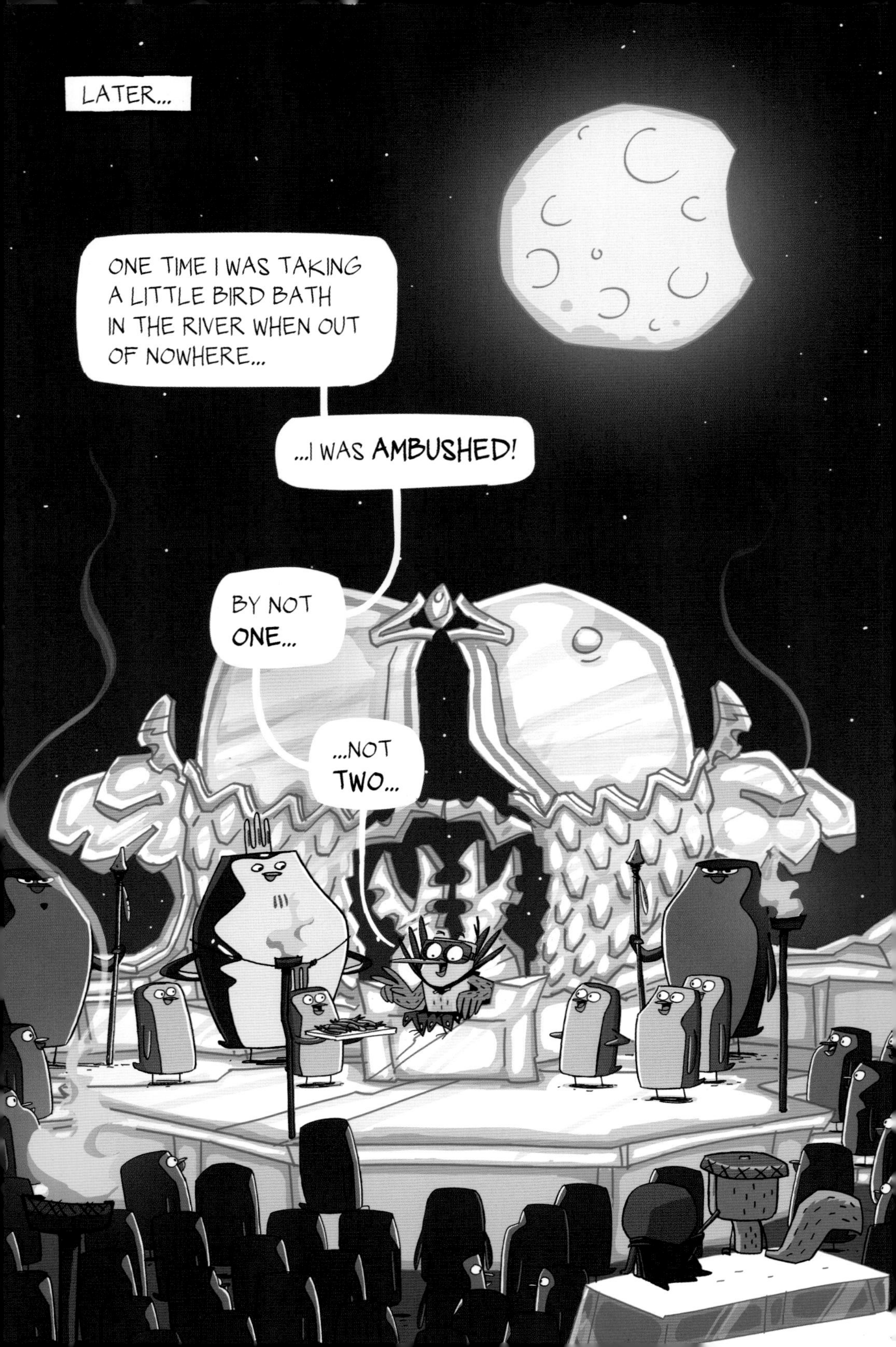
LATER...
ONE TIME I WAS TAKING A LITTLE BIRD BATH IN THE RIVER WHEN OUT OF NOWHERE...
...I WAS **AMBUSHED!**
BY NOT **ONE...**
...NOT **TWO...**

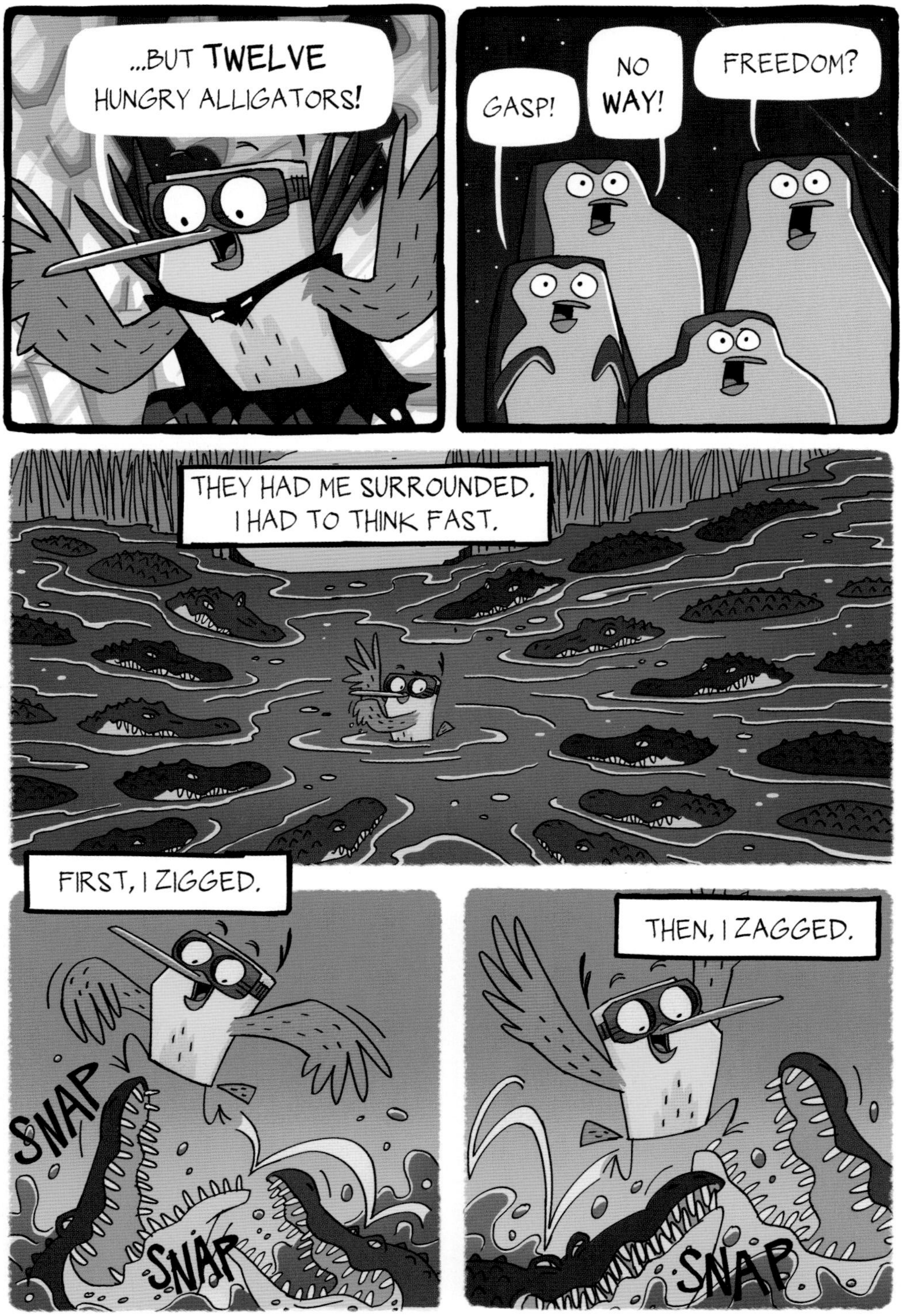

...BUT TWELVE HUNGRY ALLIGATORS!
GASP!
NO WAY!
FREEDOM?
THEY HAD ME SURROUNDED. I HAD TO THINK FAST.
FIRST, I ZIGGED.
SNAP
SNAP
THEN, I ZAGGED.
SNAP

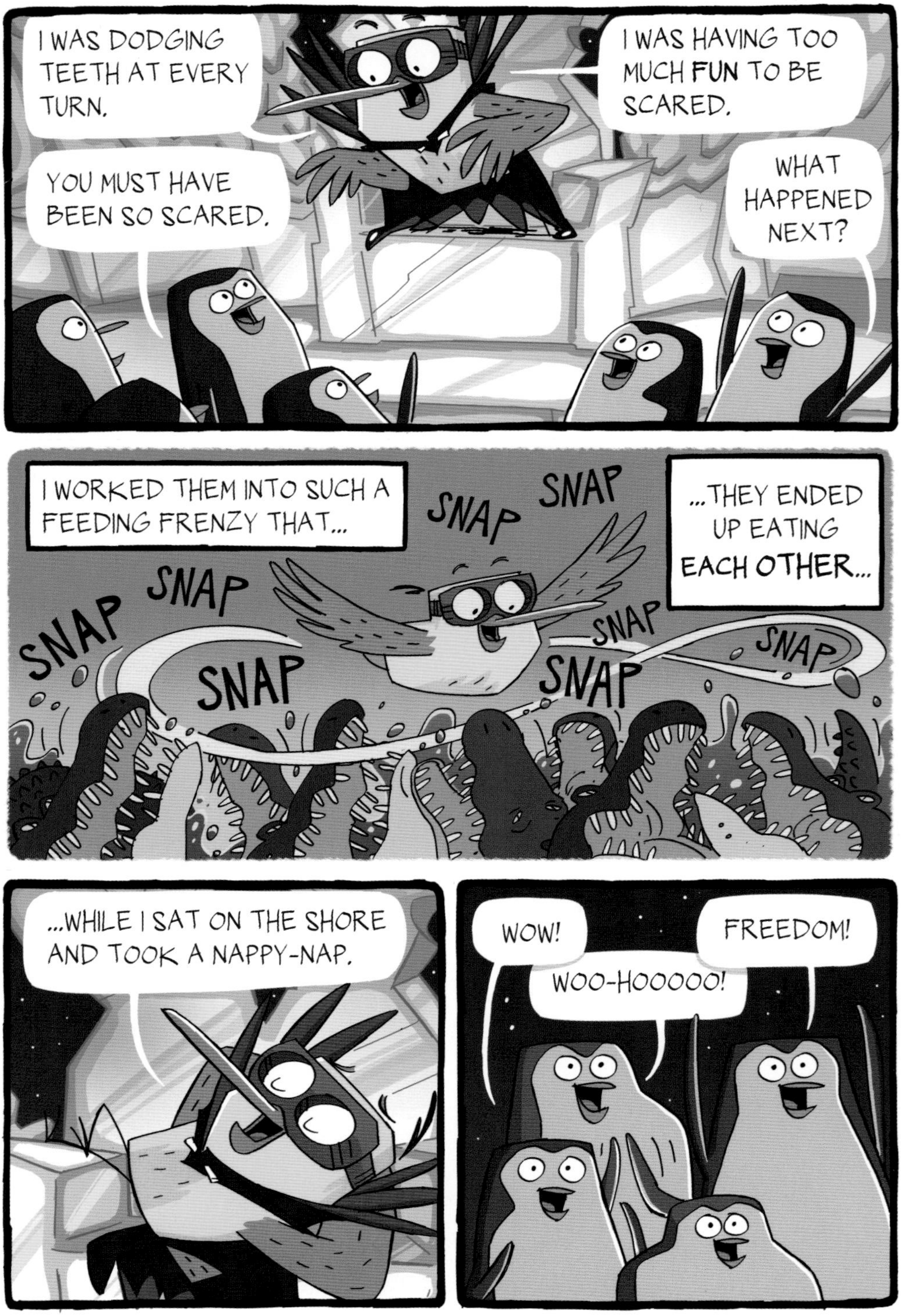
I WAS DODGING TEETH AT EVERY TURN.
YOU MUST HAVE BEEN SO SCARED.
I WAS HAVING TOO MUCH **FUN** TO BE SCARED.
WHAT HAPPENED NEXT?
I WORKED THEM INTO SUCH A FEEDING FRENZY THAT...
SNAP
SNAP
SNAP
SNAP
SNAP
SNAP
SNAP
SNAP
...THEY ENDED UP EATING **EACH OTHER**...
...WHILE I SAT ON THE SHORE AND TOOK A NAPPY-NAP.
WOW!
FREEDOM!
WOO-HOOOOO!

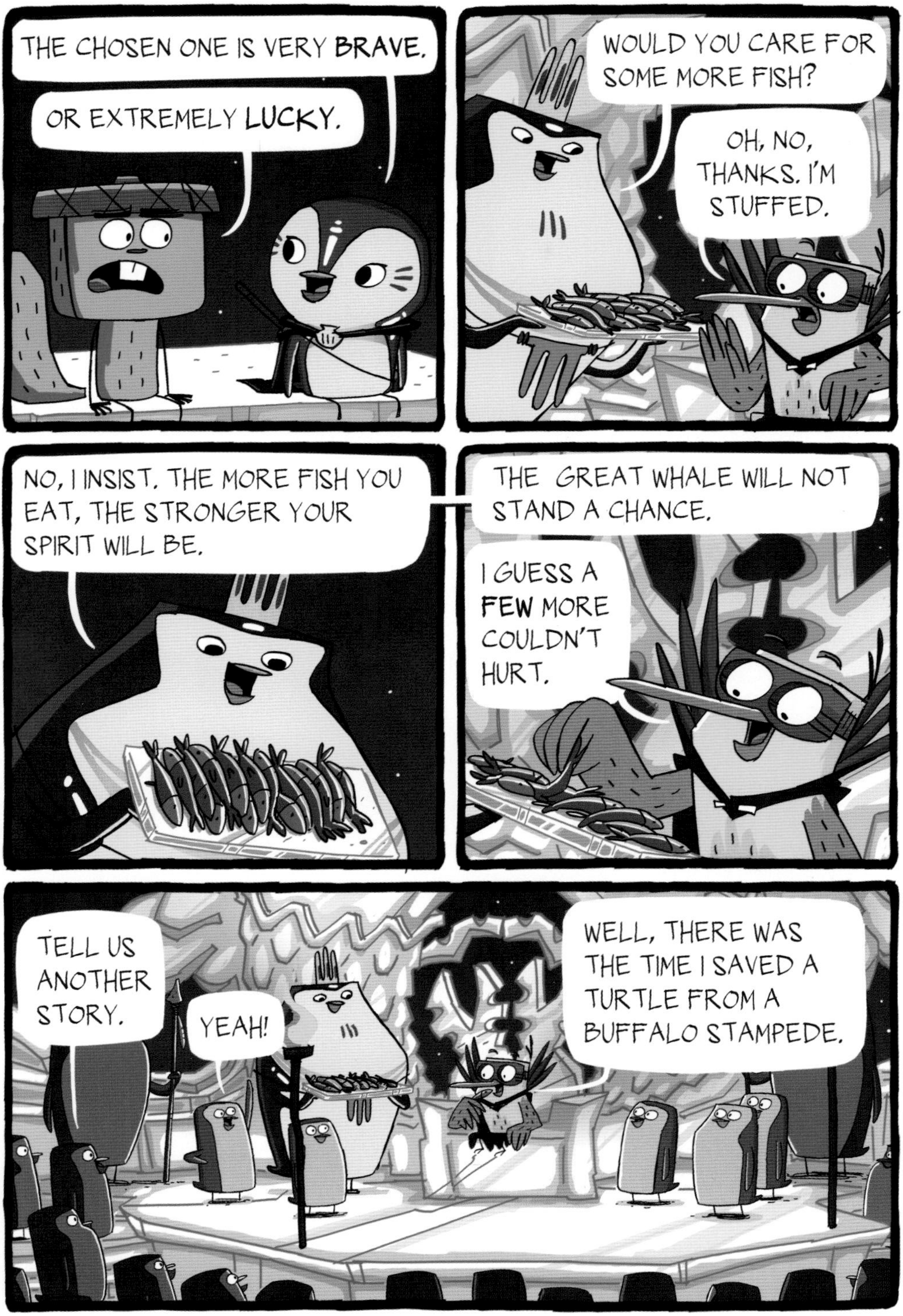
THE CHOSEN ONE IS VERY **BRAVE**.
OR EXTREMELY **LUCKY**.
WOULD YOU CARE FOR SOME MORE FISH?
OH, NO, THANKS. I'M STUFFED.
NO, I INSIST. THE MORE FISH YOU EAT, THE STRONGER YOUR SPIRIT WILL BE.
THE GREAT WHALE WILL NOT STAND A CHANCE.
I GUESS A **FEW** MORE COULDN'T HURT.
TELL US ANOTHER STORY.
YEAH!
WELL, THERE WAS THE TIME I SAVED A TURTLE FROM A BUFFALO STAMPEDE.

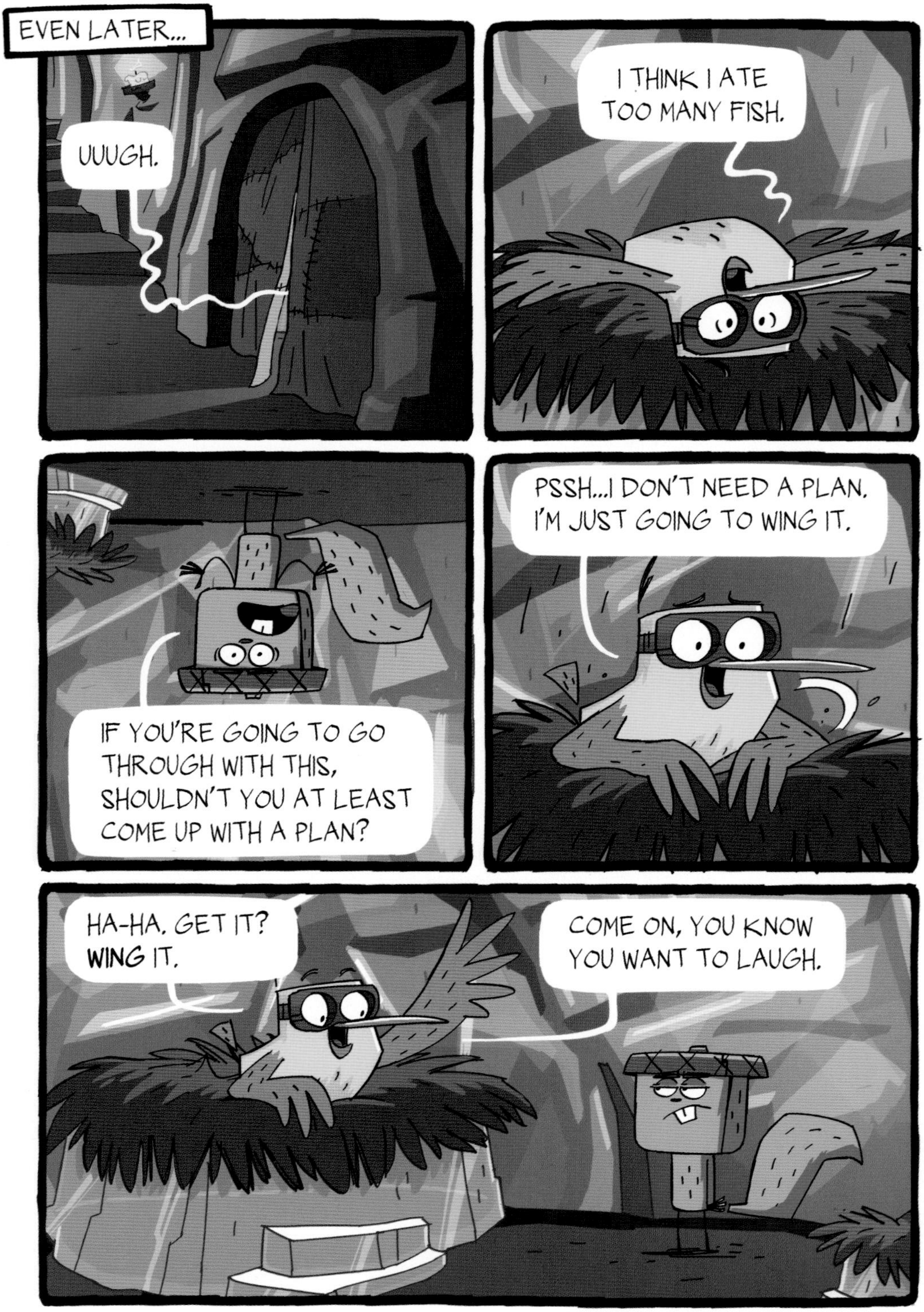
EVEN LATER...
UUUGH.
I THINK I ATE TOO MANY FISH.
IF YOU'RE GOING TO GO THROUGH WITH THIS, SHOULDN'T YOU AT LEAST COME UP WITH A PLAN?
PSSH...I DON'T NEED A PLAN. I'M JUST GOING TO WING IT.
HA-HA. GET IT? **WING** IT.
COME ON, YOU KNOW YOU WANT TO LAUGH.

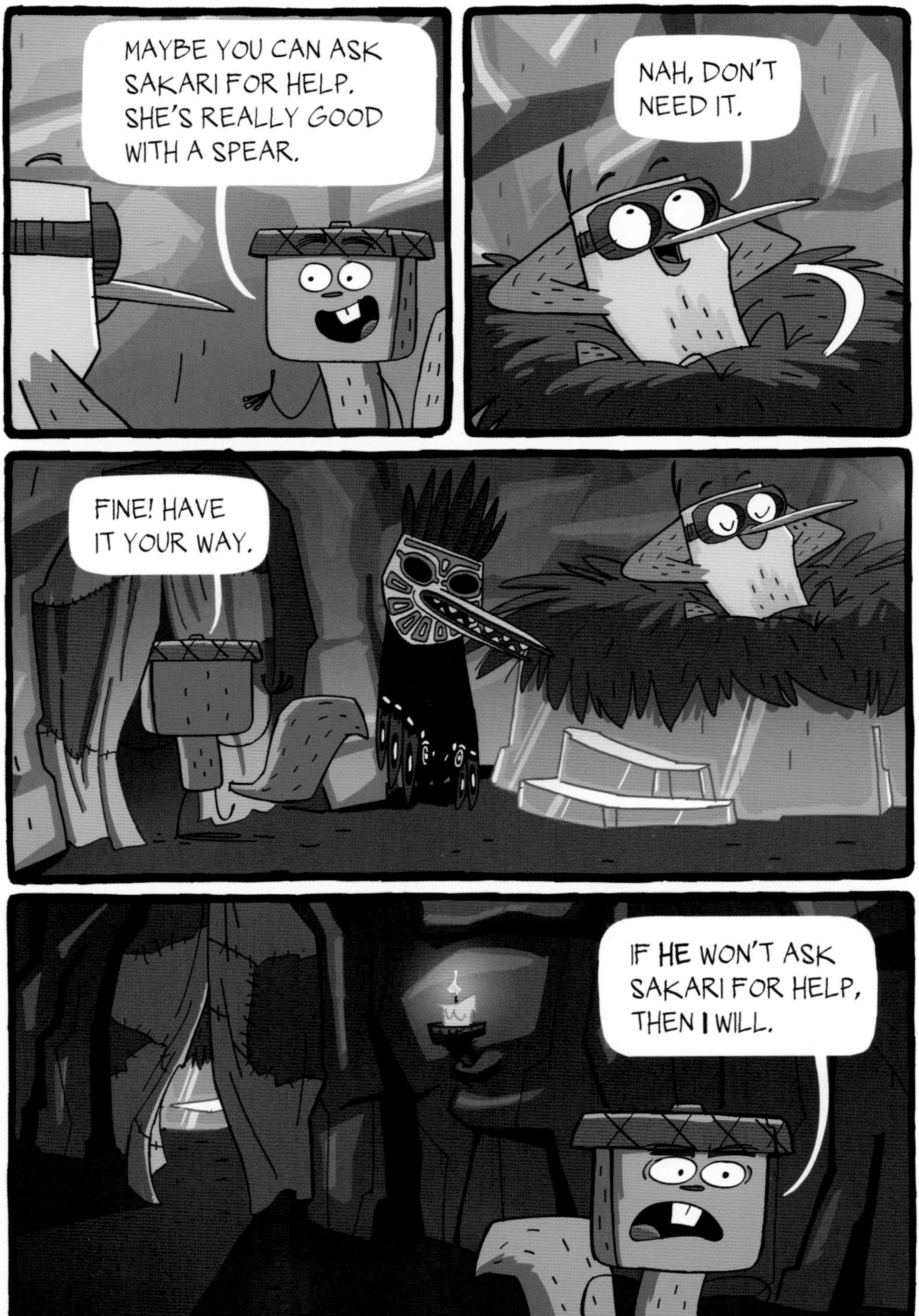
MAYBE YOU CAN ASK SAKARI FOR HELP. SHE'S REALLY GOOD WITH A SPEAR.
NAH, DON'T NEED IT.
FINE! HAVE IT YOUR WAY.
IF HE WON'T ASK SAKARI FOR HELP, THEN I WILL.

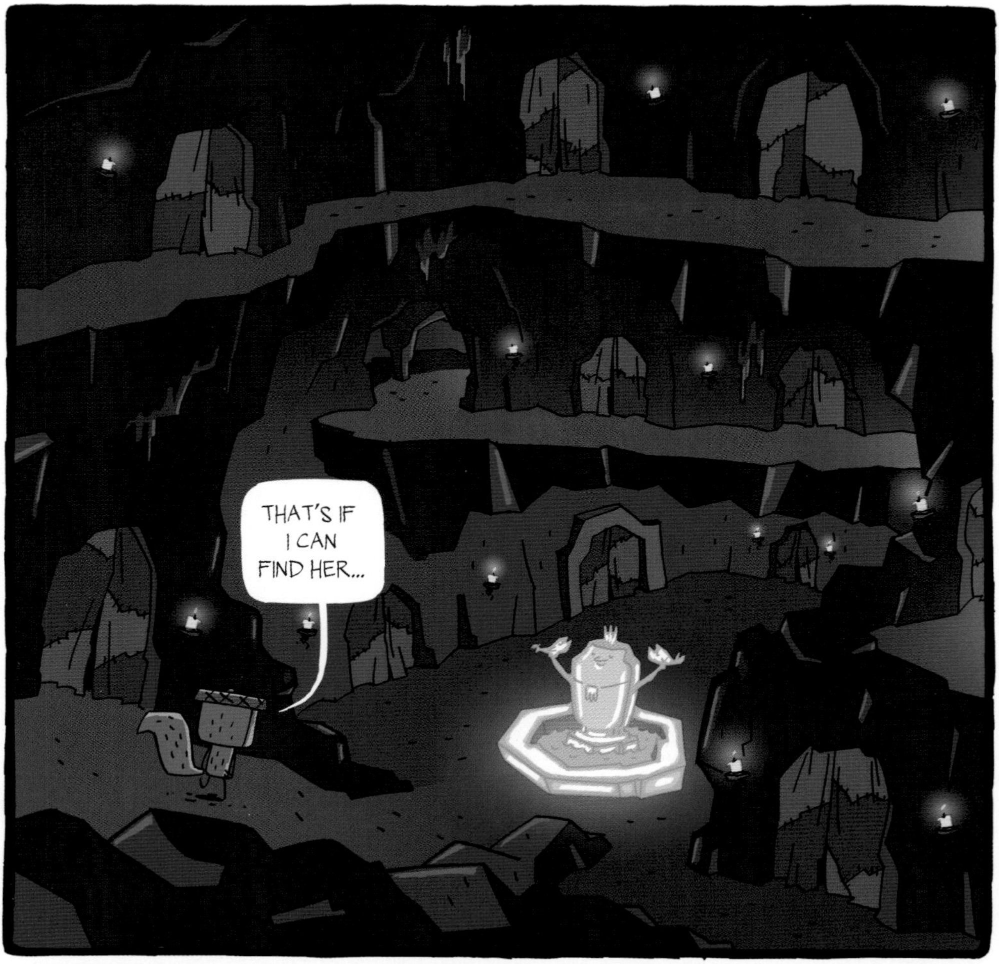
THAT'S IF
I CAN
FIND HER...

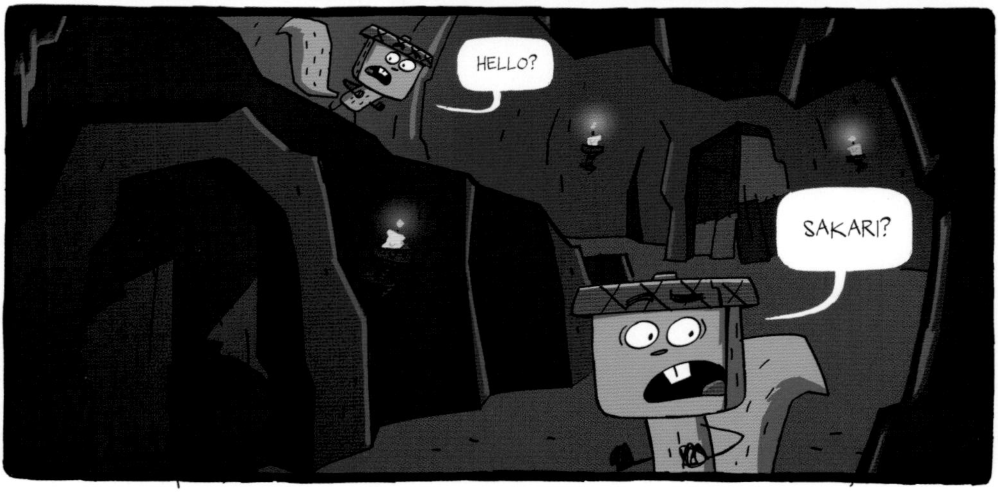
HELLO?
SAKARI?

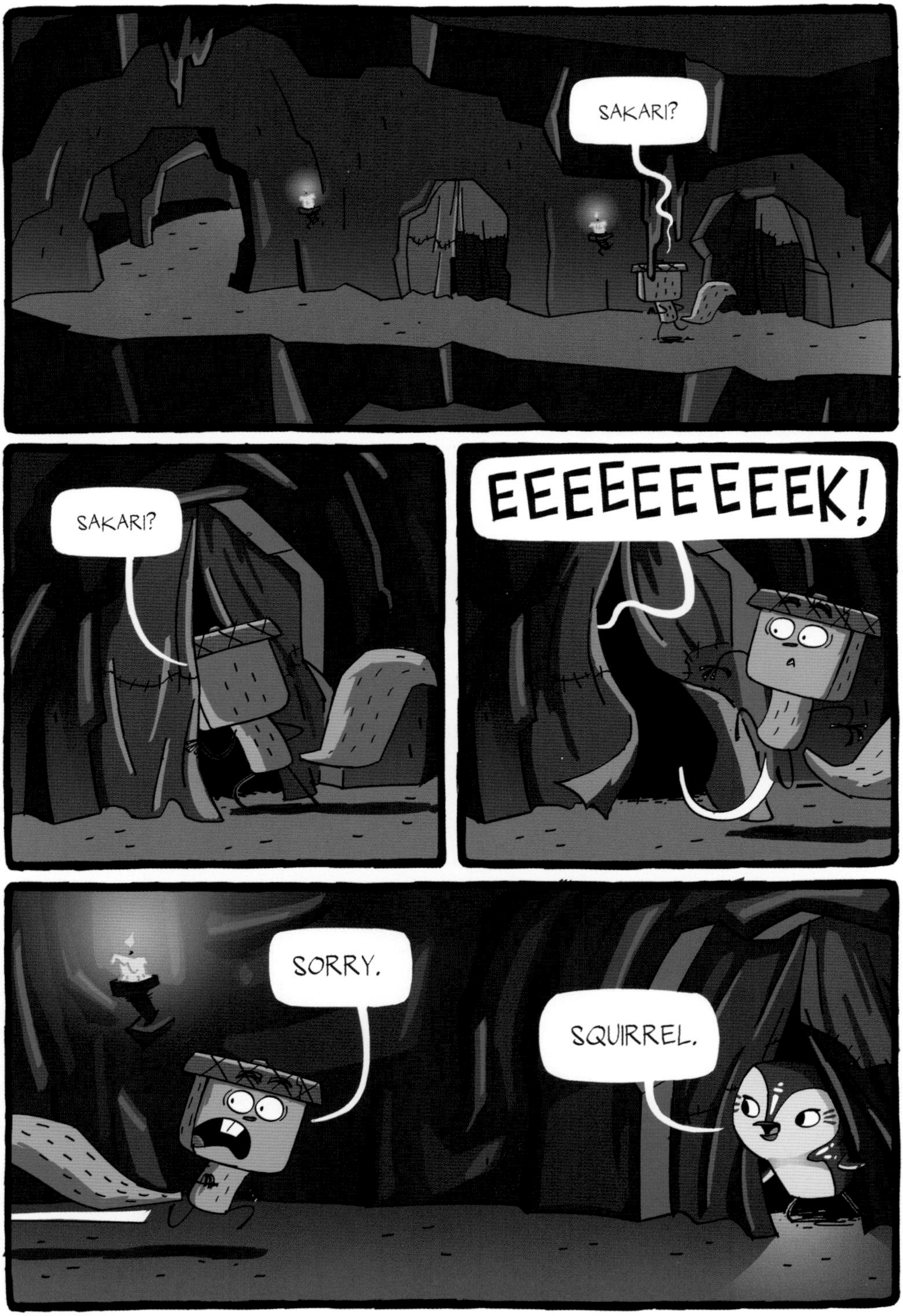
SAKARI?
SAKARI?
EEEEEEEEEK!
SORRY.
SQUIRREL.

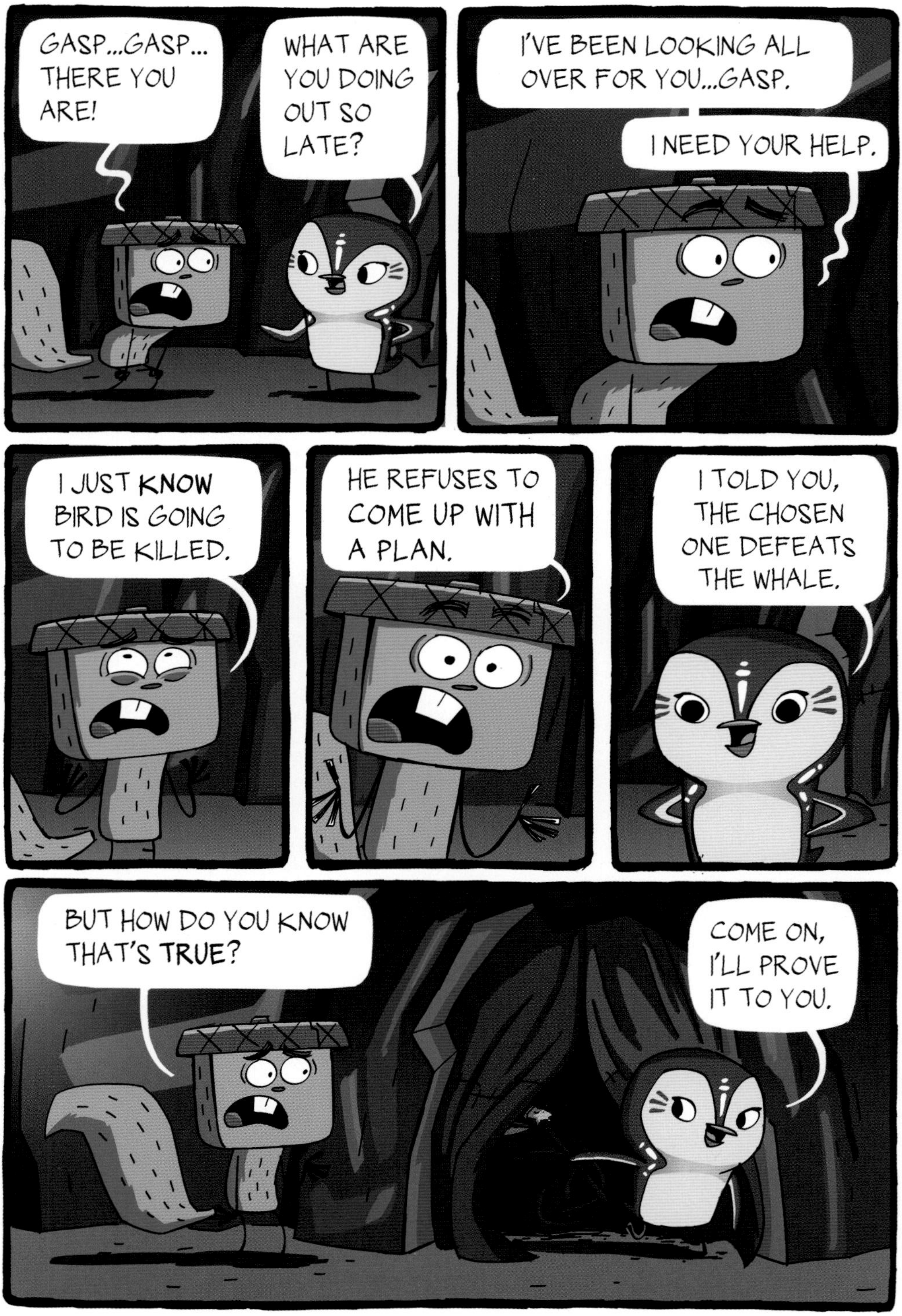
GASP...GASP... THERE YOU ARE!
WHAT ARE YOU DOING OUT SO LATE?
I'VE BEEN LOOKING ALL OVER FOR YOU...GASP.
I NEED YOUR HELP.
I JUST **KNOW** BIRD IS GOING TO BE KILLED.
HE REFUSES TO COME UP WITH A PLAN.
I TOLD YOU, THE CHOSEN ONE DEFEATS THE WHALE.
BUT HOW DO YOU KNOW THAT'S **TRUE**?
COME ON, I'LL PROVE IT TO YOU.

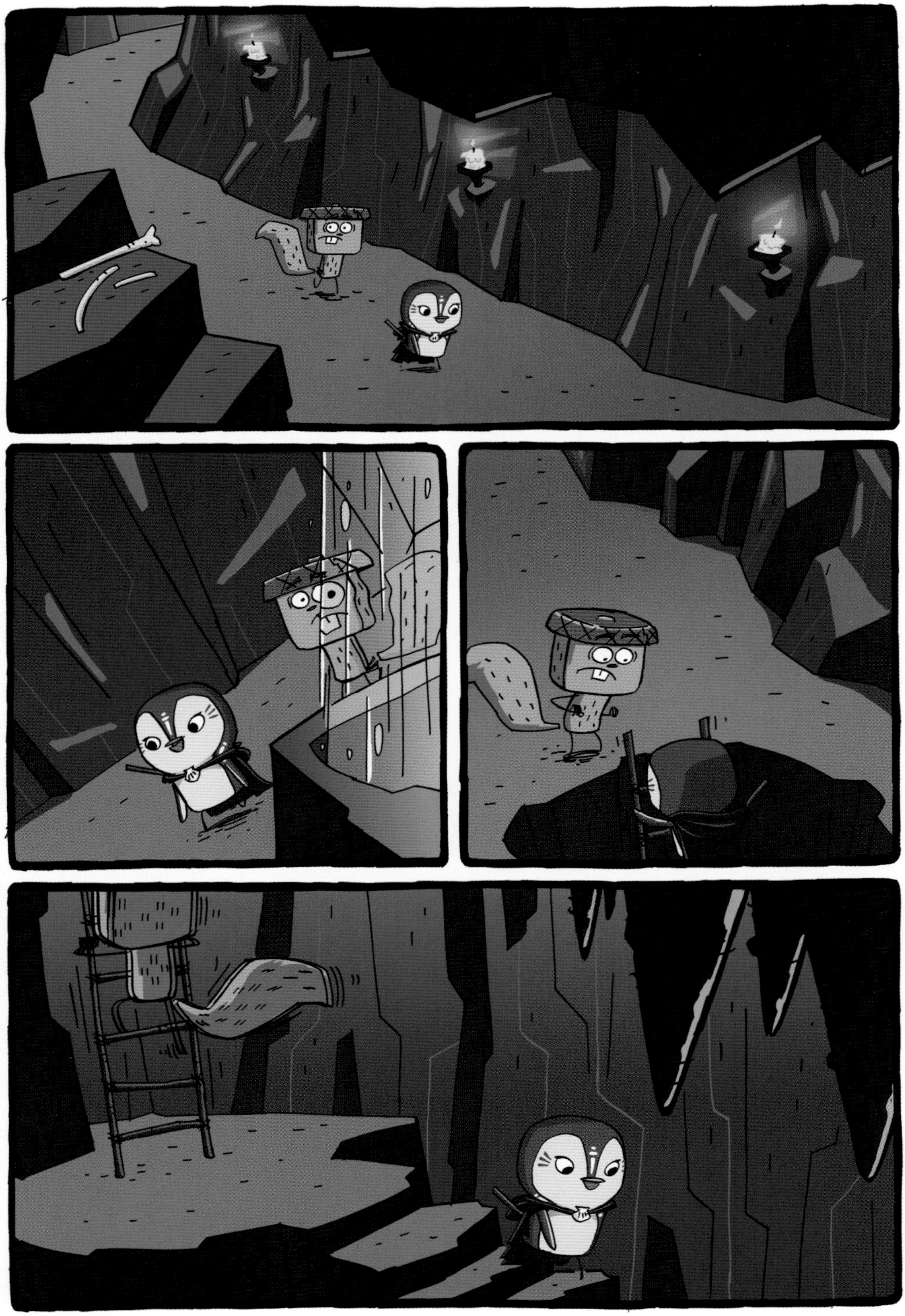

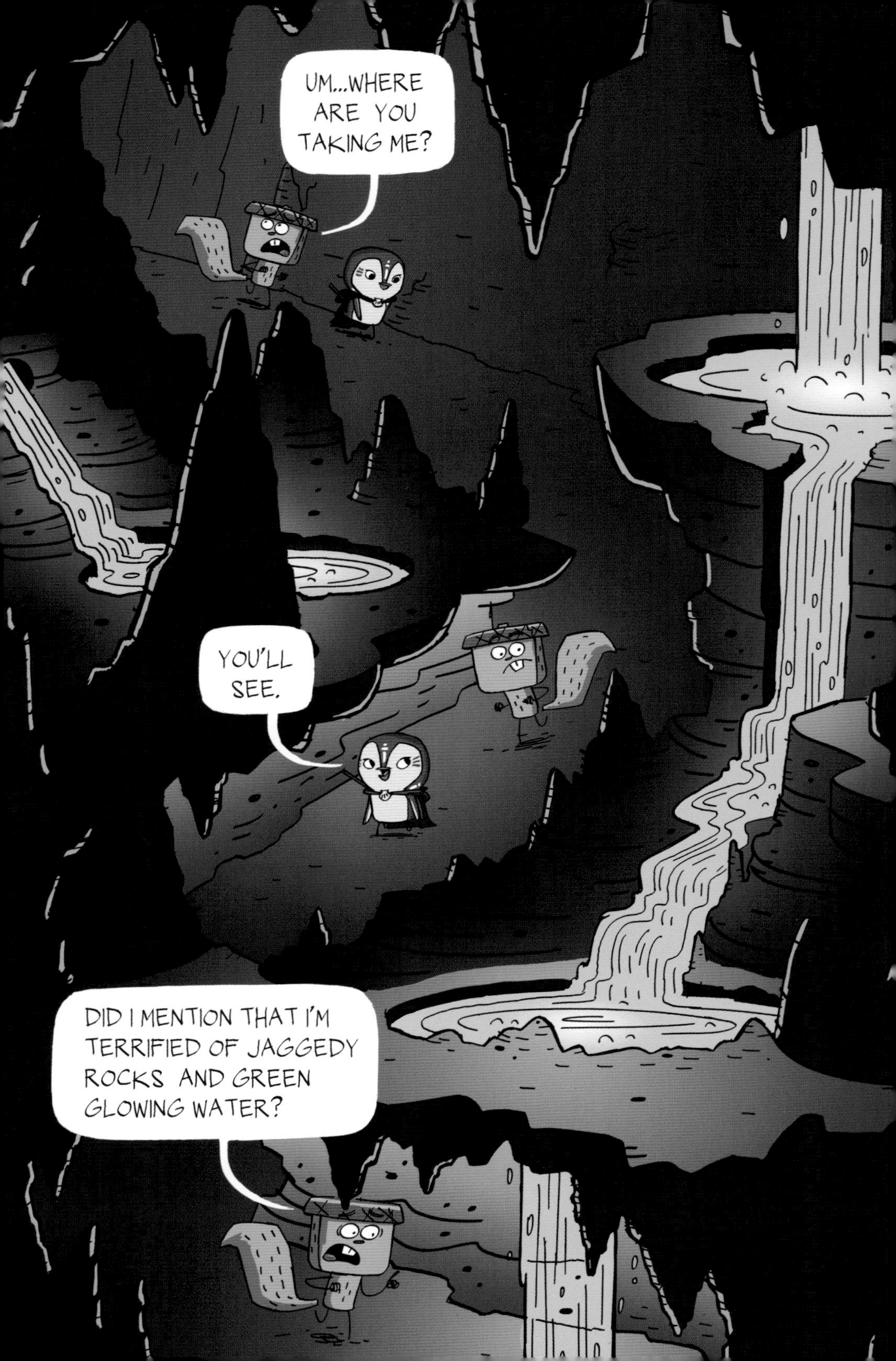
UM...WHERE ARE YOU TAKING ME?
YOU'LL SEE.
DID I MENTION THAT I'M TERRIFIED OF JAGGEDY ROCKS AND GREEN GLOWING WATER?

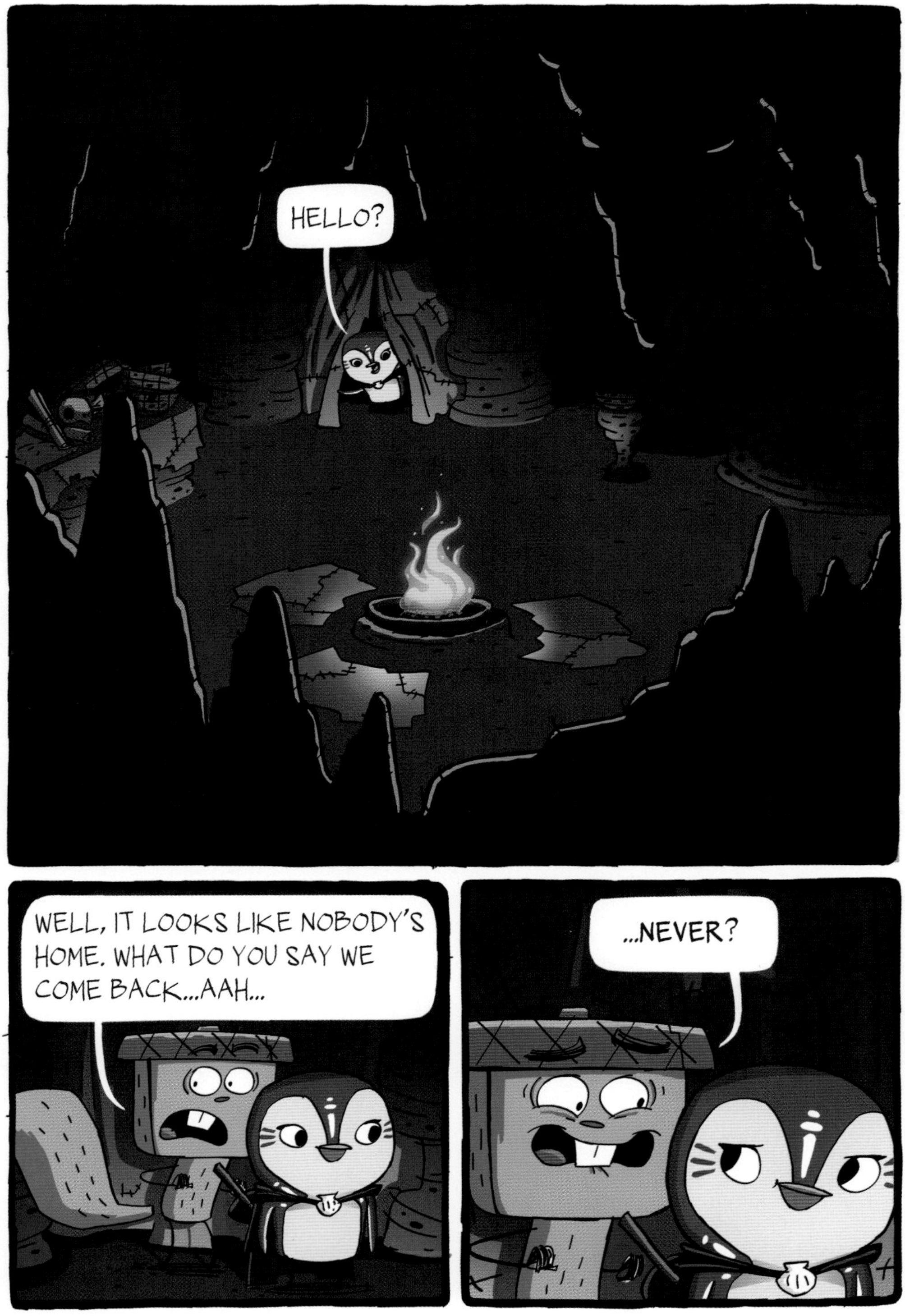
HELLO?
WELL, IT LOOKS LIKE NOBODY'S HOME. WHAT DO YOU SAY WE COME BACK...AAH...
...NEVER?

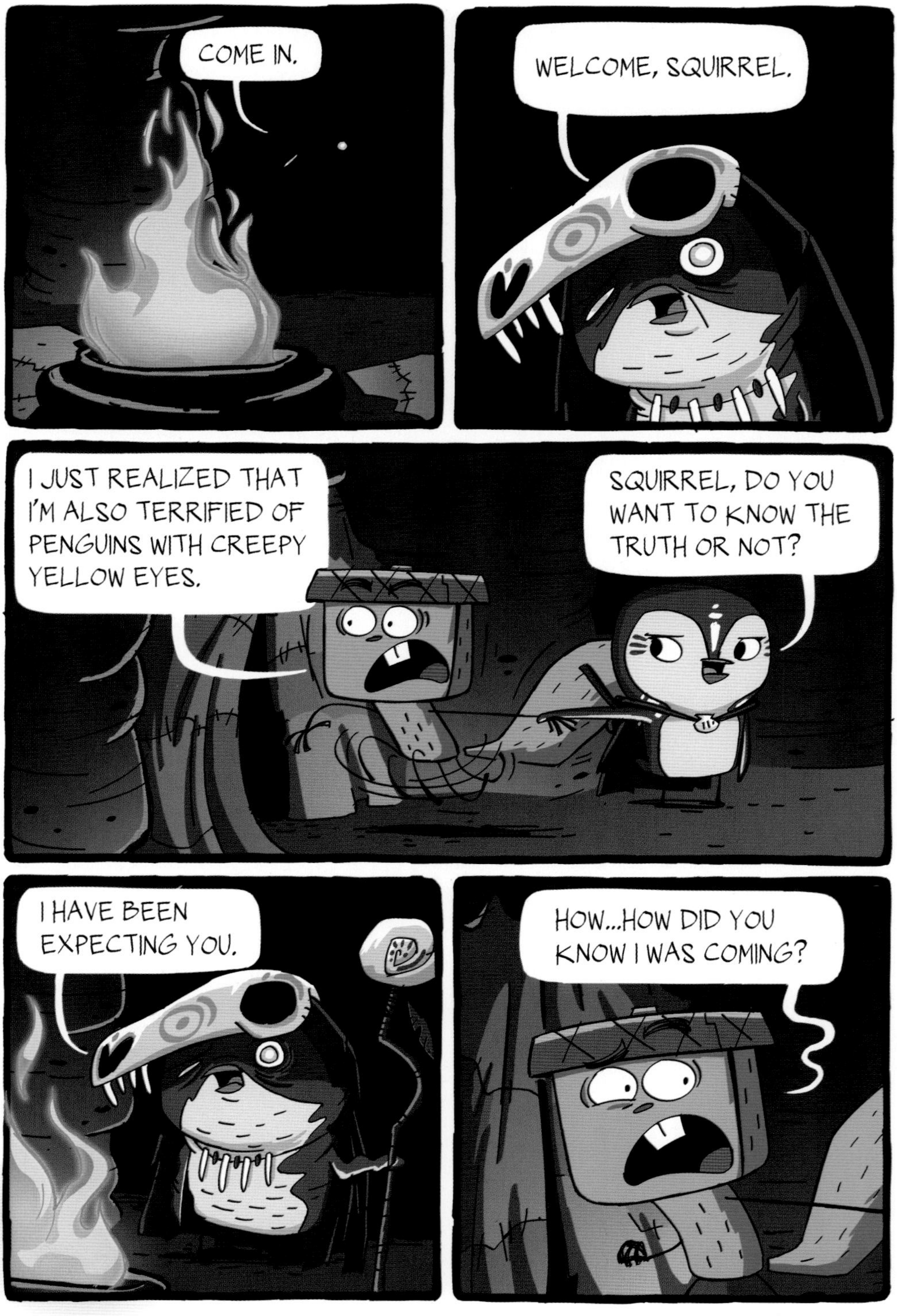
COME IN.
WELCOME, SQUIRREL.
I JUST REALIZED THAT I'M ALSO TERRIFIED OF PENGUINS WITH CREEPY YELLOW EYES.
SQUIRREL, DO YOU WANT TO KNOW THE TRUTH OR NOT?
I HAVE BEEN EXPECTING YOU.
HOW...HOW DID YOU KNOW I WAS COMING?

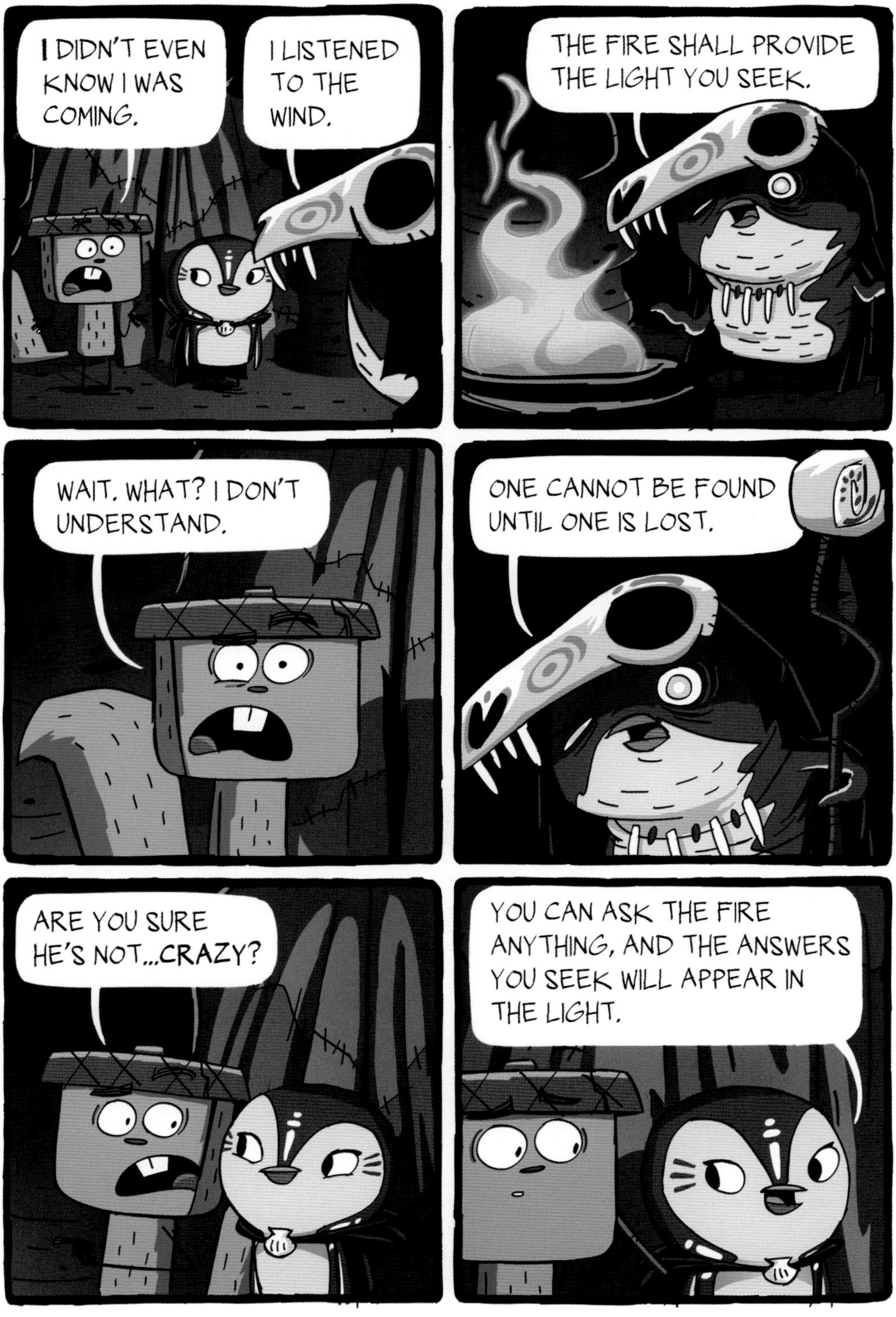

I DIDN'T EVEN KNOW I WAS COMING.
I LISTENED TO THE WIND.
THE FIRE SHALL PROVIDE THE LIGHT YOU SEEK.
WAIT. WHAT? I DON'T UNDERSTAND.
ONE CANNOT BE FOUND UNTIL ONE IS LOST.
ARE YOU SURE HE'S NOT...CRAZY?
YOU CAN ASK THE FIRE ANYTHING, AND THE ANSWERS YOU SEEK WILL APPEAR IN THE LIGHT.

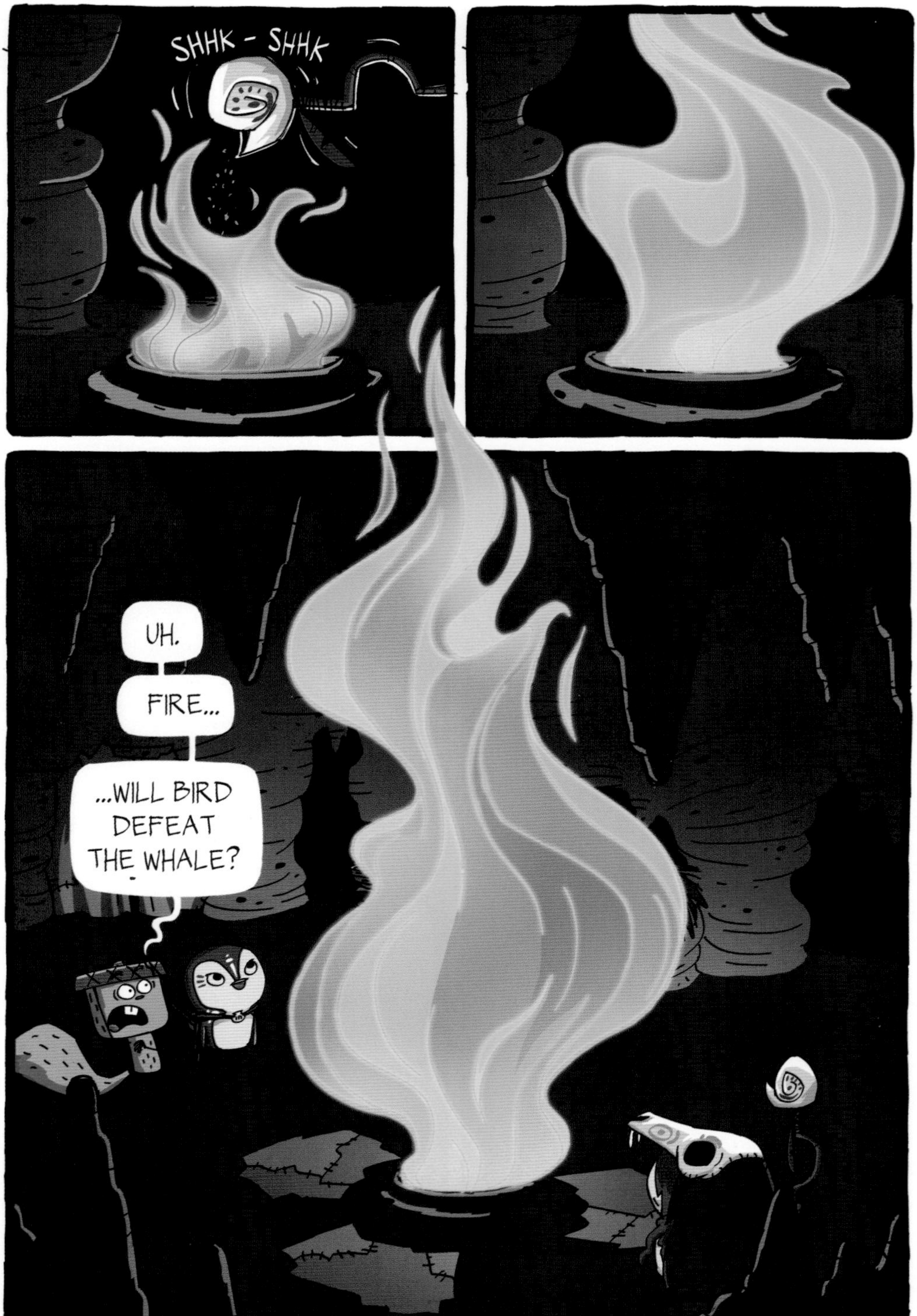
SHHK - SHHK
UH.
FIRE...
...WILL BIRD DEFEAT THE WHALE?

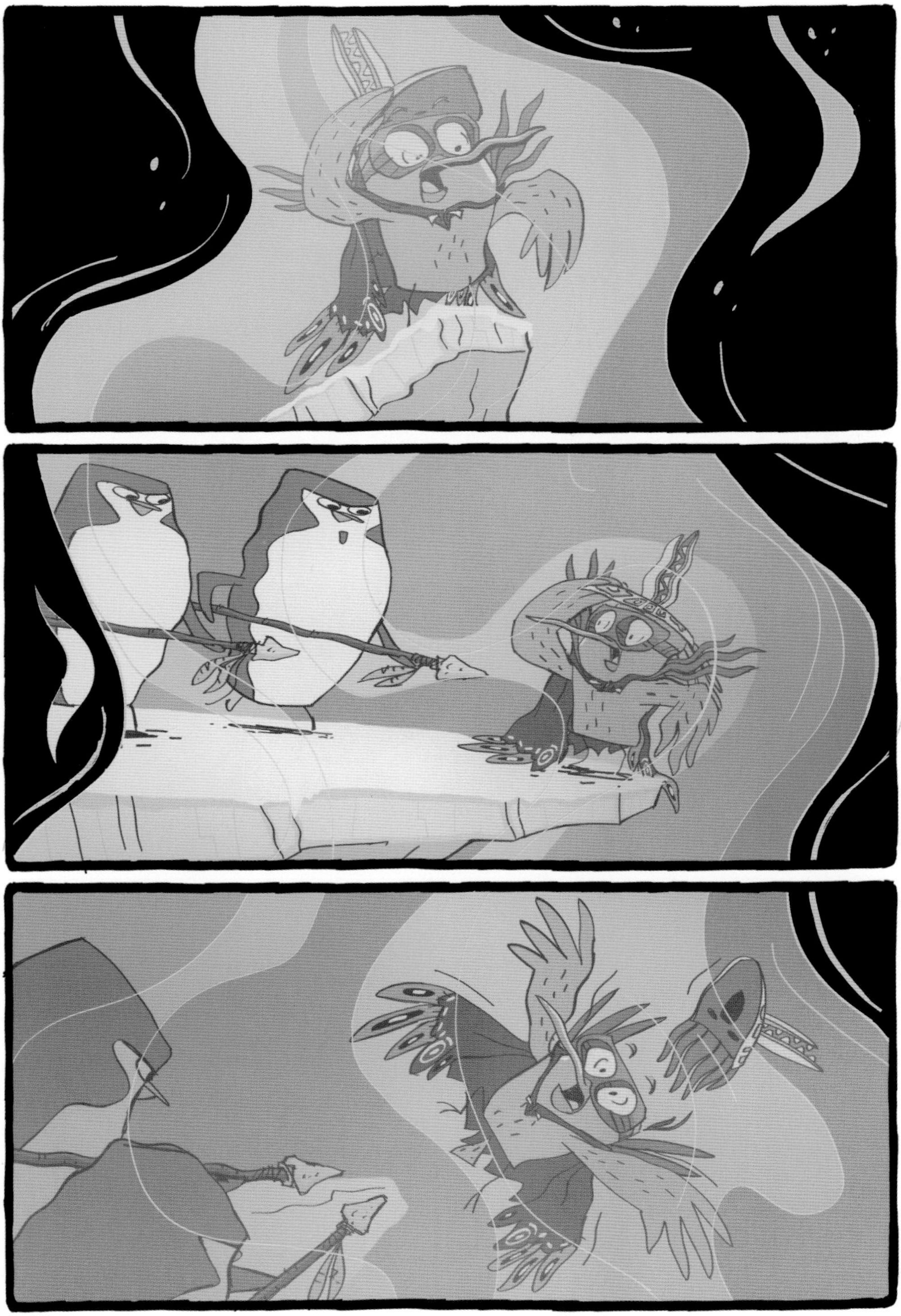

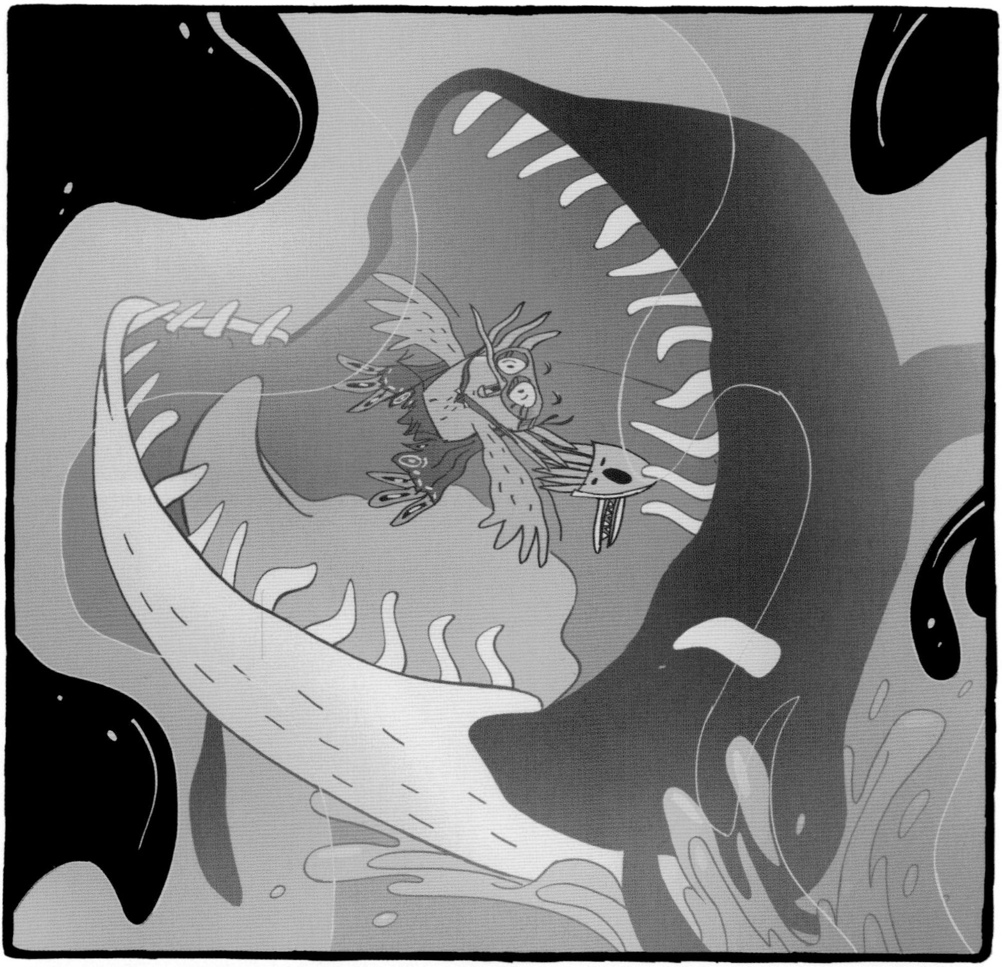

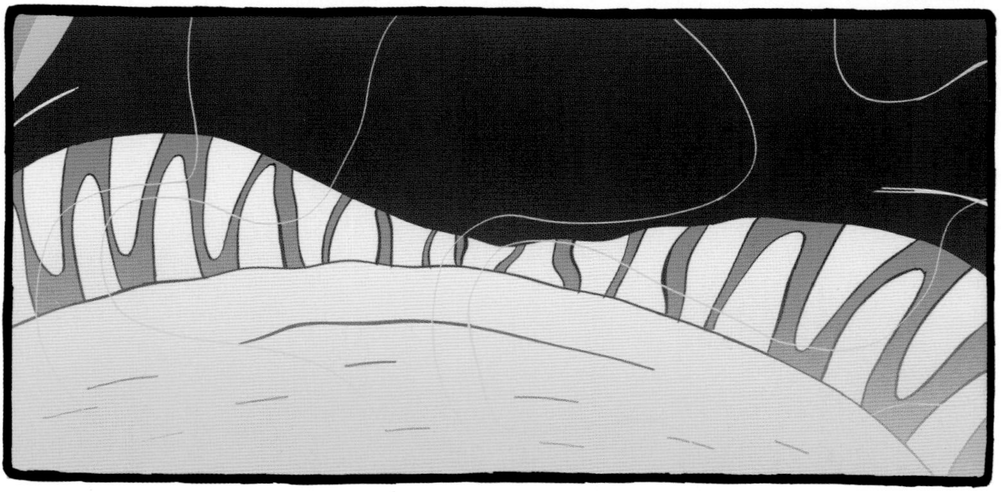

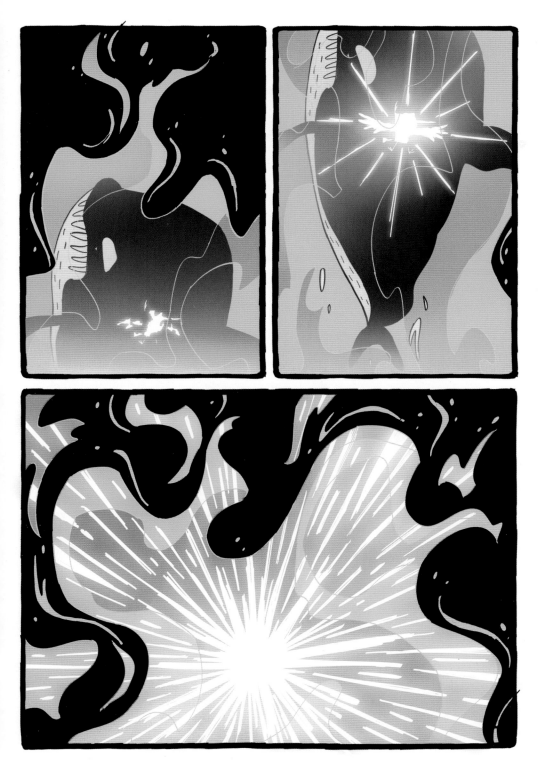

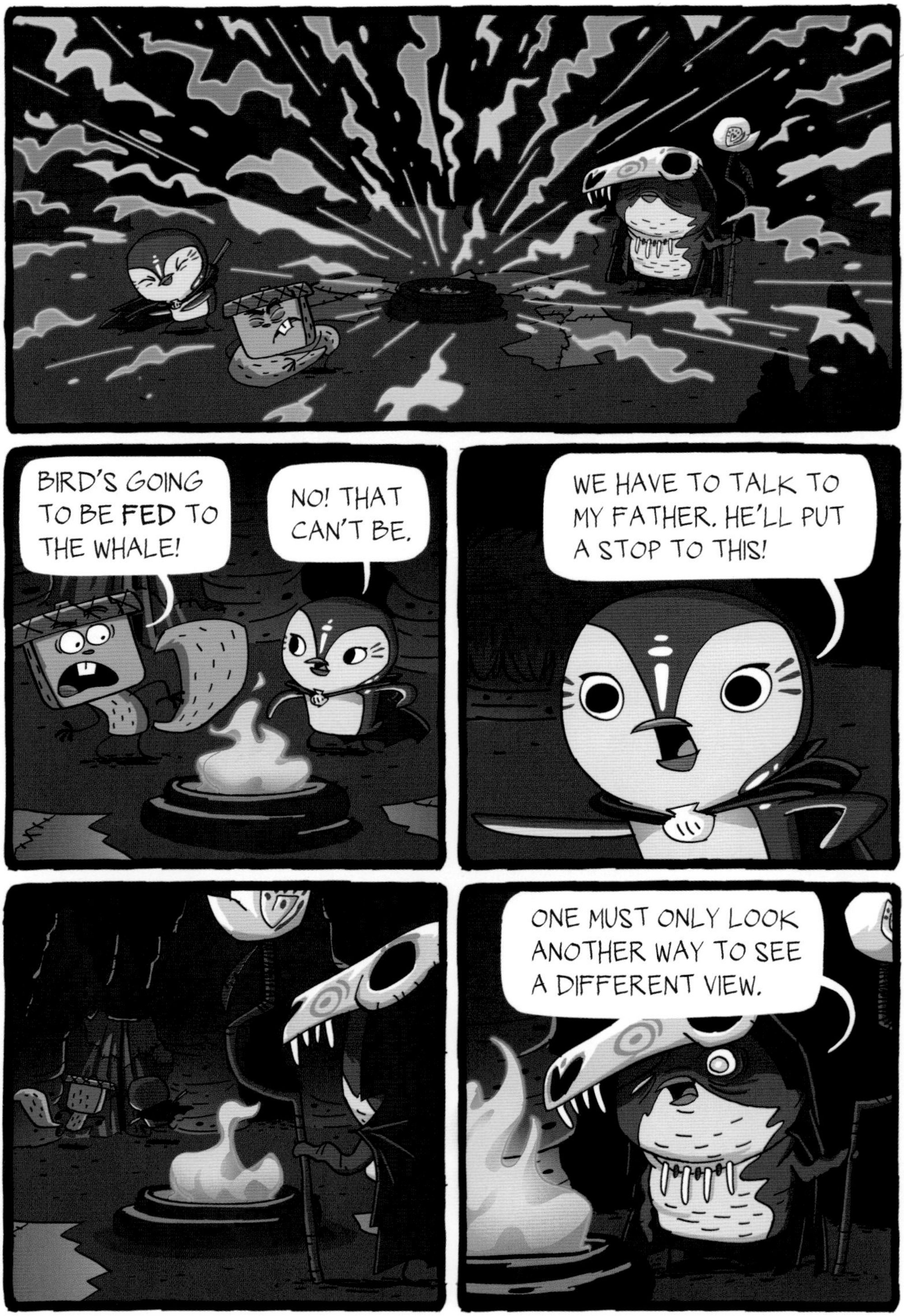
BIRD'S GOING TO BE **FED** TO THE WHALE!
NO! THAT CAN'T BE.
WE HAVE TO TALK TO MY FATHER. HE'LL PUT A STOP TO THIS!
ONE MUST ONLY LOOK ANOTHER WAY TO SEE A DIFFERENT VIEW.

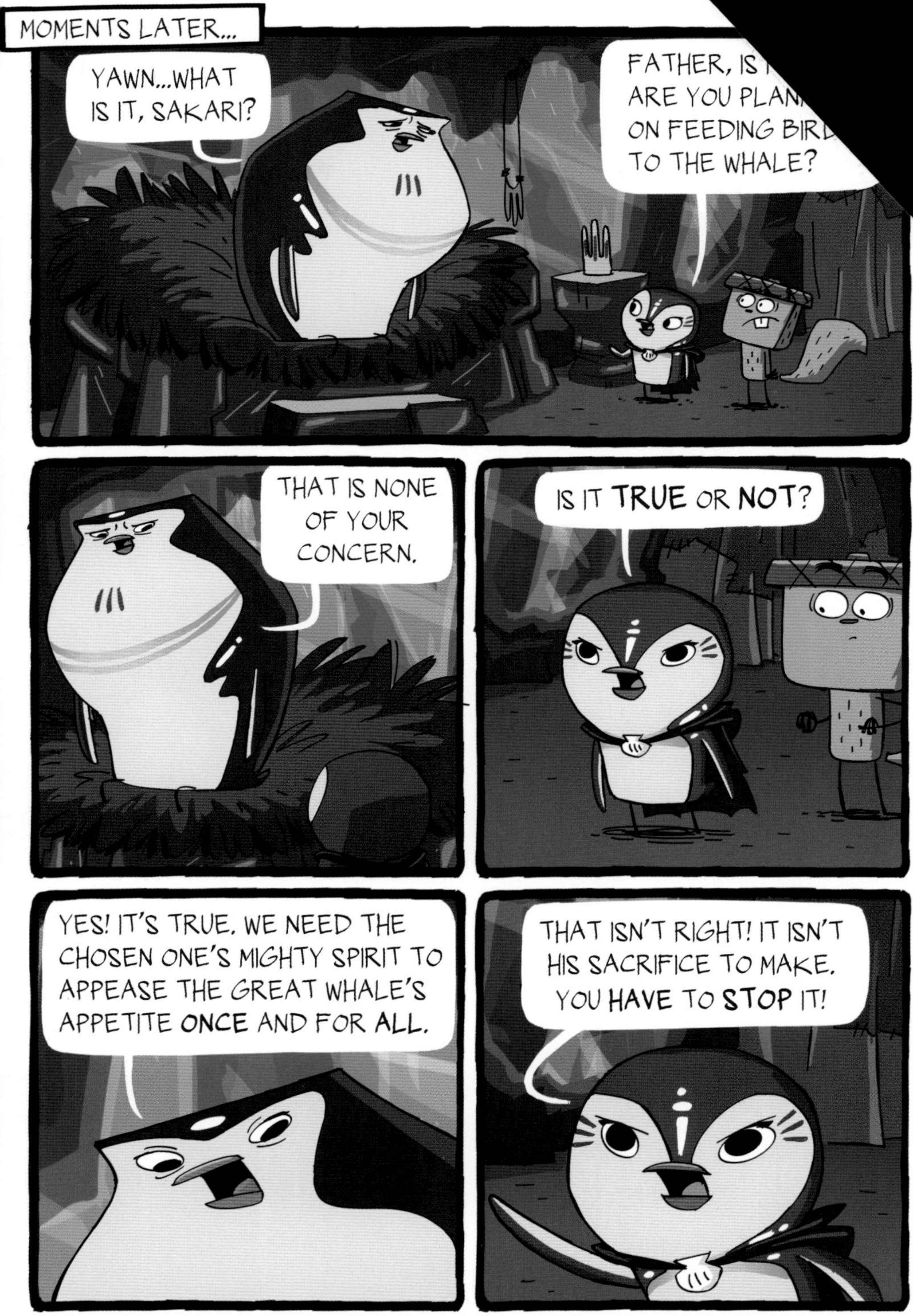
MOMENTS LATER...
YAWN...WHAT IS IT, SAKARI?
FATHER, IS
ARE YOU PLAN
ON FEEDING BIR
TO THE WHALE?
THAT IS NONE OF YOUR CONCERN.
IS IT **TRUE** OR **NOT**?
YES! IT'S TRUE. WE NEED THE CHOSEN ONE'S MIGHTY SPIRIT TO APPEASE THE GREAT WHALE'S APPETITE **ONCE** AND FOR **ALL**.
THAT ISN'T RIGHT! IT ISN'T HIS SACRIFICE TO MAKE. YOU **HAVE** TO **STOP** IT!

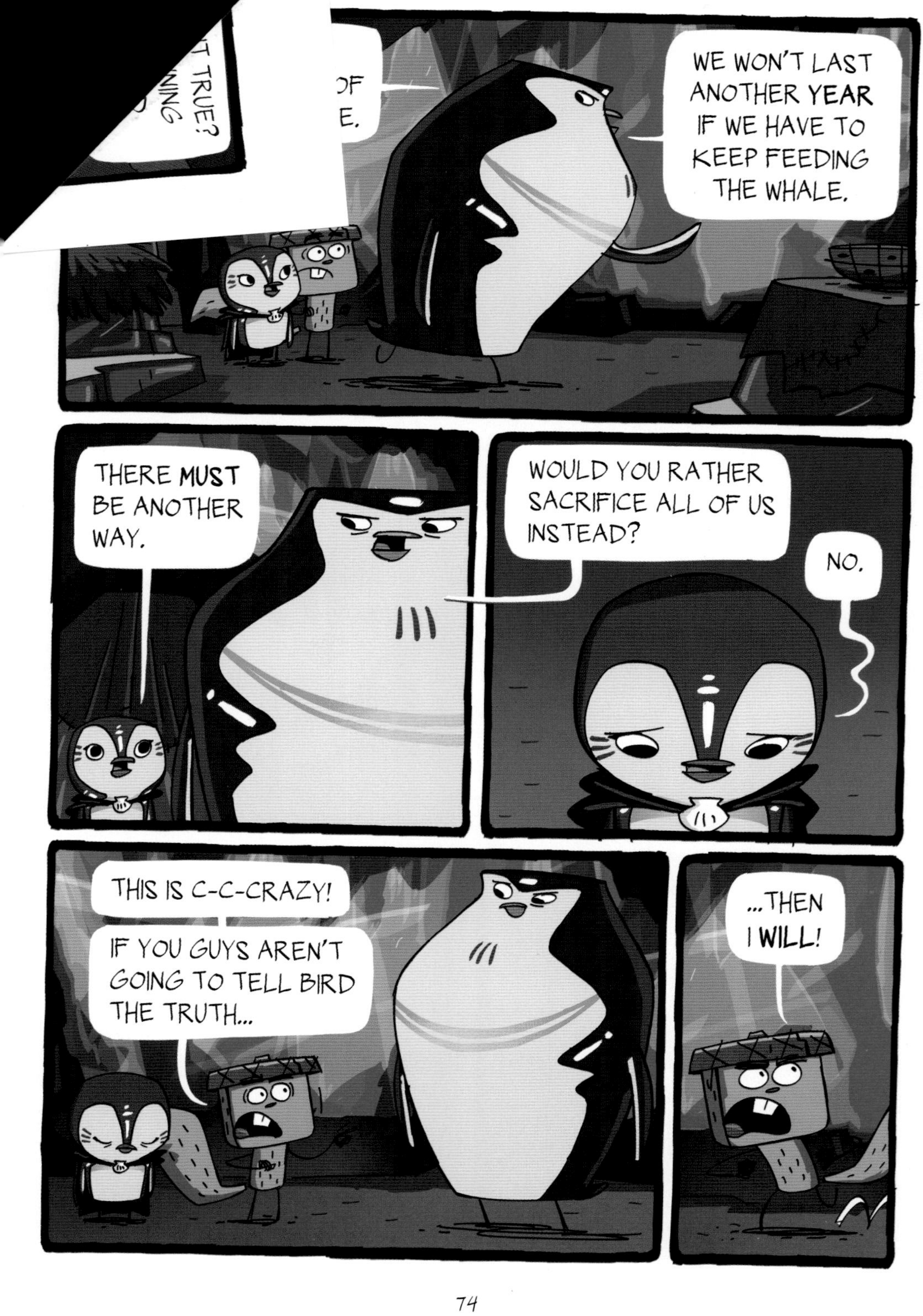

WE WON'T LAST ANOTHER YEAR IF WE HAVE TO KEEP FEEDING THE WHALE.
THERE MUST BE ANOTHER WAY.
WOULD YOU RATHER SACRIFICE ALL OF US INSTEAD?
NO.
THIS IS C-C-CRAZY!
IF YOU GUYS AREN'T GOING TO TELL BIRD THE TRUTH...
...THEN I WILL!

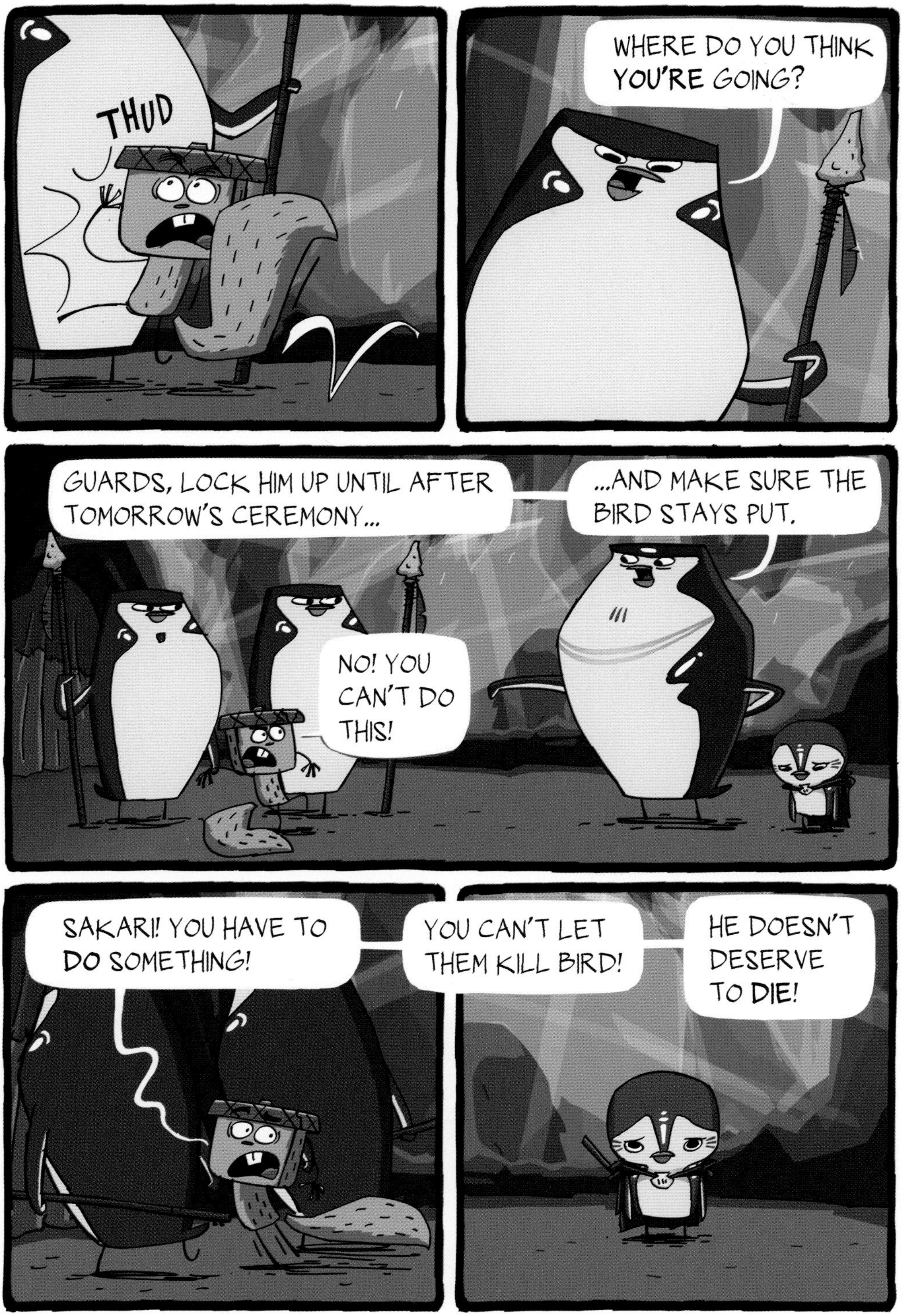
THUD
WHERE DO YOU THINK YOU'RE GOING?
GUARDS, LOCK HIM UP UNTIL AFTER TOMORROW'S CEREMONY...
...AND MAKE SURE THE BIRD STAYS PUT.
NO! YOU CAN'T DO THIS!
SAKARI! YOU HAVE TO DO SOMETHING!
YOU CAN'T LET THEM KILL BIRD!
HE DOESN'T DESERVE TO DIE!

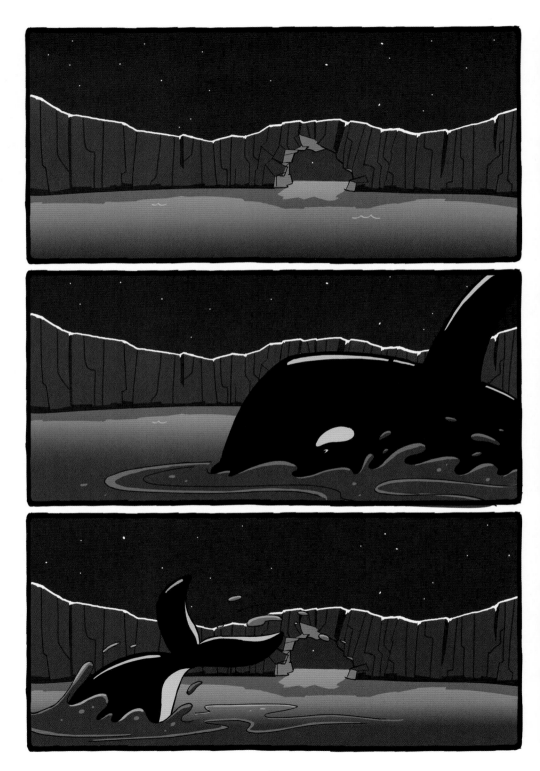

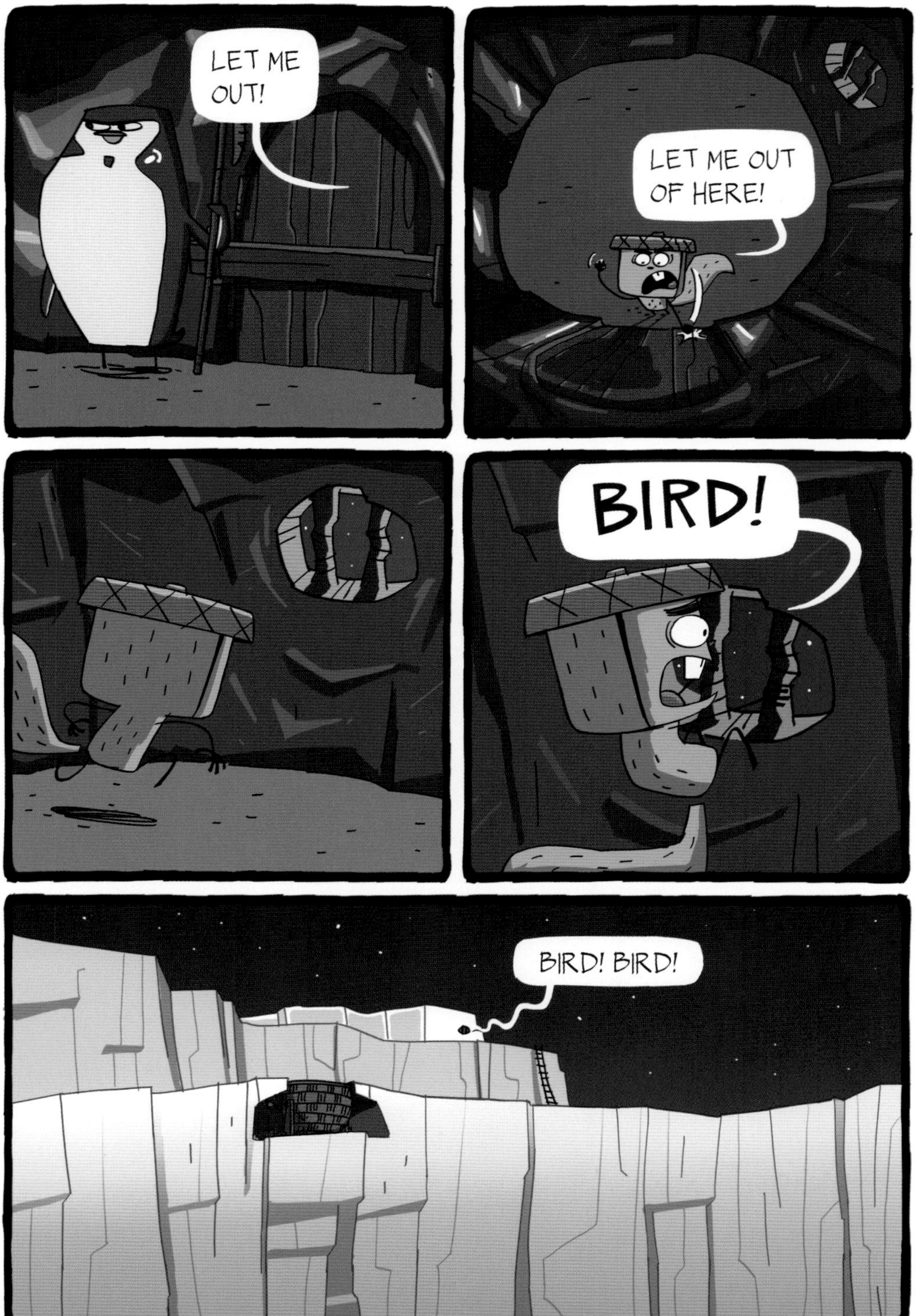
LET ME OUT!
LET ME OUT OF HERE!
BIRD!
BIRD! BIRD!

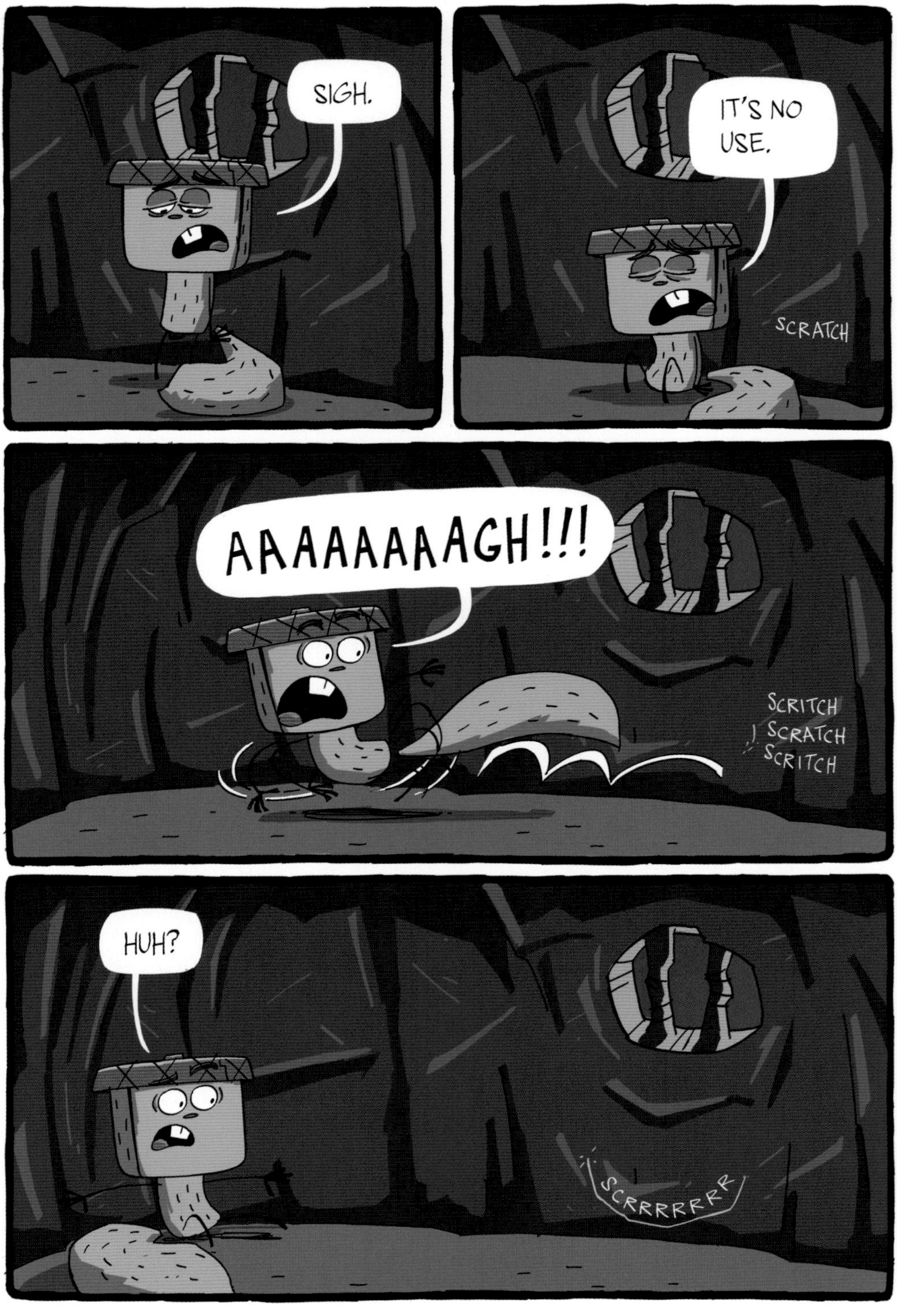

SIGH.
IT'S NO USE.
SCRATCH
AAAAAAAAGH!!!
SCRITCH
SCRATCH
SCRITCH
HUH?
SCRRRRRRR

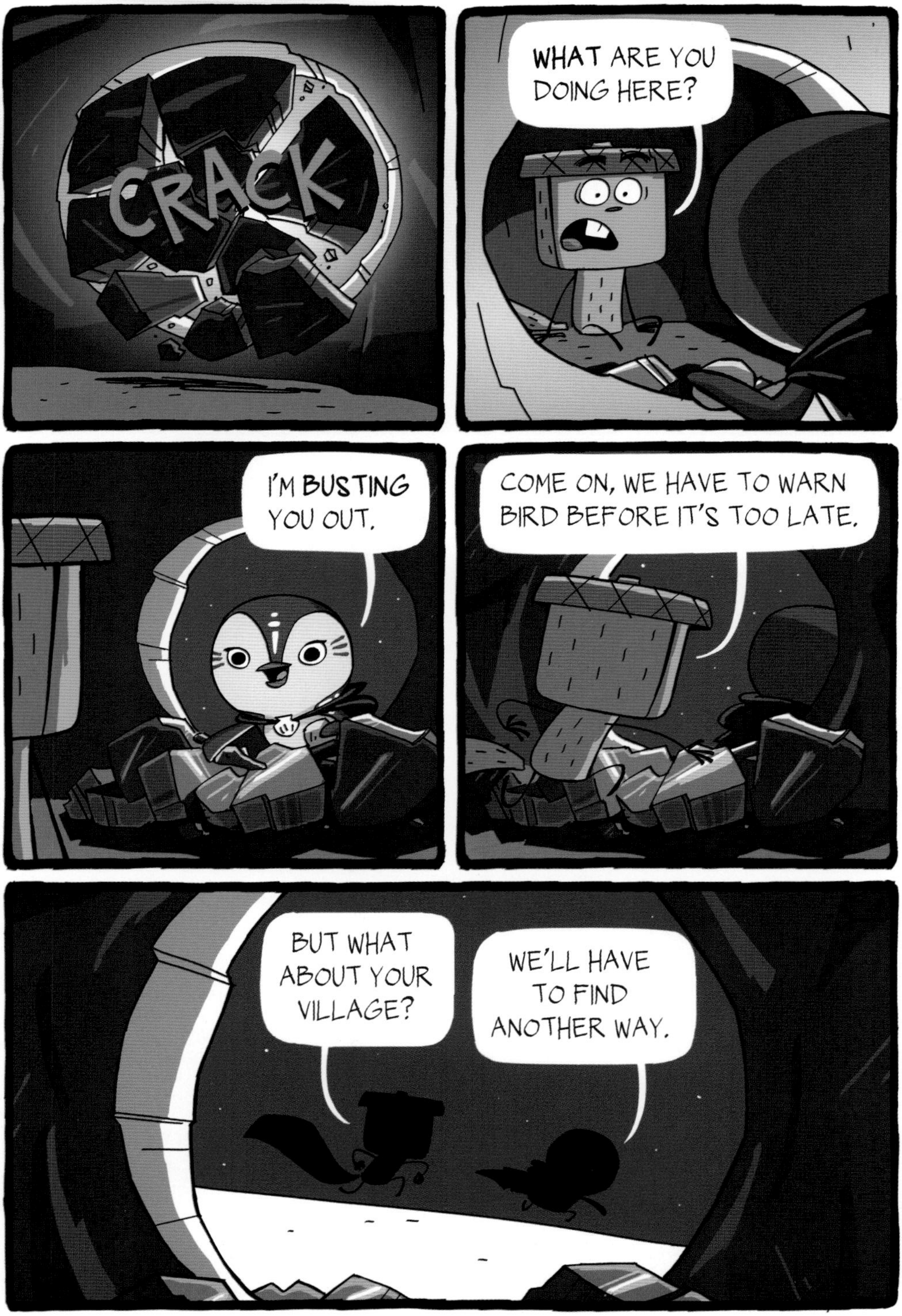
CRACK
WHAT ARE YOU DOING HERE?
I'M BUSTING YOU OUT.
COME ON, WE HAVE TO WARN BIRD BEFORE IT'S TOO LATE.
BUT WHAT ABOUT YOUR VILLAGE?
WE'LL HAVE TO FIND ANOTHER WAY.

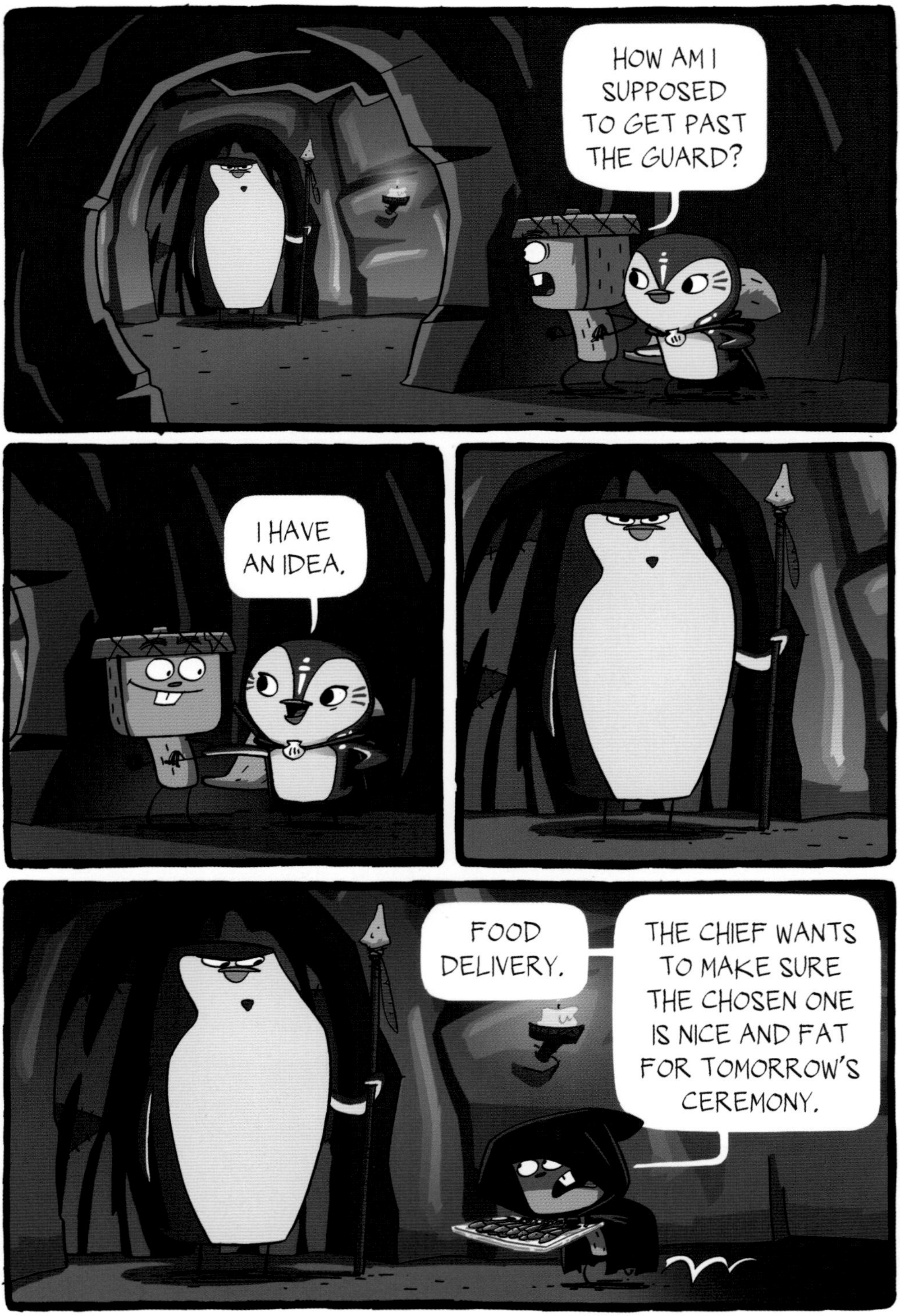
HOW AM I SUPPOSED TO GET PAST THE GUARD?
I HAVE AN IDEA.
FOOD DELIVERY.
THE CHIEF WANTS TO MAKE SURE THE CHOSEN ONE IS NICE AND FAT FOR TOMORROW'S CEREMONY.

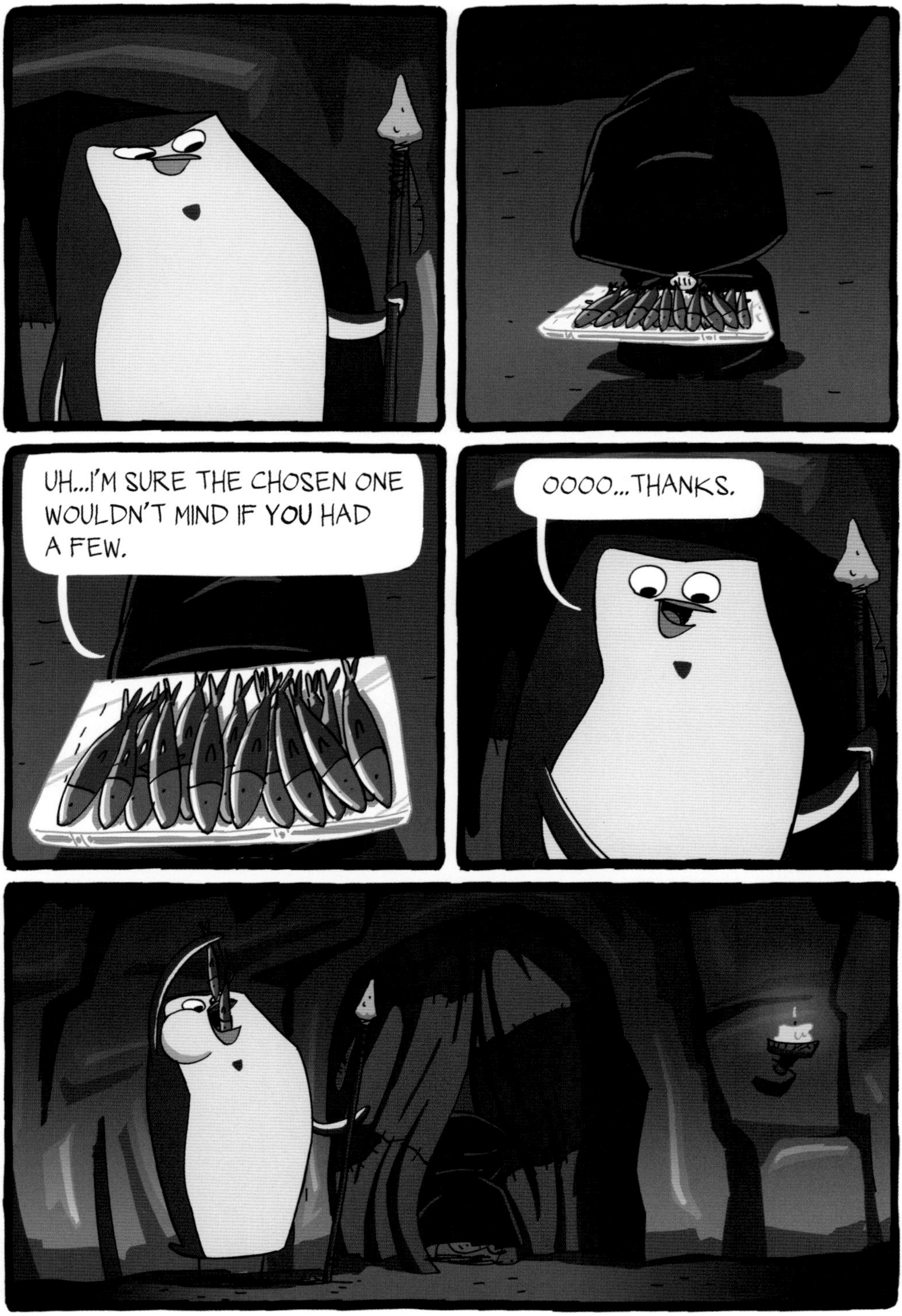
UH...I'M SURE THE CHOSEN ONE WOULDN'T MIND IF YOU HAD A FEW.
OOOO...THANKS.

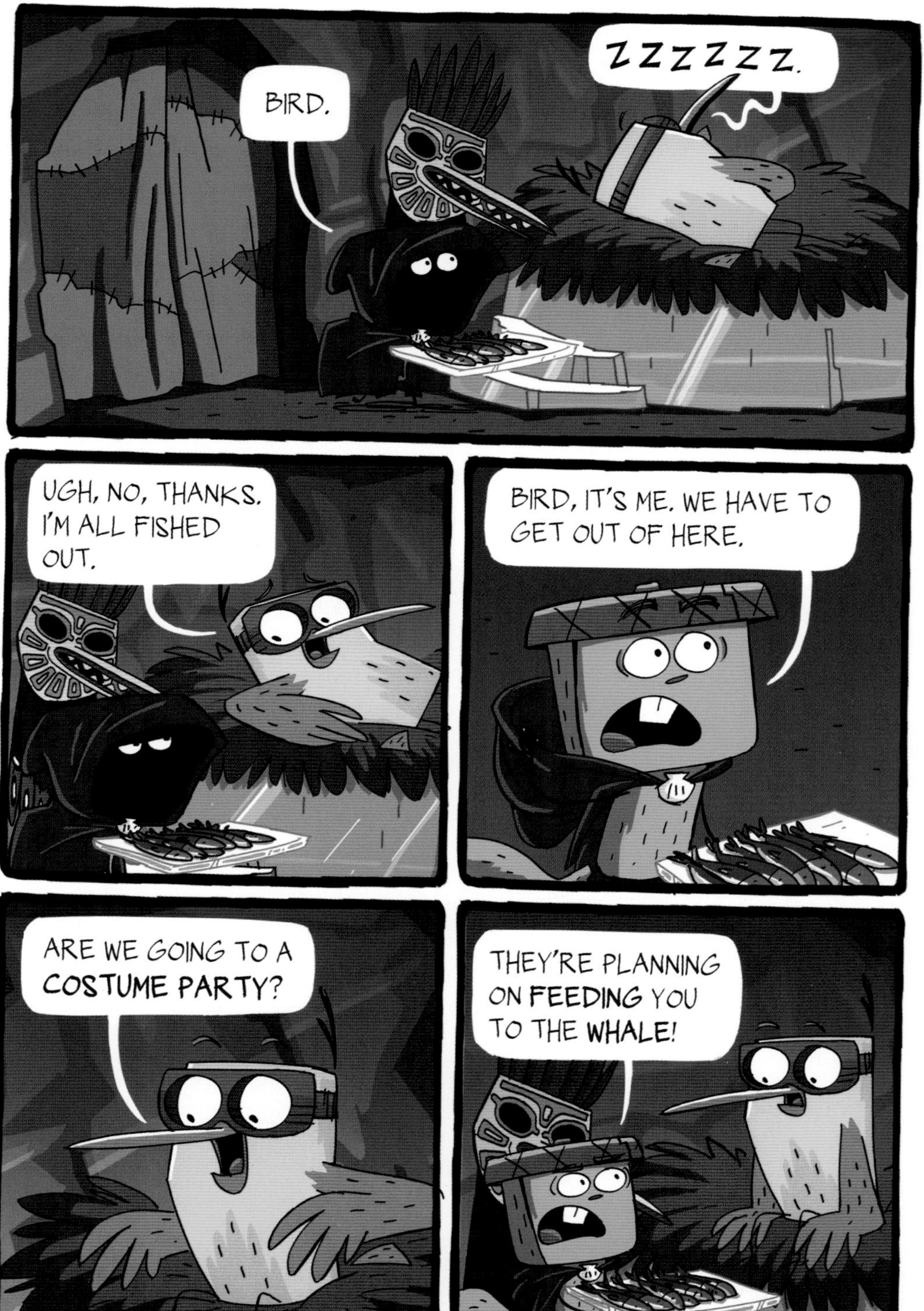
ZZZZZZ.
BIRD.
UGH, NO, THANKS. I'M ALL FISHED OUT.
BIRD, IT'S ME. WE HAVE TO GET OUT OF HERE.
ARE WE GOING TO A COSTUME PARTY?
THEY'RE PLANNING ON FEEDING YOU TO THE WHALE!

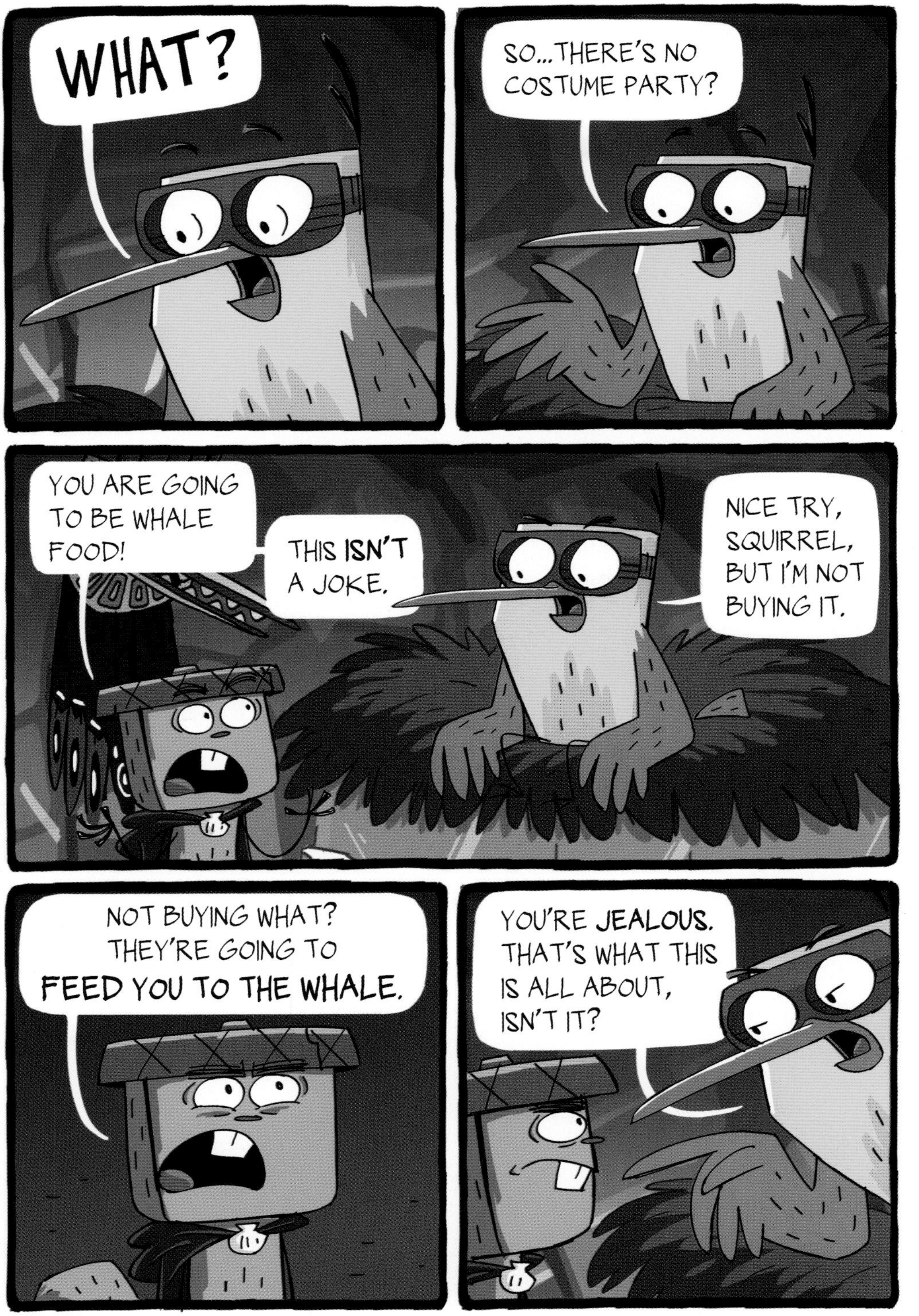
WHAT?
SO...THERE'S NO COSTUME PARTY?
YOU ARE GOING TO BE WHALE FOOD!
THIS **ISN'T** A JOKE.
NICE TRY, SQUIRREL, BUT I'M NOT BUYING IT.
NOT BUYING WHAT? THEY'RE GOING TO **FEED YOU TO THE WHALE.**
YOU'RE **JEALOUS.** THAT'S WHAT THIS IS ALL ABOUT, ISN'T IT?

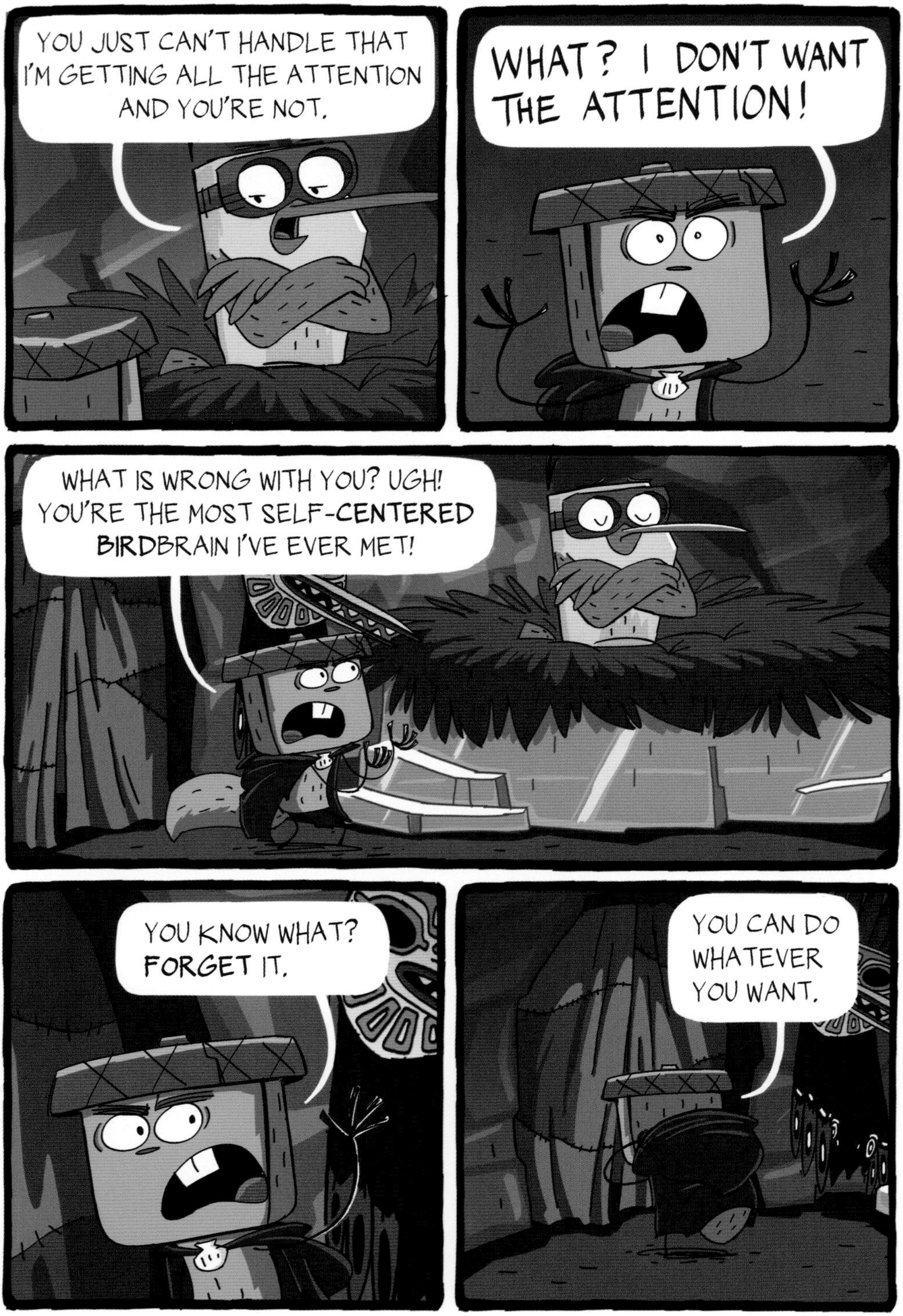
YOU JUST CAN'T HANDLE THAT I'M GETTING ALL THE ATTENTION AND YOU'RE NOT.
WHAT? I DON'T WANT THE ATTENTION!
WHAT IS WRONG WITH YOU? UGH! YOU'RE THE MOST SELF-**CENTERED** **BIRD**BRAIN I'VE EVER MET!
YOU KNOW WHAT? **FORGET** IT.
YOU CAN DO WHATEVER YOU WANT.

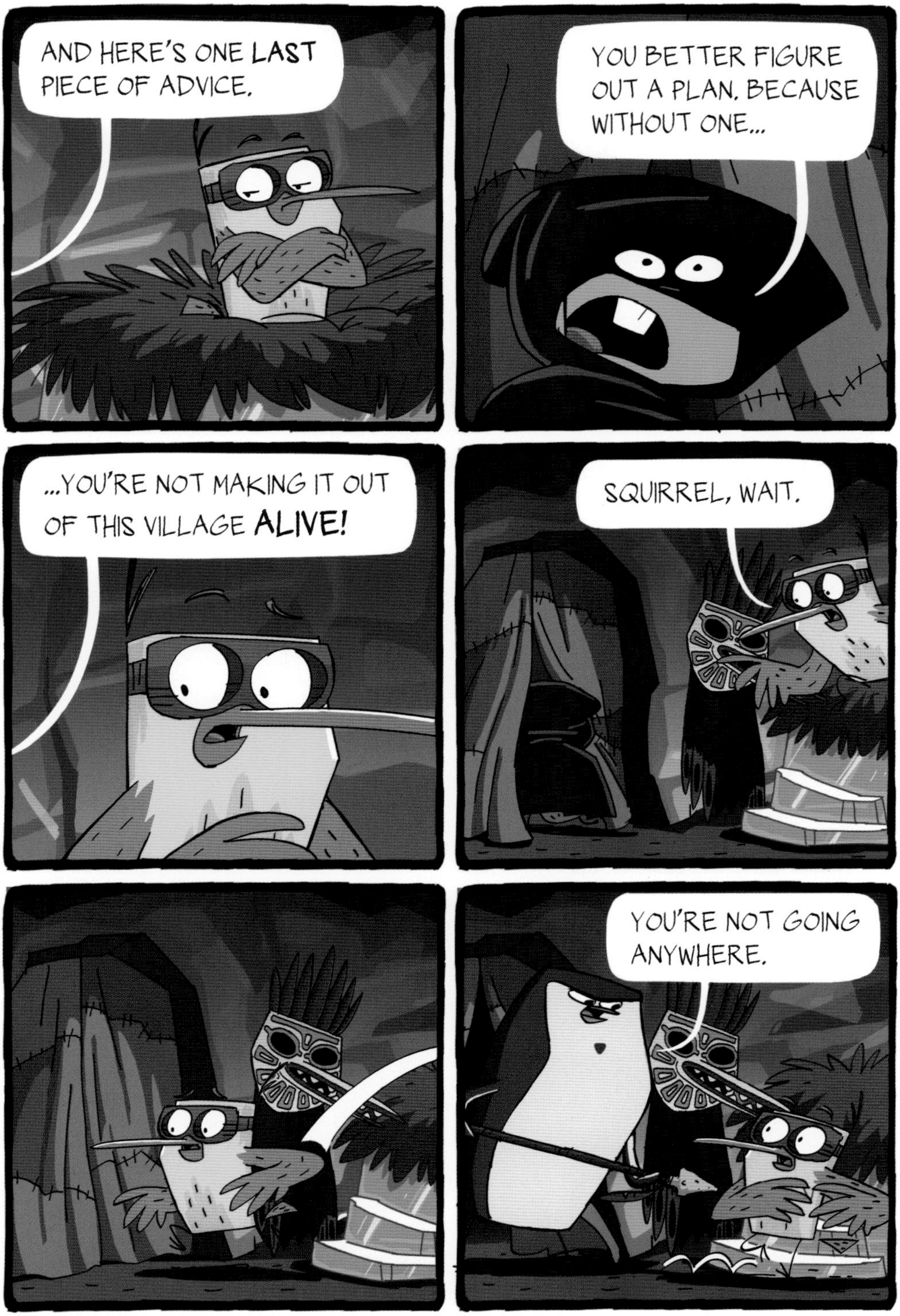
AND HERE'S ONE LAST PIECE OF ADVICE.
YOU BETTER FIGURE OUT A PLAN. BECAUSE WITHOUT ONE...
...YOU'RE NOT MAKING IT OUT OF THIS VILLAGE ALIVE!
SQUIRREL, WAIT.
YOU'RE NOT GOING ANYWHERE.

WHAT HAPPENED?

HE DIDN'T BELIEVE ME.

I'M SORRY, SQUIRREL. WE'LL FIGURE SOMETHING OUT.

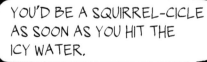

I WISH THERE WAS A WAY THAT I COULD LEAD THAT STUPID WHALE OUT OF THE BAY.

YOU'D BE A SQUIRREL-CICLE AS SOON AS YOU HIT THE ICY WATER.

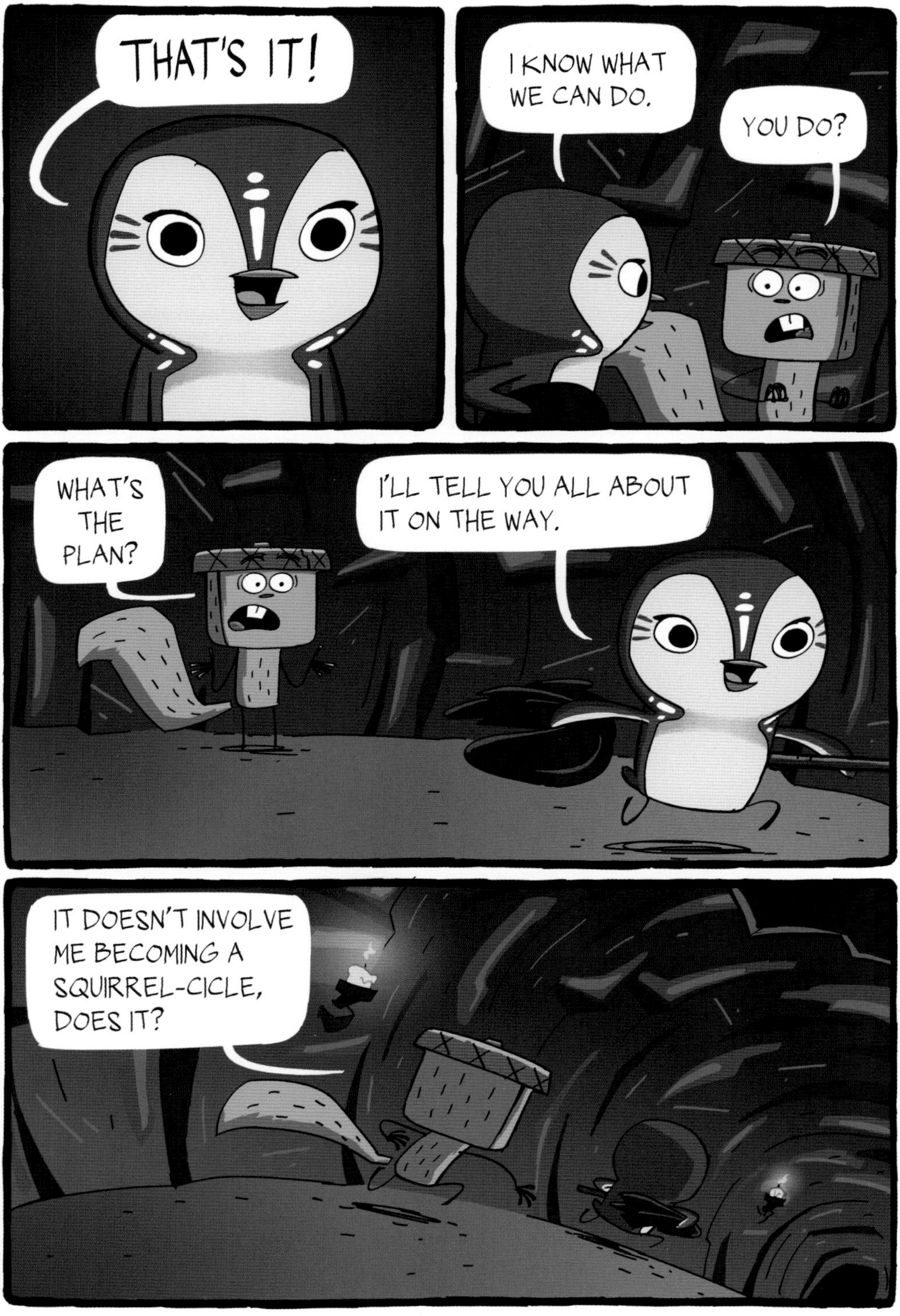
THAT'S IT!
I KNOW WHAT WE CAN DO.
YOU DO?
WHAT'S THE PLAN?
I'LL TELL YOU ALL ABOUT IT ON THE WAY.
IT DOESN'T INVOLVE ME BECOMING A SQUIRREL-CICLE, DOES IT?

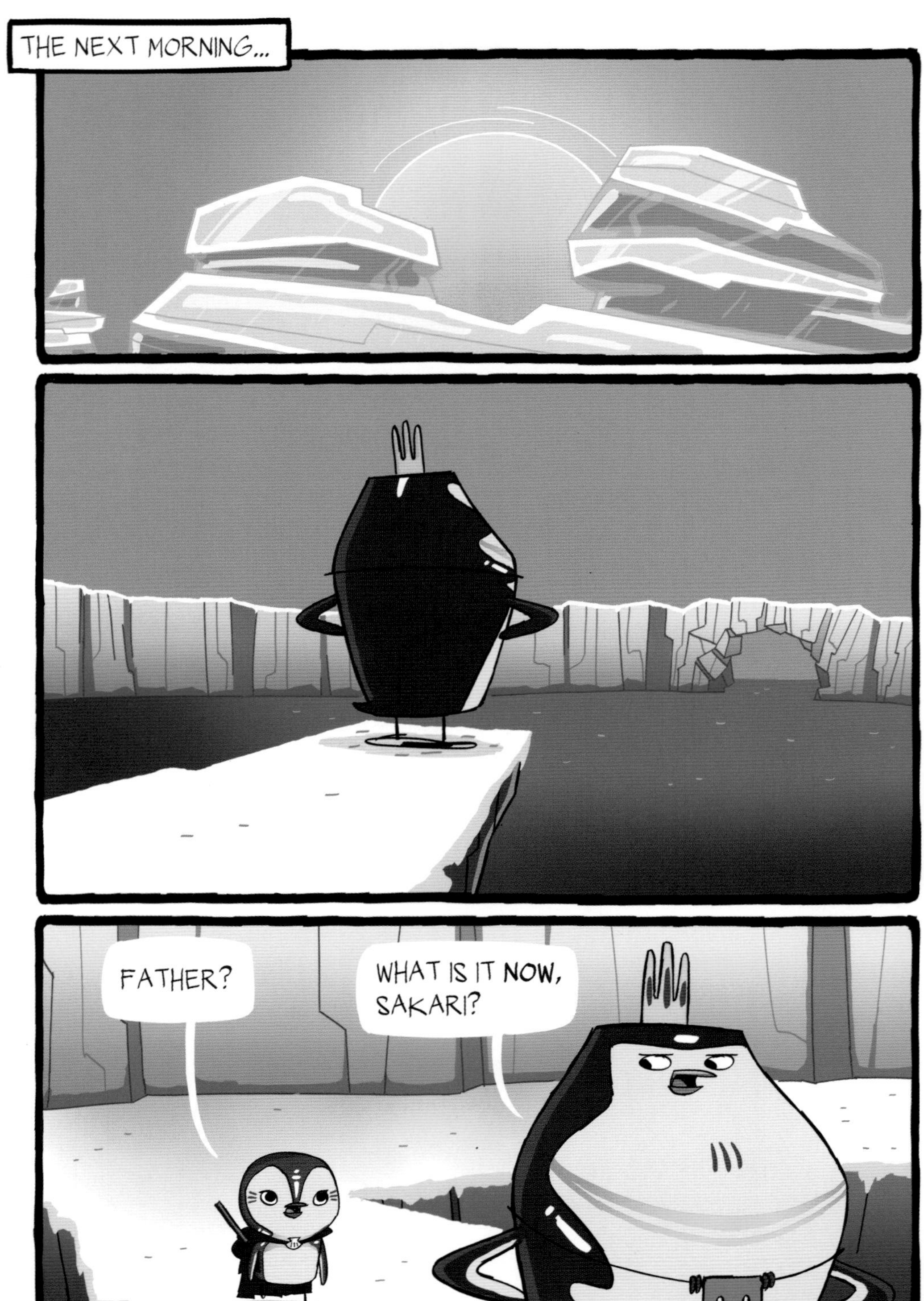
THE NEXT MORNING...
FATHER?
WHAT IS IT NOW, SAKARI?

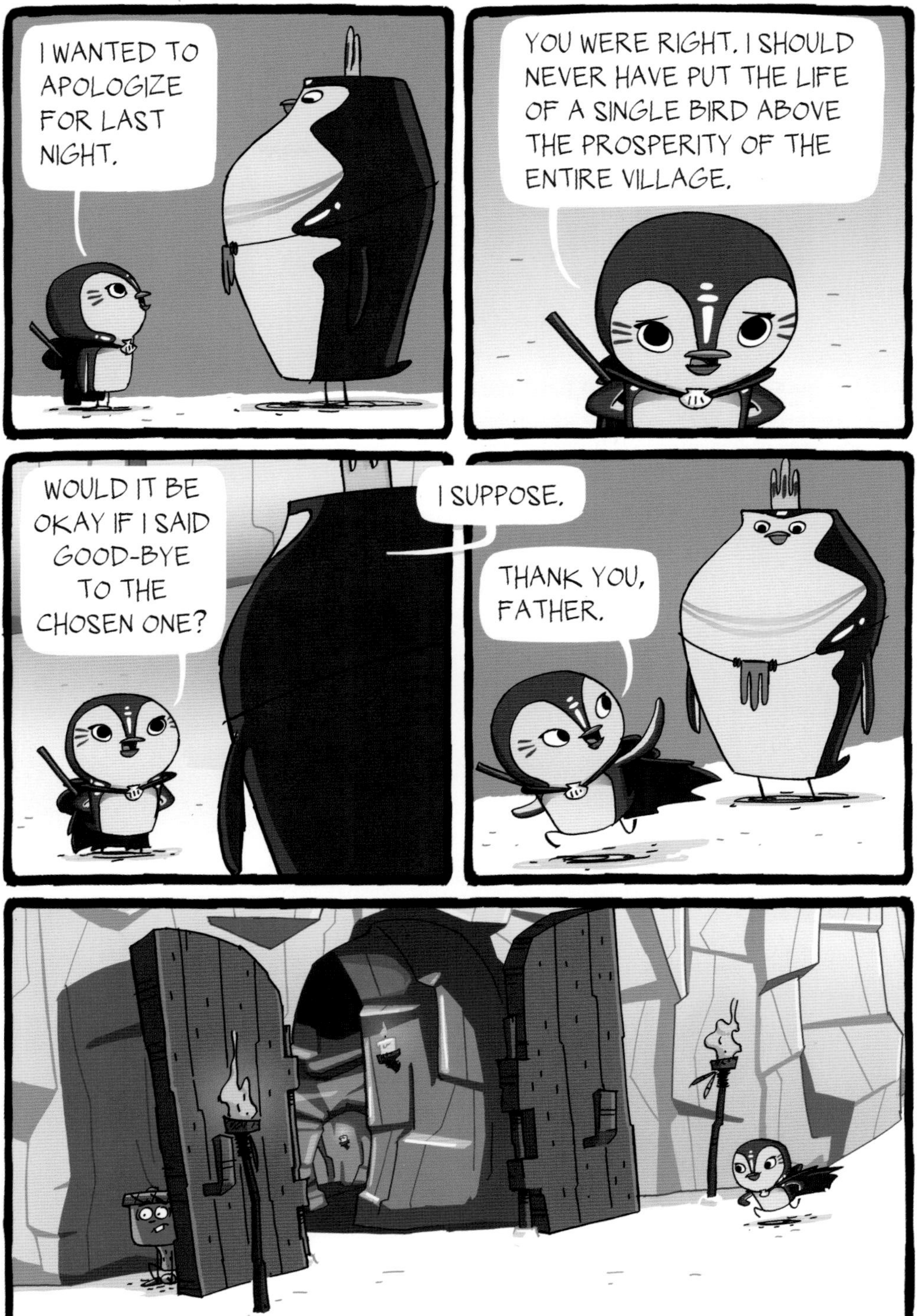
I WANTED TO APOLOGIZE FOR LAST NIGHT.
YOU WERE RIGHT. I SHOULD NEVER HAVE PUT THE LIFE OF A SINGLE BIRD ABOVE THE PROSPERITY OF THE ENTIRE VILLAGE.
WOULD IT BE OKAY IF I SAID GOOD-BYE TO THE CHOSEN ONE?
I SUPPOSE.
THANK YOU, FATHER.

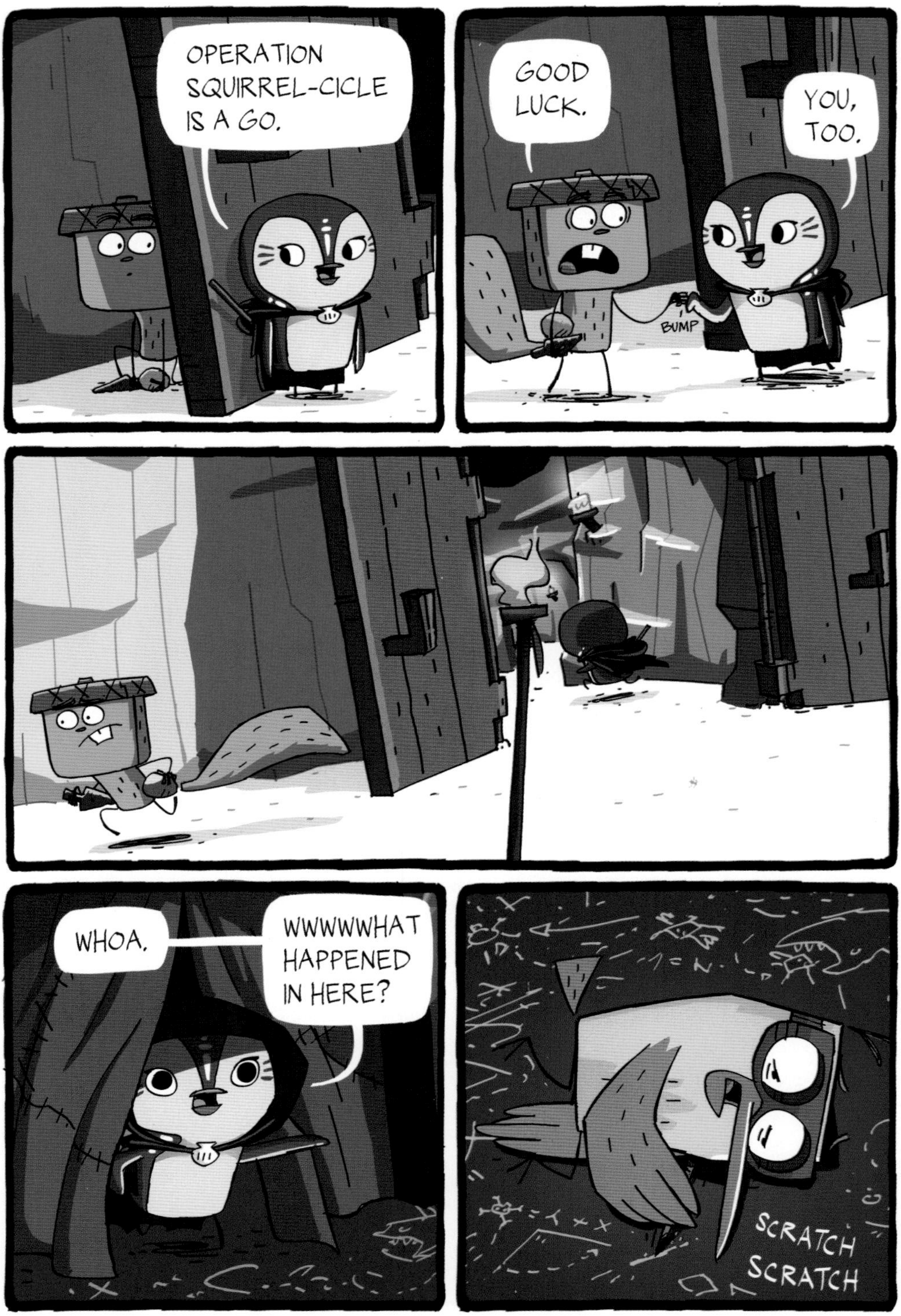

OPERATION SQUIRREL-CICLE IS A GO.
GOOD LUCK.
YOU, TOO.
BUMP
WHOA.
WWWWWHAT HAPPENED IN HERE?
SCRATCH SCRATCH

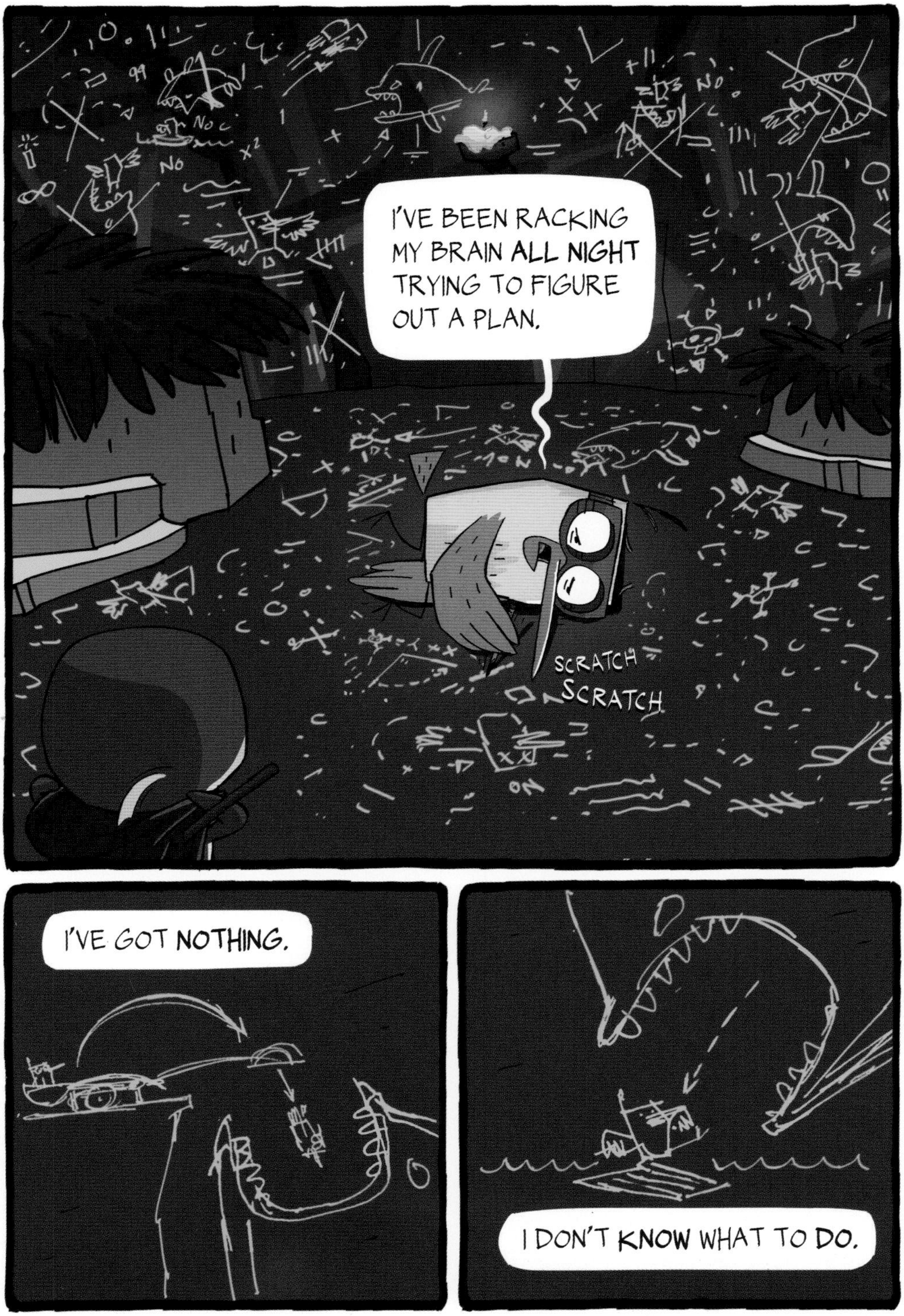
I'VE BEEN RACKING MY BRAIN ALL NIGHT TRYING TO FIGURE OUT A PLAN.
SCRATCH SCRATCH
I'VE GOT NOTHING.
I DON'T KNOW WHAT TO DO.

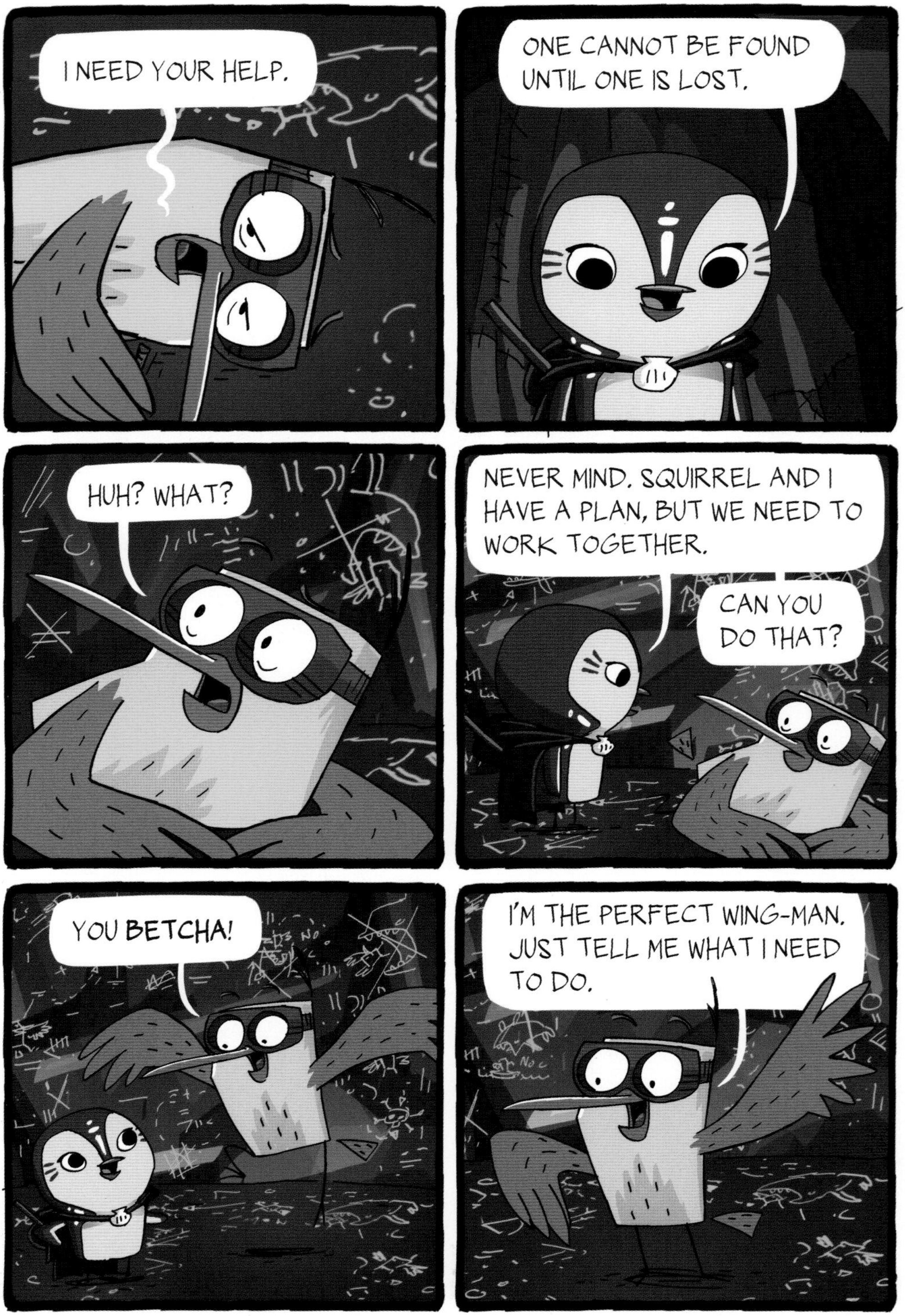
I NEED YOUR HELP.
ONE CANNOT BE FOUND UNTIL ONE IS LOST.
HUH? WHAT?
NEVER MIND. SQUIRREL AND I HAVE A PLAN, BUT WE NEED TO WORK TOGETHER.
CAN YOU DO THAT?
YOU **BETCHA!**
I'M THE PERFECT WING-MAN. JUST TELL ME WHAT I NEED TO DO.

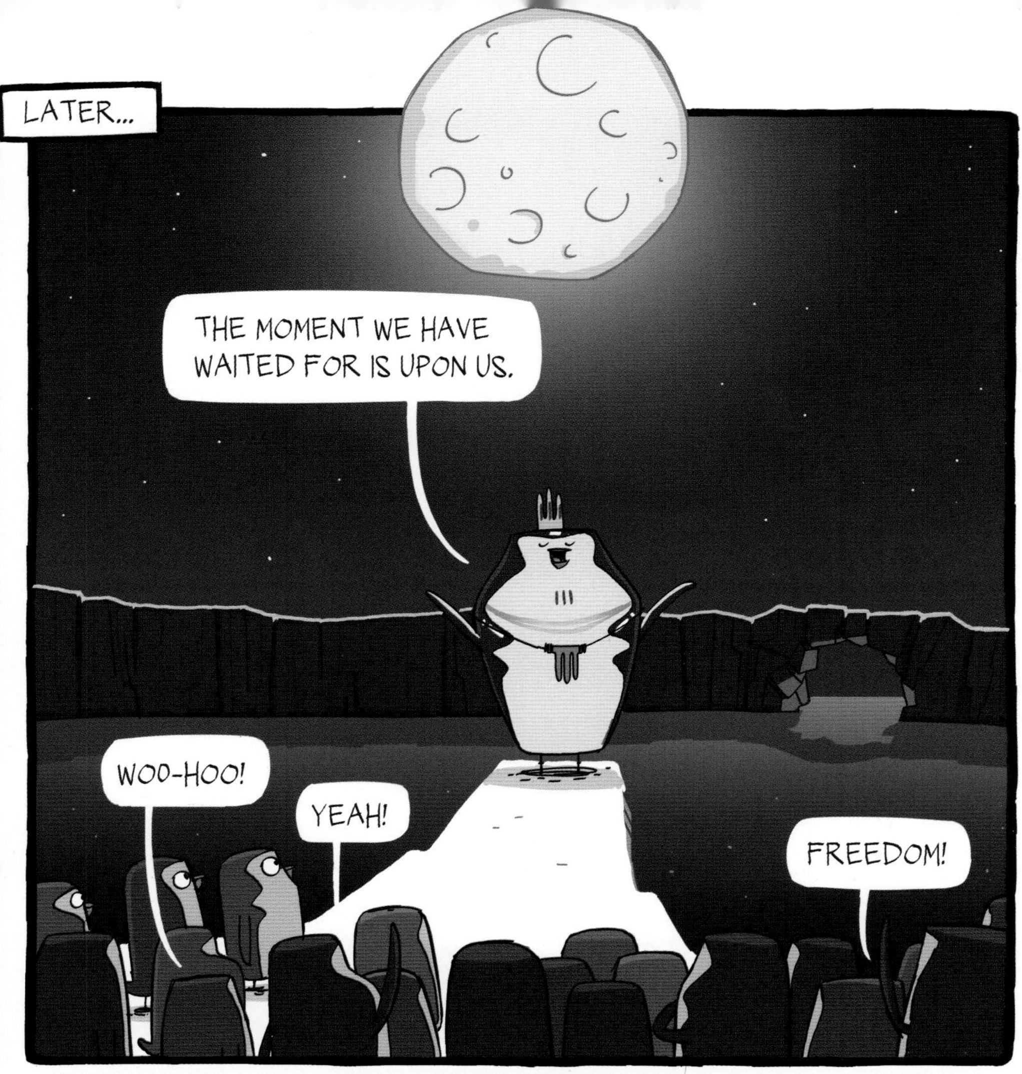
LATER...
THE MOMENT WE HAVE WAITED FOR IS UPON US.
WOO-HOO!
YEAH!
FREEDOM!

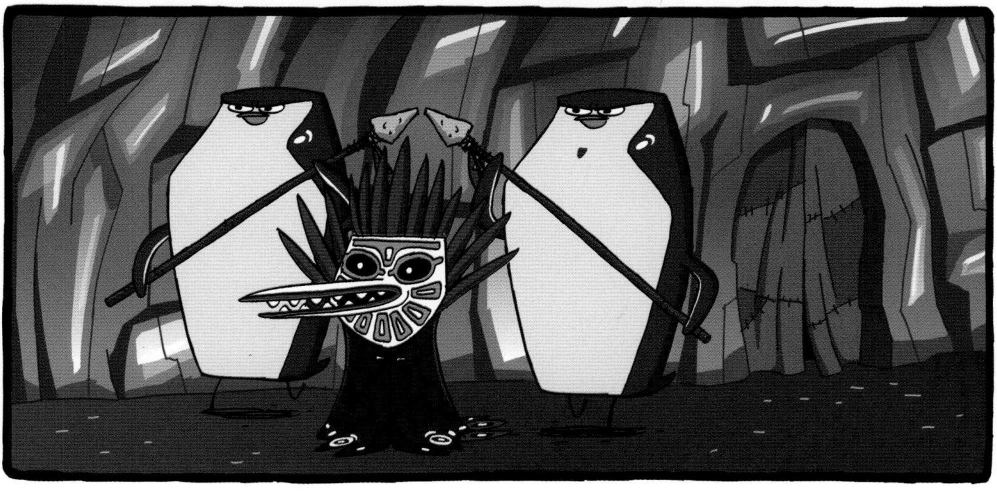

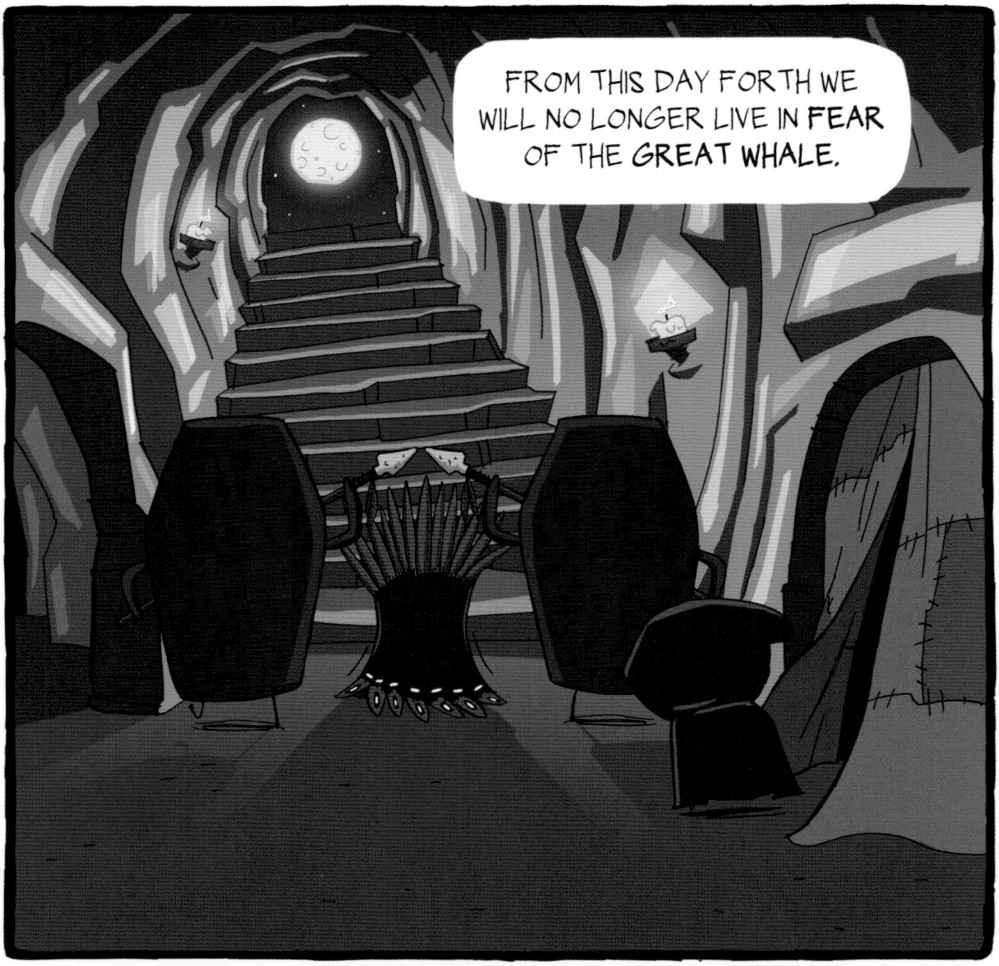
FROM THIS DAY FORTH WE WILL NO LONGER LIVE IN FEAR OF THE GREAT WHALE.

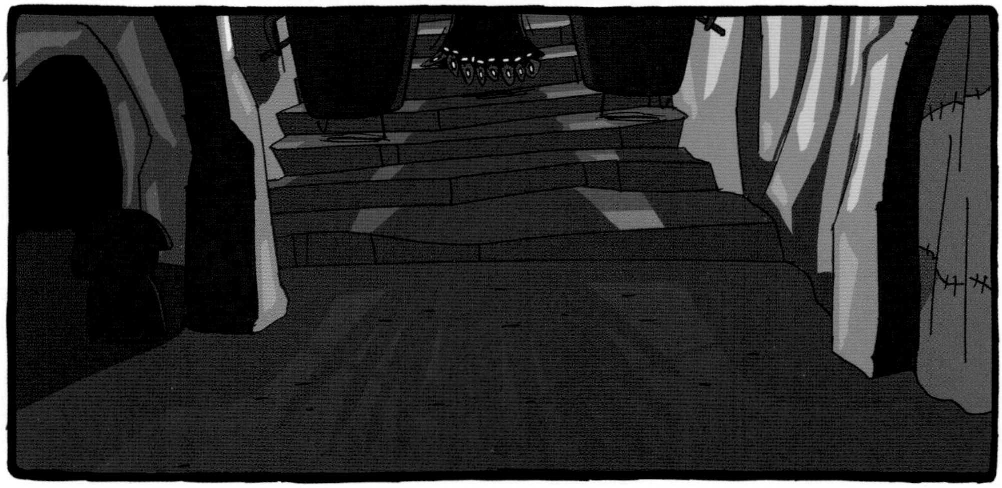

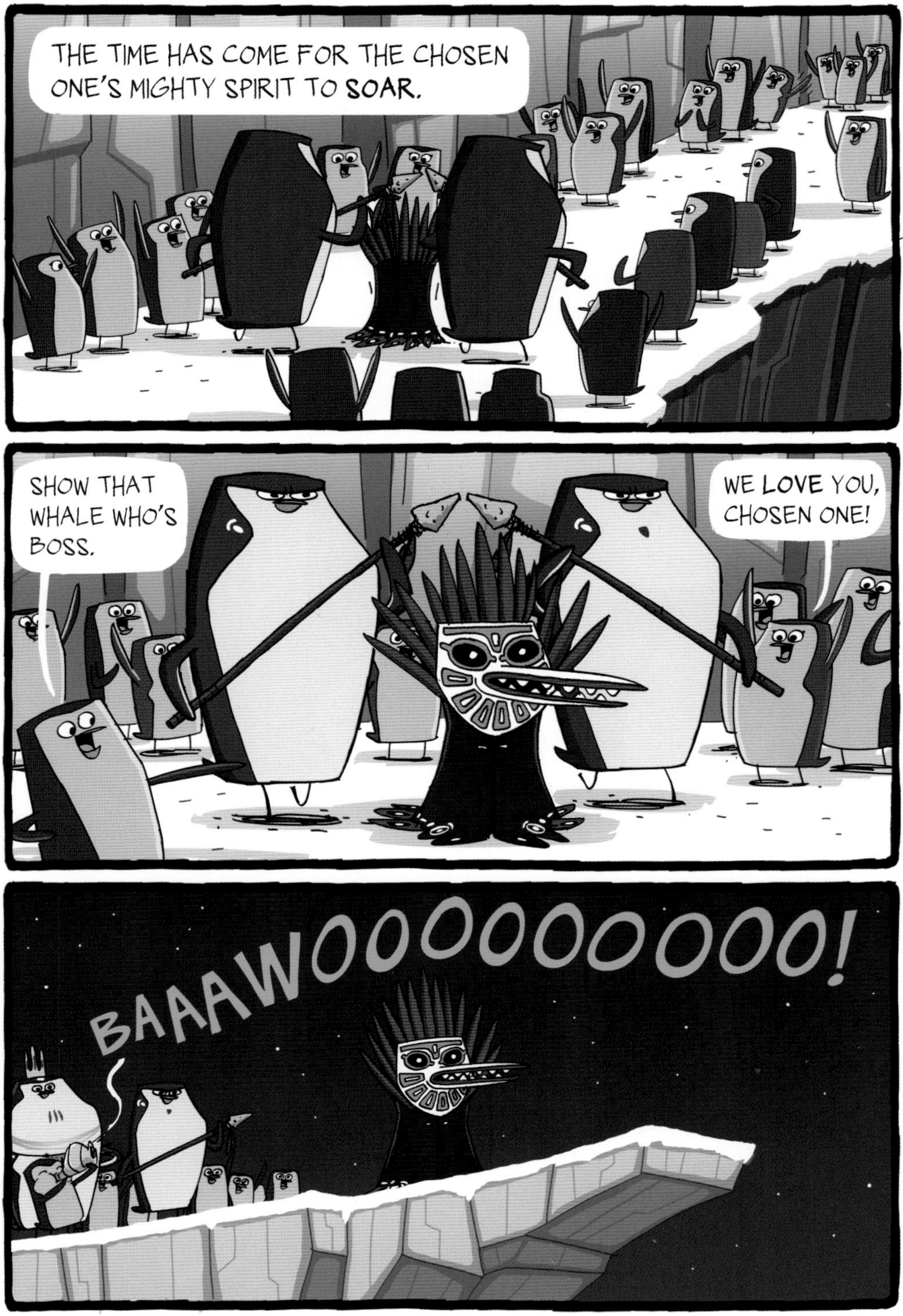
THE TIME HAS COME FOR THE CHOSEN ONE'S MIGHTY SPIRIT TO **SOAR.**
SHOW THAT WHALE WHO'S BOSS.
WE **LOVE** YOU, CHOSEN ONE!
BAAAWOOOOOOOOOO!

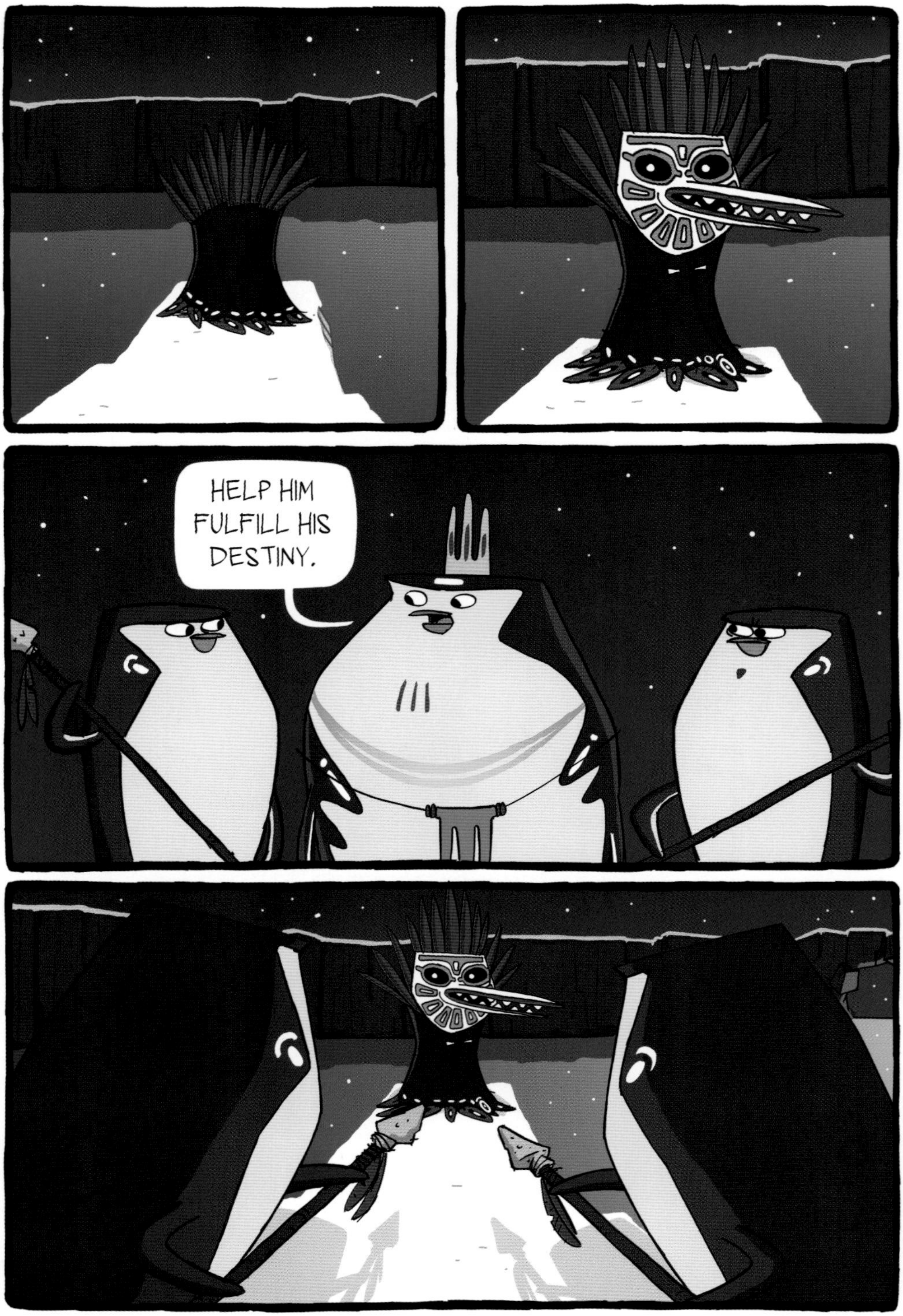
HELP HIM FULFILL HIS DESTINY.

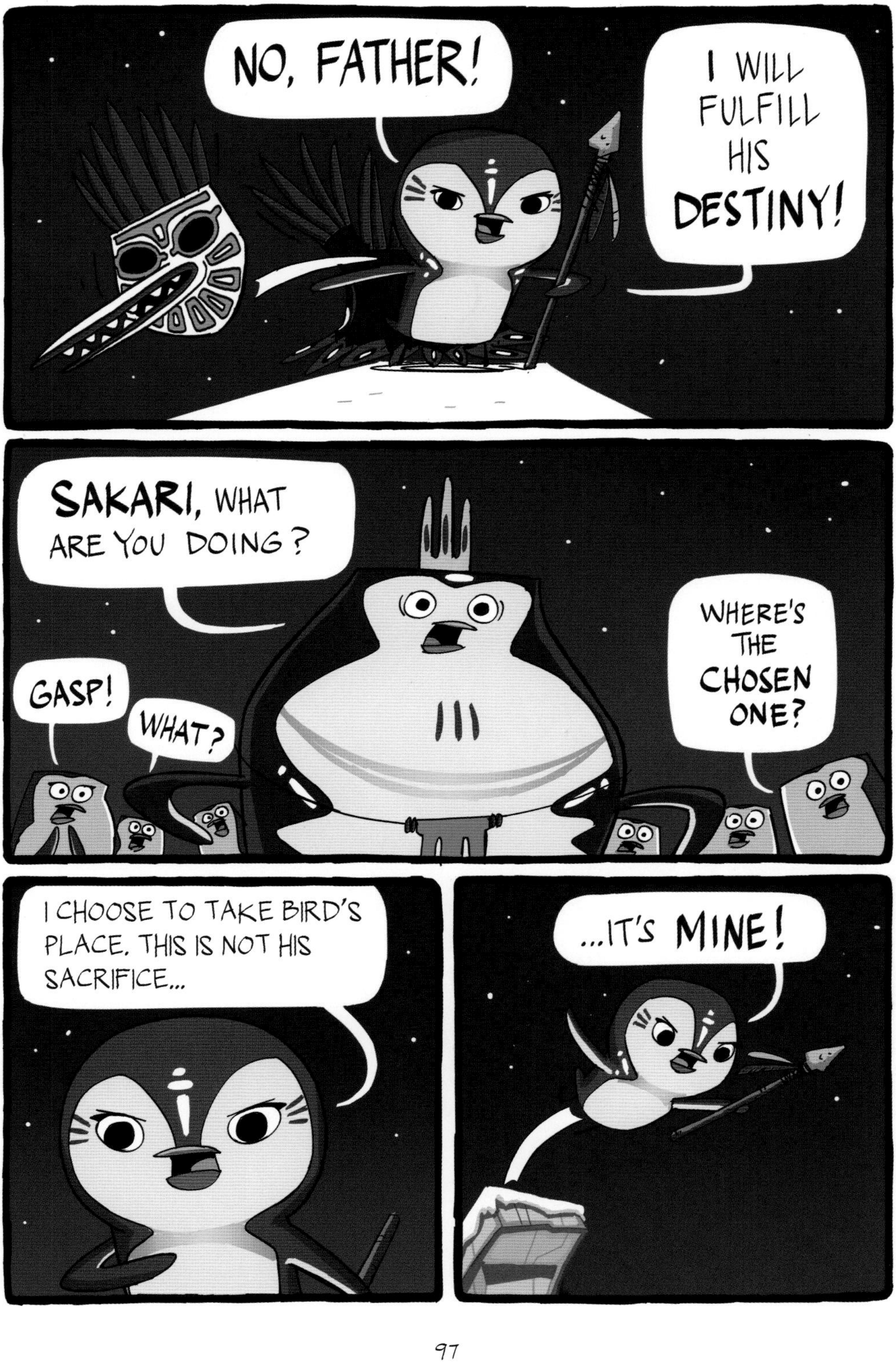
NO, FATHER!
I WILL FULFILL HIS DESTINY!
SAKARI, WHAT ARE YOU DOING?
GASP!
WHAT?
WHERE'S THE CHOSEN ONE?
I CHOOSE TO TAKE BIRD'S PLACE. THIS IS NOT HIS SACRIFICE...
...IT'S MINE!

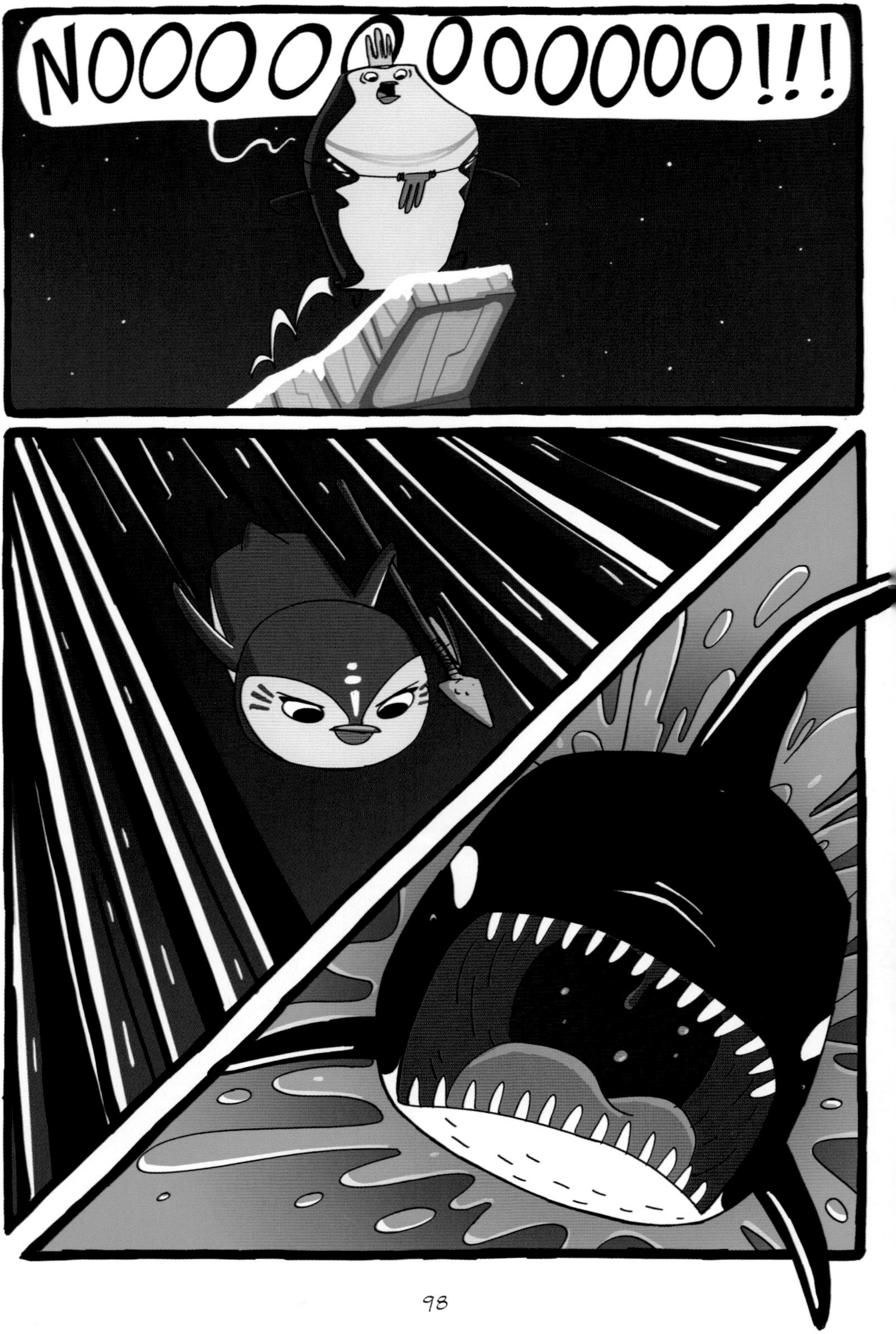
NOOOOOOOOOOOO!!!

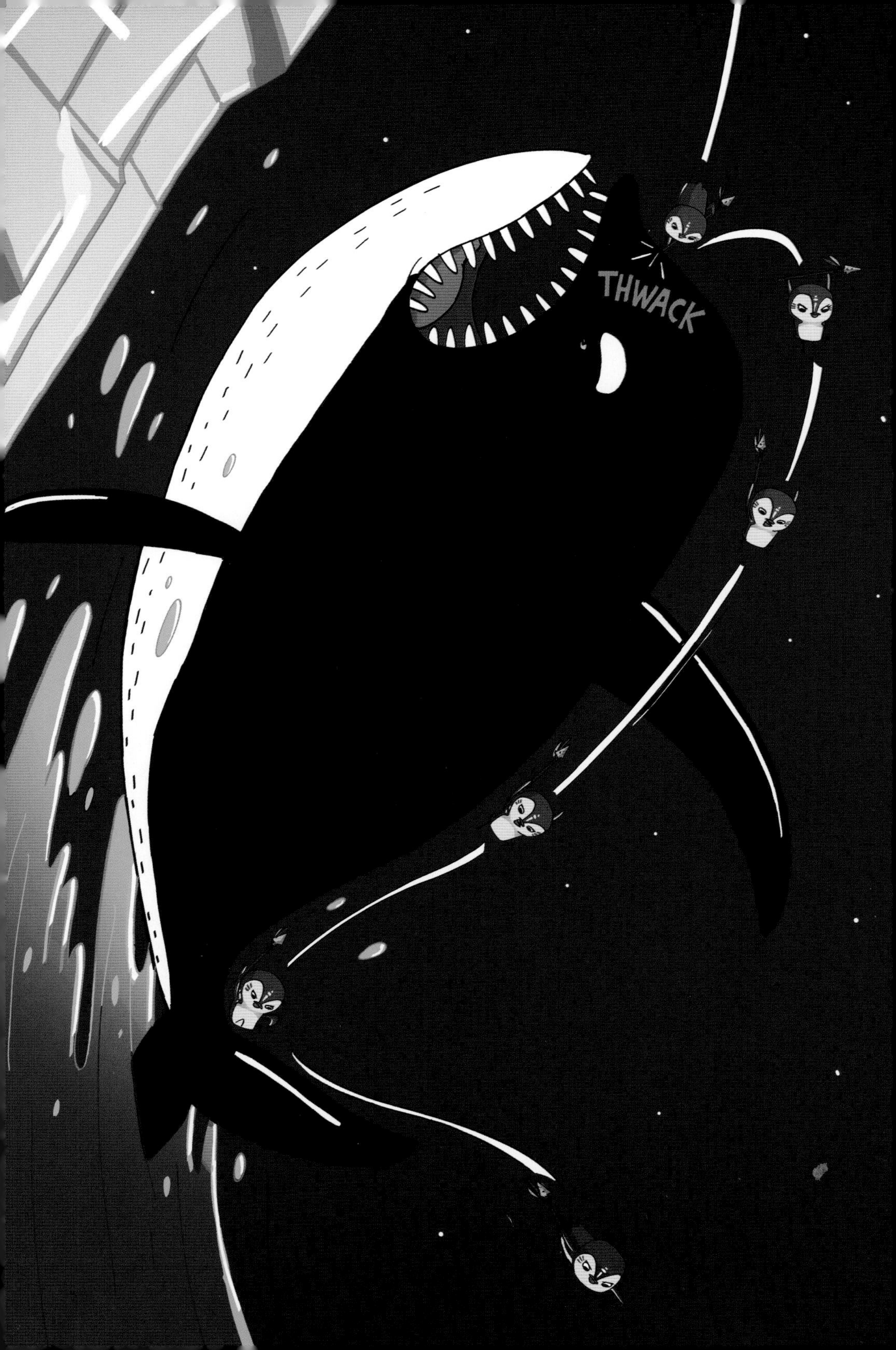
THWACK

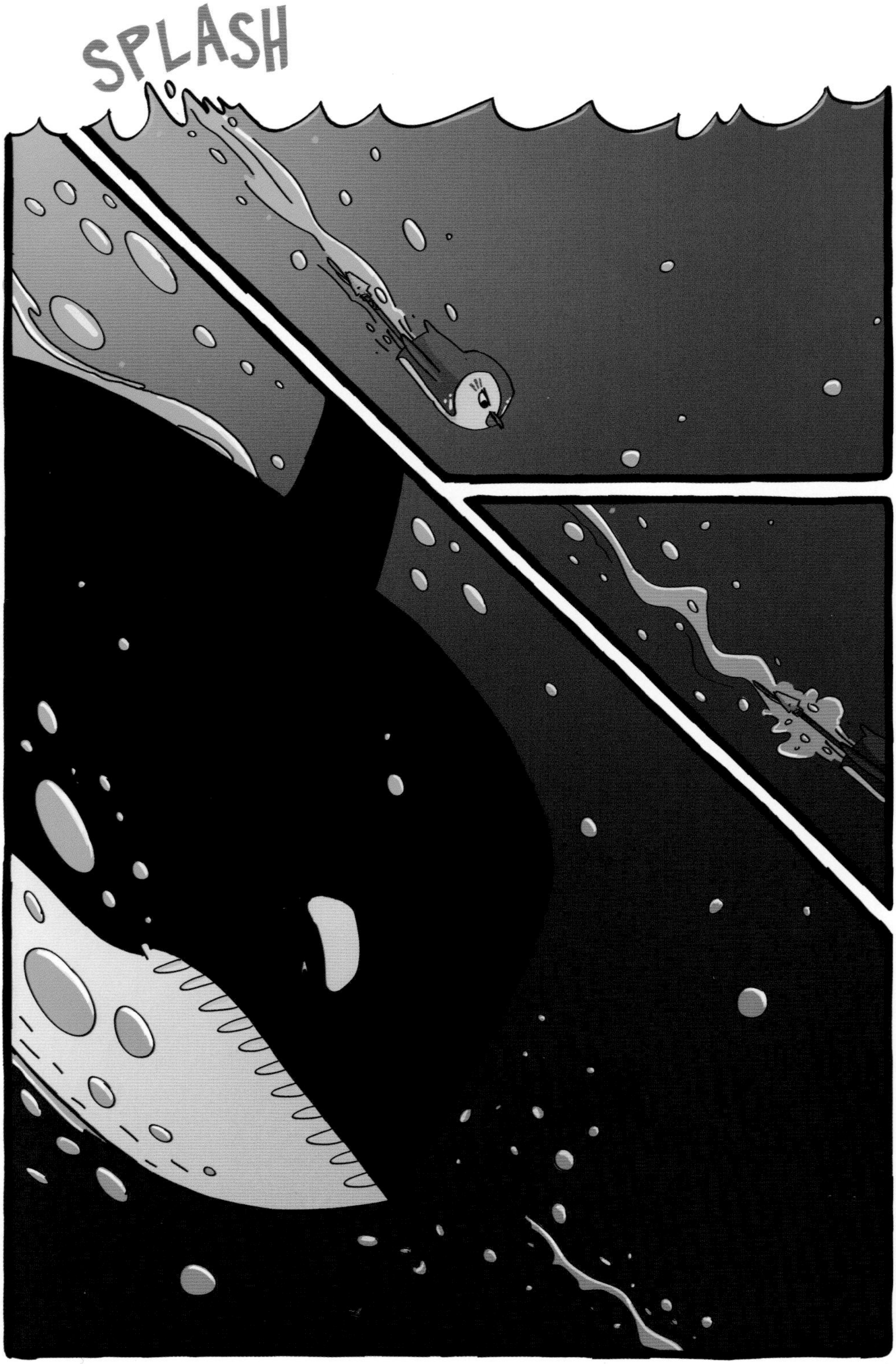
SPLASH

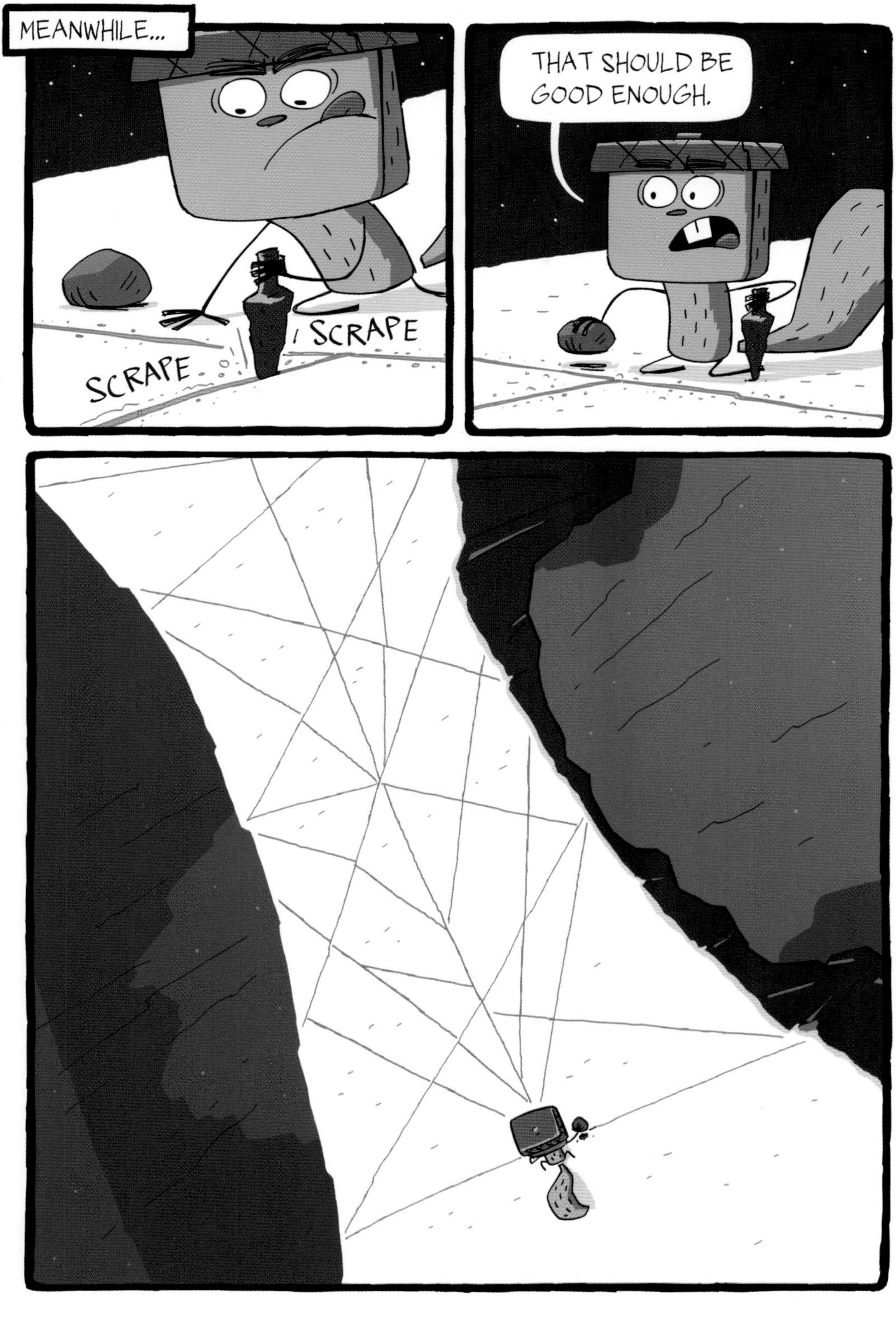
MEANWHILE...
SCRAPE
SCRAPE
THAT SHOULD BE GOOD ENOUGH.

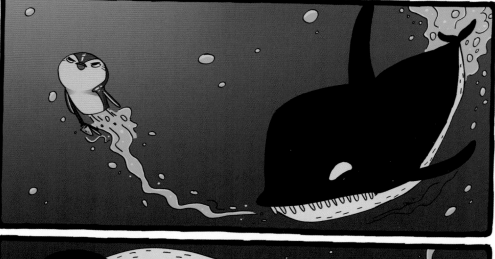

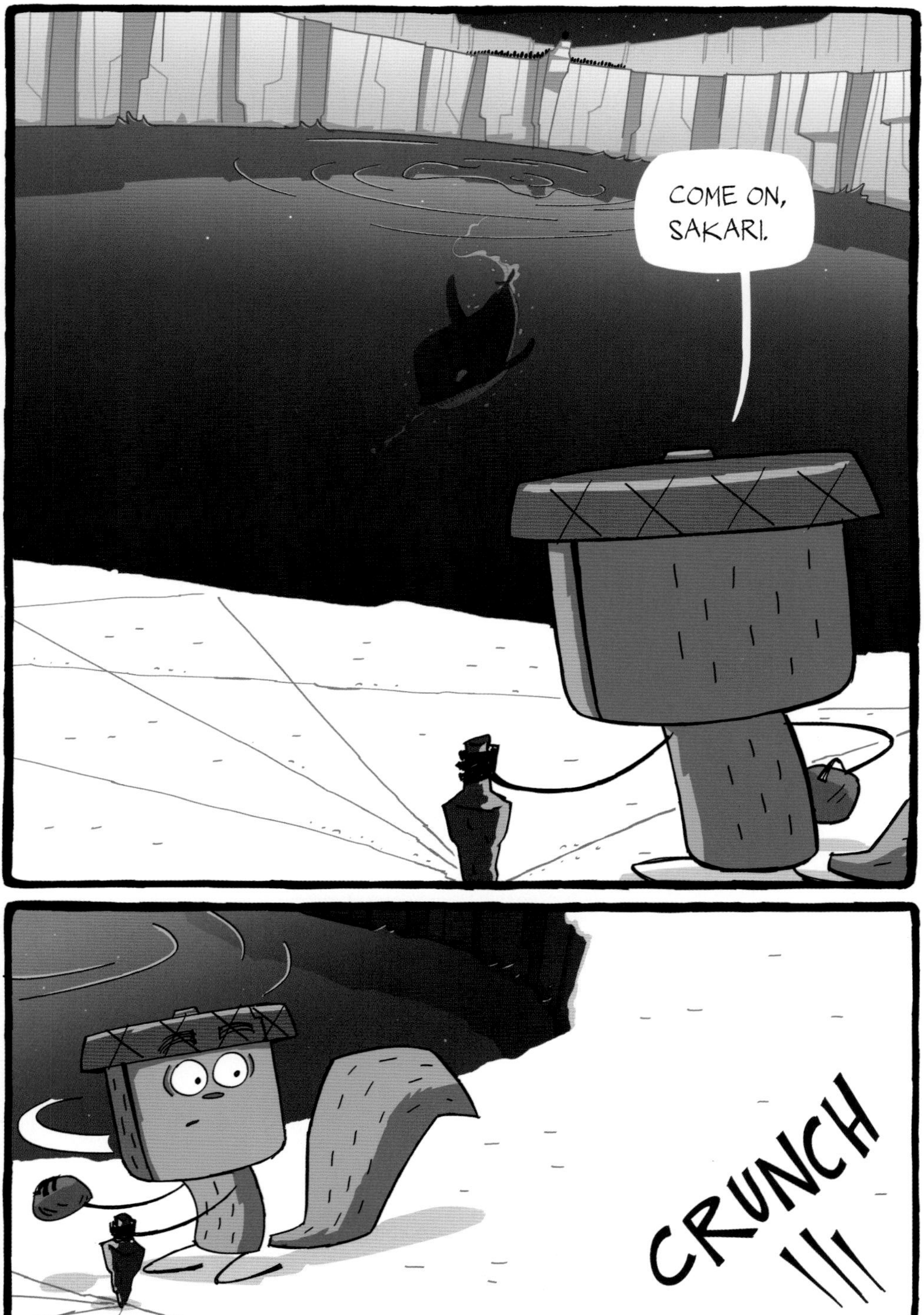
COME ON,
SAKARI.
CRUNCH

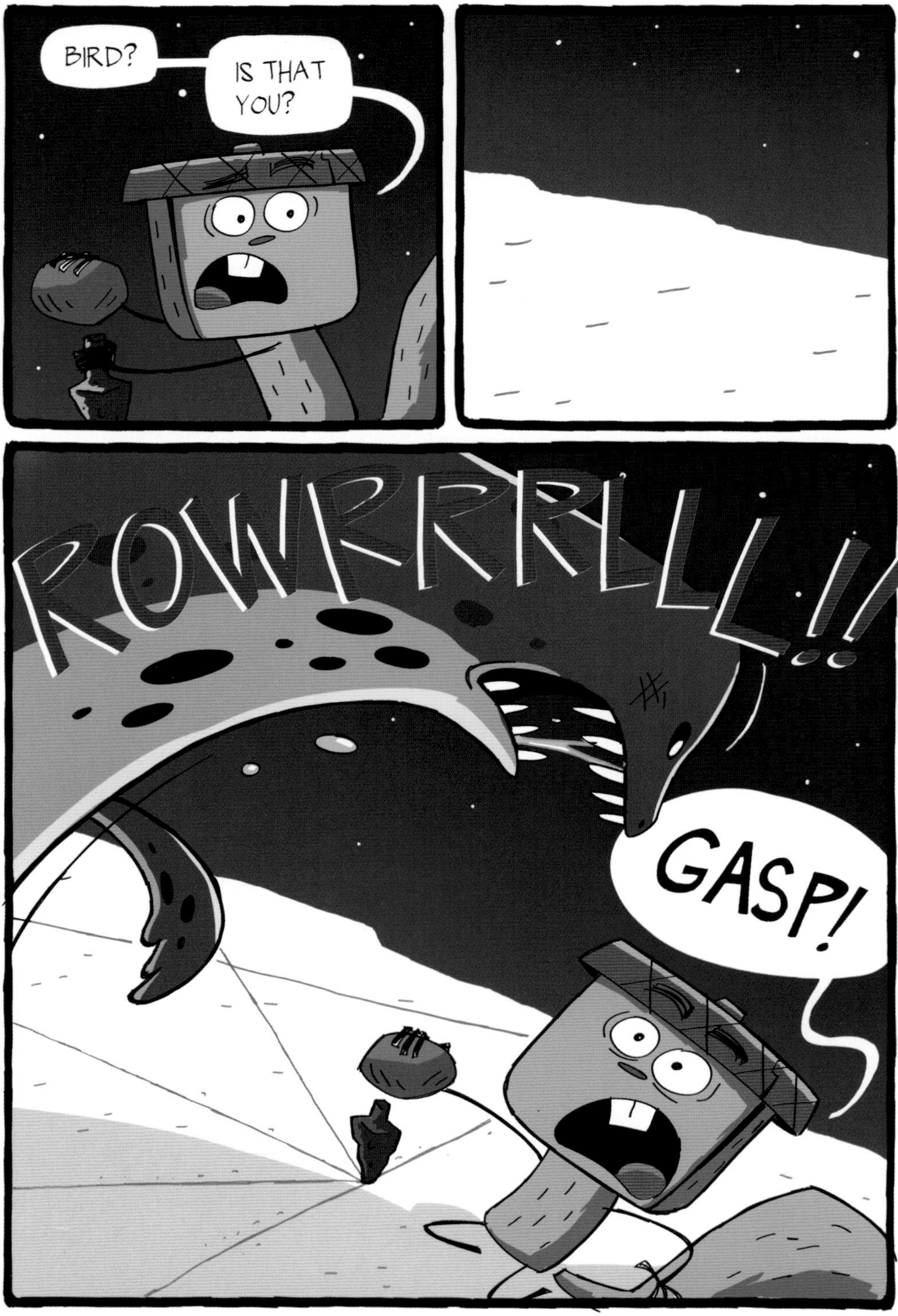
BIRD?
IS THAT YOU?
ROWRRRLLL!!
GASP!

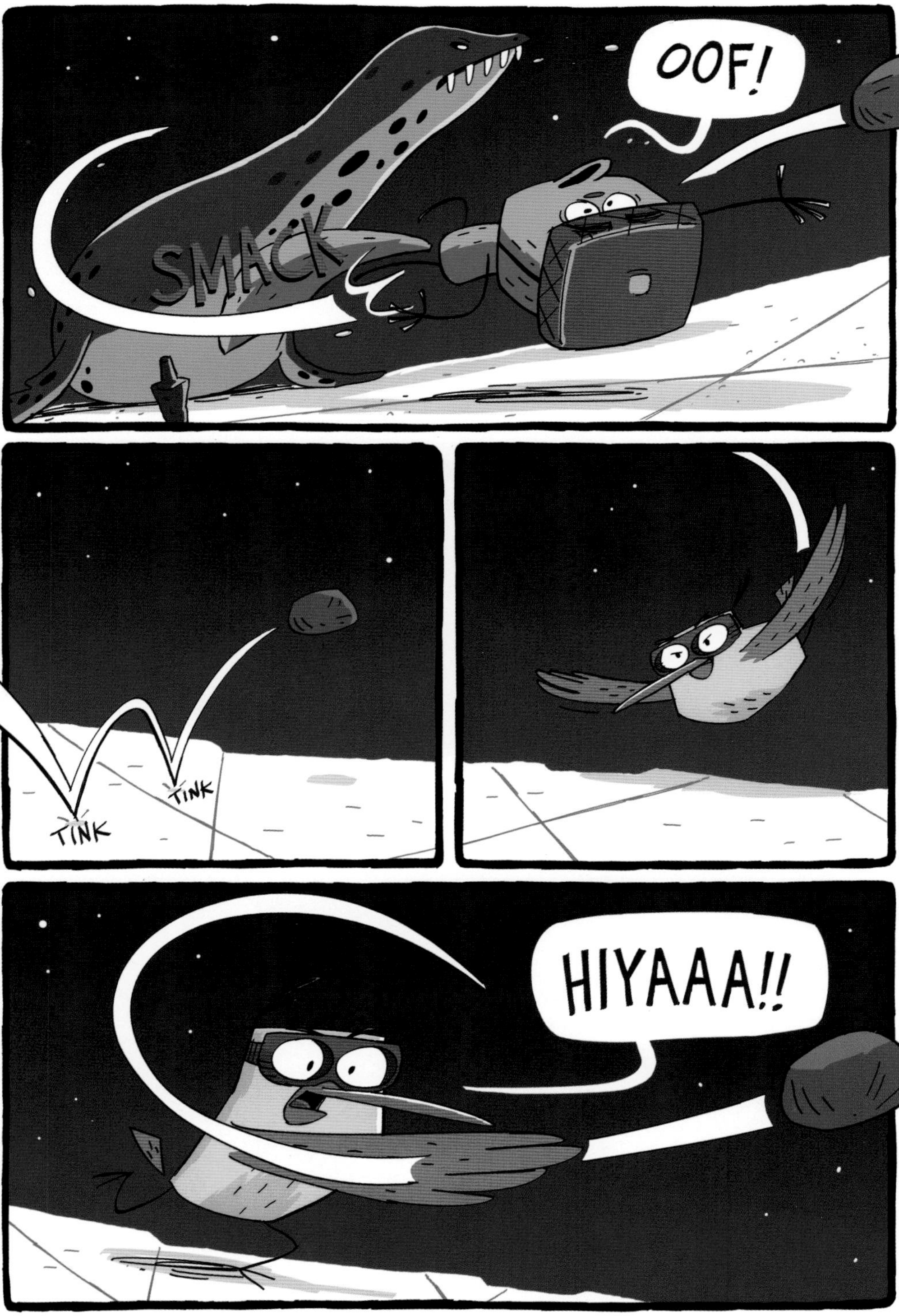
SMACK
OOF!
TINK
TINK
HIYAAA!!

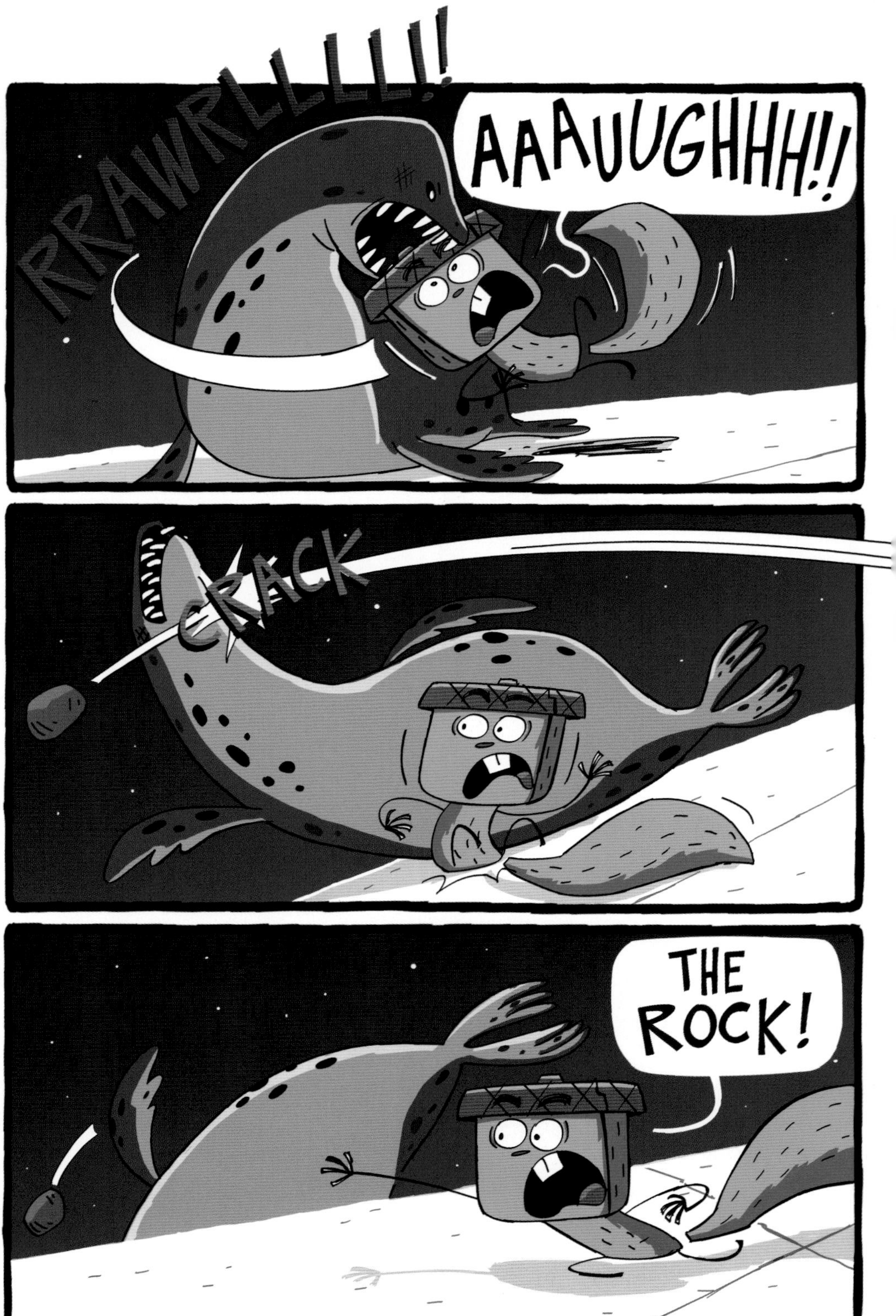
RRAWRLLLLL!!
AAAUUGHHH!!
CRACK
THE ROCK!

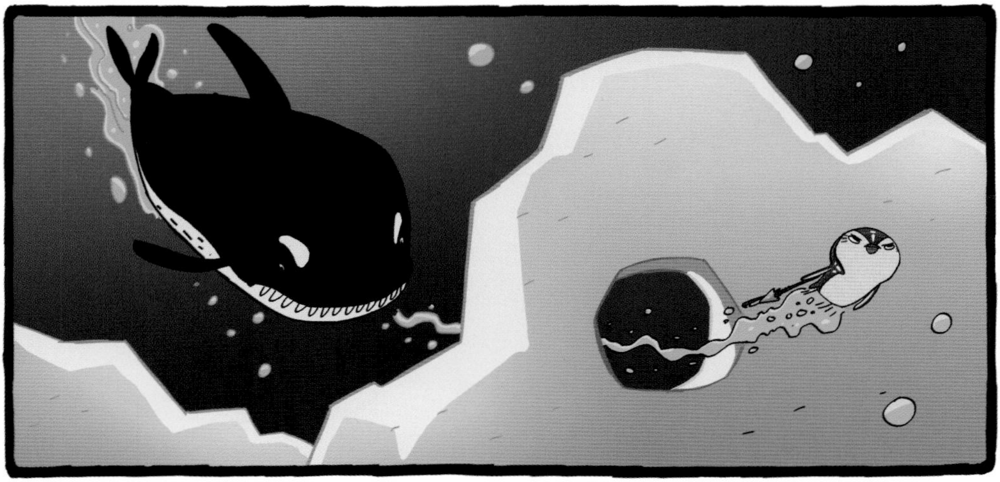

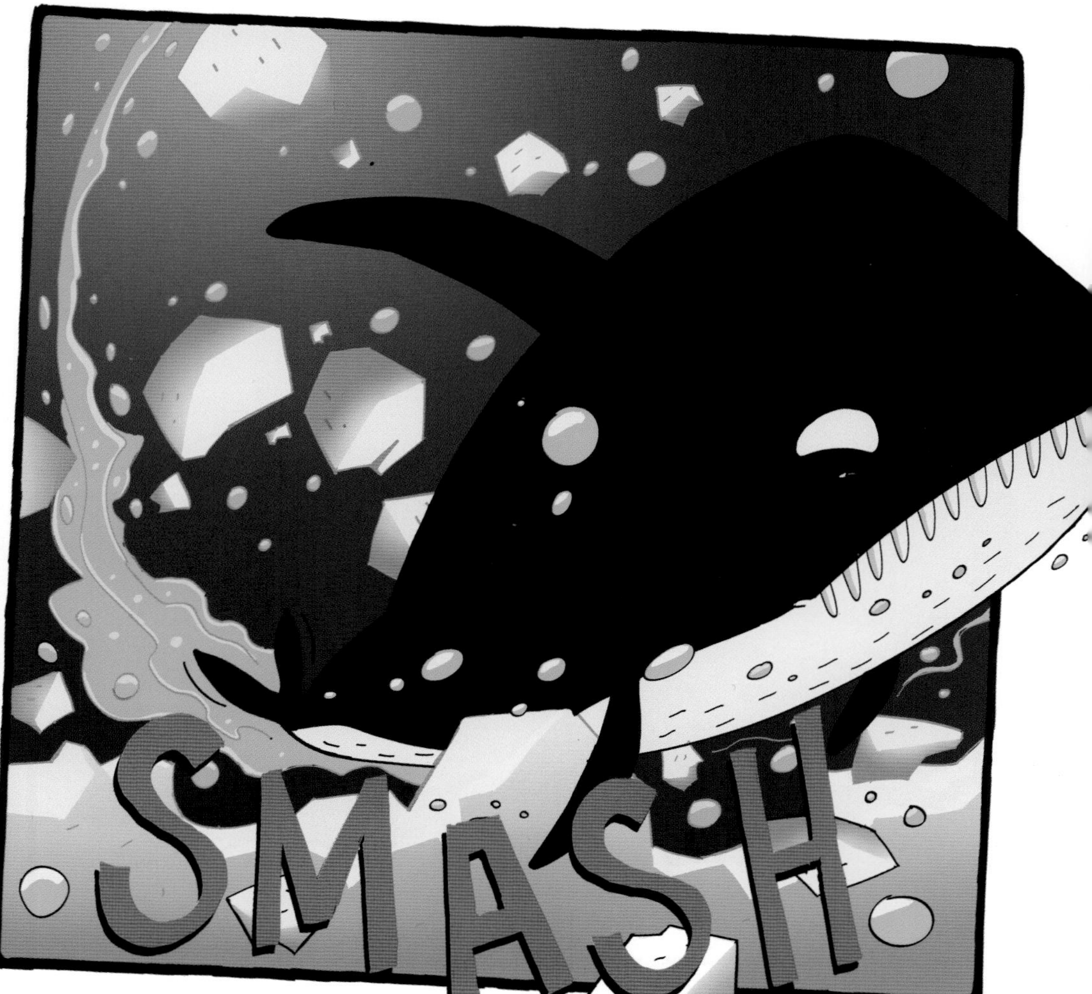
SMASH

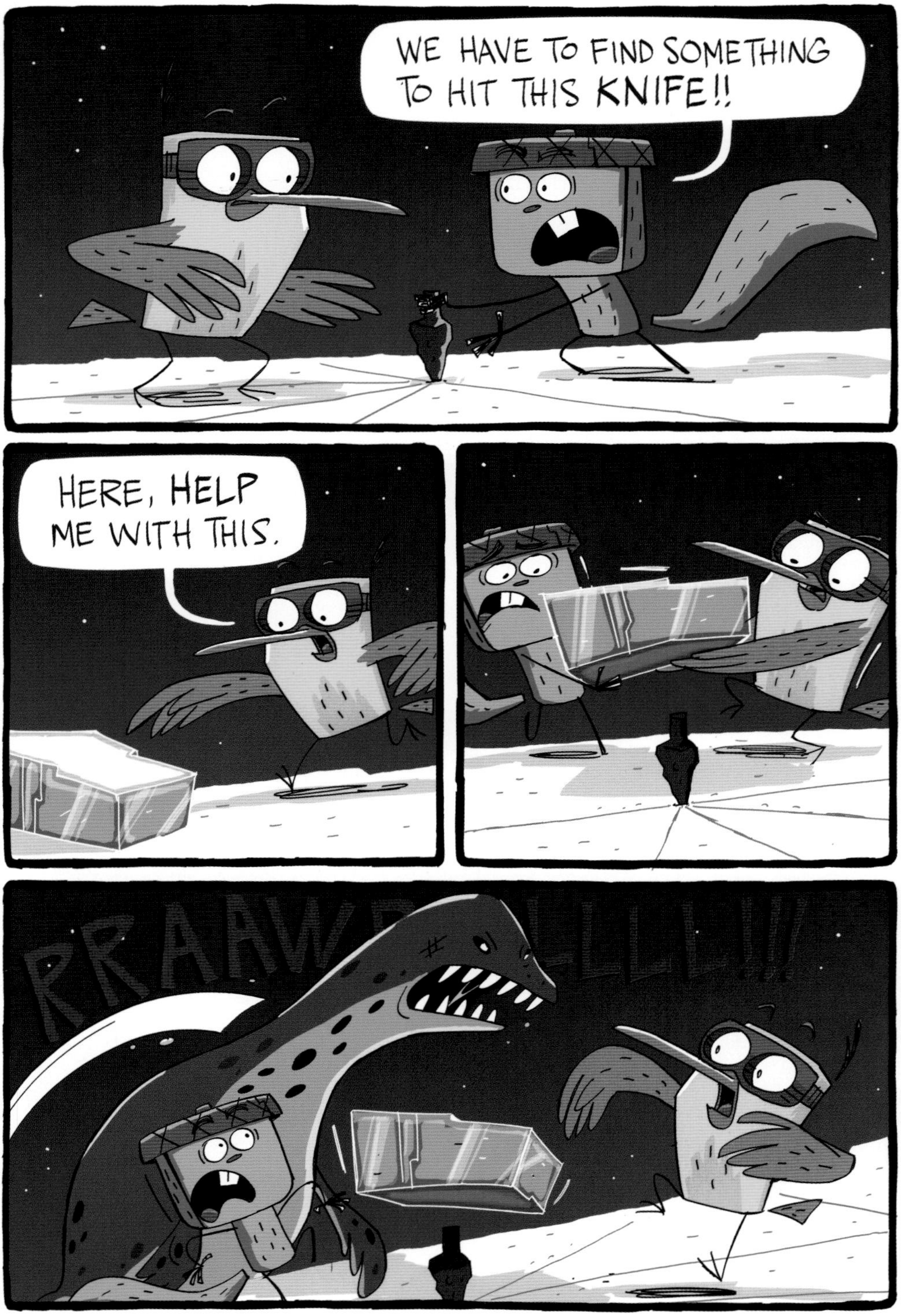
WE HAVE TO FIND SOMETHING TO HIT THIS KNIFE!!
HERE, HELP ME WITH THIS.

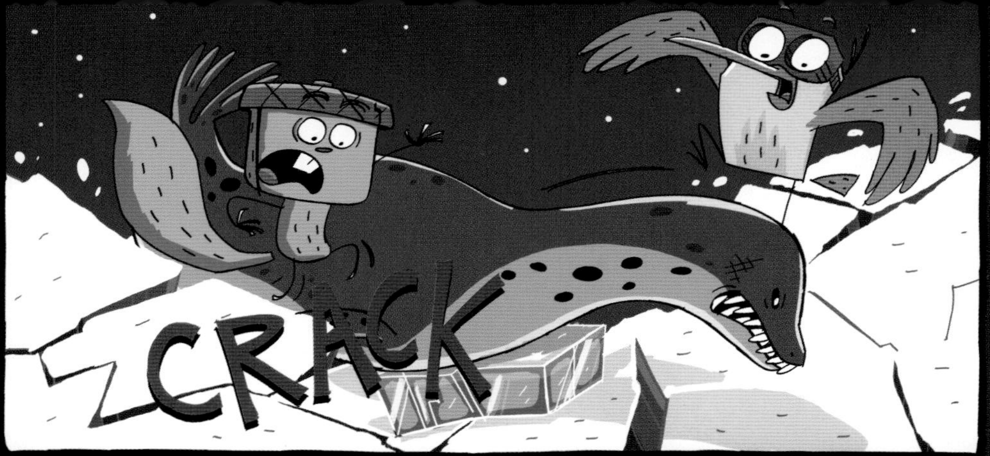
CRACK

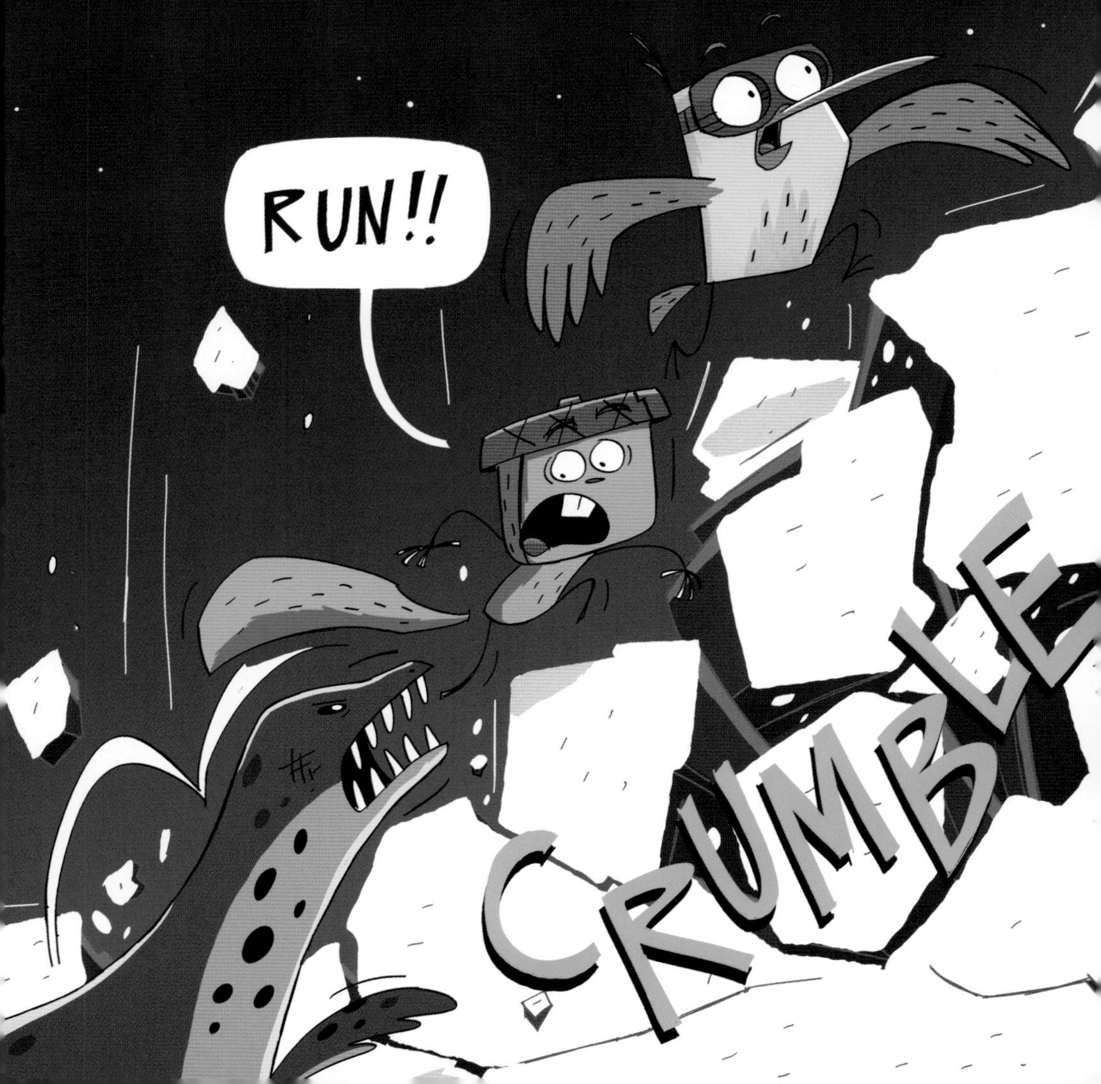
RUN!!
CRUMBLE

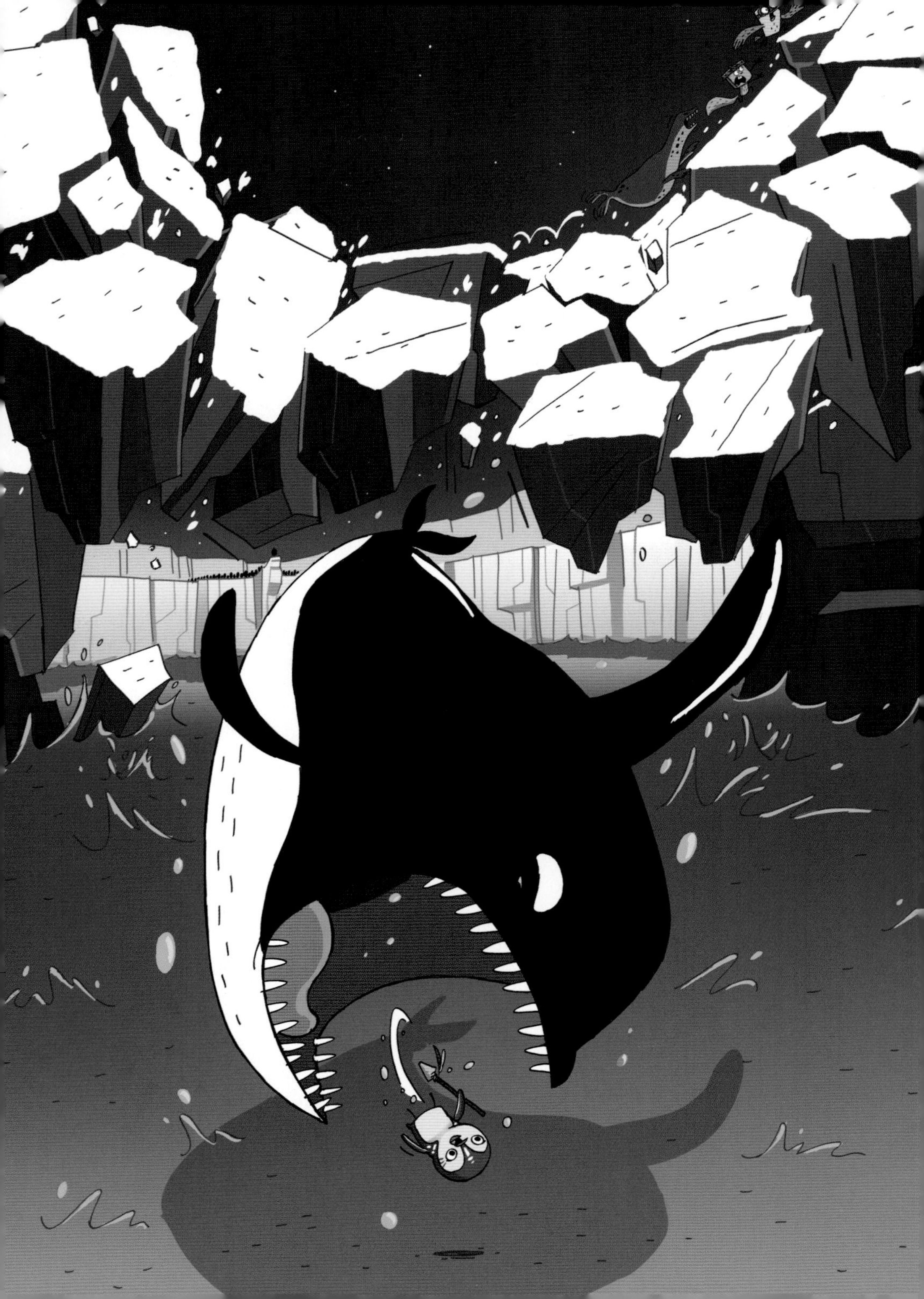

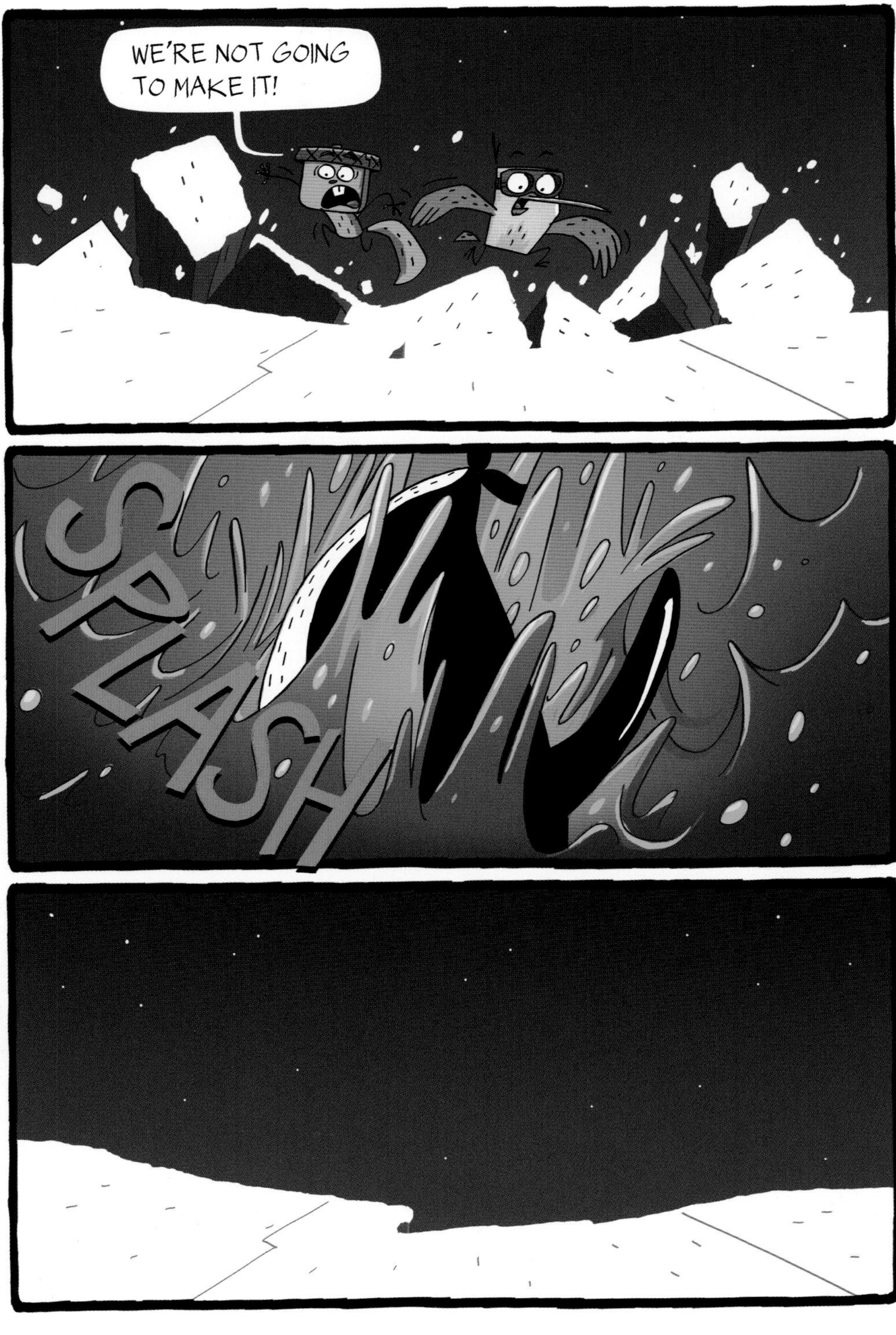
WE'RE NOT GOING TO MAKE IT!
SPLASH

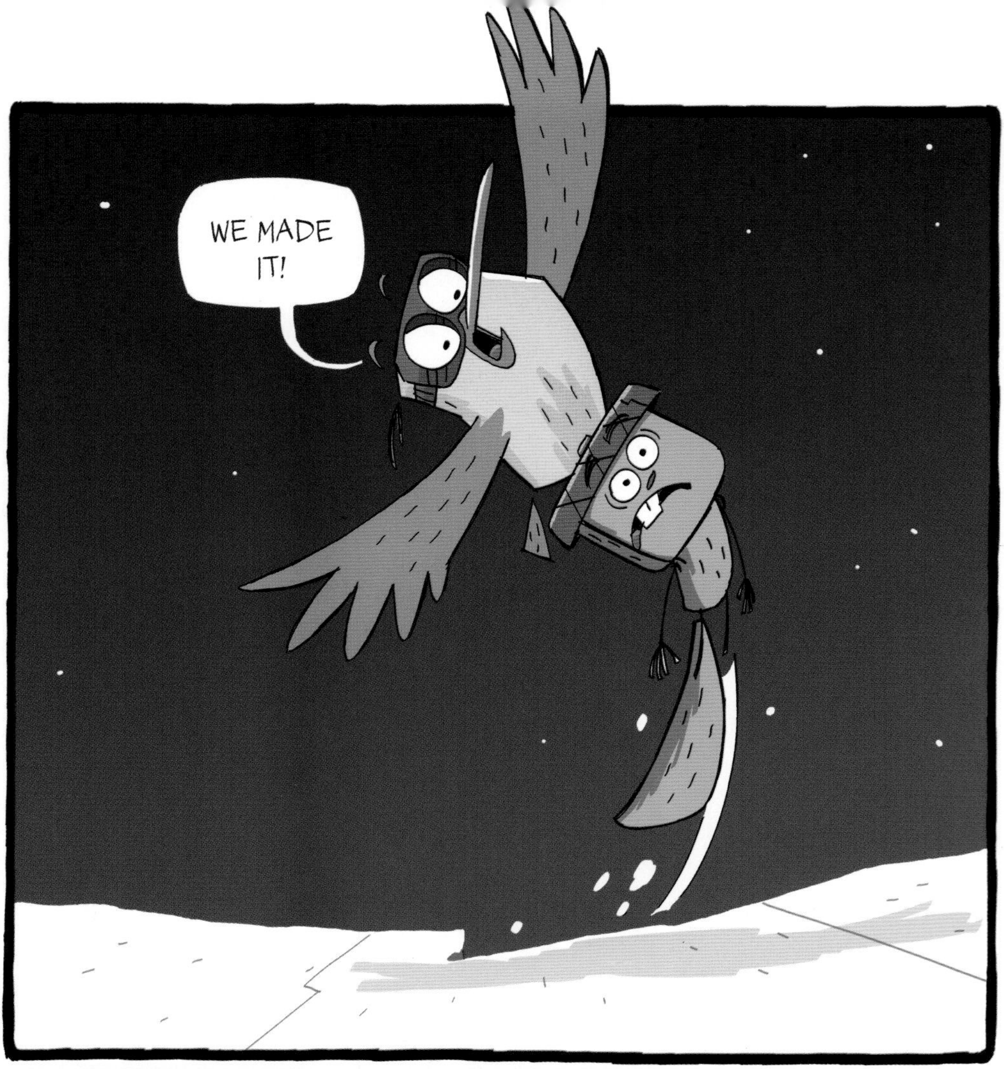
WE MADE IT!

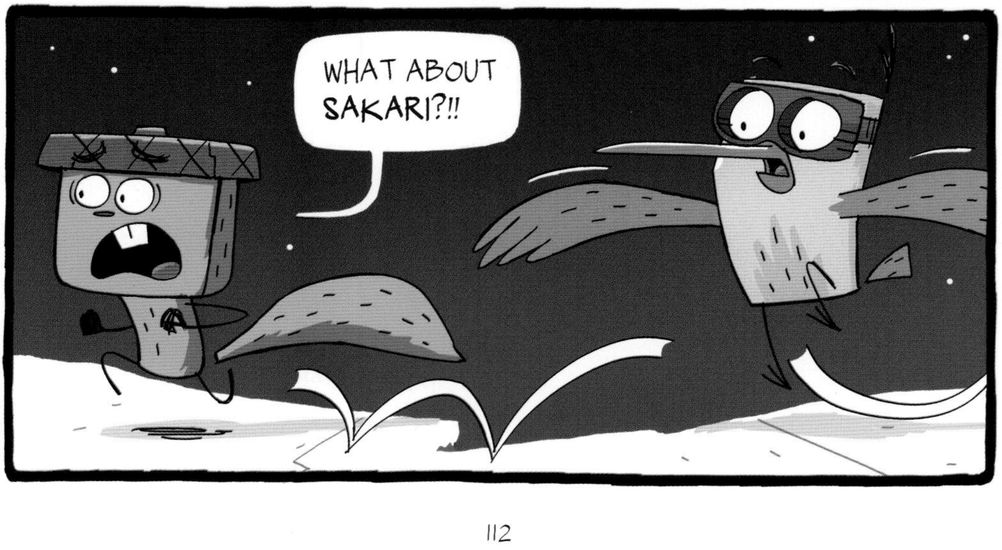
WHAT ABOUT SAKARI?!!

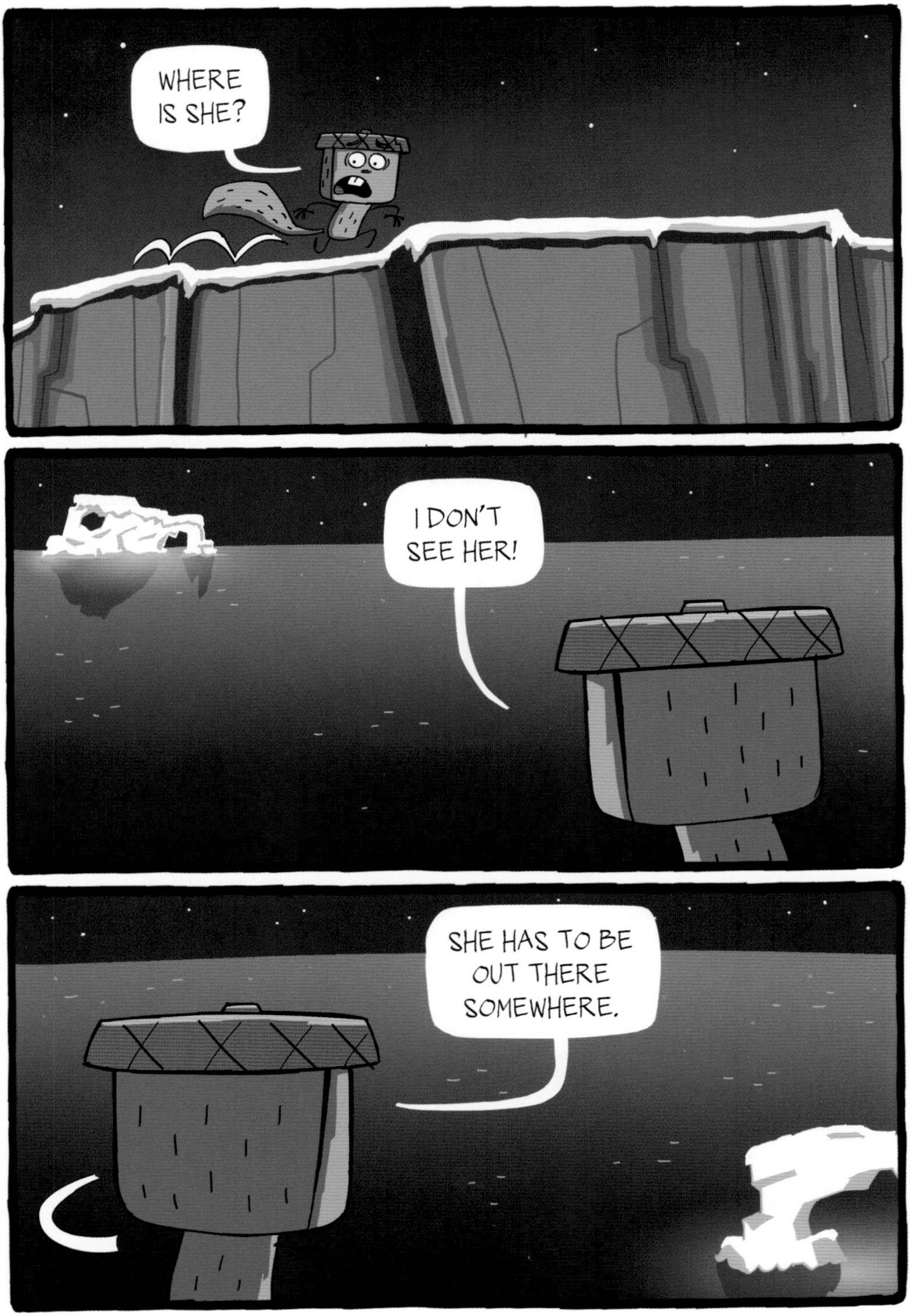
WHERE IS SHE?
I DON'T SEE HER!
SHE HAS TO BE OUT THERE SOMEWHERE.

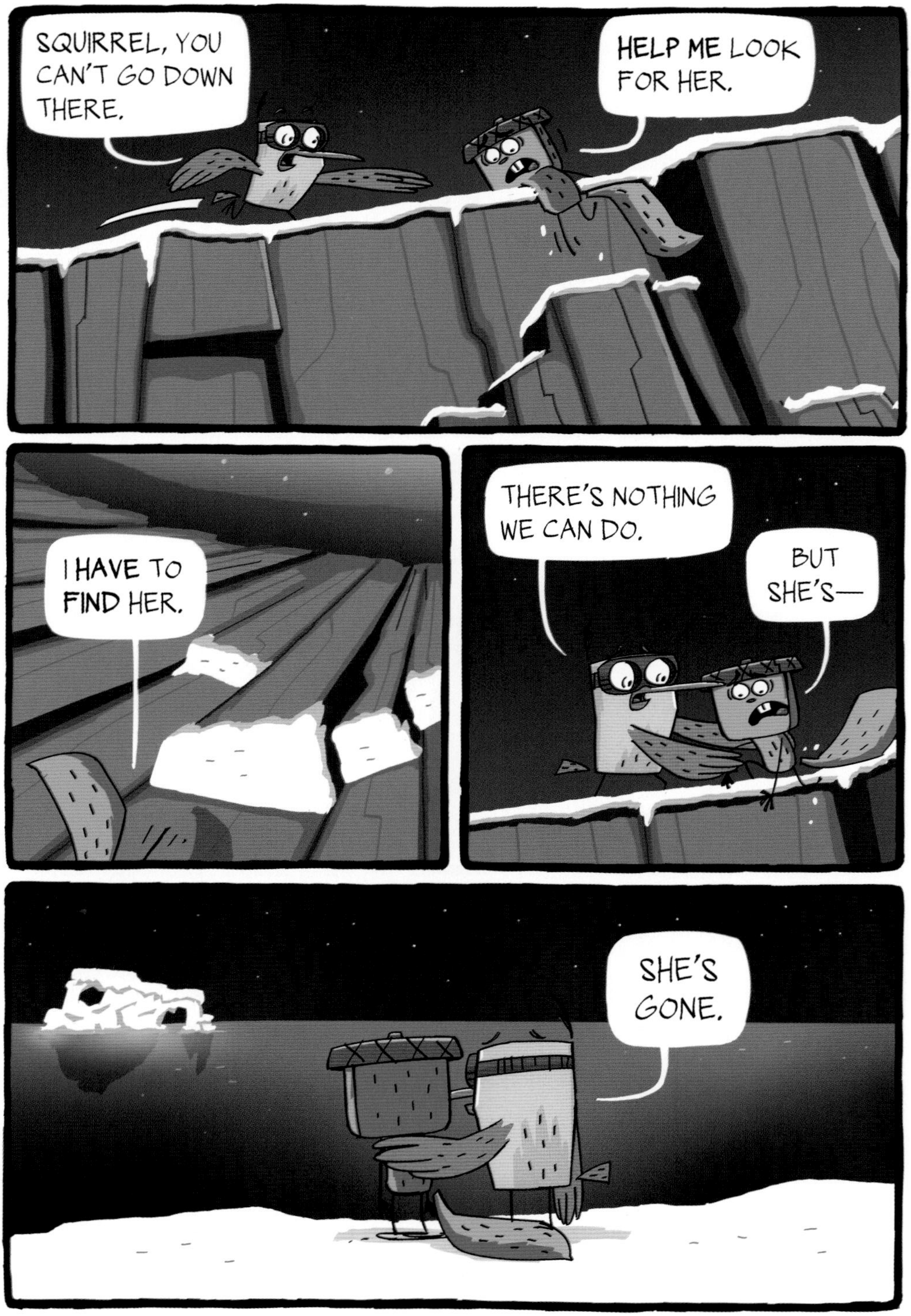
SQUIRREL, YOU CAN'T GO DOWN THERE.
HELP ME LOOK FOR HER.
I **HAVE** TO **FIND** HER.
THERE'S NOTHING WE CAN DO.
BUT SHE'S—
SHE'S GONE.

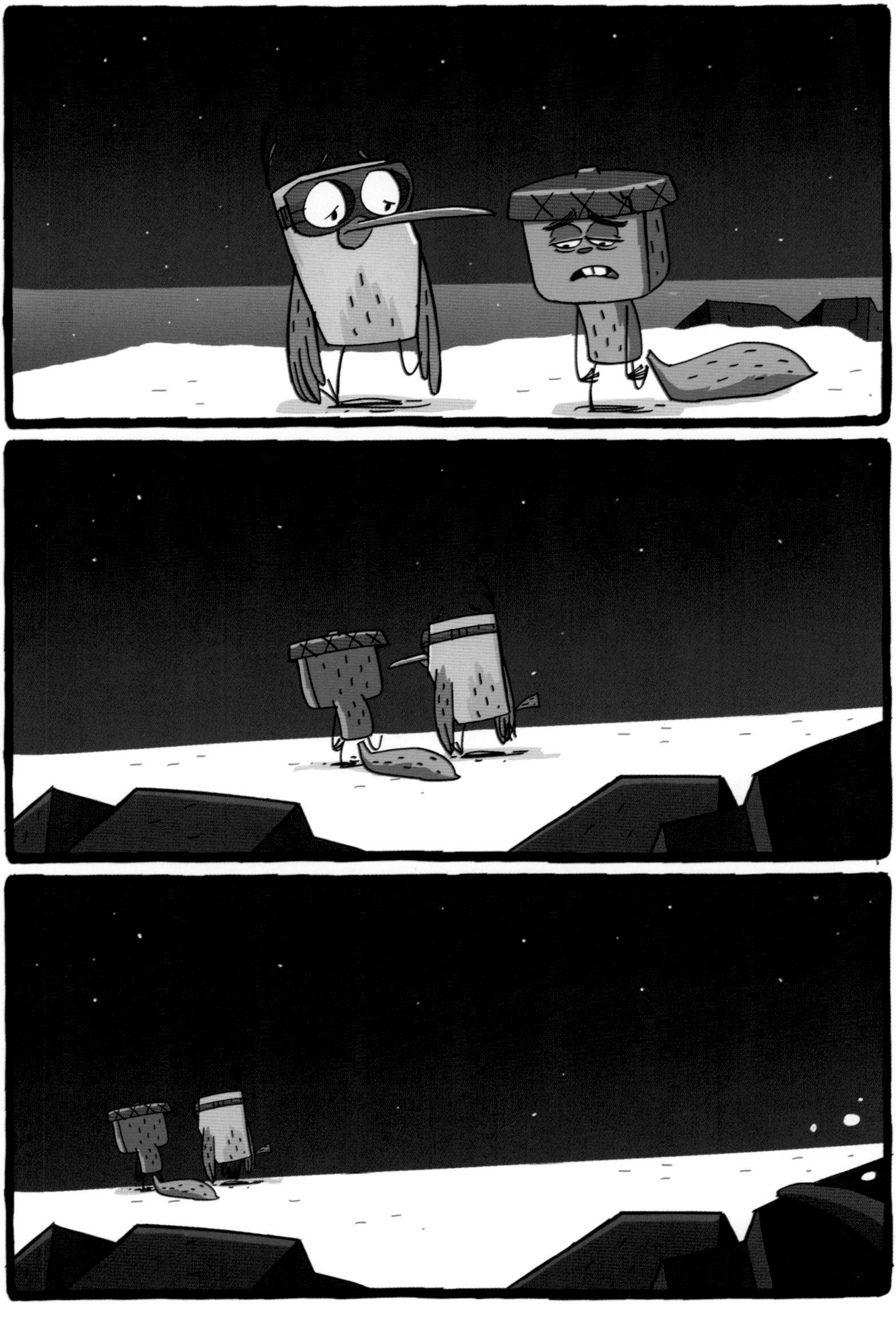

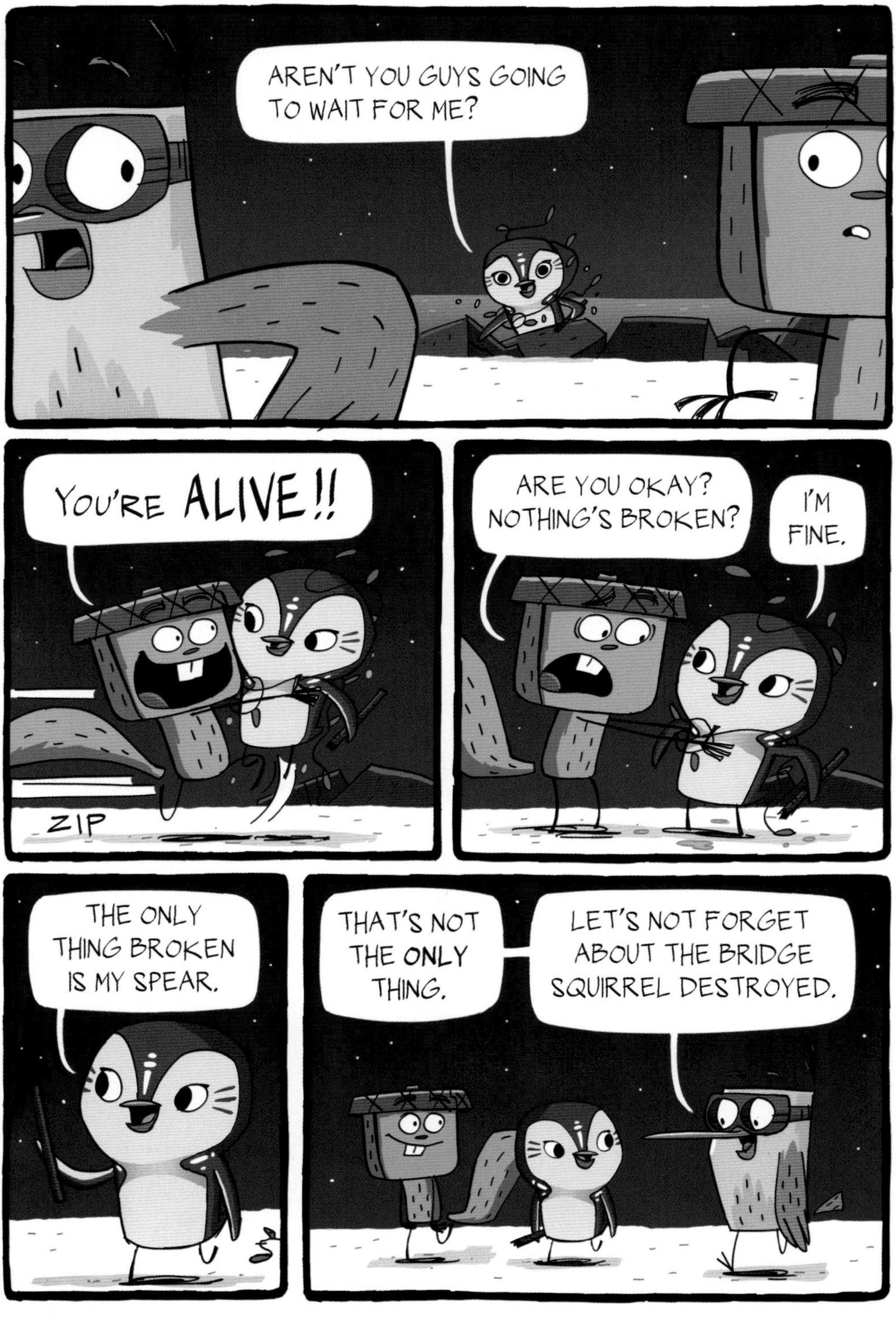
AREN'T YOU GUYS GOING TO WAIT FOR ME?
YOU'RE ALIVE!!
ZIP
ARE YOU OKAY? NOTHING'S BROKEN?
I'M FINE.
THE ONLY THING BROKEN IS MY SPEAR.
THAT'S NOT THE ONLY THING.
LET'S NOT FORGET ABOUT THE BRIDGE SQUIRREL DESTROYED.

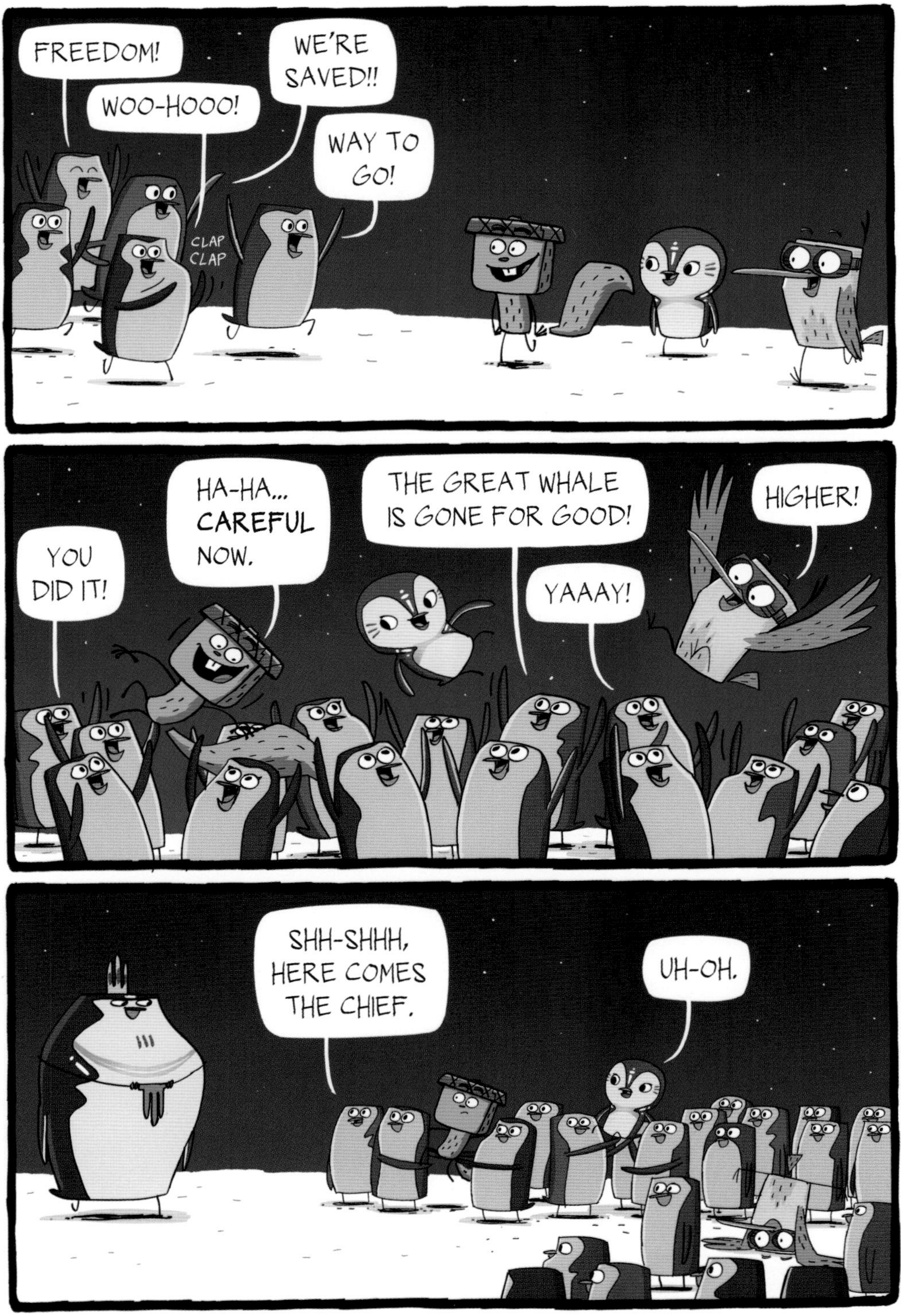
FREEDOM!
WOO-HOOO!
WE'RE SAVED!!
WAY TO GO!
CLAP CLAP
YOU DID IT!
HA-HA... **CAREFUL** NOW.
THE GREAT WHALE IS GONE FOR GOOD!
YAAAY!
HIGHER!
SHH-SHHH, HERE COMES THE CHIEF.
UH-OH.

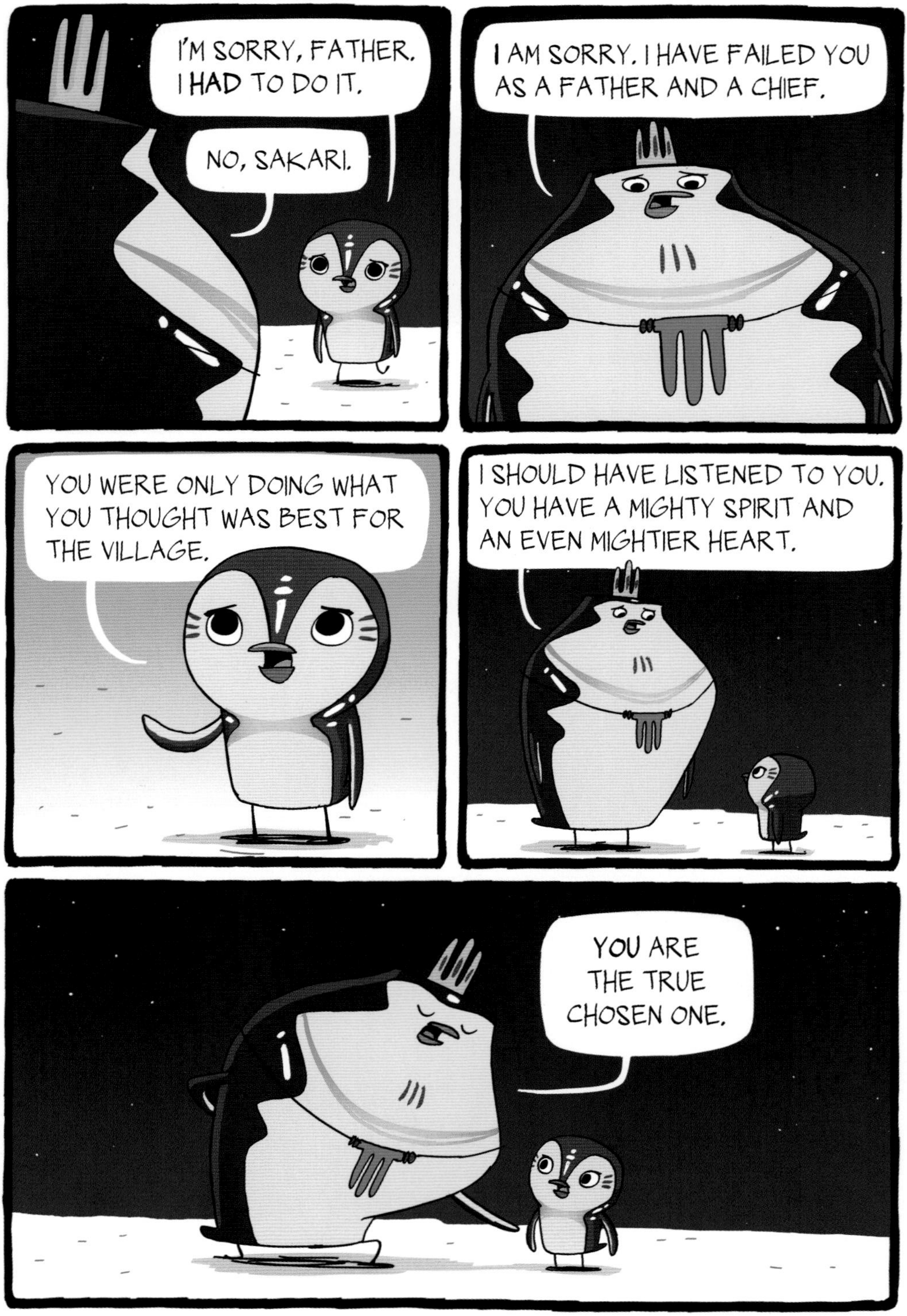
I'M SORRY, FATHER. I HAD TO DO IT.
NO, SAKARI.
I AM SORRY. I HAVE FAILED YOU AS A FATHER AND A CHIEF.
YOU WERE ONLY DOING WHAT YOU THOUGHT WAS BEST FOR THE VILLAGE.
I SHOULD HAVE LISTENED TO YOU. YOU HAVE A MIGHTY SPIRIT AND AN EVEN MIGHTIER HEART.
YOU ARE THE TRUE CHOSEN ONE.

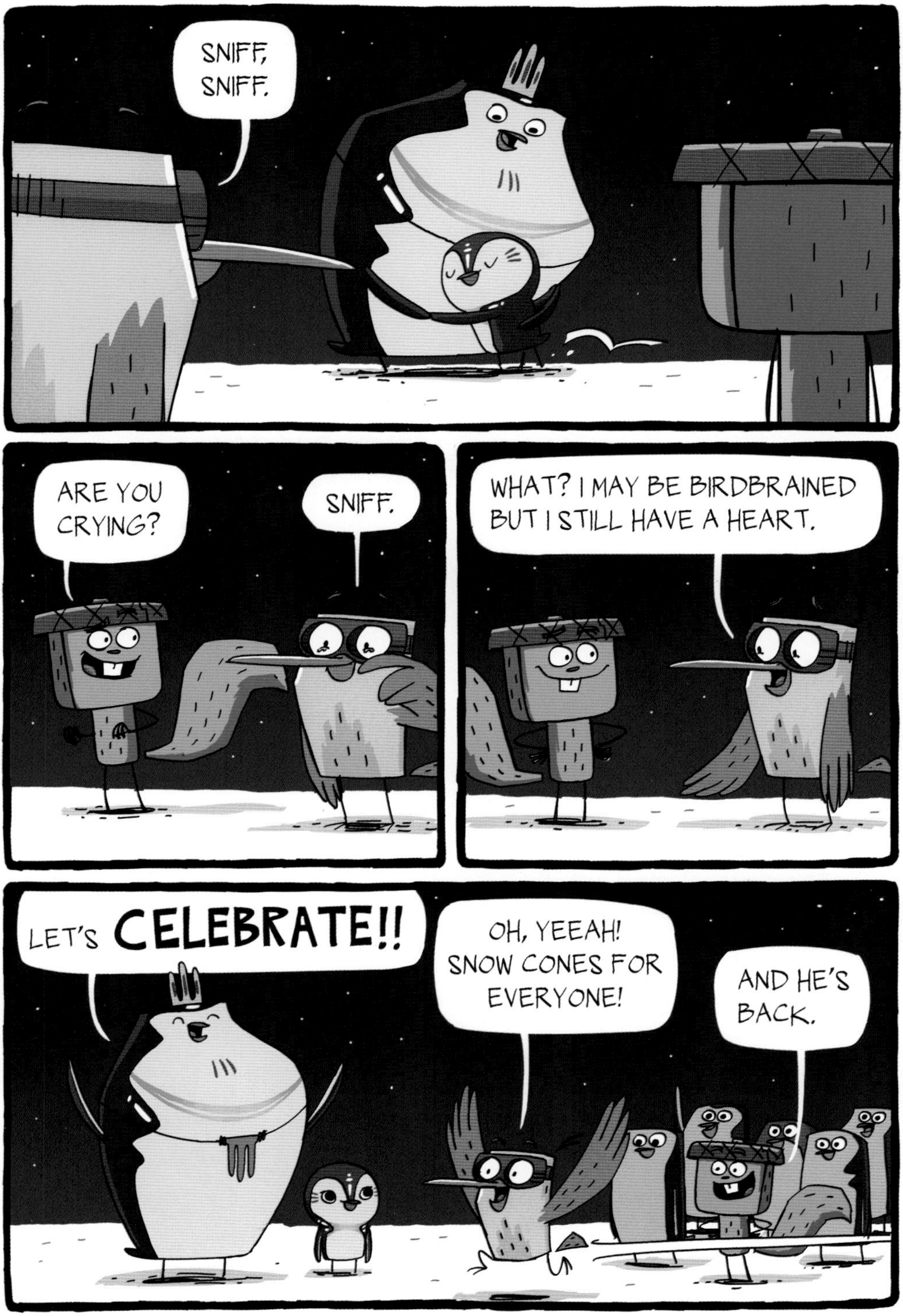
SNIFF, SNIFF.
ARE YOU CRYING?
SNIFF.
WHAT? I MAY BE BIRDBRAINED BUT I STILL HAVE A HEART.
LET'S CELEBRATE!!
OH, YEEAH! SNOW CONES FOR EVERYONE!
AND HE'S BACK.

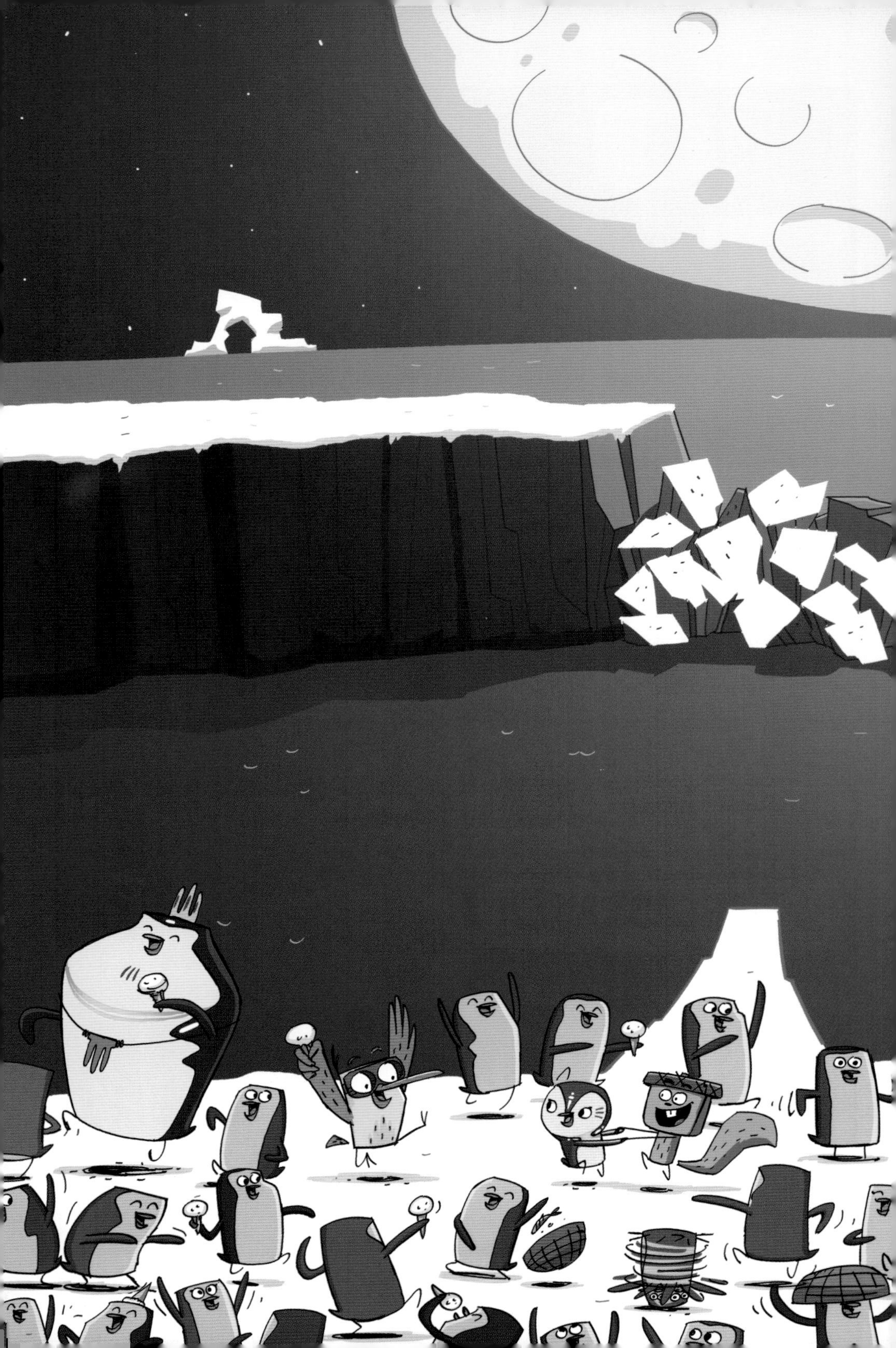

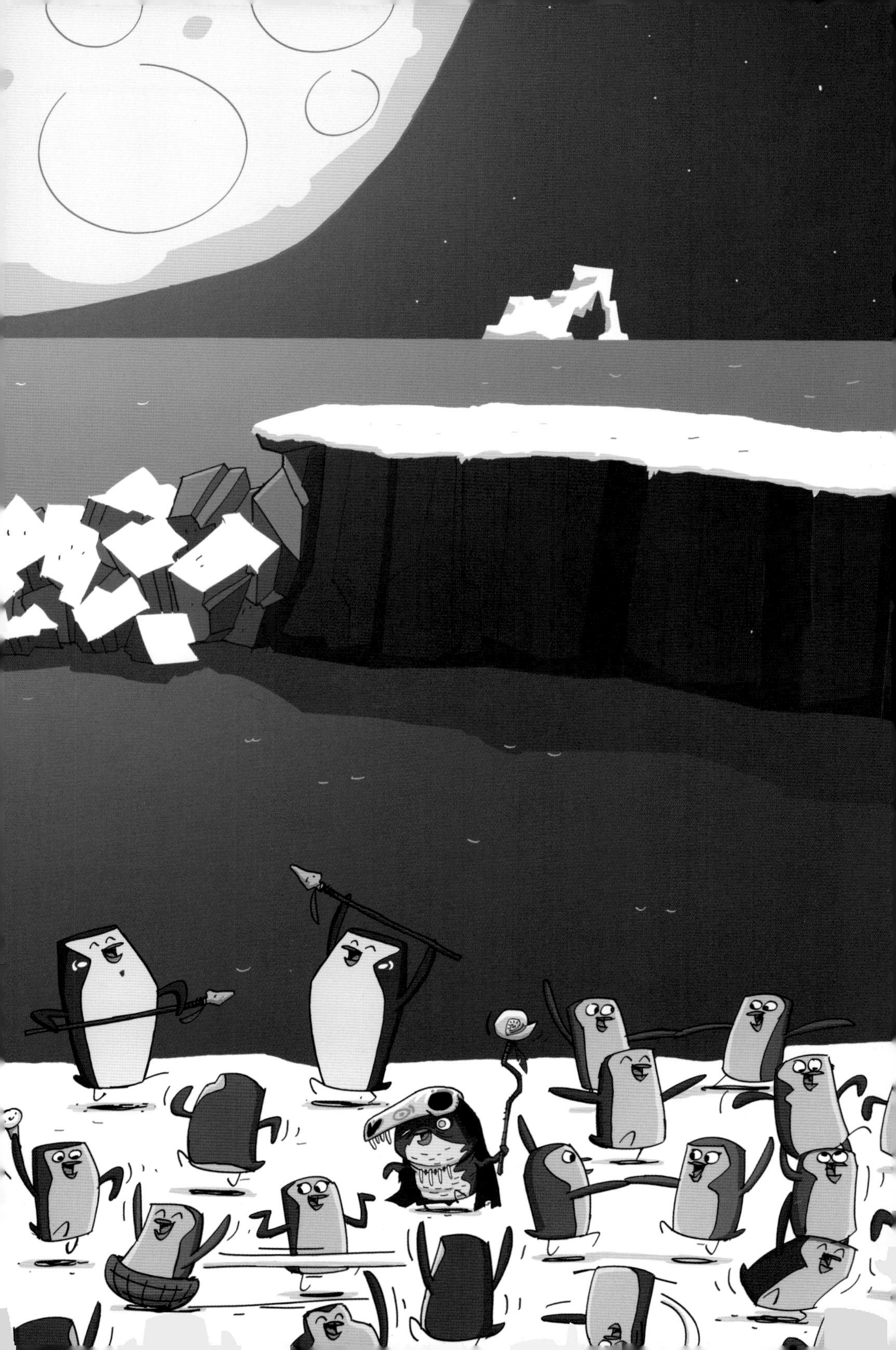

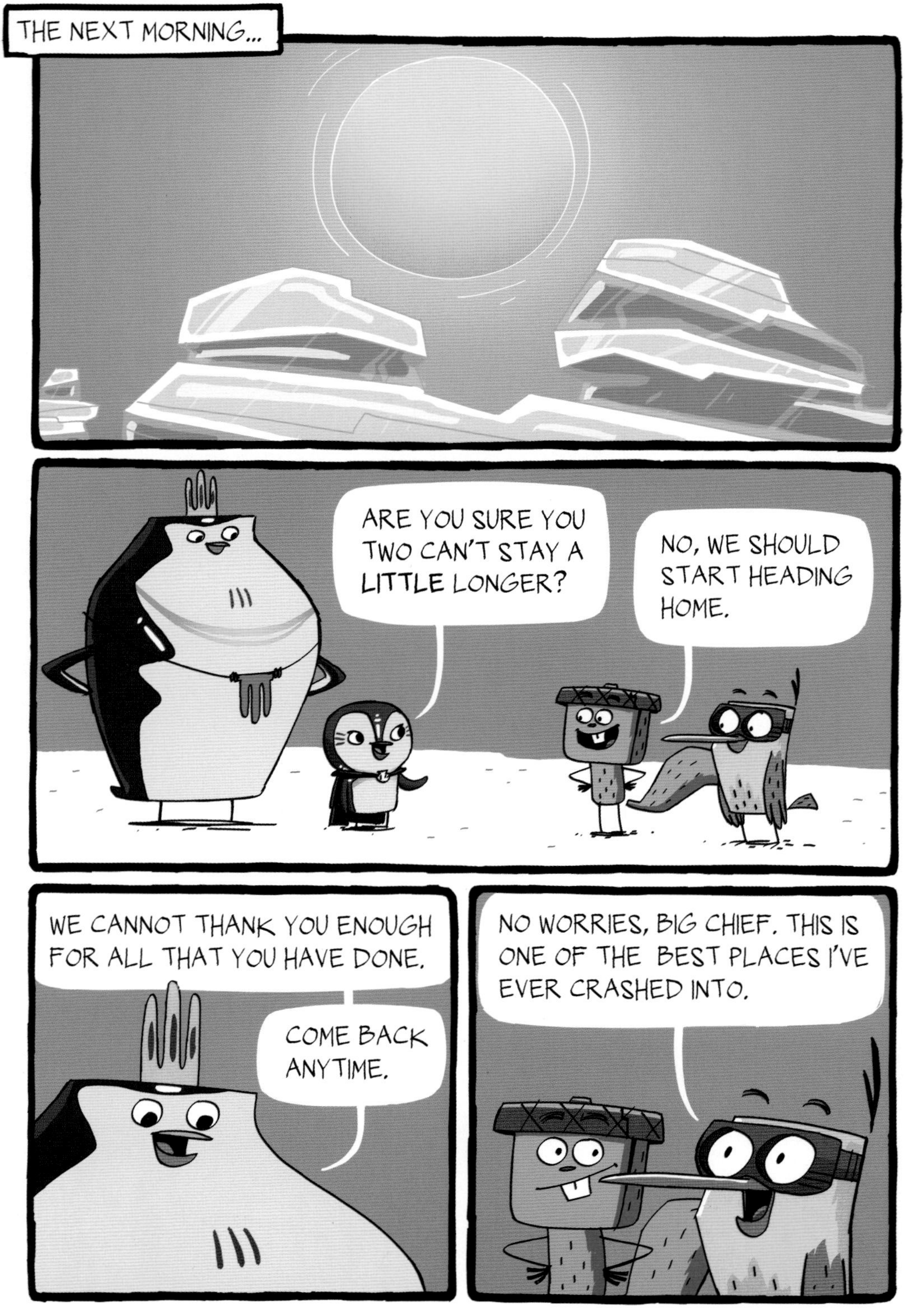
THE NEXT MORNING...
ARE YOU SURE YOU TWO CAN'T STAY A LITTLE LONGER?
NO, WE SHOULD START HEADING HOME.
WE CANNOT THANK YOU ENOUGH FOR ALL THAT YOU HAVE DONE.
COME BACK ANYTIME.
NO WORRIES, BIG CHIEF. THIS IS ONE OF THE BEST PLACES I'VE EVER CRASHED INTO.

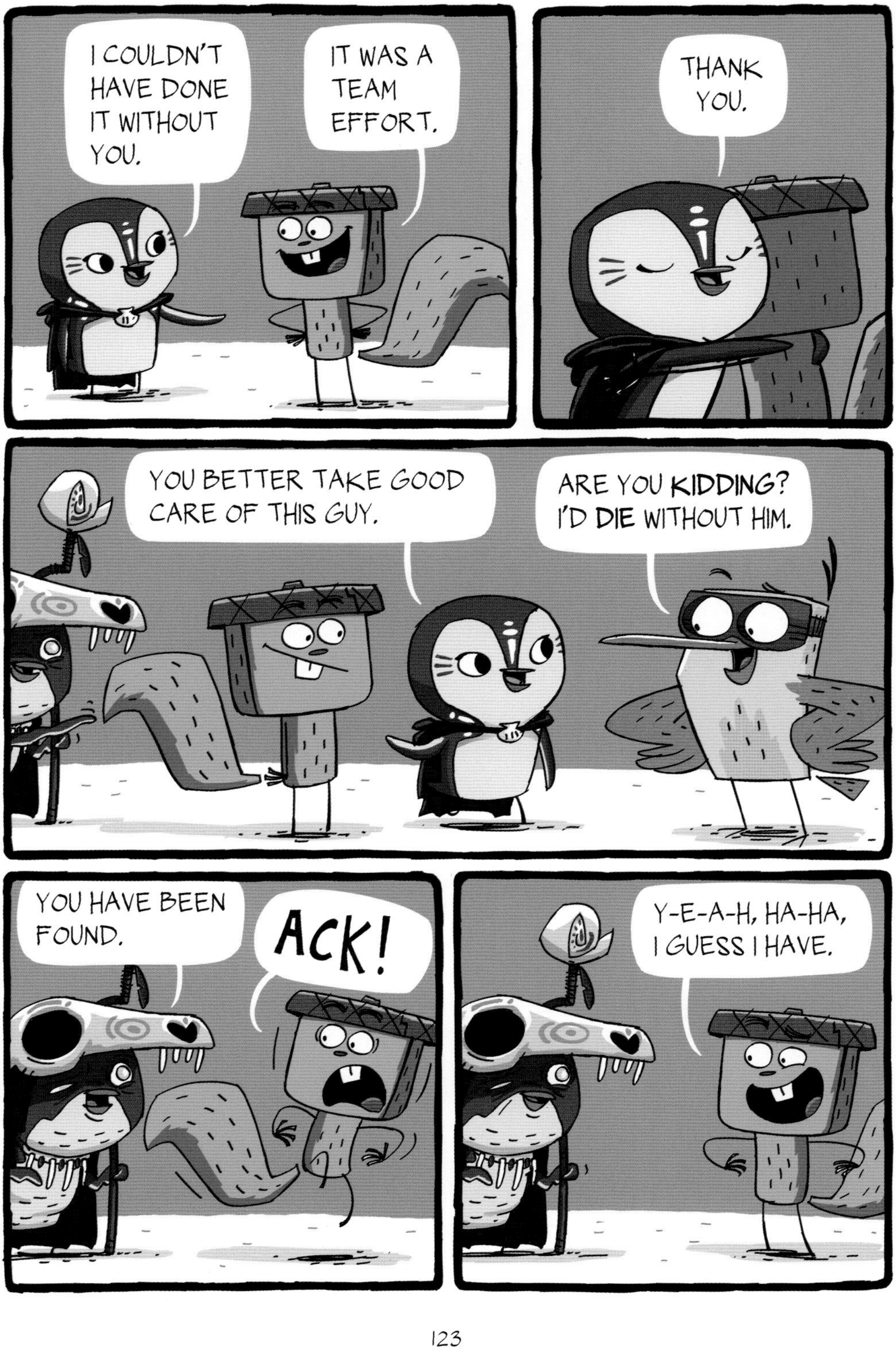
I COULDN'T HAVE DONE IT WITHOUT YOU.
IT WAS A TEAM EFFORT.
THANK YOU.
YOU BETTER TAKE GOOD CARE OF THIS GUY.
ARE YOU **KIDDING**? I'D **DIE** WITHOUT HIM.
YOU HAVE BEEN FOUND.
ACK!
Y-E-A-H, HA-HA, I GUESS I HAVE.

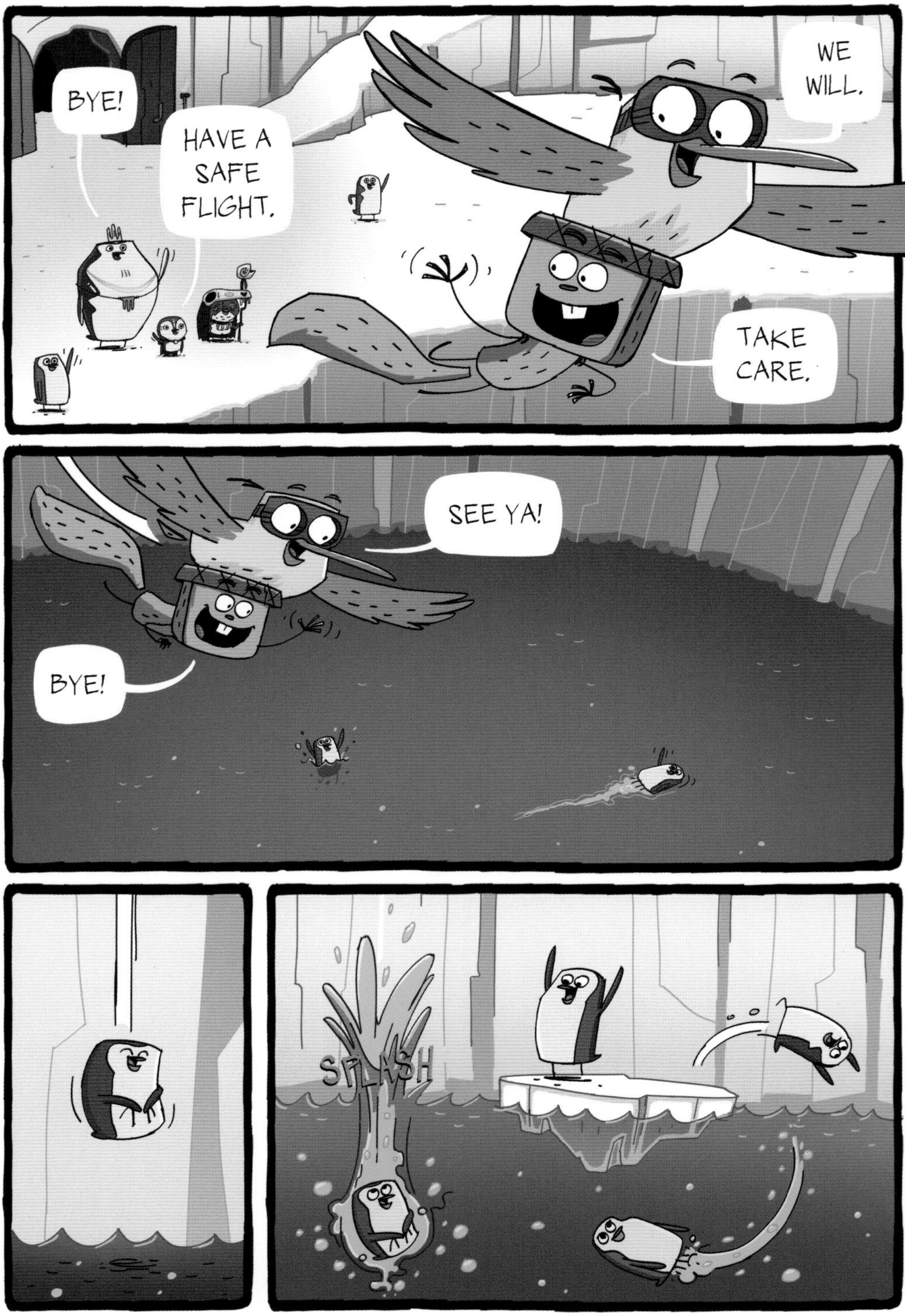
BYE!
HAVE A SAFE FLIGHT.
WE WILL.
TAKE CARE.
SEE YA!
BYE!
SPLASH

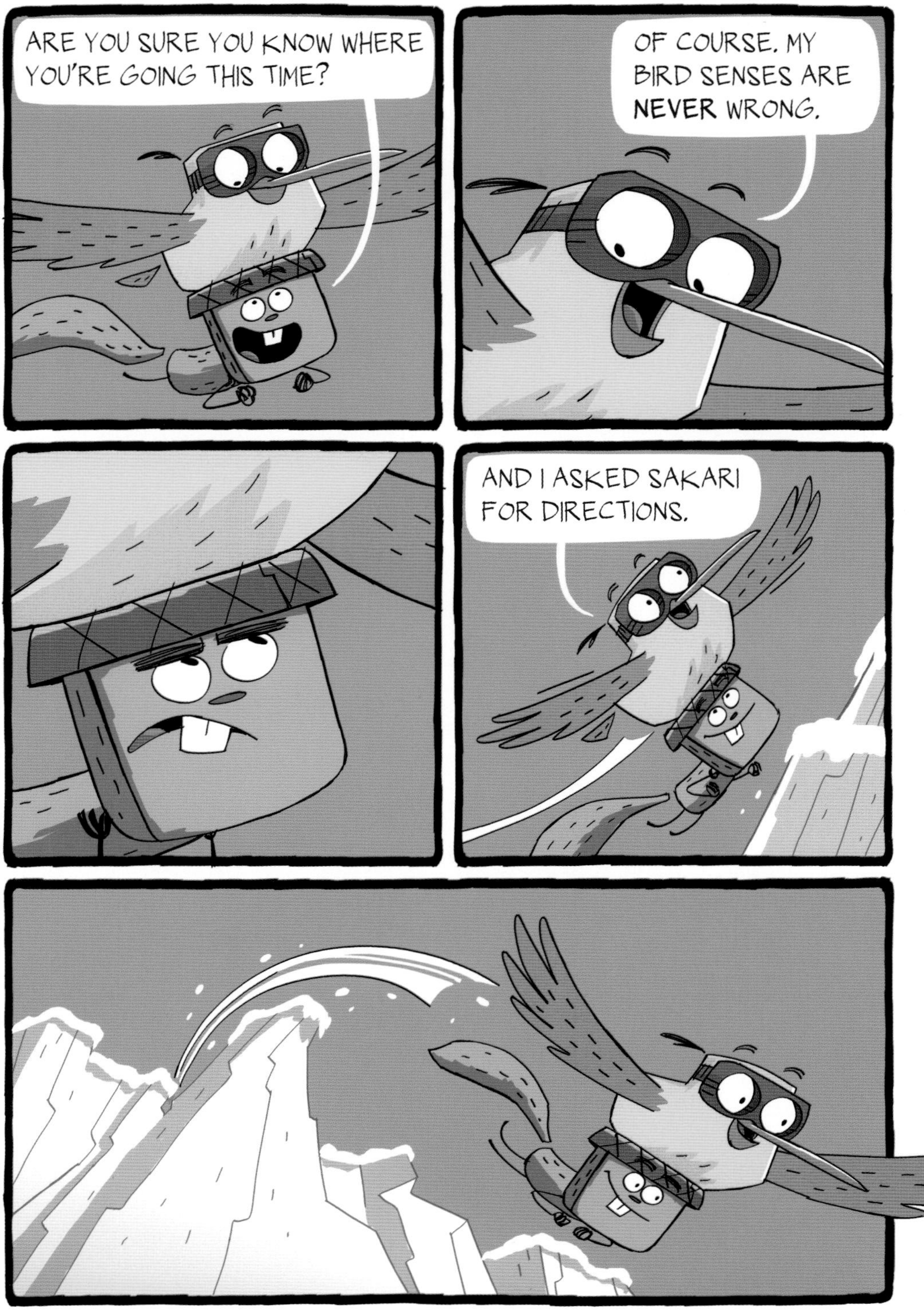
ARE YOU SURE YOU KNOW WHERE YOU'RE GOING THIS TIME?
OF COURSE. MY BIRD SENSES ARE **NEVER** WRONG.
AND I ASKED SAKARI FOR DIRECTIONS.

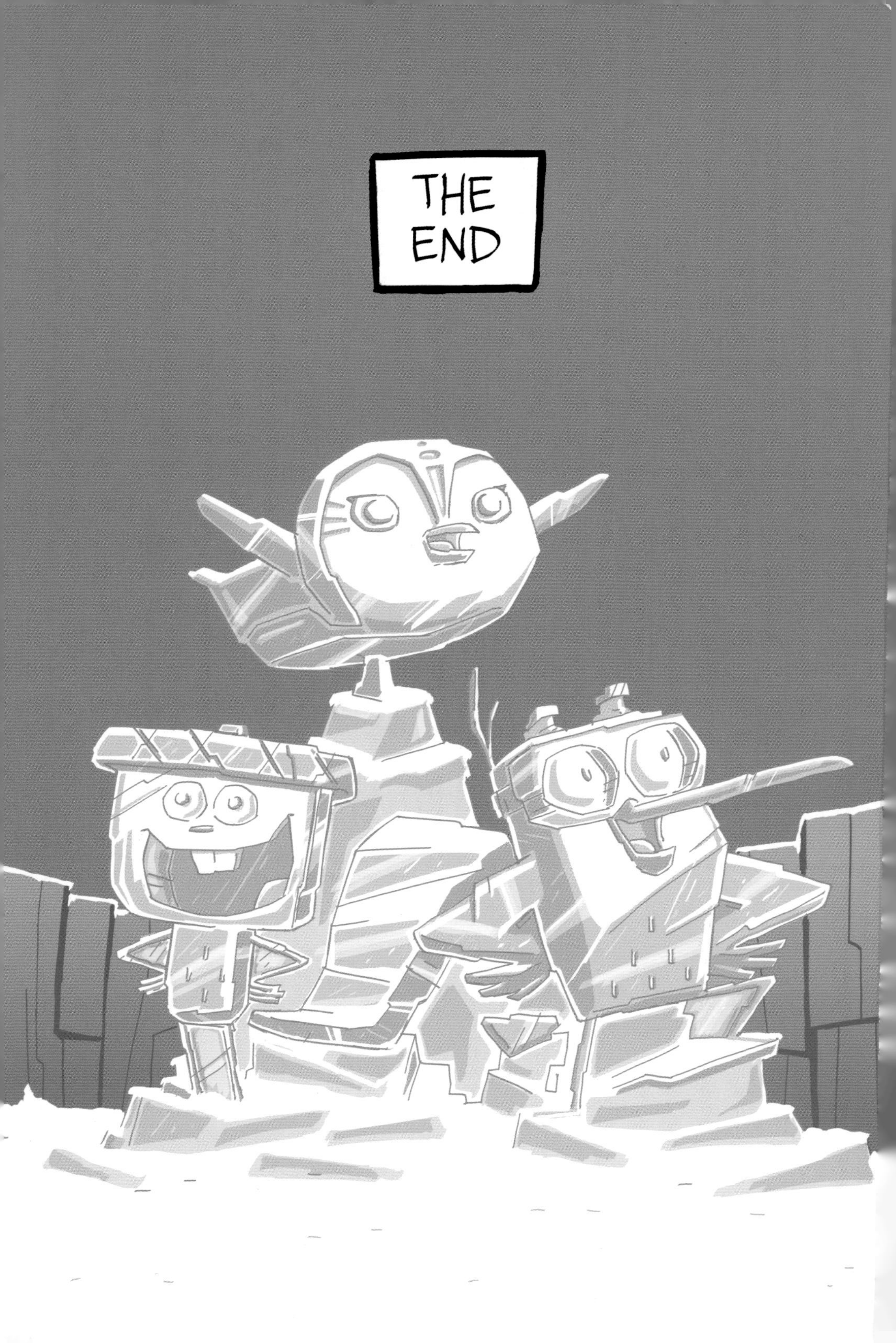
THE END